"*The Mirror Empire* is the most original fantasy I've read in a long time, set in a world full of new ideas, expanding the horizons of the genre. A complex and intricate book full of elegant ideas and finely-drawn characters."

Adrian Tchaikovsky, *winner of the Arthur C Clarke Award*

"Hurley intelligently tackles issues of culture and gender, while also throwing in plenty of bloodthirsty action and well-rounded characters. This is a fresh, exciting fantasy epic that's looking to the future and asking important questions."

SFX

"Hurley reuses old tropes to excellent effect, interweaving them with original elements to create a world that will fascinate and delight her established fans and appeal to newcomers. Readers will blaze through this opening instalment and eagerly await the promised sequel.

Publishers Weekly (starred review)

"*The Mirror Empire* is epic in every sense of the word. Hurley has built a world – no, worlds – in which cosmology and magic, history and religion, politics and prejudice all play crucial roles. Prepare yourself for sentient plants, rifts in the fabric of reality, and remarkable powers that wax and wane with the stars themselves. Forget all about tentative, conventional fantasy; there's so much great material in here that Hurley needs more than one universe in order to fit it all in."

Brian Staveley, *author of* The Emperor's Blades

"With vividly inventive world building and a fast-paced plot, *The Mirror Empire* opens a smart, brutal, and ambitious epic fantasy series."

Kate Elliott, *author of the Spiritwalker series*

"This is a hugely ambitious work, bloody and violent, with interestingly gender-flipped politics and a host of factions to keep straight, as points of view switch often. Although it is a challenging read, the strong narrative thread in this new series from Hurley (*God's War*) pulls readers through the imaginative tangle of multiple worlds and histories colliding."
Library Journal (starred review)

"Astoundingly inventive."
The Illustrated Page

"*The Mirror Empire* is a fast-paced and exciting read, and the start of quite possibly one of the greatest political dramas I have ever picked up."
Coffee on My Keyboard

"*The Mirror Empire* is a fresh, vigorous, and gripping entrant into the epic fantasy genre, able to stand toe-to-toe with any of the heavyweight series out there. I cannot recommend this novel highly enough."
SF Revu

"*The Mirror Empire* takes a look at epic fantasy patriarchy and gives it a firm kick in the balls... [It] will be the most important book you read this year."
Alex Ristea, Ristea's Reads

"In the two worlds of *The Mirror Empire*, we get Deadly Plants, Blood Magic, and yes, Brutal Women. *The Mirror Empire* is both a chance for fantasy fans to get to know Hurley's writing, and for previous fans of her work to see what she can do in a new vein. And for readers new to her work, this is in many ways the best place to start.."
SF Signal

KAMERON HURLEY

Empire Ascendant

THE WORLDBREAKER SAGA
BOOK II

**ANGRY
ROBOT**

ANGRY ROBOT
An imprint of Watkins Media Ltd

Lace Market House,
54-56 High Pavement,
Nottingham,
NG1 1HW
UK

angryrobotbooks.com
twitter.com/angryrobotbooks
Every world at war

First published by Angry Robot in 2015
This edition published 2016

Cover by Richard Anderson
Maps by Stephanie MacAlea
Set in Meridien by Epub Services

Distributed in the United States by Penguin Random House, Inc.,
New York.

ISBN 978 0 85766 565 2
Ebook ISBN 978 0 85766 560 7

Printed in the United States of America

9 8 7 6 5 4 3 2 1

This book is for Jayson,
for helping out with the plants.

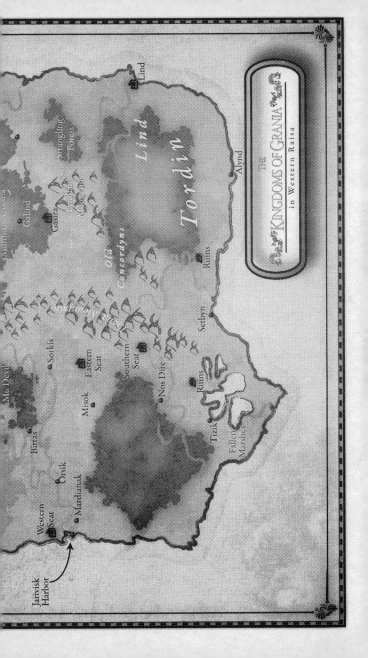

"War turns its makers mad."
                    Dhai saying

PROLOGUE

"The body's here."

Kirana Javia, Empress of Dhai, Divine Kai of the Tai Mora, gazed across a field of corpses. She gnawed at a wizened apple, pausing only to pick a fat worm from its center and flick it over the railing of the thorny broken tower she stood upon. The sky was an amber-bronze wash; it always looked like it was on fire. The blackened husk that had once been the heavenly star Para glowed red-black. It turned the light of the double suns a malevolent orange, and the tiny third sun, Mora, was no longer visible. Below, her omajistas and their handlers went body to body, gutting the deceased and collecting their blood into massive clay urns. The first few years of the Great War, Kirana had commissioned glass jars, but they broke easily, and worse – seeing the blood carted off hurt her army's morale. It reminded her people of what they were doing – bleeding out a sea of dead to save the living. You could measure the number of dead now by how many urns left the field. Carts stuffed with urns stretched across the muddy ground so far she lost sight of them in the woodlands beyond. If the infused mirror that could keep the way open between worlds had not been sabotaged, these people would still be alive, running after her army into a new world. But now she was back to killing and collecting. She told herself the deaths weren't wasted, merely transformed. This close to the end, nothing could be wasted.

She popped the apple core into her mouth and turned.

Two soldiers in tattered coats stood at attention. The slashed violet circles on their lapels marked them as lower-level sinajistas, one of the more expendable jista castes, as their star wouldn't be ascendant for another year, and this world would be dead by then. Their black hair was braided into intricate spirals and pinned in place. Hunger sharpened their faces into a grim severity. Kirana longed for the days when every face she saw was some jolly fat parody of itself. *Even my own people look like corpses,* she mused. *How appropriate.*

The soldiers carried a large brown sack between them, stained dark with blood and – from the smell – the remains of a voided bowel.

"What a lovely gift," Kirana said. She trotted down the steps to join them. The turret room was a ruin, like most of the buildings they occupied in these final days of the routing of the world. Many knew they were coming, so they burned, broke, or poisoned anything of use before her people arrived. The furniture was smashed, and the resulting kindling burned. Kirana had found a shattered mirror near the door and used a fragment to dig out an arrow head that had pierced through a seam of her armor. The armor still bled where it'd been struck. It would take hours to repair itself. She rubbed at the sticky sap on her fingers.

The soldiers yanked at the cord that bound the body in the bag, spilling the contents.

Kirana leaned over for a better look. Tangled black curls, round face, straight nose.

"It's not her," Kirana said, and she could not keep the disappointment from her voice. "Not even close. Are you just picking up random bodies and carting them over?"

The taller soldier winced. "They all look alike."

Kirana sneered. "The only face that looks like yours in that world is your double's, and I can tell you now that you'll never meet them as long as you're living. If you can't do this one thing I'll–"

The body on the floor stirred.

A stab of pain splintered up Kirana's leg. She hissed and jumped back. The formerly dead woman yanked a knife from Kirana's thigh and leapt up, spitting green bile. She slashed at Kirana again and darted between the two startled sinajistas.

Kirana lunged after her, making a wild left hook. The woman dodged and bolted out the door – a shocking turn of events if she wanted Kirana dead. Who would send an assassin after Kirana that broke away so quickly? Unless Kirana wasn't the target.

"She's after the consort!" Kirana yelled, and sprinted after her.

The assassin was fast for a woman recently dead. Kirana saw the curve of her ass disappearing down the far corridor. Kirana went after her, sliding as she rounded the same corner. Her boots were losing their tread. The assassin huffed herself from the top of the stair down to the landing. Kirana jumped the curve of the banister after her, relying on her armor to cushion the fall. The assassin wasn't running blind. She was making her way directly to the quarters of Kirana's consort and children.

Some other world had found them. Someone was coming for them.

Kirana jumped over the next curve in the stair and collided with the rail below her. It took the breath from her. She gasped and heaved forward, reaching for the assassin's bare ankle. She got a kick in the face instead. Kirana scrambled up and moved down the long hall. Now that they were clear of the stairs, she shook her wrist, and the twisted willowthorn branch nestled inside her arm snarled free, snapped out.

She slashed, searing the woman's long tunic. The

fabric fell away, hissing and smoking.

They were three doors from her consort's rooms. Kirana put on a burst of speed. She jumped and lunged, thrusting her weapon ahead of her, as far as she could reach.

The willowthorn sword rammed into the assassin's hip, drawing blood. Kirana hit the ground hard just as the assassin did. They came together in a snarl of arms and legs. Kirana climbed over her. Thrust again. The assassin caught her arm and bit her wrist. She flipped Kirana over neatly, as if she weighed nothing. Kirana headbutted her in the face. The assassin's nose popped like a fruit, spraying blood. Kirana stabbed her twice in the torso and kicked her off.

The assassin hit the floor and continued trying to scramble forward, sliding in her own blood.

The sinajistas finally caught up with them. They grabbed for the assassin. Kirana knew restraint wasn't going to work.

"Take her head off!" Kirana yelled. They were tangling with the assassin. She was a tireless ball of sinew and flesh brought back to life by Sina alone knew what.

Kirana pushed to her feet and took her weapon in both hands and swung. She caught the assassin in the jaw, ripping it free of the face. She hacked again, opening up the throat. The sinajistas dropped the body, and Kirana finished it, detaching the head from the neck while the widening pool of blood licked her boots. She bent over, trying to catch her breath. The body still twitched.

"Burn it," Kirana said. She clutched at a pain in her side; she had overstretched or torn something. She winced and straightened as one of the sinajistas went back upstairs to collect the bag for the body. A handful of the house guards she had put in charge of the hold came up now too, full of questions. She'd deal with them later.

Kirana limped down to her consort's door and knocked heavily.

"It's the Kai," she said. "Are you all right?"

The door opened. She must have been listening to the scuffle in the hall. Yisaoh stood just over the threshold. Her scarlet robe brushed the floor. She was medium height, broad, her dark hair twisted into a knot on top of her head. Her nose was crooked, broken twice during her very long apprenticeship in the army before Kirana signed her discharge papers.

Kirana leaned into her, spent. She pressed her face to Yisaoh's neck and breathed in the scent of her.

"Are you safe?"

Yisaoh pressed her hands to Kirana's hair. "This blood—"

"Not mine," Kirana said. She raised her head and searched Yisaoh's face. "You're all right? Where are the children?" She moved past Yisaoh, heading toward the nursery.

"They're fine, love," Yisaoh said. "There's a storm coming, the stargazers say. We need to close everything up."

Kirana crossed the sitting room, stumbling over a heavy piece of furniture. The room was mostly in order, though a few things were still overturned. She had had these quarters meticulously searched and set up for her family the moment the siege ended.

She opened the door to the nursery, weapon up. The children slept together in a big bed at her right. The room had no windows, making it a safe refuge from the storms. Kirana counted their three perfect heads.

Yisaoh placed a hand on Kirana's shoulder. She flinched.

"I gave them a draft," Yisaoh said softly. "They were up all night in camp during the siege, worrying over you. They needed to sleep."

The weapon in Kirana's hand softened. She released it, and it snaked back into her wrist. She let out a breath.

A low, insistent bell clanged outside. The familiar

three-by-two-by-three gong that warned of a dust storm.

"Stay here with us, you fool," Yisaoh said. She shut the door behind them, sealing all of them into the quiet black of the children's room. She rummaged around in the dark and took hold of some kind of rustling fabric.

Kirana watched her stuff it under the seam of the door, muffling the last of the light. The dull moan of the bell changed, muted by the change in air pressure.

Yisaoh grabbed Kirana's hand and pulled her down beside her in the darkness. Pain stitched up Kirana's leg, and she hissed. She had almost forgotten about the wound.

"Are you hurt?" Yisaoh asked. "Oma's eye, Kirana, I've sewn your limbs back on and seen you with half your face torn away. Don't hide an injury from me."

They pressed against one another. Kirana's breath sounded loud in her ears. She was still filled with adrenaline, ready to leap at shadows. The storm hit the hold. The stones trembled. Air hissed between the seams of the stones, and Kirana smelled the dry apricot breath of the black wind kicked up by their dying star. Getting caught exposed in storms like this could rip flesh from bone, and fill one's lungs with rot.

"Kirana?" Yisaoh again."I will sew your seat in place if you don't tell me if –"

Kirana took a lock of Yisaoh's hair in her fingers, and felt a pang of love and regret. Love for a woman she had conquered three countries to save from a fractious rival, and regret that she was so devoted to a single soul that she could not leave this dying world unless she had this woman by her side. The wind moaned through the hold.

"I'm fine," Kirana said. "We'll find her soon. You will all come with me to the new world."

"This is the second person she's sent to kill you," Yisaoh said. "That other woman, that other me, she is ruthless. She will not stop."

Kirana did not correct her, did not say the assassin had

cared little for Kirana, and run straight here for Yisaoh. "We don't know it's her. There are half a hundred worlds with–"

"It's her," Yisaoh said, and the certainty in her voice chilled Kirana. "It's what I would have done, if you had sent people to kill me."

Kirana pressed her fingers to the wound in her leg where the assassin had stabbed her. The armor had already sealed itself with sticky sap. The sap had closed the wound inside, too, or at least stopped it from bleeding. She would need to see a doctor soon. Poison was a possibility.

"You tell me they have no armies there," Yisaoh said, her voice barely audible now above the wind buffeting the hold. Kirana wondered when they would get the worst of it.

"No armies," Kirana said, "but they aren't complete fools. Not all of them. Little groups of people like the Dhai survive by being clever. I suspect she's as clever as you, and that does make her dangerous."

Yisaoh wrapped her arms around Kirana. It was awkward, with Kirana in full armor. Yisaoh's robe was crushed velvet, soft, but beneath, Yisaoh was all knobby bones and cold flesh. "You remember when I was plump?" Yisaoh said. Yisaoh never did like it when Kirana reminded her about what it was that made her so effective in the army – her ruthlessness, her cleverness. Yisaoh had given all that up to rear their children. She was tired of torture and death. But the past followed them, relentless as the burning star in the sky.

"I remember," Kirana said. She felt a stab of loss, as if she'd failed Yisaoh. Failed them all. Her stomach growled in answer. The apple was the first thing she'd eaten all day. "This isn't over yet. If they hadn't broken the mirror I'd have sent every one of my legions after her. They have wards on her, so I'll send a ward-breaker this time, and take her head for good measure. Then you and I will cross over and–"

Yisaoh pressed her fingers to Kirana's lips. Kirana remembered the day they had met. Yisaoh had emerged from the warm waters of the Shadow Sea, brown-gold and beaming at some shared joke between her and her companions. Kirana had stood on a low rise above the rocky beach, and had been struck dumb by the sight of her. Kirana was bleeding out from some wound inflicted in a minor skirmish over the next hill. Isolated on the little beach amid the pounding surf, Yisaoh and her companions had not heard the fighting. It was like stumbling into some forgotten world, like Kirana's bright childhood, carefree, before the sky imploded. Before the world began to die.

The wind wailed. The children stirred. Kirana listened to the sound of her own heartbeat begin to tick down. Surely she would have felt the poison by now, if it was a poisoned blade? She had to admire the act – the forethought to hire a lookalike good with a weapon, one not afraid to feign death through drugs or some gifted trick, and hurl herself into some other world to murder Kirana's family. It was a bold move for a supposed pacifist.

"I'm afraid," Yisaoh said.

"I'll take care of you."

"No," Yisaoh said. "I'm afraid of what we've had to become to survive this."

"We can go back," Kirana said. "When this is over–"

"I don't think we can."

Outside, the contaminated remnants of the dead star rained death and fire over the northern parts of the world. Kirana knew it would not be long now before it reached them here. Six months, a year, and the rest of the globe would be a fiery wasteland. The toxic storms blowing in the waste from the north were just the start of the end. If she had not murdered all the people she needed to fuel the winks between worlds, they would have died eventually. She was doing them a favor. Every last bloody one of them.

"Promise you'll take the children," Yisaoh said, "even if–"

"I won't leave without you."

"Promise."

"I'll save us all," Kirana said. "I promise you *that*."

Sitting there in the dark, holding Yisaoh while her children slept and her leg throbbed and the wind howled around them, she decided it was time to begin the invasion of Dhai in earnest. She had been waiting for the right time, waiting until they had enough blood, until they had rebuilt enough resources after the mirror's destruction. But she was out of time. The days were no longer numbered. The days were over.

She held onto Yisaoh, and imagined walking into the great Dhai temple to Oma, Yisaoh at her arm, her children beside her, and her people spread out all across the plateau, cheering her name, calling her savior, already forgetting the atrocities they had had to commit to see that end. It was a vision she had nurtured now for almost a decade.

It was time to see it through.

1

Lilia did not believe in miracles outside of history books, but she was beginning to believe in her own power, and that was a more frightening thing to believe in. Now she sat on the edge of the Liona Stronghold's parapet as an icy wind threatened to unseat her. She had spent over a week here in Liona, waiting on the Kai and his judgment. Would he throw her back into slavery in the east? She imagined what it would be like to topple from such a great height now and avoid that fate, and trembled with the memory of being pushed from such a distance just six months before, and broken on the ground below. The memory was so powerful it made her nauseous, and she crawled back down behind the parapet, head bowed, breathing deeply to keep from vomiting. Climbing was a slow business, as her clawed right hand still wouldn't close properly, and her twisted left foot throbbed in the cold weather. Her awkward gait had only grown more cumbersome over the last year.

Dawn's tremulous fingers embraced the sky. She squinted as the hourglass of the double suns moved above the jagged mountain range that made up the eastern horizon. The heat of the suns soothed her troubled thoughts. The satellite called Para already burned brilliant blue in the western sky, turning the horizon dark turquoise. Blue shadows purled across the jagged stone mountains that hugged Liona, festooning the trees and tickling at clumps of forgotten snow. She wasn't ready for spring. With spring came the thawing of the harbor, and worse – the thawing of the harbors in Saiduan that held the Tai Mora, the invaders that would swallow the world country by country.

"Li?" Her friend Gian walked across the parapet toward Lilia, hugging herself for warmth. "Your Saiduan friend got into a fight, and said it was important for me to fetch you."

Gian wore the same tattered jacket she had in the Dorinah slave camps. Most of the refugees who'd come over from Dorinah with Lilia's ragtag band had been fed by the militia in Liona, but not clothed properly or seen by a doctor.

Lilia said, "Wasn't it Taigan who insisted we stay out of trouble?"

"What do you expect from a Saiduan assassin, one of those sanisi? They are always fighting."

Lilia thought she could say the same about Dorinahs like Gian, but refrained. She didn't like reminding herself that Gian's loyalties had first lain with Dorinah. Lilia held out a hand. Gian took it. Lilia sagged against her.

"Are you ill?" Gian asked.

Lilia gazed into Gian's handsome, concerned face, then away. She still reminded Lilia too strongly of another Gian, one long dead for a cause Lilia didn't believe in. Lilia wondered often if she'd made the wrong choice in not joining with the other Gian's people. What difference would saving six hundred slaves make if the country was overwhelmed by some foreign people from another world? Very little.

"You should eat," Gian said, "after we find Taigan. Let me help you."

Lilia took Gian's arm and descended into the teeming chaos of Liona. Red-skirted militia bustled through the halls, carrying bundles of linen, sacks of rice, and messages bound in leather cases. Dead sparrows littered the hallways, expired after delivering messages to and from the surrounding clans about the influx of refugees. Lilia had never seen so many sparrows. She wondered if the messages getting ferried around were about more than refugees. She'd been gone for nearly a year. A lot could have changed.

Milling among the militia were Lilia's fellow refugees, often gathered in clusters outside storage rooms or shared privies. Lilia saw militia herding refugees back into their rooms like chattel, and bit back her annoyance. She wanted to send out a simmering wave of flame in their direction, boiling the offensive militia from the inside out. Her own skin warmed, briefly, and she saw a puff of red mist seep from her pores. The compulsion shocked and shamed her. Some days she felt more mad than gifted.

Omajista. The word still tasted bad. A word from a storybook. Someone with great power. Everything she felt she was not. But she could draw on Oma's power now. Omajista was the only word that fit.

Lilia kept her arm hooked in Gian's as she limped down the hall. Her hand hadn't been the only thing twisted in her fall, and even before that, her gnarled left foot had made walking more difficult for her than others. She felt eyes on her even now. What did she look like to them? Some scarred, half-starved, misshapen lunatic, probably. And maybe she was. She opened her left fist, and saw a purl of red mist escape it. What did it feel like to go mad? They'd exiled gifted people for going mad with power, like the Kai's aunt.

As they rounded the corner to the next stairwell, Lilia heard shouting.

A ragged figure loped up the stairs on all fours. Lilia thought it was an animal. She saw filthy skin, a tangle of long hair, a shredded hide of some kind that she only realized was a torn garment when the figure barreled into her. The thing thumped its head into her stomach, knocking Lilia back.

The creature snarled at her, tearing at her face and clothes. Lilia lashed out with her good hand. Hit it in the face. It squealed. The face was young, the mouth twisted. Where its eyes should have been were two pools of scarred flesh.

"What is it?" Gian shrieked. She cowered a few feet away, hands raised.

Lilia called Oma, pulling a long thread of breath and knotting it into a burst of fire. The breathy red mist pushed the thing off her. It tangled with the spell, growling and snarling as it tumbled down the steps.

Ghrasia Madah, leader of the militia in Liona, rushed up the steps just as the thing began to tumble. She caught it by the shoulders, shouting, "Off now!" as if the feral thing was a dog or a bear.

Lilia pressed her hand to her cheek where it had scratched her. The thing began to whine and tremble at Ghrasia's feet, and it was only then that Lilia realized it was a real human being, not some beast.

Gian hurried to Lilia's side and helped her up.

"I'm sorry," Ghrasia said. She held the little feral girl close. "She hasn't attacked anyone *here* before." Ghrasia straightened. The girl crouched beside her, head hanging low, hair falling into her face. She nuzzled Ghrasia's hand like a dog. "She was treated badly," Ghrasia said. "She's my responsibility."

Lilia smoothed her dress. She was still wearing the white muslin dress and white hair ribbons she had put on to give her the appearance of the Dhai martyr Faith Ahya. In the shadow of the rising suns, her skin glowing through a gifted trick, and flying to the top of the wall with the aid of several air-calling parajistas bound to her cause, the ruse had worked to sway the Dhai of Liona to open the gate. But in the stark light of day, Lilia suspected she looked filthy, broken, and ridiculous.

"Why are you responsible?" Lilia said. "Surely you aren't her mother. She doesn't have a clan, does she? She is not Dhai at all."

"Many would say the same of you," Ghrasia said. "When I took up a sword, I accepted that there were some bad things I'd have to do. I wanted to temper them with good. It was up to me, now, to decide who was the monster, who the victim. That's harder than you might think, and it's a terrible power. One must use that power for something better, sometimes." The feral girl nuzzled her hand.

Lilia could not bite back her retort. "That girl attacked me. It's not as if I left thousands of people to die, crushed up against that wall, the way you did during the Pass War."

Ghrasia said nothing, but her expression was stony. Lilia regretted what she'd said immediately. But before she could recant, Ghrasia called the girl back, and they walked down the long curving tongue of the stairs.

"Let's find another stairway," Gian said. "I want to find Taigan before she makes a mess. Her jokes don't go over well here."

But Lilia stayed rooted there, looking after Ghrasia. "She thinks she's better," Lilia said, "because she guards some monster. I'm protecting hundreds of people. Innocent, peaceful people."

Lilia imagined all of Dhai burning, just the way the Tai Mora wanted. She needed to speak to Taigan more urgently than ever, because choosing sides was becoming more difficult.

"Let them make their own mistakes," Gian said, pulling at her hand again. "They aren't your people any more than they're mine."

But Lilia had lost track of who her people were supposed to be a long time ago.

They found Taigan tussling with a young man on the paving stones outside the dog and bear kennels. Lilia thought for a moment that Taigan had indeed started telling her morbid jokes, and gravely offended him.

"Tira's tears," Lilia said. "Who is this?"

Taigan gripped the man by the back of his tunic and flung him at Lilia's feet. "Ask this man where he's been," Taigan said.

The man wasn't much older than Lilia – maybe eighteen or nineteen. His face was smeared in mud and bear dung. She saw blood at the corner of his mouth.

For a moment, the sight of the blood repulsed her. Then she squared her shoulders and said, with a voice surer than she felt, "You should have known better than to provoke a Saiduan."

"You'll both be exiled for this abuse," he said. "Violence against me. Touching without consent. These are crimes!"

"I caught him in your room," Taigan said, gesturing behind her to the storage room off the kennels that they had been housed in by the militia.

"They say you're Faith Ahya reborn," the man said. "My grandmother is ill, and with Tira in decline, there's no tirajista powerful enough to save her. But they say Faith Ahya could heal people, even when Tira was in decline. Can you?"

"He's lying. He's a spy," Taigan said.

"Where is your grandmother?" Lilia asked. His plea reminded her of her own mother. She would have given anything to save her mother, but she had not been powerful enough, or clever enough.

"Clan Osono," he said.

"Perhaps I will see her," Lilia said, "when things have settled here. I have a responsibility to the Dhai as much as the dajians I've brought here."

Taigan said something harsh in Saiduan, and whirled back toward their shared room.

"Forgive Taigan," she said. "She has a very strange sense of things. It may be a few days before I can see your grandmother. There is much to sort out here, and the Kai may still condemn me to exile."

"It won't happen," the man said. "We won't let it." He scrambled to his feet and ran off, clutching at his side. Lilia wondered if Taigan had broken his ribs. Violence would call even more attention to them than bad jokes.

"Can you help him, really?" Gian asked.

"Maybe," Lilia said. She knew that helping the Dhai in the valley would go a long way toward the acceptance of the refugees. If she had turned him away, he would have brought back stories to his clan about some arrogant little no-nothing girl and her stinking refugees. She needed to create another story, or the refugees would find no welcome in Dhai.

Gian stroked her arm. Lilia pulled away, annoyed. She had gotten used to touching without consent in the camps – it wasn't considered rude in Dorinah – but that didn't make it easier to tolerate. In that moment she found it deeply offensive. Something about seeing Taigan's brute rage at the young man had shaken her. It reminded her of who she could be.

Gian said she would get them food, though Lilia knew they needed none. Gian had become obsessed with food since they arrived in Liona, and had started secreting bits of it away in their sleeping quarters. Lilia once found an apple under her pillow.

Lilia walked back into the musty storage room they had called home for nearly a week. Taigan sat on a large barrel, muttering to herself in Saiduan. She ran a stone across her blade.

Lilia sat on the straw mattress on the floor. She saw a brown wrapper peeking out from under the mattress and pulled it out. It was a hunk of rye bread wrapped in brown paper.

Taigan grunted at it. "She's going to start drawing vermin."

Lilia tapped at the flame fly lantern, rousing the flies to give them some light. "You sit in the dark too much," she said.

"This Gian girl is like your dog," Taigan said. "Dogs hoard food and lick their masters' feet. You trust a dog?"

"That's unfair."

"You know nothing of her."

"I know less of you. But I put up with you too." In truth, her feelings about Gian were confused. Did she like this Gian for who she was, or because she reminded her so strongly of the woman who died for her? She tucked the bread back under the mattress. She didn't want to know what else was under there.

"Which is just as curious," Taigan said. She balanced her blade on her thigh. Her mouth thinned. Lilia saw her arm flex. Then move.

Taigan's blade flashed at Lilia's face.

Lilia reflexively snatched at Oma. She caught the end of Taigan's blade in red tangles of breath.

Taigan blew a puff of misty breath over Lilia's tangles, disintegrating them. "Still so much to learn," Taigan said. She began to sharpen the blade again.

Lilia pillowed her hands beneath her head. Taigan's little tricks were growing tedious. Some days Lilia wanted to bundle Taigan up with some clever spell while she slept and leave her there. But most of what she knew of Oma now was self taught. There were hundreds, if not thousands, of songs and litanies to learn, and all she knew were those Taigan had taught her in the mountains and here during their long wait together.

"I don't have a lot of friends," Lilia said. "Don't try and make Gian mean."

"It's a sorry day," Taigan said, "when a young girl's friends are an outcast sanisi and some politicking snake."

Taigan jabbed the sword at the wall now, feinting at some unseen enemy. Lilia wondered what enemies she fought when she slept. Taigan cried out in Saiduan at night, wrestling with terrible dreams that made her curse and howl. Lilia had taken to sleeping with a pillow over her head.

"Not everyone is like you," Lilia said, "some spy or assassin trying to use other people."

"You and I disagree on many things, bird," Taigan said. She sheathed her blade and stood to look out the tiny window at the back of the storage room. Motes of dust clotted the air. "But we must agree on what comes next. You cannot stay here mending people's mad mothers." A blooming red mist surrounded her.

Lilia countered with the Song of the Proud Wall, a defensive block, mouthing the words while calling another huff of breath to build a snarling counterattack.

Taigan's spell crashed into her barrier. The meshes of breath wrangled for dominance.

Taigan deployed another offense. Always offensive, with Taigan. Lilia knotted up another defensive spell and let go.

"These are my people," Lilia said. "We won't let that other Kai win."

"This country doesn't know what to do with you," Taigan said, and Lilia recognized the Song of the Cactus right before she spoke, and muttered her own counterattack. She released it before Taigan got out her next sentence. Ever since she had learned to draw on Oma, using the songs Taigan had taught her was easy. "I can take you away from here under the cover of dark. The Saiduan would welcome you. We know what you are, and how to…"

"How to use me?"

Lilia leaned forward, concentrating on the Song of the Mountain, trying to call it up and twist the strands she needed without mouthing the words and giving her move away while Taigan's Song of the Cactus and her Song of the Water Spider warred in great clouds of seething, murderous power.

"So indelicate." Taigan said. Six tendrils from the Song of the Cactus kicked free of the Water Spider defense and grabbed Lilia's throat. She huffed out another defense. She was sweating now.

Taigan neatly deployed another offense, a roiling tide of red that spilled over their tangling spells and wafted over Lilia's protective red bubble. Lilia had four active spells now. If she panicked, if she lost her focus, Taigan would overwhelm her. She did not like losing.

"And what will they do here without us?" she wheezed, calling another huff of Oma's power beneath her skin for a fifth offensive spell. Taigan had no defenses. All Lilia had to do was switch tactics long enough to overwhelm her.

Taigan shrugged. But Lilia saw the movement of her lips, and the spell she was trying to hide with that shrug. Defensive barrier. It was coming.

Lilia released her offensive spell, six brilliant woven balls of Oma's breath, hurtling at Taigan like moths to claw lilies.

"If I leave," Lilia said, untangling the spell at her throat. "The Kai will throw my people back into Dorinah, and everyone left will be killed by the Tai Mora."

Her red mist collided with an offensive spell, something Lilia hadn't anticipated. But one of hers got through, curling back behind Taigan's left shoulder, half of it slipping through before Taigan's defensive Song of the Pearled Wall went up.

Taigan hissed, flicked her hand, and mitigated the worst of the damage. But Lilia felt a burst of satisfaction on seeing the shoulder of Taigan's tunic smoking.

"I am a sanisi, not a seer," Taigan said. "I cannot see all futures." Taigan clapped her hands, and deployed some song Lilia didn't know, neatly cutting Lilia off from calling on Oma.

Lilia's warring spells dissipated, as did Taigan's. The air smelled faintly of copper. Lilia sneezed.

"It's unfair to use a trick you won't teach me," Lilia said.

"I'd be a fool to do that," Taigan said. "The Song of Unmaking is all a teacher has to control a student. If I let you keep pulling, you'd burn yourself out."

"I wouldn't."

"You would. You seek to win at all costs, even when the odds are against you. But drawing on Oma isn't some strategy game."

"That's exactly what it is."

"The stakes are higher."

Gian pushed in with a tray of food – lemon and cilantro rice, steamed vegetables, a decadent platter of fruit spanning a surprisingly wide range of colors, considering the season. She pressed the tray at Lilia.

Seeing so much food made Lilia nauseous. "Where did you get this?"

"I said it was for you. More people here like you than you think." Gian set the tray on the floor. She pulled two sticky rice balls from her pockets and crawled to the edge of the mattress. Lilia watched her a moment, wondering where she would think to put them, but Gian simply held them, contentedly, in her lap.

"What do you think about helping the Dhai fight?" Lilia asked.

"I don't know," Gian said. "What does it mean to be a god, Faith Ahya reborn?"

"Bearing babies," Taigan said.

"Oh, be quiet," Lilia said. "If there's a war, I will win it. I'm not afraid anymore."

"Heroes are honest cowards," Taigan said, "who fight though they fear it. Only fools feel no fear."

"I was afraid my whole life, and it got me nothing."

Taigan muttered something in Saiduan. Then, "Fear tempers bad choices, bird."

"I've made my decision," Lilia said. "You can help me convince the Kai to let the refugees stay, and to help me get them accepted here so we can fight the Tai Mora, or you can go. Both of you."

Gian said, "If you aren't going to eat–"

"Take it," Lilia said.

Gian picked up the tray. Taigan stood, muttering. "Bird, this choice changes everything. The whole landscape of your life. If you come to Saiduan…"

"I made my choice," Lilia said.

She heard footsteps outside, and turned just as two of the militia stepped up to the door.

Taigan moved to block them as the smallest one drew herself up and said, "The Kai is on his way to pass judgment, and Ghrasia Madah wishes to see you immediately."

2

Ahkio had stumbled into the belly of Oma's temple looking for the secret his dead sister had kept there. Now that he had arrived within the temple's rapturous beating heart, he feared he had made a terrible mistake in pursuing this particular mystery.

The light blinded him. He covered his eyes. Warmth suffused his body, and for a moment he thought he had fallen through the stone monolith in the temple's basement into some bright day. There wasn't supposed to be anything below the temple basements. Yet here he was, bathed in ethereal light, and clearly not alone.

"Kai?"

The voice again.

Ahkio pulled his hands from his face. Squinted. He sat at the center of a circular stone room. The light came from a bank of windows twice his height. As his eyes adjusted, he saw a tall woman with intricately styled white hair bound in jeweled silver pins and combs standing a few paces away. The cut of her long skirt and belted tunic was wholly unfamiliar. She did not move toward him so much as she floated, hands clasped behind her. There was something uncanny in her demeanor. When she moved, nothing else moved – not her dress, not her hair. Even her serious expression remained fixed.

He moved slowly to his feet. His hands hurt from his fall. He saw a great streak of crimson and violet bands of light tangling with one another above the windows. They wove strange characters in the air. He couldn't quite make out what they were meant to be.

"We are almost out of time," she said.

"I just got here," Ahkio said, confused.

She gestured to the tangling bands of light. "I have been compromised," she said. "That's our water clock. Quickly now. I am the heart of the temple, and your predecessor warned me you would come. She said she would educate those who came after, but now that I have been... altered, I suspect much has gone wrong."

"My predecessor... My sister, Kirana, the former Kai?"

She withdrew her hands from behind her. They fluttered. It wasn't a motion she was making, but some kind of distortion of her form, as if she were reflected on a pool of water.

"Has Oma risen?" she asked.

"No," Ahkio said. "What are you and how did I get here?"

"We built these beasts to take us to the moon, but that's pointless now, listen–"

"What are you talking about?" He was beginning to think this was a hallucination. He remembered seeing his sister's ghost. He remembered how she had ripped herself from Sina's maw to deliver a message that had, eventually, brought him here. Was this Sina? Had he been transported to the star that carried the souls of the dead?

Her expression did not change, but her tone was not as confident. She pointed to the vast bank of windows. "We broke the sky."

Above her, the snarl of figures continued to whirl. Instructions? Numbers? A ward losing its integrity? He still wasn't certain.

Ahkio went to the windows. They were not the

smooth skin of the temple he knew, but metal. Had he stepped through a door to some other world? He gazed at the jagged teeth of the mountains beyond the windows, ringed in wreaths of cloud. It was a foreign vista, but not a foreign place. Mount Ahya rose high from the cloak of mountains, its crown so tall it lost itself to the sky. He saw cities now at the base of the slopes and along the river. Was that the Fire River? The same one that circled Oma's temple? Shimmering blue tiles seemed to seethe along the rooftops. Brightly clothed figures moved over sinuous roads the color of obsidian. And something else was circling in the sky, too large for a bird.

"Where is this?" Ahkio asked.

The woman floated toward him. She had no feet. He shrank away.

"This is a shard of time, stuck between spaces. When we broke the sky, we broke a good deal more. Broke reality itself. Do you understand these concepts? Your predecessor had some knowledge of the parallel theory of worlds, but many before her have not."

"I've met people with our faces," Ahkio said. "Is this some other world too?"

"Not another world," she said. "Another time."

"I don't–"

She pointed at the flickering light above the window again. "I have been sabotaged. One of your number put a ward here tailored to your presence. If you do not leave now, you will perish with me. There is no telling what will happen when the heartstone breaks. It could fracture us into a hundred different times or realities."

"Who could get down here but me?" he asked. "I'm the Kai. Only Kirana and I–"

"Only a Kai can cross over into this space," she said. "Only a Kai can speak to the heart of the temple. But she did not set the ward on the heart, only the stone. It will break, Kai, and when it breaks, you will be trapped here with me. Please go."

"Not until I have answers." He pointed to the sky. "Where's Para, in this time? You said this wasn't another world, so where are the satellites, then?"

"The satellites are…" She brought her hands together. "Let us pretend the gods were once one creature. They were a creature we did not understand, one that brought great strife and madness. The effects of this god were felt across the whole of the world. It hung in the sky for years, poisoning us. We had already been planning our escape, there." She pointed to the edge of the eastern horizon, where a massive rising crescent blotted out the edge of the world. "See how large it was? The moon. We planned to escape there through transference. You understand?"

"You wanted to open a door to another world. To the moon?"

"See, you're not so dense. So many Kais I have told this to, so many, and here I am again, repeating it. You never learn." She sighed and turned to stare again at the bands of light. "Not once."

"How many have you spoken to?"

"Since the breaking of the world? At least a dozen."

"Do you know what date it is? What year?"

"I told you – it doesn't matter."

"Before Kirana, who was the last Kai you saw here?"

"They blur together."

"Please."

Her form went still. He thought for a moment she was ill or having some kind of fit. Then she spoke. "They came after the battle of Roasandara. Kai Saohinla. But after Roasandara was far too late. Oma was in decline. They found me far too late. And the time before that, and before that… always, they came too late. My life is just this. This conversation. Over and over."

"What did Kirana speak to you about before she died?"

"Kai Kirana asked how to control the transference

engines to prevent the other worlds from colliding here."

"Engines?" When he thought of an engine, he thought of the devices like wind and water mills that converted energy into motion. Something told him she wasn't thinking of a water mill.

"The beasts."

"You created beasts?"

"The engines are sentient beasts. Surely you know that by now? You have been living inside our beasts for centuries."

Ahkio thought of the warm skin of the temples. Many believed they had souls. "Your beasts, your engines, are the temples," Ahkio said. "This is the literal heart of the temple."

"I have said that at least three times already. Listen, properly controlled, the engines act as great conductors for the energy from the satellites," she said. "We thought we were able to kill the thing infecting our sky and harness its power. But it broke apart instead, and now its pieces travel across our world and many, many others. It poisons a new world every cycle. When Oma rises, all of these disparate worlds come together again. All the stars. All the worlds. Only the engines can stop it."

"How?"

"I am not an engineer, Kai. Now our time is over. Quickly, move to the center of the room."

"Please, I–"

"I am not a god, Kai. Just a woman unstuck in time." She waved at him. He refused to move back. Her hands passed right through him, and he yelped. She really was a ghost. He stepped back to the center of the room, a few inches from a symbol on the floor that matched the one on the stone.

"How do I stop the worlds coming together this time?" he said.

"I can only tell you how we broke the worlds, not how to fix them. I was lost before anyone learned how to do that. Perhaps they never did."

Ahkio stared at the rising moon. It tinged the sky lavender. The double suns were the same – their hourglass form in the sky comforted him. He saw the smaller red sun, Shar, riding high up over their left shoulder. Whatever thing had killed this world, or this... time, was not visible in the sky, unless it was the moon itself. With all that he had seen and experienced since his sister's death, maybe this wasn't so remarkable. She could be a hallucination, a dream. He could have been spirited off to some other world, or some other time, as she said. Reality had become a questionable thing. Nothing would surprise him.

The figures above the windows consisted of fewer characters now. Counting down? Unraveling?

"Not everyone is prepared to make the sacrifices necessary to win," she said. "What will you sacrifice, to stop these worlds from entering yours. Do you know, yet?"

"I don't," he said.

She smacked her lips, making the motion but no sound. "You are the first to give me such an honest answer," she said. "It's time to go back. Step back."

"Who sabotaged you?" he asked.

"An Ora," she said, "one of your own."

"Nasaka?"

"No." Her form flickered. The room trembled, out of focus. Ahkio rubbed his eyes. "Step back, or die here."

"Almeysia," Ahkio said, and stepped back onto the symbol on the floor–

–and woke on the basement floor in Liaro's trembling arms.

"What will you sacrifice?"

Ahkio stabbed his sister Kirana in the eye. Blood gushed from her face, smearing his clothing and skin, until he could not tell where he ended and her body began. She screamed at

him with his mother's voice – the same screaming he had heard
when his mother was burned alive, and he could not save her.

The same screaming…

Ahkio woke in a drab stone room, shivering but
soaked in sweat. The presence of the stone told him
he was no longer in one of the temples, which meant
someone had moved him a great distance. He pushed
out of bed, and found he was wearing little more than
a linen shift. He moved groggily to the narrow window
and looked out. He was high enough up to gauge that he
was gazing west into massive woodlands of bamboo and
bonsa and giant everpine. Above it all was the peak of
Mount Ahya, its crown lost to cloud. The only place in
Dhai with a view like that was the Kuallina Stronghold,
at the center of Dhai.

He heard raised voices in the hall. The door burst open,
and Liaro and Caisa entered, arguing with a woman who
wore the green and violet apron of a Clan Osono doctor.

"How long have I been here?" Ahkio asked.

The three of them stopped short when they saw him.
Liaro was the first to break away. He ran to Ahkio's side
and embraced him. "I thought you were lost," Liaro said.
"You're the greatest fool in all of Dhai."

"Have I finally usurped that title from you?" Ahkio
said.

"A joke! Tira, it can't really be you if you're telling
jokes," Liaro said, and though his tone was light, Ahkio
noticed that Liaro's brow furrowed, and he peered into
Ahkio's face as if half expecting to find a stranger there.

"We've kept you almost a week," the doctor said.

"It was necessary," Caisa said quickly, and Ahkio
sensed the length of his stay may have been what they
had been arguing about.

"We couldn't leave you with Ora Nasaka," Liaro said.
"We got you out on the Line, just the two of us and
some novices Caisa trusted. If Ora Nasaka thought you
harmed, she'd have done some other awful thing like

light a kitten on fire."

"There's rumor she's…" Caisa began, and then came up short, staring at the doctor.

The doctor frowned. "I'll see myself out, then," she said, and left them.

"She's looking for your Aunt Etena," Liaro said. "Or that's what we've been hearing. She put out word to her little spies about it. No one looks for Etena if they want to keep you on the seat. So if you wondered what she was doing all that time we were hunting down Tai Mora spies, now you know."

"And there's Liona!" Caisa said. "And the emissary."

"If you're well enough," Liaro said, "You should go to Liona first. Your friend Ghrasia says there are refugees swarming the wall. It's a disaster."

"One disaster at a time," Ahkio said. "Who's minding Nasaka in the temple? Has she had full run of it?"

Caisa and Liaro exchanged looks. "We've been busy saving *you*," Liaro said, "in case that wasn't clear. All your Oras from Raona are there, though – Ora Ohanni, Ora Shanigan, your third cousins–"

Ahkio said, "Liaro, I want you back at the temple. Find out what's changed, and dig more into what's happening with Etena. I can't imagine it will be any easier to find her now than it was before I took the seat. Also, let people at the temple know I'm traveling to Liona. The last thing we need is rumors I'm dead. There was an emissary coming, wasn't there? Gods, if Nasaka's handling that… put off the emissary, too. Caisa, come with me to Liona. I'll need militia to accompany us, and a couple good jistas."

Caisa sniffed. "I'm a good jista."

"Another good jista, then. Move now. We've tarried long enough."

Caisa ran to the door, but Liaro lingered.

"What happened to you, Ahkio?"

He shook his head. "I went somewhere… else."

"But that's the thing," Liaro said. "You *didn't* go anywhere. You slopped against that stone like a dead man. I couldn't rouse you until the thing cracked."

"It's broken?"

"I thought you were dead, Ahkio. I thought you wouldn't wake up."

Ahkio embraced him again. "Get things prepared for Liona," Ahkio said. Was he mad? Was Liaro? "I can talk more about what I saw later."

"Don't keep me in the dark."

"Don't argue with me!" Ahkio said, more forcefully than he meant to.

"You don't know what it's been like," Liaro said, "loving a dead man."

Ahkio sat back on the bed. "I'm exhausted, and I'm doing the best I can."

Caisa sent clothes and broth, and Ahkio stumbled his way down into the banquet hall to meet with the head of Kuallina and assure her he was all right. Within a day he and Caisa and their little party of militia and six jistas were on the road to Kuallina. The party was too big to take the Line, the great organic transit system that linked the temples and holds. The way to Liona was perilous. Spring was rousing the snarling plant life of the valley, and they fought nests of floxflass and ambervine and pulled two of their number from hidden bladder traps, their mouths newly engaged. They heard roving bands and semi-sentient walking trees nearby for two days, and had to alter their route twice to avoid them. Caisa came down with a hacking cough their last night on the road, and one of the tirajistas coaxed up a great flowering plant tendril from her throat.

"Bad season for traveling," Ahkio told her as she shivered in bed. He fed her broth and took her hand when she asked and told her she wasn't going to die.

"I have too much to do before I die," she said.

"We all do," he said, and pressed her hand to his face

and wondered what Liaro would do. Tell some fine joke. Lighten her mood. But his mood was so dark he could see no light as far as he could glimpse into the future.

Ahkio remembered the temple keeper's words again as they approached the great wall of Liona. He was exhausted and drained, full of worry about Caisa, Ghrasia, Liaro, Nasaka, the clan leaders, the impending war, and gods, what had happened to Meyna – too many things for a mind already stretched to the edge of sanity. Liona was a fortress three hundred feet high made of massive cut stones and tirajista-trained vines. Ahkio rode at the head of the party astride his bear just outside the massive gates of Liona. Liaro was right that this was the immediate issue – the threat of more people pouring in at the borders as the Tai Mora escalated their war was very real. They could be sending anyone in with the refugees. All that killing in Raona meant nothing if they could not secure their borders.

"What's that noise?" Caisa asked. She rode beside him on a great brown bear.

"I don't hear it," Ahkio said.

Caisa rode ahead. He called after her just as their party broke through the woods and into the great meadow burned clean around the wall of Liona. He came up short as they did, struck dumb by the sight ahead of them. Four walking trees, the tallest over a hundred feet high, crashed across what should have been a bare clearing. But it was not empty. It was very much occupied. Camped all along the outside of the wall were hundreds of members of the militia, all dressed in red, and clumps of what must be the refugees, all of them hemmed in by a makeshift thorn fence. The trees bludgeoned their way through the mass of humanity, stirring them like a terrified hive of insects. The trees swung great sinewy tendrils, plucking up the defenseless people below them and depositing them into the great, poison-filled sacks swinging from their massive crowns.

Ahkio waved back at his party. "Help them!" he yelled, and urged his bear forward, though he had no weapon. "Caisa!" he yelled as his bear galloped to catch up to her, its great tongue lolling.

She already had her hands raised. He saw a small whirlwind skitter across the meadow, heading straight for the smallest of the trees.

One of the militia behind him caught up to Ahkio and offered a big machete. He took it and raised it high, barreling at the same tree that Caisa had targeted. The largest of the trees whipped its sticky tendrils at him, moving laboriously into their path on its great undulating roots to protect the smaller tree.

Ahkio glanced back at his jistas. He had no sinajista strong enough to produce a flame – the only thing the trees were truly afraid of. They would need to turn them back with brute force, a slow and dangerous thing with so many untrained people on the ground.

He caught up to Caisa. She yelled, "Get inside!"

"No," he said.

She huffed at him. The air was already heavy as cream. He saw the loop of the main gate open up, allowing him a brief glimpse into chaos as half a dozen figures came out to assist in the fray. He hoped one of them was a sinajista. He saw hundreds more dirty, haggard figures camped inside the lower courtyard. Sina's breath, how many had Ghrasia let in?

He turned his attention back to the big tree. "We need to coordinate with the ones at the gate," Ahkio said. He raised his machete and gestured for his party to come forward.

"Dangerous run," Caisa said. "We didn't bring you back just to–"

"Go," Ahkio said, and slapped his bear forward.

They made a breakneck run across the melee of militia and screaming refugees. A sweeping vine swung past Ahkio's head and caught one of the militia behind him.

She screamed as she was hoisted a hundred feet into the air and neatly dropped into one of the poisonous bags at the top of the tree.

Ahkio gritted his teeth and circled back behind the figures that had come out of the gates. He recognized Ghrasia immediately. She was shouting orders to three jistas who broke away from the group. He saw the little feral girl with her, the one from Raona, barking madly at her side.

On seeing him, something in Ghrasia lit up, briefly, before going out, like watching a candle flame flicker and die. He didn't understand it.

"Fire!" he said.

"We have no sinajistas," she said. "We're loading fire archers on the wall. We need to herd them together. Take your party back around the other side and flank them. I'll come up behind them. I have parajistas who can help contain the fire. I can't risk it catching the woods."

Ahkio relayed the order to his group and circled them back around to the north. The trees were spread widely now, grazing at random all across the broken encampment. He rode with Caisa and their companions in a long line, seeking to herd the trees back against the wall. The big tree nearest them turned its attention away from feeding and lashed at them with its sinewy appendages. Ahkio clung tightly to his bear. He wrapped his wrist around the reins twice, hoping he and the bear together would be too massive to draw up into the waiting pods.

The air was heavy, and a strong wind blew from the east. He glanced over and saw Ghrasia at the head of her party, and two parajistas coaxing vortexes to come up behind the herd.

Ahkio waved Caisa and the others closer to the tree, yelling at them to keep up the long line of their formation. Just as the big tree began to move inward, the smallest made a break between the two at the center, trying to run diagonally at them.

Ghrasia broke formation and charged after the littlest one. Ahkio raced to meet her, hoping they could pin it back in with the others.

He saw a few dozen fiery arrows flame across the sky from the parapet. One landed just ahead of his bear. It spooked and veered out of control, nearly colliding with Ghrasia. Two of her people had caught up to her. Ahkio's charging bear enraged the other two, and they broke.

Above them, the trees' appendages snapped and shivered. One grabbed hold of Ahkio and pulled. He clung to the bear. The resistance seemed to dissuade the tree. It lashed away and plucked one of the parajistas from his mount. The man screamed. A heavy whump of air slammed into Ahkio, nearly taking him from his seat.

"That's my parajista!" Ghrasia yelled. She urged her bear forward and reached up for one of the lashing vines. Ahkio watched in a mixture of awe and horror as she grabbed the vine and started climbing it toward the pods in the treetop.

He took a great breath and yelled at his bear for another burst of speed, but the bear was already running at full tilt, slavering. Ahkio raised himself up in his stirrups and took hold of a swinging vine. It was tough and slippery, but he found purchase, and began a stuttering climb after Ghrasia. As the tree tried to tip him into the lip of the pod, he hacked himself free with his machete. Ghrasia perched on a pod opposite him, sawing away at it. She firmed her mouth when she saw him, but said only, "Don't cut open the pods. Cut them loose. The stuff inside will cushion the fall. We may be able to save a few."

Ahkio swung back onto the long branch from which the pod dangled and began to cut. It was hard and fibrous. He glanced back at Ghrasia. "Why did you open the gates?" he said. "All these people drew the trees."

"Are we honestly going to talk here?" Ghrasia said.

Her bundle came free, spilling to the ground. She jumped to the next.

"Exile, Ghrasia! You put me in a place to exile you!"

"You haven't seen her," Ghrasia said, but Ahkio had no idea who she was talking about. "Your world is good and evil. But mine is far more complicated than that."

"How do we know they're dajians and not Tai Mora?"

Below them, the feral girl was barking.

Ghrasia gestured to the girl below with her dagger. "I'm responsible for her now, too. Should I kill her as well, like some trash because of what someone else did to her? Those refugees were shaped by Dorinah. She was shaped by the Tai Mora. People aren't born monsters. Monsters are made."

The pod Ahkio worked on finally came free, dropping its contents. He dodged one of the tree's knotted appendages. Smelled smoke. Turned. Some arrows had found their mark, but the fire wasn't taking hold. "I think the wood's too wet!" he said. "Do you have oil?"

"We're out," she said. "Used it all to fuel the refugee fires."

"Curse that, Ghrasia!"

"Exile me or don't," she said. "I can put Arasia in charge of the militia in addition to Liona. But you must make that decision now."

"After all we've–"

"Don't you bring that up. Don't you dare." The vehemence in her voice surprised him.

"But aren't we–"

"No," she said. "I made a mistake."

"Ghrasia–"

"We need to get off this tree," she said. "We're almost at the woods."

He glanced back. The other four walking trees were still well behind them, circled together now by their combined forces. "This isn't working," he said. "We need sinajistas."

"I would conjure one for you if I could," she said.

As she said it, one of the trees behind them burst into brilliant flames. "Oma!" he said, pointing.

Ghrasia gave a determined little smile. The other two trees went up. Ghrasia's smile faded. "Off the tree!" she yelled.

"But–"

"Off the tree, she'll light it up!"

"Who?"

Ghrasia grabbed the vine next to her and swung out toward Ahkio. She caught him around the waist and yelled, "Let go, for the love of–"

The tree's crown burst into flame.

Ahkio let go.

They slid more than seventy feet before the vine began to wave frantically. It came alive again, and curled around them while the smoking detritus of its crown fell all around them in ashy whispers. Ghrasia cut them free. Ahkio held her tight. They fell another fifteen feet to the soft, loamy ground, and landed with a huffing thud.

Ahkio lost his breath. He turned just as the flaming tree crashed into the woods.

Ghrasia crawled to her feet, yelling for parajistas, but they were at the far end of the encampment now, at least five hundred paces from its edge.

"Ghrasia," he said, scrambling to his feet, still winded. "If there was anything between us–"

She rounded on him. "It was a mistake. I know I can rely on you to respect that I've made my decision and leave it be."

"I thought–"

"You thought incorrectly," she said. "When I made the decision I did to open the gates, I also made a decision about our potential future. If you don't know it now, you will." She gazed back at the tree. It crashed into the great rooted trees of the woodland, thrashing. It emitted a terrible hissing sound as its sap bubbled. "We need to contain that fire." She started back down to the encampment, limping.

He ran to catch up with her, and reached for her arm. She yanked it away.

"I revoke consent," she said.

He stopped dead still, as if struck. "It's done, then?" he said, still not understanding.

"It's done," she said. "You're Kai and I lead the militia, and no more."

They strode down into the camp as Ghrasia called for doctors and tirajistas to help cut out the people they had released from the pods. Ahkio was still confused and breathless, uncertain as to why Ghrasia had wanted to change their relationship so suddenly. Yes, the world was mad, but that was a good reason for two people to stay together, not break apart.

Another line of people walked across the battered ground toward them while the great blazing mass of the dying trees guttered at the center of the camp.

A small, hunched figure limped along at the head of the group. Beside her was a very tall Saiduan person who looked very familiar.

"Faralis!" Ghrasia said to one of the men beside them. "That tree in the woods–"

"We're containing it," Faralis said. "I have two on it now."

"We freed people from the kill pods," she said. "I'll need doctors to care for them, if they lived."

Faralis turned and sprinted back toward the hold. All around them the survivors of the attack milled about with glazed eyes. Some shrieked, but most wandered around in shock.

Ghrasia said to the limping girl, "There were people in those kill pods. We could have cut them free."

"There's a reason they're called kill pods," the girl said.

"You're welcome," the Saiduan said, and Ahkio realized why the figure had seemed so familiar. It was

Taigan, the Saiduan who had visited the temple and carted away a scullery maid almost a year ago.

Ghrasia grimaced. She turned to Ahkio. "Here she is," she said.

Ahkio still wasn't sure who she meant. The little limping girl had scars on her face, and a serious, graven expression, though she could not have been very far into her teens. Her hair was tangled with frayed white ribbons that matched her dirty dress. She wore an oversized coat that made her look even smaller than she was. When she squinted at him, he felt as if he were being weighed and measured like one of the trees. Burn him or save him?

Realization dawned, then. "You're the scullery girl," he said. "Oma's tears, *you're* the one who brought these people here?" He looked at Taigan. "What have you done to her?"

Taigan shrugged. "She did this to herself."

More people were crowding up behind the girl. Some were grinning and whispering.

"You're a sinajista?" Ahkio asked the girl. "You took out those trees?"

"I'm more than that," she said.

"She's Faith Ahya reborn!" some young man from the crowd yelled, and a little cheer went up. Ahkio felt more fearful then than he had halfway up a blazing tree. This could get out of hand.

"There's something else," Ghrasia said as the crowd swelled.

He wasn't sure he could bear any more surprises.

Ghrasia gestured to someone from the crowd who began to wend her way forward. "Your wife is here," Ghrasia said.

Mohrai cut between Taigan and the scullery girl. She was as Ahkio remembered, a plump, soft-faced woman with a gaze that told him she was used to getting her way. Her low brow and pinched features put him in mind of an owl. She wore a knee-length purple tunic cinched with a leather belt and embroidered with silver stars. The extravagance was not lost on Ahkio, especially when paired with her flamboyantly curled hair.

"Catori," he said.

"Kai," she said. "I've been looking for you for days. My family's closed the harbor gates."

They all stared at her, including Ahkio, and he wondered if this was the best place to relay this news. "We need to go inside," he said.

"The Tai Mora have blocked the harbor," Mohrai said. He caught a hint of fear in her voice then, "and they are making demands for our immediate surrender."

3

Zezili fought death. She thought, for a time, that she had won. But her body still failed her.

Zezili's face and hands and torso swelled. The wounds inflicted by the Empress's cats oozed a thick yellowish pus. A fever shook her body and left her sweaty and delirious. Zezili remembered the Empress picking up Zezili's bloody severed thumb and painting her own white lips with it. The doctors said Zezili raved for three days and screamed that the Empress had eaten her whole.

Zezili's sisters clustered around her body, warbling in sticky voices as tangled as Zezili's dreams. The room smelled of shit and morbid flesh. When she roused herself for a few stolen moments, her youngest sister, Sorana, said they believed they sat at her death bed.

Her sisters had gathered to watch her die.

Taodalain, the last of her sisters to hover at her side once living seemed a possibility, asked if Zezili wanted her to read the letter the Empress had sent to her bedside.

Half of Zezili's face was bandaged, one eye shredded or swollen shut, she did not know which. She kept her hands beneath the heavy folds of her bedding. Even bandaged, she did not want to see what had become of the hands that once held her sword.

She nodded to hear the letter.

Taodalain read:

Zezahlia, my dearest;

As of the thirty-eighth of Seara, I have released you from sworn service. I allow you to choose, upon this unbinding, to retire to your estate until the end of those days my cats have left you, or – upon your renewal – I grant you leave to return to me, to renew your oath to Dorinah, and let us see what we can make of you.

Tordin is next, my love. It's your campaign if you'll take it.

Forever I am,

Empress Casanlyn Aurnaisa of Dorinah–

"Et cetera, et cetera," Taodalain said. "She is kind. She offers you a way out of service."

Zezili closed her good eye, and slept.

It was three weeks before the doctors allowed Zezili out of bed. By then she had seen what remained of her right hand. The doctors had stitched the thumb back on and covered it in leeches. They coaxed the wound closed with organic salve and the help of some backwoods tirajista of middling talent, but she could not move the injured digit. She could barely feel it. The swelling was so bad her hand looked like nothing so much as a discolored hunk of meat. The first joint of her index finger was missing, and the nail and most of the flesh had been ripped from her middle finger. The other wounds she did not look at.

Her housekeeper, Daolyn, and Taodalain removed her from the public infirmary in Daorian to her estate. She rode for hours in the back of a dog-pulled cart. Zezili asked where Dakar, her loyal dog, was, and Daolyn reminded her he had been slain in the dajian camp at the pass into Dhai.

"And my husband?" Zezili asked. "Where is Anavha?"

"We have heard nothing of him," Daolyn said. "His family has declared him dead."

Zezili cried, then – the first time she had cried since her mauling. It was all gone. Everything was ash. What use was saving the world when you had nothing?

The journey was painful. Zezili saw her estate from a strange vantage, lying prone on her stretcher. She gazed up at the tiles of the roof and turned her bruised head to look in through the round gate. A stir of shadowy dajians shifted quietly about the grounds.

Daolyn washed and dressed her wounds. The Empress sent a doctor from Daorian each week to prod at her. It was another kindness, Taodalain reminded her. The Empress could have left her to some rural surgeon.

When Zezili could sit up without blacking out, she hobbled to her wardrobe. She pushed open the door with her good hand. Daolyn had left a coat draped over the door, shrouding her view of the long mirror on the inside. She saw her bandaged hand, the end of her torso, but her face and chest were obscured. She took hold of the end of her tunic, and tugged at it awkwardly. She stretched and strained and shrugged her shoulders until the tunic came free. The exercise left her panting, shaky.

Stripped to the waist, she reached forward and pulled the long coat from the mirror.

The coat trembled down the glass.

Zezili gazed at an alien face, the rent visage of a stranger.

The right side of her face was a morass of bluish-red swelling, distorted, the right eye like a dark wound. Four long red gashes quartered the face. The longest mark ran from the inside of the eye to the jaw, catching flesh again along the shoulder. A series of slashes had loosened the skin from muscle and bone. That side of the face would sag and weep, and heal into a twisted parody of a face. Her torso was worse. Two cats' bites had left punctures along her stomach, and on her upper arm. Another had gnawed meat from the top of her rib cage, tore and twisted at the breast, left behind a pool of scarring tissue.

The partner of the claw that rent her face had taken her along the chest, scoring deep lines from the ruined left breast to her navel. There were lighter scratches, bites, claw punctures, but by now those had all but healed, and left their own shiny scars.

She had been eaten by a god. She had pulled herself from its belly. Now she had to find out what it had left of her.

Zezili shuffled to the doorway. "Daolyn!" she called. "Bring me my sword."

Daolyn did. Zezili picked up the sword in her left hand. She moved through defense positions, slowly, agonizingly slow. Had her sword always been so heavy?

She went through the forms again, until sweat poured from her face and her wounds throbbed, threatening to spill open. She lay back in bed, resting with her sword beside her, and called Daolyn for tea.

After tea, she stood. Brought up the sword again.

It was three days of this haphazard dialogue with her new body before Zezili stepped into the cold courtyard and ran through forms on the bare stones. She had the dajians lay out her armor in her room so she could see it each morning as she rose. Before bed, she spent time examining the helm and breastplate. The cats had gnawed at the leather straps and relieved her of her armor before they ravaged her. She called in the armorer from Dryan and had her hammer out the dents and repair and polish the scratches until it shone. That week, the doctor's visit consisted of the woman's barely concealed horror at the idea that Zezili had had the wherewithal to be out of bed and walking, let alone training.

"Pardon, Syre," the doctor said, "but you have come back from death itself. Your body needs–"

"My body needs to live," Zezili said. "I am in service to the Empress of Dorinah. She owns this body, and a dead thing in bed is of no use to her."

The doctor closed her mouth.

Soon the swelling of Zezili's wounds abated, which left no error in the reading of her reflection. The scarred right side of the face was hers, a face torn through by the mark of a cat. But in profile, from her left side, there was no visible damage.

She tried on her helm for the first time after the mauling. She fastened the chin strap. The scored cheek was still painful, though whether it was a real or remembered pain, she did not know. Instead of hiding the scars, the helm seemed to make them stand out all the clearer, the one sunken eye, the twisted, shiny flesh. She looked fierce, frightening – like the face of a Saiduan sentinel.

"I will need a new coat," Zezili said. "Long. Purple. Stitched in silver. A white under- tunic. Dark trousers. Bold. Stark. A feminine cut."

"Of course," Daolyn said.

"I will also need a new mount. Some strong, fit dog. Two or three years old."

"Yes, Syre," Daolyn said.

Zezili continued her exercises. She took her new mount out on rides inside the grounds of the estate. As yet, she avoided the roads. It was not time to be seen. Her sisters sent her letters detailing the gossip about her in Daorian, Janifa, Ryn. It was said that Zezili had been devoured by a cat. Others said the Empress had marked Zezili herself, gouging out both her eyes and tossing her out of her service. They said that her missing cousin Tanasai's body had been found, or said Zezili had eaten it. It was likely, they said, that if Syre Zezili were still alive, she would not live out the year.

Zezili let the rumors boil. She had indeed parted with her cousin Tanasai's body some weeks past, before spring broke. Daolyn had called Taodalain to the estate in the wake of Zezili's illness, and the two of them had carted the body to Lake Morta, weighted it down, hacked a hole in the ice, and watched Tanasai sink to the bottom of the lake.

It was the Empress, finally, who broke Zezili's fugue.

"An invitation," Daolyn said, handing her the familiar purple paper.

Zezili sat in her study and opened it. It was an invitation to a banquet in Daorian with the other legion commanders, to plan the upcoming campaign against Tordin.

A sliver of moonlight cut through the room from the parting in the heavy curtains, and fell across the wardrobe, shimmering in the mirror visible just inside the door. It reminded Zezili of another type of mirror, and another type of invasion; one slowed, but not stopped.

A powerless former general could do nothing in the face of such an enemy. The most trusted of the Empress's tools could do much, though – a hardened, bitter general could even be used to topple the Empress's reign. But only if Zezili could succeed in banishing the thought of her true intent from her own mind, and do what the Empress bid. Zezili could bide her time. She had died once already. She wasn't afraid of dying again, if she could destroy the Empress with her last breath.

Zezili went to the desk. She penned a missive to the Empress with her good left hand.

She wrote:

I am yours.

She signed and sealed the letter.

4

Lilia had once stood in front of Kai Kirana of this world, the sister of the man who stood before her now. And that Kai had assured Lilia that she was in a peaceful place, a world without an army, a world that would welcome her into its temples with open arms, and provide and care for her no matter who she was.

Now she stood in front of a Kai who wanted to throw her and the people she'd saved back into slavery on the other side of the wall. How quickly things changed, when a people was no longer at peace.

His militia escorted her up four painful flights of stairs to a great foyer, apologizing the whole way for not considering how difficult stairs would be for her. What they really meant, of course, was that they felt silly and impatient because her pace was so much slower than theirs. Neither Taigan nor the militia offered to help her, which was just as well. She needed to get used to stairs again. In truth, she believed the militia were a little frightened of her now. It was one thing to fly to the top of a wall. It was quite another to burn down a grove of walking trees like so much kindling.

The foyer opened up into the hold's religious sanctuary, much like the one at Oma's temple. Instead of a dome over the top, it looked out into the inner courtyard where a hundred refugees huddled in tents and nested in straw beds. The latticed windows of the room were open, and the refugees' voices filtered up through the slatted shutters.

The Kai stood in the center of the room at the altar to Oma, which was a great silvery claw gripping a red orb with an orange-and-black center, like an eye. Altars to the other gods flanked it – purple Sina, blue Para, green Tira, their great glass orbs twinkling with inner light. Lilia wondered if they had some kind of bioluminescent flora or fauna inside of them, self-contained colonies living and dying for generations inside the confines of the glass.

The Kai's face was no longer dirty, and he wore new clothes. For some reason that rankled. She had not bathed or changed in weeks now.

"I invite you to sit," Ahkio said.

She thought it odd he was alone. The militia who escorted them stayed, though, taking up places at either side of the door. She was exhausted, still filthy, and not ready for an audience with this man, the most powerful person in Dhai. What would she do if he turned them away? Surely that was what he meant to do. She had no plan for that.

"I have stood a long time," Lilia said. "I can go on standing a while longer." She halted a few steps away from the altar, two rows of seats back. The aisle was just big enough for Taigan to stand beside her. She had left Gian behind, though she'd protested. Lilia feared she might say something impolite. Taigan was going to say things that were much worse, she knew, and she did not want to try and rein them both in.

It was strange to see indecision written so plainly on Ahkio's face when she refused to sit. He was a tall, wiry man with soft eyes and a full mouth that, she admitted, made her breath come a little faster. She felt she had no time for such a distraction, and despised herself a little for even noticing him. People like him, with clear skin and easy confidence, struggled less to be noticed than people like her. When he spoke, people would listen, and not just because he was Kai. His hair was longer than she remembered from her brief glimpse of him in Oma's temple, before Taigan took her away, and his hands bore the same terrible scars. But there was something in his face now that was different. It looked haunted, hungry.

"You look exhausted," Ahkio said. "They told me you haven't slept."

"I have many responsibilities here," Lilia said.

"Like burning up walking trees and vexing Ghrasia Madah's conscience?" he said.

"Among other things," she said lightly.

She was aware of the murmur of voices from the courtyard four stories below. She heard raised voices. The militia and the refugees had already gotten into several heated arguments, and the mess outside the gates with the trees wasn't helping. She had already heard rumors that the refugees thought the militia had called the trees there on purpose to murder them. The refugees didn't have the same laws related to touching and consent, either, and it was creating problems. Grabbing a woman's arm to get her attention in Dhai was a grave offense, like spitting in someone's face, or punching them. Lilia had gone down with Gian the first few nights, trying to communicate the necessity of consent, but many of the refugees found the idea bizarre. How would you get someone's attention? Show affection? Gain trust?

"Just ask," Lilia had told them, but, as with her relationship with Gian, trying to change a behavior so ingrained was difficult.

Lilia wanted to put Ahkio out of his obvious discomfort, so took charge of the conversation. His fidgeting made her nervous. Fearful people did bad things. She knew.

"You can sit if *you* want," she said.

She had practiced things to say, or tried to, for the last few days while the militia at Liona figured out what to do with them. She was so tired.

"You need to understand something," Ahkio said, "in case it hasn't been put to you. You've called yourself the incarnation of a god, and ordered around militia at Liona on your behalf. As far as I remember, I'm Kai, I already have a Catori, and there has been no prophet since Faith Ahya, and no martyr since Hahko."

"It's about due then, isn't it?" Taigan said, waggling her eyebrows.

"Would you leave us, please?" Ahkio said to Taigan.

"She'll stay," Lilia said. "You have your militia at the door. I have Taigan."

"She," Ahkio said, correcting his use of pronoun for Taigan. Lilia suspected no one knew what to make of Taigan. She had heard many use the gender-neutral Dhai pronoun to refer to her. It was probably more appropriate. Taigan was Taigan, and the longer Lilia knew her, the more she felt "Taigan" was the only pronoun that fit. Taigan had shifted the pronouns she used to refer to herself three times since Lilia had known her. That was common among young people, but most settled by the time they reached adulthood.

The shouting beyond the windows grew louder. Lilia gazed past Ahkio and the shining altars but could see nothing from this height.

"You haven't left me many choices," Ahkio said. "I've consulted the Book."

He rattled on for some time longer, quoting from the Book, but Lilia ignored him. The voices outside were growing now, a slow rumble. Lilia limped to the windows. Below, a knot of refugees in tattered coats, most without shoes, shoved and shouted at militia in red tunics and skirts. Someone threw a rock. She heard the exhale of the crowd, like a great beast that had been waiting for the order to charge. They surged forward. The militia at the back started drawing weapons.

Lilia pulled herself up into the window frame with her good hand and yelled, "Enough!" but her voice was small, and did not carry. She called on Oma, fast and deep, and spun a simple tornadic spell. She flicked it into the melee below. The misty red mass hit the center of the roaring crowd and burst, sending a puff of hot air in all directions, knocking back militia and refugees alike. Surprised cries. Many looked up and spotted her.

She called again, "That's enough! There will be no violence here."

The crowd hummed. A few of the refugees sketched hasty bows in her direction. Some put thumbs to foreheads, a very Dhai sign of respect and understanding.

"You," she said, pointing to the militia. "All of you come up here. Your Kai is up here."

Ahkio came to her side, so close she felt the heat of him. "You're much more spry than I thought," he said.

She gripped the windowsill so tightly her good hand hurt. She glanced back at Taigan. "Help me down?"

Taigan offered a hand. Lilia stepped out of the sill, catching herself against Taigan when her bad leg nearly gave out. She rested a hand on the lattice, leaning carefully against it for balance.

"*The Book of Oma* gives fair choices," Lilia said, "if I said I was Kai. But I didn't. I didn't say I was anything at all. They follow because they believe in me."

"And they will do as she says," Taigan added. "As you can see."

Ahkio frowned, and she saw him reconsidering her. They would all underestimate her. This Kai and the Tai Mora. Their prejudices were her greatest advantage. "Is that why you chose the color?" he asked. "Faith Ahya's? So they would follow without questioning?"

"Didn't you take your title for the same reason?"

"Don't argue religious ethics with me," Ahkio said, and she noted the hard edge in his voice. "You'll lose."

"The two of you would be greater allies than foes," Taigan said.

Ahkio waved a finger at Taigan. "Your counsel is not requested. I have to send you both back to Dorinah."

"You would kill me, and six hundred other Dhai?"

"Dajians, not Dhai."

"Slaves are not people?"

"There must be rules."

"I know the Tai Mora are coming," Lilia said. "I know bringing these people here puts you in a bad position. But Faith Ahya and Hahko did as I did. I can help you build a stronger country, Kai. They listen to me. Others will, too."

"Why?"

"I'm an omajista," Lilia said. "That should have been obvious out in the meadow. In a year, maybe less, that will mean something beautiful and terrible."

"Exile doesn't serve either of our interests," Taigan said, and Lilia gave her a sharp look. Taigan's tongue would get them into trouble.

"I know some things about your enemy," Lilia said. "I can use that to the advantage of Dhai. Just as Faith–"

"Don't say her name," Ahkio said.

Lilia reconsidered her approach. "I know how to turn back the Tai Mora," she said. "I have been to the other side. I've met our enemy. I can turn them back now from the harbor. You saw what I could do to those walking trees. That's just a start. And Taigan is like me."

"I am nothing like her," Taigan said.

"And I have Dorinah Seekers bound to me," Lilia continued, ignoring Taigan. "I can bring you an advantage in this conflict."

Ahkio said to Taigan, "When you took her, she was a scullery girl. What did you make her into?"

"I didn't," Taigan said. "She made herself."

"If I'm just a stupid drudge," she said, "you can turn me and the others back. But if I can save six hundred dajians as a scullery girl, what can I do as something more? Ghrasia already believes in me."

Ahkio pressed himself against the windowsill. The refugees below had gone back to their tents and knotted circles.

"The season is changing, Kai," Lilia said. "They will come for you. *The Book of Oma* doesn't have a quote for that. There is no battle plan. No strategy." She tapped her head. "But I have one. Give these refugees safety in Kuallina, and I can help you."

The doors opened. The eight militia from the riot downstairs came in. One pointed an accusatory finger at Lilia. "Kai, that woman used the gifted arts against her own people!"

Ahkio waved his hand at the militia, asking for their silence. Lilia waited, trying hard to still her trembling. She had gotten used to getting hit in Dorinah, and defending herself from Taigan's unpredictable attacks. She had done the best she could. If the Kai struck out at her now, she would defend herself. She would defend them all. She feared what she would need to do if she had not convinced him with words.

"We are peaceful people," Ahkio said. "I've been asked what we will sacrifice to win this war, and I don't want to sacrifice what we are. But someone has to fight."

"I can fight," Lilia said, and a great feeling of satisfaction came over her. She had done it. He was going to put her in a position to fight the Tai Mora. She saw all the terrible things she had already done – pulling the young girl Esau through a gate that cut her in half, burning up legionnaires, using her gift against her own people – and instead of hating herself for it she saw it as one long line of horror that prepared her for just this moment. For revenge.

"I'll let you go to Asona Harbor," he said, "but you're not in charge of anything. You're to put yourself and the omajistas at the disposal of Catori Mohrai and her family in defense of the harbor."

"And Taigan. And Gian. And the Seekers. They must come."

"Who in the world is Gian?"

"She's my friend," Lilia said.

"You'll find she treats her friends very well," Taigan said, pulling a wedge of potato from her pocket, and Lilia wondered if it was another one of Gian's hoarded rations. "And her enemies much differently." She munched on the potato, watching the still seething militia with amusement.

Lilia was not paying much attention to Taigan anymore, though. She was already moving toward the next stage of her attack on the Tai Mora. She had gained some measure of power. She intended to use it.

A few hours later, after relaying news to Mohrai about Lilia's place at the harbor and going over Liona's defenses and current supplies with Arasia, Ahkio found Ghrasia at the bedside of the parajista they had cut from the boughs of the walking tree. She bowed over the woman's still body, muttering a prayer to Sina. The parajista's skin was slimy, her eyes sightless. Ahkio saw that the ends of her fingers were melted, like soft butter. Two doctors stood some ways distant, conferring quietly as they snuck pitying looks at Ghrasia.

A door was open on the other side of the ward, and he could hear a lute playing. Someone was singing an old ballad about Faith Ahya in a high, clear voice.

"I'm sorry," Ahkio said, low.

Ghrasia did not raise her head. "She torched those trees without a thought for the people in them," Ghrasia said. "We could have saved them. Not this one, no, but others. And she burned them up without a thought." She shifted in her seat. "I heard you're sending her to the harbor. I hope you are able to take responsibility for whatever she does there."

"Word travels very fast in Liona."

Ghrasia rose and took her blade from the edge of the bed. Sheathed it. "You should know that my daughter is dead."

"Oma's breath, I didn't know. Was she out there?"

"No." Ghrasia moved past him without meeting his look. "She killed herself. Ora Nasaka has held a great deal over the two of us, her and me, for some time. That's over now."

"Is it really? Or is this some new game?"

Ghrasia finally met his look. Her eyes were red from crying. "No games," she said. "Those are over. Ora Nasaka ruled my life for far too long. Now she's trying to rule yours. You best stop her before she meddles any more with your life."

"I intend to exile her."

Ghrasia laughed lightly. "So did your mother. You see how that turned out. And my daughter... she felt there was only one way to free us from Ora Nasaka, too." She marched from the room without a backward glance. It took a great deal of effort for him not to reach out for her.

Ahkio stared at the body on the stretcher. There were more wounded on the far side of the infirmary, and dozens more downstairs who had been too fragile to take up. The sound of the singing from the hall both attracted and repulsed him. Who would be singing at a time like this?

He crossed the infirmary and went out into the hall. He followed a broad band of golden light spilling out from an archway, and stepped into the rays.

Mohrai sat in the music room playing the lute in a deep padded chair. She was bathed in the brilliant light of the double suns streaming through the windows. She sang a very old ballad that brought him back to his childhood. It was called *The Lament of Hahko*. He had a memory of an old woman sitting over him, singing the very same ballad. His grandmother, maybe? His grandparents had died when he was very young, three of them dead from a run of yellow fever that had swept through the country, taking mostly the old and infirm.

Mohrai stopped singing when he entered.

She set the lute aside. "Do you play an instrument?"

"I never had the talent or the time for it," he said. "I need to discuss–"

"My family insisted," she said, cutting him off. "It teaches discipline, they said. Dancing or defense forms would teach the same thing, but I suspect my father hoped I'd be a singer instead of... whatever I am now."

Ahkio did not have the time to soothe her bruised ego over the defense of the harbor, but knew he needed to make it. He sat on the long chaise opposite her. He was preparing to leave Liona and go back to the temple, now that the situation in Liona would be eased with the movement of the refugees to Kuallina. He didn't want to believe a word Lilia had said, but the other jistas in Liona verified that Lilia called not on Sina but on Oma. There was no other star that could give one the powers she wielded with such ease and force during Para's ascendance. Everything was coming together now.

"You didn't have much to say when I told you to escort Lilia to the harbor," he said.

"It didn't seem like something up for discussion. I don't see what you expect some dajian scullery girl to achieve there that my family hasn't. She's a child."

"I'm aware of that."

"You trust she isn't the enemy?" Mohrai said. "After what you've told me about them?"

Ahkio tried to figure out a way to avoid the question, as it would needlessly prolong this conversation, and he had an urgent message in his pocket from Liaro telling him that the Tai Mora emissary at Oma's temple was growing increasingly impatient. He suspected that if he didn't meet with them soon, they would simply storm the harbor gates instead of blocking the piers, and then it wouldn't matter if one little omajista girl was there or not.

When he did not answer, Mohrai leaned forward. "We have defended the harbor for centuries. With enough Oras–"

"Who will lead those Oras in battle?" Ahkio said. "We don't teach Oras how to use their gifts in fighting scenarios. She can, though. You and your family have done an admirable job at the harbor, and I am sending you someone who can help you do an even better one. Ghrasia will stay here in Liona, and I'm moving twenty more militia to assist in Kuallina as well. We'll be moving the refugees there."

"Is that wise?"

"Which part?"

"Any of it!"

"Dorinah remains a threat," he said. "Liona is also the only other possible incursion point for an army, any army. I want our best people at the harbor and in Liona."

"It won't matter if they just open some gate between worlds and push through," she said.

"If they were going to do that," he said, "they would have done it. They wouldn't block the harbor."

She set the lute aside and stood. "I'll listen to her ideas. But if she's a fool–"

"She isn't."

"Best hope you aren't making a mistake, Kai." She started to the door.

He raised the lute. "You don't want to ask to take this with you? It seemed to give you pleasure."

"I gave all that up," she said, "when my family told me I was to protect Asona Harbor. Best think about *your* priorities, Ahkio." She shut the door.

Ahkio took a long moment to compose himself, wondering if he would ever see her again, and wondering if he could have spoken more compellingly. As he pulled on his pack, he noted his hands were trembling. An emissary of the Tai Mora at Oma's Temple, and Tai Mora at the harbor, while his head buzzed with questions presented to him by the temple keeper. He had to hold off the Tai Mora long enough to puzzle out the riddle of the temples, and that meant putting himself at the temple, not the harbor, however much he wished to see how Lilia meant to hold back an army that the Saiduan could not. The threat of civil war he had battled the year before seemed trifling now. A petty distraction. Now he faced so many enemies and priorities that he feared he was no longer making the best decisions.

"Kai?" Caisa came in, tone sharp. He suspected she still had not forgiven him for following Ghrasia up into the tree. "Our escort is leaving for Oma's Temple."

The keeper's words bubbled up again. *What will you sacrifice?*

Everything. They would destroy everything.

But if survival meant destroying everything, he should just give up now, and let the Tai Mora win. He gazed at Caisa's broad, eager face, and found he did not have the heart to tell her that the reason he had sent a horrifyingly powerful young girl to Asona Harbor instead of going himself was because he knew she would be able to do what none of them could – she could become the very thing they were fighting against. She could be the evil that he could not be.

And, perhaps, she could win.

5

Wrapped in the shroud of winter in the abandoned prison called Shoratau, Roh studied, and brooded, and wished he had made better decisions. He and Luna sat up most nights with the other sanisi in the dining hall, huddled together in their own stink because it was so much warmer than going out and exploring the hold on their own. But Roh had never been one to stick close to the herd. Sometimes he needed time away from them, so he climbed the towers and explored the old cells, and when he was too cold, his energy expended, he came back to Luna and they sat over the Talamynii book. The book could hold the key to unlocking what the Tai Mora wanted in Saiduan, but they still couldn't figure out how to read it. It was his only real diversion, besides training with Kadaan and Wraisau.

During the four weeks of winter's siege, they lived on the prison's meager store of root vegetables and rice. Roh was so sick of rice and onions that the smell of it made him gag, but he choked it down every morning and every night because the alternative was starving.

With very little to do but endless dice games and fighting exercises, the book became his focus. He and Luna sat over it every morning, and much of the evening, until they ran out of candles, and then they sat up against the windows, huddled together against the cold drafts, soaking up as much daylight as possible.

It was during the tail end of one of these cold evenings, Luna nodding to sleep against his shoulder, that Roh realized what had eluded him about the text for so long.

He was reading it backwards.

It seemed like such a stupid mistake, and the way Roh noticed it was even more foolish. He was so tired he dozed off next to Luna, and the book fell out of his hands. He woke at the sound of it. He pulled the book back into his lap, not paying attention to the orientation, just peering at the columns as he ran his fingers down the line of letters again, reading them left to right instead of right to left. That gave him pause, because he realized he'd never used the Kai cipher while reading it in the opposite direction. It just hadn't occurred to him that the Talamynii would write anything in the other direction. Luna said every other Talamynii text read in long columns, right to left.

He pulled out the characters according to the method he'd been taught as part of the Kai cipher, and then arranged them into words. The first word sent a shiver down his spine.

Worldbreaker.

"Luna," Roh said, shaking him awake. "I figured it out, Luna."

"Sure," Luna said, "and I figured out gravity."

"Really," Roh said, and pointed at the Dhai word on the page in front of him.

Luna looked dubious. They had been close too many times. "Do another one," he said.

It took another week to translate the book. After he learned that they had cracked it, Kadaan came in nightly and asked for updates on their progress. He fairly loomed, expression as grim as their living situation. He was much leaner now. He looked hungry all the time. When Roh pulled off his tunic to wash himself in a basin of warm water once a week, he could see his own hip bones poking painfully out from under his skin. They were becoming walking skeletons.

"It's some kind of instruction manual," Roh said. "Let us get to the end."

They made it halfway through the book, untangling references to coteries of jistas and their arrangements inside temples, and some great spiraling game of spheres, before the Tai Mora came to Shoratau.

Roh leaned over the broad edge of a busted window high up in the west tower, trying to spot the group of Tai Mora the scouts had reported. He was wrapped in a thick, foul-smelling ubel coat and hood, his face covered from throat to nose. Eight sanisi stood watch along the walls below him, but he had not left the window in hours.

"Roh?"

Luna entered the broad doorway behind him. It had been a recreation hall for the prison's staff. They had cleared out all the furniture and burned it for heat. One sanisi had already died of exposure – caught in a storm, blinded, unable to get back before it overtook him. That left just twenty of them, plus Luna and Roh.

"They're here," Luna said. He was bundled up as Roh was, narrow little face nearly lost in the great hood of his ubel coat. He held a large pack in one hand. Roh suspected it held the Talamynii book. Luna went nowhere without it. He slept with it under his head every night.

"How many Tai Mora in the party? Does Kadaan know?"

"Forty, at least."

Roh gazed back out the window.

"Kadaan wants to see us. About the book, and what we do next."

Roh slid out of the window. The cold and waiting had been much worse than fighting. If this was where he was going to die, gutted on some frozen tundra, among Saiduan who considered him a slave, he just wanted it over with. The waiting – that was too much.

He followed Luna downstairs. The halls were mostly dark, and they had to make their way by feel for much of it. Finally, they came to the main floor where the sanisi had set up house. Roh glanced into the great hall as they passed. Another sanisi, Wraisau, was coming out as they went by, so Roh could see inside. Flickering torches. Bowed heads. Empty plates. Endless games of dice.

Luna knocked at the door to Kadaan's office. It was a former storage closet, not a proper study.

"Yes," Kadaan said, and Roh felt a surge of anticipation at his voice even now, cold and hungry and on the edge of dying. He dreamed often of Kadaan taking him aside and declaring his passion for him, absurd as all that seemed here. Many of the sanisi had taken one another as lovers. It took the edge off their confinement, and gave them some comfort. It's why Roh slept next to Luna every night, though their relationship was purely friendly.

Kadaan stood behind a battered table brimming with candles. Empty sacks and crates littered the room. There hadn't been much food in storage to start with, and twenty sanisi had made neat work of what was left. Roh worried they would begin to eat each other without going through the proper rituals next. When he had brought it up with Luna once, Luna had looked so horrified he never spoke of it again. But to Roh, it wasn't eating the flesh of others that was horrifying. The horrifying part was not planning for it, and eating human flesh as if it were the offal of some dark animal.

"What do you want?" Roh asked.

Kadaan regarded him coolly. "I'm often comforted that it was I who claimed you, and not a man with a taste for subservience."

"I don't know that you've claimed anything," Roh said. He squared his stance and clasped his hands behind his back, expression as neutral as he could make it.

Luna gave him a sidelong look.

Roh had not been able to figure out Kadaan. He had

taken Roh as a slave, claimed him after the death of the Saiduan Patron and Roh's companions in a bloody brawl. But Kadaan's interest ended, it seemed, after that. Roh wondered if he had imagined the kiss Kadaan had given him in the Patron's banquet hall. It felt like an age ago.

"Luna still hasn't taught you deference," Kadaan said.

"I was never good at that."

And you like that I'm not good at it, Roh wanted to add, but thought that might be a bit much, especially in front of Luna. Kadaan was almost a decade older than him – twenty-five, maybe – and some days it seemed like an impossible chasm. Roh wondered if it was culture or age or just the fact that he was a sanisi that stood between them.

"I want progress on the book," Kadaan said.

Roh glanced over at Luna. "You need both of us?"

"Yes," Kadaan said. "You're the Dhai. You have one duty. And it's put us here, in the middle of a raging storm with forty Tai Mora slogging toward us."

Roh said, "We've learned that there are gates, engines of some kind, in the temples."

"I've ascertained that much," Kadaan said. "How do we control them?"

"Omajistas," Luna said. "But we knew that, too."

Roh knit his brows. "You knew that?"

"We always knew that," Kadaan said. "Omajistas open gates. It's why we went south to look for more of them."

"How long have you known?" Roh asked.

Kadaan said, "We knew who, but not how. We've lost nearly every omajista who could open a way between the worlds. That's why this work is important. It's why we called you."

"But... we didn't even know–"

"Roh," Kadaan said. "We need to know how to open them. Having an omajista means nothing if we have no way to open, or, more importantly now, close the tears between our worlds. These people are getting through.

If this can stop them–"

"The temples of Dhai are the key, as far as we can tell," Luna said. "Having omajistas is important – we'll need to have one for each temple that powers whatever this… process is."

"So bringing omajistas to Saiduan–" Kadaan began.

"Was probably not the best use of time," Luna said. "There are four temples in Dhai. There used to be a fifth, in the northwest, but it disappeared during the last rising of Oma, when the Dhai and the Saiduan ripped the world apart. We can spend years trying to find an omajista to successfully open or close a tear, or end everything using the temples. They magnify Oma's power."

"But there's no instructions," Roh said. "At least not that we've translated yet. I think that's the second half of the book. There's something about spheres and mathematical equations that's–"

A shout came from outside.

Roh called Para. Calling Para had become almost like breathing, if breathing meant you sometimes drew enough air to drown, and sometimes took three breaths just to get air. Para, like all the satellites, was fickle. The gods liked to remind them who was actually in control.

Luna opened the door. The sanisi from the main room were pouring into the hall. Wraisau drew his blade and shouted, "Breach downstairs!"

"Stay here," Kadaan said. He leapt over the desk and sprinted after Wraisau.

Roh started after him, but Luna grabbed his sleeve. "He said to stay."

"He was talking to you!"

"He was talking to us. We aren't them, Roh. Stay."

Roh shook him off, angrily. "They can call me a slave, but I'm not one. You choose what you want."

Luna made a face so angry Roh thought Luna was going to hit him. "Only a man who's been free would say such a thing."

"I'm not a coward. Not like you."

Luna crinkled his face; a rush of unshed tears glistened in his eyes. "Cowardice isn't what keeps me here," Luna said. "You have no idea what it is to belong to someone. I've run a hundred times before."

Roh pushed past Luna into the hall.

The other sanisi had disappeared down the stairs. Roh barreled after them, holding onto Para's breath. He got four steps down before he saw blue mist crawling toward him. He fell back, too late. A roiling thread caught at his ankles. Bound him. He fell over. He'd been holding the Litany of Breath, and preparing other litanies, but none would help him with this. The curling tendrils of Para's breath snaked up his body and bound him like a vise.

Roh gasped. Choked. The litany. What was right? Litany of Unmaking, Litany of Breaking, Litany of... He fell on the stairs, gasping.

Luna came up behind him. "Who hit you?"

Roh flailed.

Luna coughed and recoiled. He drew a deep breath, hooked his arms under Roh's, and pulled him up the stairs.

Roh hacked up great gobs of blue mist. Litany of Unbinding. That was it. He called Para, mouthing the words between heaves, and broke the triangular bindings of the deadly trap. The balls of mist burst apart and dissipated.

Noise on the stairs. Cries. The clash of metal.

"They're coming up," Luna said. He tugged at Roh's tunic and headed toward the dining hall.

"There's no way out that way," Roh said. Too late. Luna was already inside. Roh struggled after him.

The sounds of fighting reached the hall. The doors burst open, and a wave of fighting sanisi broke in. The tables blew off the floor, upturned to serve as barricades. Ten sanisi took up positions behind the tables.

Roh pitched himself backward. He rolled over the

table behind him and used it for cover. Vortex, vacuum, blast... the litanies for binding Para's breath tickled the edges of his mind, just out of reach. All around him, blades clashed. People screamed. Furniture flew about the room, cracking against the walls. Roh saw the bubbling blue mist of Para suffusing everything, a roiling stir of conflicting litanies.

Roh recited the Litany of Breath, drawing Para beneath his skin and holding it. He drew his sword. Peeked above the table.

Two Tai Mora took out the legs of a sanisi four paces distant. One of them looked right at him. Roh let out his breath, forming a wall of air with the Litany of the Balustrade. One held up a hand and blasted an impossibly powerful glut of Para's breath at Roh's wall, tearing it apart.

The parajista advanced, a little smile on his face that turned Roh's stomach.

Roh drew his weapon. Pulled Para. He made a simple litany and created a wall. He struck with his weapon while pushing the wall forward.

He saw the misty blue defenses of the Tai Mora swirl to counter, and called a new litany. A cyclone. But the parajista must have been able to read the pattern of his cast, and retaliated with a burst of air that broke the cone of the call.

All the while, the parajista advanced, his weapon snarling out ahead of him. Roh parried, countered, but he was stuck in a defensive position. Behind him, one of the Tai Mora fell into the open fireplace. Screamed. He crawled out, his coat aflame, and fought on, a blazing specter.

Roh tried to put a table between him and his attacker. His stamina was not what it was, cooped up in this hold so many weeks. His breath came hard. His concentration wavered. The parajista thrust forward again, faster.

Roh pivoted – and smacked right into the wall behind him, face first. Pain exploded across his face. He went down hard. Blood poured from his burst nose. He tried to push away from the parajista. Pain drowned out the litany for a shield.

The parajista raised his weapon. Kadaan came from behind and gutted him like a fish.

Roh hocked blood and snot.

Kadaan took Roh by the collar and yanked him up. He hauled him across the body-strewn floor, slipping in blood as he did. Roh's face throbbed.

"Take your feet!" Kadaan yelled, then – "Luna!"

Luna scrambled out from under a table and came after them. Several sanisi followed. The Tai Mora in the room were dead, but Roh heard more below.

Roh stumbled after Kadaan into the stairwell.

"Here, stop," Kadaan said, and gestured to one of the sanisi, a parajista.

The parajista knocked out the wall with a burst of air.

Roh yelped, expecting it to come down on them, but Para's blue mist suffused the outer edges of the wound, keeping it sound.

Luna leapt out first, then Wraisau and another sanisi. Kadaan pushed Roh. Roh pin-wheeled his arms and fell the ten feet to the ground. The breath left his lungs. He gasped for air that wasn't there. Tasted more blood and snot.

The sanisi were already moving. Luna helped him up. Roh looked back, once, and wished he hadn't. Dozens of Tai Mora were pushing through the scar in the stairwell.

Wraisau ran ahead to the outer wall and broke it open with another blast of air. Without the protection of a jista or an especially powerful ward, walls and doors and gates meant little.

Wraisau waved at Kadaan.

Kadaan grabbed at Roh's collar again.

"Stop that!" Roh said.

"Go," Kadaan said.

"What?"

"Go!" He pushed Roh ahead. "Take Luna, and that

fiery book, and find Maralah in Anjoliaa. If she hasn't retreated there yet, she will. Do it."

"I'm here to fight!" Roh said.

"You'll be here to die."

"I can't–"

"Roh!" Luna grabbed his sleeve. "Please!" Luna slid through the break in the wall. Held out his hand.

Roh saw the storm of Tai Mora running across the yard. Wraisau and the five remaining sanisi held their ground.

Kadaan glanced back once at the Tai Mora, then grabbed Roh by the collar. Pulled him close. Kissed him fiercely.

Roh had been waiting for it for so long it took his breath from his body. Or maybe he was still recovering from the fall. No matter. He gripped Kadaan tightly.

Kadaan released him. "I will meet you in Anjoliaa," Kadaan said. "We'll hold them for you. Go."

Roh ran after Luna, to the kennels.

Luna worked at the dogs' tack with trembling fingers. Roh helped saddle them.

"I'll scatter the rest," Roh said.

"Tie an extra dog behind. We'll run them."

"But–"

"Do it."

Roh did as he said, then pushed wide the kennel doors. But the dogs weren't stupid. Beyond the shelter of the kennels was a blasted white tundra. They had nowhere to go. He cursed and crawled up onto his dog's saddle and whistled the animal forward.

Luna trotted off ahead of him into the late afternoon light. They would be easy to track in the daylight. If they were lucky, these Tai Mora wouldn't care anything for two Dhai slaves who escaped Shoratau. But if they'd come specifically for the book...

Roh tried to banish that thought. The sun on the white tundra was blinding. "You know the way?" he shouted at Luna.

Luna yelled back, "I've been planning an escape my whole life! I know what way is south!"

Roh held on tight as the dogs leapt forward. Not even a year in Saiduan, and already he was running back home. He glanced back, once, at the dwindling hulk of Shoratau. He called Para to settle in beneath his skin. The blue mist gathered about his own body. He said a prayer to Para and released its breath. The wind picked up, catching icy particles of snow and sending them into a swirling vortex. It would not last, but it would cover their tracks.

Roh's resolve faltered in the face of the unending tundra. They were just two slaves, running across a wasteland into some uncertain future.

Luna lay still and silent against the belly of the dog, wrapped firmly in a thick coat. It was the first night in ten years Luna had slept without fear of a fist or a whip or a noose or a drunken master. Luna woke up twice in the night, expecting Kadaan or Wraisau or the Tai Mora, but there was only the cold, cold wind. It sounded like something Luna remembered from hir childhood – dogs howling in a kennel, or maybe the sea. Luna had grown up near the sea… maybe? Sometimes Luna confused old memories with things ze had read about Dhai. Luna had spent hir whole life clinging to those memories, hot and muddled, all tangled together with accounts Luna had read in the great libraries when trained as a runner and translator as a child.

Luna and Roh dared not light a fire. They had circled the dogs for warmth instead and bedded down with them. Roh pretended to know a lot of things, but it was difficult for him to pretend he knew anything about the north. So Luna had to tell him to let the dogs dig down into the snow, and when the little shelter was built, Luna pulled Roh down at the center of the mass of dogs, and they slept as a soft layer of snow drifted all around them, covering their tracks and their burrow. To an untrained eye, their snowy mass would look like just another snow drift. A kink in the landscape. Luna had grown used to the soft weight of Roh against hir, and the comfort was painful sometimes, because ze knew that's all it was to Roh. Luna was a coward, a slave, in Roh's eyes. He never saw hir, just the idea of hir, like a figure in some old dusty text, a slave from his books, maybe. He never once asked about Luna's life, about what ze liked to eat, or what ze did as a child. Roh talked about himself, and Luna put up with it because Roh was so beautiful he made Luna's heart ache. But here in the wind and the cold, Luna realized how little that beauty mattered. What they needed now was to be clever and resilient, and ze worried that Roh did not have enough resilience to make the journey they needed to make. Riding from Shoratau to Anjoliaa would take months during the winter, longer if they lost the dogs and had to go by foot. Ze worried over Roh more than ze should have. Why should Luna care what happened to him? But hir heart hurt when ze thought about making this journey alone. Ze wanted to protect hir the way ze had never been protected. Ze spent much of hir time in Shoratau trying to shield Roh from how bad things could be for him. Luna distracted the sanisi who talked about him in low tones, and told Kadaan whenever ze heard someone meant to do Roh harm. But Roh went through life in Shoratau merrily and arrogantly, as if his safety was assured. Luna knew, more than anyone, that being small and enslaved meant nothing was assured.

The wind had died down. Luna blinked snow from hir lashes and shifted uncomfortably against the dog. Luna needed to piss. Always the worst part of nights on the tundra. Ze crawled a few paces away from their circle and found a place to squat. Hir urine turned to ice far too quickly, and ze yanked hir trousers back, chilled to the bone. Luna dug back into their circle, squeezing hirself in between the dogs and Roh.

Luna began to tremble, so hard hir teeth rattled. Roh stirred beside hir.

"You all right?" Roh asked.

"Cold."

Roh wrapped his arms around Luna. Luna thought hir body would tense, but ze was so chilled the warmth was welcome. Luna instinctively moved in closer. Roh was strong, stronger than he looked, even thin and hungry. He held Luna tight, and Luna closed hir eyes and imagined they were living together in Dhai, married to half a dozen spouses, raising children on some farm far, far from here.

As the trembling subsided, Luna considered how strange it would be in Dhai. Ze could be whatever ze wanted, not ataisa or slave or some fisher's girl. In Dhai, Luna could be like Roh. They called hir ataisa here, but it never fit right on hir. Ze wanted to be a man, desperately, but people laughed when ze said it, and pointed out all of hir shortcomings, all of hir differences, all the things that made hir ataisa, so ze pushed that away, tried to forget about it. But Luna remembered a time when ze could choose what ze was, instead of having it thrust upon hir.

"Roh? Promise me something?"

"Sure."

"If I die first, don't eat me, all right?"

"I'm not going to eat you."

"Well, I know that Dhai–"

"I wouldn't eat someone who said it wasn't all right. You think we murder babies, too? Cook them?"

"Do you?" Luna had little memory of what Dhai was like when it came to funerary practices. But what ze knew was bad enough.

"No. After all this, you'd ask that?"

"It's important."

"You're all really upset about that. It's not what you think it is. We don't just go around killing people. It's how we honor people, Luna. Family and friends. So no, I wouldn't eat you."

"We aren't friends?"

"It's complicated," Roh said.

Luna kept the silence. Above them, the stars were brilliant; a jeweled blanket across the heavens. All three moons were up. The largest was full and round, and the red moon was in half-shadow. The smallest was a mere crescent, ringed in its tiara of satellites. Para had gone down just before the suns, and would not rise again until they returned. Luna liked the stillness. Freedom, Luna imagined, felt like stillness.

So did death, though. Luna closed hir eyes.

When Luna woke next, it was morning, and ze was very cold. Frost rimed hir lashes. Ze sat up and stretched and found Roh rubbing the frost from the dogs' coats.

"We need to go," he said, and Luna noted the twinge of fear in his voice.

"What is it?" Luna asked.

"Riders," Roh said. "Far, still, but they could catch us if we don't move."

Luna crawled to hir feet and surveyed the landscape. Ze could not see the riders Roh mentioned. The tundra here was hilly, shot through with stunted trees bowed over in snow and ice.

"We'll go north," Luna said. "They'll expect us to go south. Only a fool would go north."

"So what does that make us?" Roh said.

"Clever fools," Luna said.

Luna shrugged into hir pack, checking reflexively to ensure the book was still secure in its waxed linen wrap. Ze was going to get to Dhai, and ze was going to keep Roh alive long enough to get there, too, no matter how relentlessly Roh tried to sabotage his own survival.

6

Blood poured down Anavha's arm, thick and dark as honeyed wine. The injury from the animal that had attacked him before he opened the black gate was severe. He could barely move his fingers. Natanial stood over him, gripping Anavha's uninjured arm in one hand and his own weapon in the other. Natanial peered out at the unfamiliar landscape, cursing the black gap in the world that had closed behind them. Natanial started up a slurry of Tordinian curses while Anavha wept.

It had happened again – blood, fear, a door to nowhere…

Natanial took him by the shoulders and shook him. Anavha imagined Zezili over him again, yelling "What did you do?"

Anavha gasped. "I'm sorry, I'm sorry…"

"What happened?" Natanial said.

"I… I don't know."

"There was a door. You opened a door. You must have closed it. Open it again. Laine curse you, where did you take us?"

"I… don't know." The sky was black. Anavha saw something very far in the distance, some purple glowing orb that put him in mind of Sina, but Sina was at least two years from rising. It winked out, and the sky was clear again. He wondered if he was going mad.

"Where are the moons?" Natanial said. "Stars, yes, but the moons…?"

Anavha trembled. "Please, take me to my wife. Take me to Zezili. She'll know what to do."

"Laine's eye, you're an *omajista*," Natanial said, breathless, and started muttering in Tordinian again.

"Please, don't–" and Anavha wanted to finish by saying, "don't tell anyone!" but this man answered to no woman. He was lawless. He would do whatever he liked, and there was no woman here to stop him.

"Where did you take us?" Natanial asked. "Do you know that much? How do you use the power to navigate?"

The air was cool, not cold. There was no snow like there had been in Dorinah. They sat in a great meadow of trampled reddish-brown grass.

His arm throbbed. He clutched it to his chest while he bled. A soft wind started, blowing his hair from his face, and the clouds away from the sky, and there were the moons – big Ahmur and its tiara of satellites, and Zini and Mur.

Natanial gave a whoop when he saw them, and raised his fist to the sky. "We are not so far lost on the web, then," he said. The moons' light illuminated the clearing. Anavha saw the bunched blackness of scrubland on the horizon, but mostly it was broken grass as far as he could see.

"Let's attend to your arm," Natanial said. He crouched next to Anavha and took his arm gently. Anavha shuddered. The pain was intense, as if his arm were on fire. "Get your tunic off," Natanial said.

It was difficult, so Natanial helped him. Natanial got behind him and unbound the girdle, then pulled off his tunic. The chill night air met Anavha's skin, and he shivered. The tunic was off, but Natanial remained behind Anavha. Anavha turned. Natanial was staring at his back.

"Did your wife do that to you?" Natanial said softly.

He must have seen the scar on Anavha's back – Zezili's initials, carved into his skin. In the light of the triple moons, it would be easy to see. "I am hers," Anavha said.

Natanial said nothing. He knelt beside Anavha and began tearing up the already shredded sleeve of the tunic. Anavha held out his arm. It looked very thin and pale in the milky light.

"Did she do these as well?" Natanial thumbed the scarred slashes on the inside of Anavha's arm.

"No," Anavha said.

"Someone else?"

"I did," Anavha said.

Natanial grunted and bound Anavha's arm. "I took you for a foppish Dorinah man," Natanial said, "but this is something else. Not all men in Dorinah are treated this way."

"Zezili loves me."

"She hurts you."

Anavha's face felt hot. "Sometimes... sometimes that's all right. Sometimes I deserve it. I even... I even like it, sometimes."

"Some do," Natanial said. He knotted the makeshift bandages. "I will grant you that. But far more common are those who fetishize the abuse they endure because living under the alternative is too much to bear."

"Don't tell me what I feel." Tears burned Anavha's eyes again, and for the first time in a long time, he hated himself for it. Hated to cry about his own life in front of a stranger. "You don't understand anything."

"I understand more than you know," Natanial said. "Come, we need to go on. If this is Aaldia we have a much longer distance to travel back to Tordin."

"Aaldia? How do you know it's Aaldia?"

"The stars," Natanial said.

They traveled all night. When Anavha collapsed, Natanial carried him, lifting him up over his shoulders as if he weighed nothing. And perhaps he did not. He was no one, of importance only to Zezili, and then only if he pleased her. Natanial carried him because Zezili would pay for him.

Finally, Natanial came to a stop. He set Anavha back on his feet. The moons had risen and nearly set.

"What is it?" Anavha asked.

"Lights," Natanial said. "Stay here. I want to make sure it's safe."

"Don't leave me!"

"Anavha."

"Please!"

"Stay three paces behind, then. Laine's bloody spit."

Natanial crept across the broken grass and onto a worn path. He called out in Tordinian. An answering call came from the house in another language, one Anavha didn't recognize.

Natanial yelled something else, then returned to Anavha. "There's a village two miles further on," he said. "We should find a tavern and a room."

"So we are in Aaldia?"

"Yes."

"How did we get here?"

Natanial cocked his head at him. "You took us here, you tell me. Let's just hope it's our Aaldia."

"What does that mean?"

"You really have no idea? Has no one trained you?"

"Zezili would never let the Seekers take me. Never."

Natanial swore again.

When they walked down into town, the moons were high in the sky, and Anavha was exhausted. His arms throbbed and his feet ached. He would give much for a warm meal and a bed.

Anavha expected the tavern they entered to be a loud, raucous affair, full of drunks and people selling their bodies, but even from the outside, this place looked different than a tavern in Dorinah. The town was very small, just one main street. It was paved in clean oblong stones, their seams filled with sand. One half of the village was built into a broad hill. The few buildings with two stories all had their first nestled within the ground, windows and broad doors peering out into the streets. The roofs were flat, not sloped, and Anavha saw a few figures glance down at them from nearby roofs where milky blue fire burned on long poles. Insects buzzed around them, their bodies blinking green, then white, then blue, each as big as Anavha's thumb. They rested on doorframes and hitching posts, giving the whole street a merry glow, as if it were decorated for some festival.

Natanial stepped into a large two storied tavern at the far end of the street. Anavha gasped as he disappeared into a black shroud. Natanial poked his head back out. "It's an illusion. To keep out the bugs. Come in."

Anavha stepped gingerly forward. "Illusion?"

"A parajista-trained door, hexed into place. It will admit you, just not the bugs. Aaldians have the best tricks. Come on, it's warmer in here."

Anavha took Natanial's hand and stepped through. He smelled jasmine and cloves. A small crowd was gathered at the far side of the room, attention rapt on a figure standing on a low dais, surrounded by misty multicolored spheres. The figure was tapping and moving smaller floating spheres and dragging them through the air into the larger ones. As the smaller spheres touched the larger spheres, the small ones disappeared. The room was still but for the low murmur of appreciation when a sphere disappeared, or a collective gasp when the manipulator chose a new orb.

Anavha was drawn to the game. Natanial went to a broad opening in the far side of the room that looked like it opened into the kitchen. A dark woman with a lean face and stout form gave him a warm smile as she wiped her hands on her apron.

The person on the dais was, Anavha assumed, a

woman, like the proprietor. Anavha wasn't sure, as his vocabulary gave him just two choices. The woman was lean and dark, with expressive hands. Her low brow was furrowed in concentration as she selected another small sphere. Anavha could see no pattern to the game – the larger spheres were scattered widely just outside her arm's reach, so she had to lean out to place them. The small red scattered spheres were all inside the sweep of her arms. He thought the object of the game had something to do with colors, at first – matching the small purple to the large purple – or maybe it had to do with size, but the only size discrepancy was between small or large sphere. His inability to understand what was going on actually made the game that much more interesting.

"It's a game that the Aaldians play, with doors," Natanial said. "Each projected sphere is a door. Each of the pieces on the board matches one of the doors. They have to choose which piece goes with which door. An old game, but even the young people play it. It's part of the entrance exam for government officials."

"But how is it played?"

"It's something to do with mathematics," Natanial said. "It takes a long time to master, unless you have a head for it. It's calculating the distances between the doors, I believe. Certain ranges of numbers are assigned colors, and the color corresponds to the pieces on the board." He waved a hand. "Not my talent, alas, but Aaldians have a particular passion for numbers. It makes them very good tradespeople. They are mad for this game."

"Do you travel to Aaldia a lot?"

"I am Aaldian, originally. I was born here, anyway."

Anavha looked at the small, black-skinned people around him, then back at the broad, bronze-skinned Natanial. He was uncertain what to say to that. Surely there were Saiduan people born in Dorinah, but they were always Saiduan. No one could be a citizen in

Dorinah without... looking like someone from Dorinah. "You don't look like it," Anavha said.

"If you're born here, you're Aaldian," Natanial said. "My mother looked more local than my father, though, to be sure. Just so happens I look more like him than her. You can't always tell a person's parentage in their face."

"How many languages do you speak?"

"Eight."

"Eight! There aren't that many languages in the world."

Natanial laughed. "Sheltered Dorinah child. There are three languages in Dorinah alone – high Dorinah, spoken by your priests and empresses; low Dorinah, spoken by most everyone else; and Daj, the patois the dajians speak. Dhai has two – Woodland Dhai and Valley Dhai. Saiduan has seven – let's not get into that. But it's a big country, and with those kinds of distances, it's inevitable that languages proliferate. Tordin has at least five, and Aaldia, though it recognizes only one common language, has five provinces with very distinct ways of speaking that language. And we have not even discussed the southern continents, like Hrollief, or the eastern kingdoms–"

"I'm foolish, then," Anavha said. "Does that please you?"

"You're not foolish," Natanial said, glancing over at the woman playing the sphere game, frowning as the crowd drew a collective gasp as another sphere winked out. "You're just ignorant. The wonderful thing about being ignorant is that it can be resolved very easily. Foolishness cannot. Once a fool, always a fool."

Anavha turned back to watch the game too. Only three large spheres remained, but there were over two dozen smaller ones left. As he and Natanial watched, the woman chose a small gray sphere, and flicked it into a large one over her left shoulder. It winked out. A hush descended over the crowd.

She hesitated, fingers hovering over the final pieces. Then she plucked out a small sphere and popped it into the larger one at her right.

The misty spheres all turned purple. The crowd howled; some hooted, many groaned. The misty game burst apart. Anavha wondered what parajista had conjured it. Like the bug screen on the door, it all had to be some elaborate gifted invention, though he had never seen a jista in Dorinah do anything like it. The look of defeat on the woman's face was so palpable that it gripped Anavha's heart.

"She chose wrong," Natanial said, rising.

"What happens?"

"They play again tomorrow. Lucky for her, this was a casual game. She wasn't playing for an entrance exam, or the fate of the world, or anything like that. She'll try again. Come. I got us a room."

Anavha followed him upstairs. "I'd like to learn that game," he said. There was something about the complexity of it, the geometry, that captivated him. It was easy to lose yourself in a game like that.

"We have more urgent places to start with your education. On the upside, it's a long way back to Tordin. I'd prefer we didn't rely on your spotty ability with your gift to get us back. There are few things I distrust more than an untrained jista."

"Why would you teach me anything? Aren't I a prisoner?"

Natanial hesitated, his hand on the banister. "I have seen the fear in your eyes before," he said. "I know what can be achieved when knowledge replaces fear."

"You think I'll become a killer, like you?"

"Not at all. I'm an artist. The killing has its purpose. There's a greater goal. Come, I asked the matron to send up a medic for your arm. I'd prefer you didn't lose it before I delivered you to Saradyn."

"Zezili will come for me."

"I don't doubt it. Saradyn won't either."

"Am I worth a lot, you think?"

"Likely more than Zezili will pay."

"I don't think so."

"It won't matter at all if we're in the wrong world," Natanial said. "Until then, let's work on your mathematics, and your Aaldian. You may need both before the world ends."

Anavha thought that an odd thing to say.

7

Harajan was a city of faces, a wintry Saiduan city far enough south of Kuonrada to give the retreating Saiduan army some comfort that the Tai Mora were not nipping at their heels. Maralah entered the city of faces showing her most fearsome one: a graven expression she had seen on broken statues of Patrons from the early days of the Empire, when the Dhai who once ruled what would become Saiduan still held out in small groups on the frontier. Over the centuries the Dhai were slowly eradicated and enslaved. Now the Dhai were returning – or, rather, a darker version of them, from some other world.

She supposed there was a great cosmic irony in that, to find her people slaughtered by those with the same faces they'd destroyed over a thousand years before. But mostly it wearied her, because in the end, it did not matter what face an enemy wore – an enemy was an enemy.

As she and her brother's army stumbled into Harajan during one of the worst winters she could remember, she kept the same expression, though few had cause to see it inside her snug furred hood and wrap.

She bore that expression all through the winter, until the false spring, when her brother started to hack his guts out and Taigan still had not answered the messages she had sent. Some part of her worried the missives were being intercepted by the Tai Mora. But the part that knew Taigan suspected he was merely resisting, and would resist until she compelled him through the pain of the ward.

The army was hungry, as were the civilians, but the Tai Mora advance had halted in the face of the weather. The weather, for all its horror, gave her a comfort she had not known in seven years.

Now the weather was lifting.

"You promised him Taigan would come," Morsaar Koryn, the second-in-command of her brother's army, said.

Maralah found him not with the army, nor with her brother, but in the scullery baking bread. He wore a stiff leather apron better suited to the butchering of ubel – the giant bear-dogs of the tundra – but his hands were nimble as they pinched and kneaded the dough. This was a man with long practice at an oven. She remembered some half-story Rajavaa had told her about Morsaar starting out as the assistant cook for the army when he was very young. Morsaar was a slim, wiry man, his hair braided back and twisted up into three tights knots on the top of his head. His most arresting feature was a long scar that stretched from the corner of his left eye and parted the upper edge of his left lip. She had known him when he was still unblemished, but had to admit the scar made him interesting as opposed to ugly. Infused weapons didn't make scars like that, which led her to wonder what man he'd tussled with in their own ranks to earn that bit of interesting.

The only other person in the room was tall, handsome Kovaas, one of the sanisi she now counted among hers after the schism in Kuonrada. She trusted very few now, less every day, and she admitted that seeing his broad, glowering face here in this sea of misery soothed her. If she lost the sanisi, she lost control of her mastery over those in the hold, and then she lost control of what remained of the country. She needed every one of them.

Kovaas seemed bemused, at best, by the baking.

Maralah came to the end of the long stone table as Morsaar began to shape his first fist-sized loaves, pinched at the ends to resemble almonds. Maralah knew that shape well – standard issue for the army.

"Don't we have cooks for that?"

"We are short a cook," Morsaar said. "He fled during the night."

"Then he will have no better luck leaving than Taigan has had in arriving," Maralah said. "The weather is bad. He couldn't cross between here and Anjoliaa." It was not a lie, precisely. It was an assumption.

Morsaar cut a neat slit in the side of his first loaf and tucked a pickled olive inside. She admired his long, deft fingers. For the first time she considered what it was Rajavaa found so attractive in him. He took up a wooden cutout of a leaf and pressed it firmly into the top of the bread, smoothing the edges of the raised dough with a finger. Perhaps Rajavaa loved this – a neat attention to detail. An exacting concentration.

"I don't see why he can't take a ship up the coast," Morsaar said. He placed the first loaf on the baking slab and pinched out another blob of dough to begin the next. Behind him, the big oven blazed merrily, emitting a slow heat.

"There are any number of things he should do," Maralah said. "What I can't tell you is which one he's chosen."

"Do you own him or not? You told Rajavaa he was yours." This loaf came out lopsided. He mashed the dough into a ball and began again.

"You mean the *Patron*. I'm as troubled as you are, Morsaar. The Patron told me he had a year."

"Illness doesn't adhere to a neat schedule, no more

than the satellites."

"Is there any other mundane thing you'd like to explain to me, as if I'm a child at your knee?" she said. "You forget your place." It was a trick often employed by men years her junior, to explain to her some trivial or obvious detail, expecting her to nod along like some honor-bound wife or slave instead of War Minister of Saiduan.

Morsaar straightened his spine. His fingers ceased their shaping. He peered at her from the corner of his eye. "I apologize," Morsaar said. "Do you cook?"

"Never," she said.

"A shame," he said, "you have the bitter bite of a woman who would do well ordering about a kitchen."

"I do hope you order your army better than a kitchen," she said. "I know I do."

"They are much the same," he said. He patted the loaf into shape and cut it open, inserted the olive. Pressed the leaf shape into the top. There was a preciseness to the routine that Maralah found oddly mesmerizing. Perhaps she should have learned to cook. "Hungry armies are useless armies," he said, "and we are low on onions and tubers. Bread helps."

"You'll need far more than this."

"The other cooks will be up soon," he said. He placed the second loaf, and took another gob of dough for his third. "I'm beginning to understand how the Dhai became cannibals."

"We're not done yet, Morsaar."

She heard footsteps in the hall outside, and raised voices. Her hand went instinctively to her infused blade. Kovaas moved to block the door, but it was just Driaa.

"Let hir enter," Maralah said.

Driaa inclined hir head and strode in. Ze looked worse for wear – hir long coat was tattered, and still damp from the matted snow and ice that had melted on entering the keep. Hir boots were worn. Maralah made a note to direct hir to the pile of gear they'd collected from the few dead they managed to pick up before the Tai Mora.

Morsaar raised his head from his work and smirked. "So the pass is open after all," he said.

"Spring's early," Driaa said, frowning at the growing line of loaves. "Just our luck, no? I intercepted a runner from Shoratau on the way." Ze pulled a leather-bound pack from hir coat and handed it to Maralah.

"What, they die on the way?" Maralah asked. She opened the case.

"Frostbite," Driaa said. "They say he'll lose a leg."

"Unfortunate," Maralah muttered, but her attention now was on the missive. It read simply:

Shoratau is fallen. All lost.

"Did you read this?" she asked Driaa. Losing Kadaan and Wraisau and the last of the Dhai scholars would be a blow to her and the people here. The last of their slim hope still rested on that gambit.

Driaa shook hir head. "Why didn't they send an infused missive? Seems a waste of a runner."

"The Tai Mora have started intercepting them," Maralah said, and thought again of the messages to Taigan, the tardy replies.

"When did that happen?" Driaa asked.

Morsaar made another liberal dusting of flour on the stone slab. He slapped another pinch of dough off and mashed his fists into it. "The Patron split his forces right before Harajan. We tested them by sending a missive that said the majority of our forces were headed southeast to Sorvaraa."

"How many died on the way to Sorvaraa?" Driaa asked.

"Three hundred," Maralah said. Decoys, all, though they had not known it. Some things were better left unspoken. She imagined they thought their deaths poor luck, in the end. But she often wondered what their commander had thought, facing what must have been thousands of Tai Mora waiting for them outside Sorvaraa. Another log thrown onto the fire of the cause.

"If the pass is open, the Tai Mora aren't far behind," Morsaar said. He wiped his hands on the leather apron, smearing flour across the front. "I'll tell Rajavaa."

"The Patron can hardly piss straight," Maralah said. "I'll go to him. Driaa, Shao Sindaa has command of the sanisi. You can find him in the Wailing Hall. Let him know about the pass. Who's leading our retreat to Anjoliaa?"

"I've put Ren Huraasa in charge of shoring it up. He's been running patrols. There's something else you should know. A week ago, we spotted ships off the coast. Tai Mora ships. Not a large fleet. But they were headed south."

"To Grania?"

"Yes. If I had to guess, they're assaulting Dhai or Dorinah."

"Why divide their forces now, when we're almost done?"

"Maybe they think we *are* done," Morsaar said.

"I will tell the Patron," Maralah said. She turned to follow Driaa. If Rajavaa died they lost not only a Patron, but the man who commanded the loyalty of what remained of the army. Morsaar was a capable man, but she suspected his loyalty was to Rajavaa, not Saiduan. And certainly not to her. She glanced back as he lifted his first batch of loaves into the big oven.

"Don't burn yourself," she said.

"I never do," he said, and promptly hissed as his finger caught the edge of the oven.

She smirked and went upstairs.

In the vestibule outside her brother's quarters she could already hear him hacking. Two flat-headed slaves exited the room, carrying bloody linens. Those born into service were the only slaves she let care for him. Even then, rumor was difficult to quash. The Patron of Saiduan dying bloodily from a rotten liver was a hard thing to keep quiet. She pushed into Rajavaa's quarters. His personal surgeon knelt at his side, drawing fluid from his extremities. Rajavaa was a slim man, but in the advanced stages of his disease, he had swelled.

"Leave us," she told the surgeon.

The surgeon finished bandaging the wound and stood, without meeting Maralah's gaze. When she was gone, Maralah sat at her brother's bedside. She took his hand.

"What can I get you?" she asked.

He rolled his eyes at her. They had taken on a yellow tinge. "A drink," he said, and showed his teeth.

"You told me you stopped drinking when you became Patron. That was months ago. Yet here we are."

"Got the rot. Told you."

"Surgeon said if you stopped drinking immediately you could have–"

"Where is Taigan? You promised Taigan could heal me."

"I promised Taigan, so you kept swilling a barrel a day? You're a mad man, Rajavaa." She released his hand.

He moaned. "You haven't seen what I've seen."

"I've seen more," she said. She wanted to call him weak, like their mother, a man who could not stop drinking even when he poisoned his body, and the country with him. But what she saw now was not a cowardly man with no backbone. She saw the last of her kin, dying from an illness neither of them could combat while Tira was in decline, and Taigan a continent away. He would always drink. He would never stop.

"The pass is open," she said. "Taigan will be here soon."

"Soon enough?" His eyes were wide, his tone hopeful, like a child's. Her heart clenched.

"I thought you'd resigned yourself to die of the rot."

"Morsaar could not survive that."

She could, though, and he knew that, didn't he? She could survive the death of everything.

"Who will take your army, then?"

He broke into a fit of coughing. It racked his whole swollen body. Blood flecked his lips. "Who? Who will take the army? You will take the army, Maralah. What is left of it. You keep spinning us all around, trying to avoid it. But it's coming. You know it, don't you?"

"They will not listen to me. An ataisa, maybe, but not a woman. *You* know that."

"Dire times," he said. "Times for miracles."

She leaned over him. "Then perform a miracle," she said. "*Live.*"

He gazed at the twining branches of the living hold that made up the ceiling, all painted in red and amber stripes. "Para is in decline."

She patted his hand. "Para is ascendant for another year. It will be some time before we see Sina, and without my star I am just a sanisi like any other."

"You could kill me cleanly, then, take my soul and arm yourself with it."

"You promised me at least a year. Taigan will come."

"You say that," Rajavaa said. "But I don't think it's me you're saying it for." He broke into another fit of coughing.

She needed Taigan. But would he really come when she called him? That was the fear of every master – that one day the dog would no longer answer the call.

8

Zezili fought her way out of her own house like a woman eager for her first bedding. She argued with Daolyn, and the dajians, and once she was on the road, she argued with the keepers of the way houses she stayed at, though most of those arguments were one-sided. The moment people glimpsed her face, they shut down, like cheap puppets with broken strings. She rode across Daorian as spring woke across the country. It was her first solo journey since her mauling, and everything hurt. When she heaved herself off her new dog in the courtyard of the Empress's hold, her boots crunched across dead and dying plants poisoned by the hold's fastidious dajians. She had a tremor in her left hand. She had not been able to still it.

She was dressed for her meeting with the Empress – a short red coat embroidered in silver, long dark trousers. She wore her sword. She kept her hair knotted back, no matter that the simple style made her look like a servant. Let the world see her face.

Zezili had spent the morning practicing in the yard of the nearby way house to loosen her up for this walk. She had burned most of the stiffness from her body. Now she pressed her left hand to her side to still the trembling.

The Empress's dajian secretary, Saofi, greeted Zezili

outside the banquet hall. But instead of ushering her into what was sure to be a vacuous affair stuffed with pretty ministers and profiteers, Saofi said, "The Empress awaits you in the vestibule with Syre Storm."

"Storm? You mean Lasli, that *man*?" Syre Storm – given name Lasli Laodysin – was the Empress's only male legion commander. He was not permitted to pick up a sword and do violence, but he could send others to do it in the Empress's name.

Saofi inclined her head.

"Well," Zezili said. "This should be interesting." She watched Saofi's face for any hint of disturbance at Zezili's appearance, but Saofi betrayed nothing, as ever. Those who served the Empress a long time had to be too loyal to consider treason, or too fearful. Zezili once considered herself somewhere in between. Now she wasn't so sure. If all went as Zezili hoped, she would never see Saofi, or Daorian, ever again.

Saofi led her to the common vestibule outside the banquet hall, a long walk for Zezili. She was breathing heavily by the time they arrived, and paused outside the door a moment, looking for a way to catch her breath.

"You know invaders are coming," Zezili said, stalling. "Will you stay here in Daorian?"

Saofi's gaze got as high as Zezili's shoulder. "You speak as if there's a choice for people like us," Saofi said.

Zezili raised her brows at that, but it was no longer worth denying that she and Saofi were different. In the eyes of the invaders, they were both dajians. Perhaps in the eyes of the Empress, too.

"I'm not property," Zezili said, tapping the wall. "Not like the hold. I have legs. As do you."

Saofi played with the bands of her chatelaine. "Don't let the Empress think you believe that property has choices." She opened the great banded iron door of the vestibule. The room was long and narrow. Zezili heard laughter and music from the banquet room adjacent.

The Empress stood motionless as a statue on a dais at the far end of the room. Her mouth was a painted red smudge, drawn down at the corners. She had caked on a thicker layer of bronzer that matched the belled fabric of her dress. Her head was tilted toward Storm, who stood uncomfortably next to her at a low table near the blazing mouth of a hearth so grand Zezili could stand upright in it. Storm was a broad, tall man, easily fifty pounds heavier and two hands taller than Zezili. She despised men who took up space. Storm slouched, showing abhorrent posture, but typical for large men who sought to minimize their sprawl. When he saw her, something like relief passed over his face. Difficult to tell with the scraggly black beard he wore, but it was certainly less strained. He ceased his rambling and raised a hand in greeting.

No one had ever shown relief in her presence, and it concerned her immediately. It meant whatever the Empress was talking to him about was far worse than Zezili's face.

"Syre Zezili," he said. He winced when she stepped into the light. Ah, so he'd not caught the full measure of her face yet.

The Empress beckoned Zezili forward.

Zezili halted a few paces from the Empress. She stooped painfully to one knee. Bent her head.

"I am, as ever, yours."

"Join us," the Empress said, and gestured expansively to the table. On the table was a great map of Grania, and the countries it hosted – Dorinah, Dhai, Tordin, Aaldia.

As Zezili took up her position opposite Storm, she saw he was sweating profusely. How long had he waited here for her? What had they spoken of before she arrived? Her skin crawled at the idea. She didn't like being kept in the dark.

"I've chosen you both to take on a most glorious task," the Empress said. She scratched at the map with one of her gold-powdered fingers, rigid and unmalleable, like a claw.

A tingle of fear rode Zezili's spine. She peered at Storm. He was a good tactician – any woman would give him that – but he was barred by law from committing direct violence. Men who committed violence were sacrificed to Rhea without exception. He was dressed for a festive dinner, not battle, but so was she, and she wore a weapon. He did not. Not even a utility knife. He wore billowing black trousers and a broad purple tunic and long coat stitched in silver. Lovely work, no doubt. Both his mother and his wife's families were terribly wealthy, and despite his size, they ensured that he dressed the part of a noble man of standing. His face was powdered in gold, his eyes lined in kohl, and his black hair was carefully curled and bound in silver ribbons. Storm was not the Empress's best asset. And Zezili, the traitor, wasn't a shining paragon of virtue either. Whatever the Empress wanted the two of them to collaborate on wasn't going to be glorious. Why choose them?

The voices in the banquet chamber opposite rose. A heated argument had broken out.

"Who's in attendance?" Zezili asked, tilting her head at the wall.

"No concern of yours," the Empress said. "I have called together my many friends for a discussion of our situation. Look to your own task today. I have many pieces in motion, and your pieces are integral to the rest. I have a weapon, if you will, that has been waiting for me to awaken it. You will go south to Tordin with a force of two hundred to its resting place. All you need do is uncover where it lies and awaken it. The rest will happen in its own time." She, too, tilted her head at the banquet room, as if in mocking imitation of Zezili.

"How do we awaken this weapon?" Zezili asked. "Is this why you let them kill the dajians? Did you make a bargain?"

The Empress smiled and pressed a clawed finger to her lips. Then said, "When we first arrived, my sister Penelodyn and I put this weapon in Tordin for safekeeping. Then that fat man, Saradyn, made a mess of things. A few of us had to wait for Rhea to return. Now she is rising. And we will rise again with her. Myself and my... weapons."

"This is a heavy responsibility," Storm said. Zezili glanced sharply at him. He must see how suspicious this looked. Why was she sending her half-dajian and her single male legion commander to Tordin? Maybe sending Storm made sense – the man who called himself King Saradyn was said to be more sympathetic to men – but Zezili's part in this was shadowy.

"Why two legion commanders?" Zezili said.

The Empress was blunt. "I expect losses."

"Oh," Storm said.

"You wish to win this war against the Tai Mora, Zezili? My dearest one, this is what I planned from the start. It is why I could sacrifice Seekers and dajians. This was my end goal, do you see it now? I am not so strange, am I? Not so impossible to understand? You will save this country, Zezili. The two of you together will preserve Dorinah to take its glorious place in ascendance when Rhea's eye once again beams over this world."

"Why send me?"

The Empress brushed Zezili's cheek. Zezili flinched. "You have been punished for your disobedience, but I know you acted as you did to protect Dorinah. Now the astromancers tell me Rhea is close enough that they can sense it in their lenses. It won't be long now. You must set my weapon free."

"How do we awaken it?" Zezili said.

"Storm and I have already discussed that," the Empress said sharply. "There will be some wards that need cleaning up. I have five very special jistas who will accompany you – they have already been instructed on what they must do after you open the way."

"I had hoped we'd be leading a campaign to take Tordin," Storm said.

Zezili was glad he'd said it before her. If she could burn down Dorinah and Tordin at the same time, she'd do it.

"All in time," the Empress said. "As of this moment we must look to our shores. First we secure Dorinah, then we take the world."

"The world?" Zezili said.

The Empress smiled. Her teeth were long, slightly yellow. "The world," she said, and needled one of her cold golden claws into Zezili's soft stomach. "Are you hungry?" she said absently, and sashayed to the door leading into the banquet hall. The voices had subsided. "My friends are eager to meet you."

Meet me and eat me alive, Zezili thought. She saw the flash of the cats' teeth again, felt the searing pain of their claws.

"I'm not hungry," Zezili said.

The Empress smiled delicately. "No," she said, "I expect you are not." She licked her fingers. "Guard your thoughts, Zezili. This is not going to turn out the way you imagined."

9

The dying woman stank like a moldered corpse. The stink was so strong Lilia smelled her from ten paces away. Taigan stood when she saw the woman and her litter bearers approach, and drew her blade. Lilia thought drawing a blade was a foolish thing – what was the old woman going to do, bite them?

Lilia and the caravan of refugees were still three days away from Kuallina, the great stronghold at the center of Dhai where the Kai had agreed to house and feed the six hundred until they could be assimilated into the clans. That put them just outside Clan Raona, eating rice and camping out along a very contaminated stretch of road. She had requested parajistas to accompany them, but the Kai only gave them one, and she had a very long night of running up and down the road killing virulent plant life that tried over and over again to devour the people camping along the road.

The militia boy who had asked Lilia to cure his grandmother had met them there with a gaggle of his relatives, pulling the old woman behind them. Now Lilia stood at the entrance to the tent they had placed her in, trying not to gag at the smell.

Beside Lilia, Gian put a hand to her own nose. "I told you it was very bad," Gian said.

The militia man stood well outside with his other family members. Lilia glanced back just once at him, then entered the tent where Taigan was already kneeling.

"I'm Lilia."

The old woman winced. Her face was a doughy, wrinkled map. But though her face and belly were plump, her hands were withered claws. Lilia thought perhaps Oma's breath would allow her to see some part of the woman she could not see through her other training, but when she pulled on Oma's breath, it gave her no special sight.

She sat back on her heels.

"I am Mahinla Torsa Sorila," the woman said.

"You have pain?" Lilia asked.

"Always."

Taigan leaned into Lilia, so close she nearly brushed Lilia's ear with her chin. "You intend to heal her?" she said. "You can see it's cancer."

Lilia shook her head.

"Oma is a fickle star," Taigan said. "You haven't been trained. It's like wondering why you can't speak a word you've never heard."

"You can cure her?"

"The cancer? I can kill it, yes. But then her body must reabsorb it. She also has arthritis, two failing kidneys, and an aging digestive system. She is, in a word, old. Bodies fail. They are imperfect things."

"But we can save her?"

"For a year? Two? Certainly."

Mahinla raised her voice. "Girl? Lilia?"

Lilia bent back over the woman. "What is it?"

"May I take your hand?"

Lilia looped her good hand into the old woman's. Mahinla moved her arm, but did not try to close her fingers. Lilia imagined it hurt terribly.

"My grandson is a good boy," she said. "Takes me to good jistas."

"We will help you," Lilia said.

"No, no," the woman said. She sighed. "I am a hundred and forty-three years old. It's enough."

"He's asked a favor," Lilia said, and caught herself. What he wanted had no bearing on this woman's wishes.

"I, too, am asking a favor," Mahinla said.

"You do not consent to being healed?" Lilia said. "Why? I would give–"

"I am tired," Mahinla said. "You don't know what that is, yet, to be tired of this world."

"But why did you–"

"I wanted to see the girl who opened the gates of Liona."

Lilia glanced over at Taigan. Taigan shrugged. "I know what it is to want to die," Taigan said. "You'll understand one day, too."

It took some time to sort things out between Mahinla and her grandson. Great-great-grandson, Lilia amended. After some tears and a few soft words from Gian – who gave them each a sticky rice ball she had secreted away in her tunic pockets – they called the boy's sisters and the three of them hauled Mahinla away.

As they did, Mahinla called Lilia over one last time.

"I had stopped believing," Mahinla said, "when my granddaughter was killed on the other side of Liona. I thought Faith Ahya had turned her face from us. But she has not. She gave us you."

Lilia watched them go. Taigan came up behind her. "Good stories, there."

"Is everything political?" Lilia asked, disgusted.

"Of course," Taigan said. "All you have to decide is whether you'll take advantage of it or let it run its course. In this case, I suggest you pursue it."

"How?"

"I can take care of it, if you wish."

"You won't hurt anyone?"

"Not every task I perform is that crude. What do you

think, Gian? I suspect planting stories in people's ears is something you have some skill at."

"What do you know?" Gian said. She rummaged through her pack and triumphantly pulled out an apple.

"Gian and I will take care of it," Taigan said. "It's a long way to Kuallina still, and we can spread very good stories about you as we go."

Lilia watched the little family trundle off into the woods.

"There will be two stories," Taigan said, pressing her. "The story the Kai and his people tell, of a mad refugee girl pretending to be Faith Ahya, trying to fool the country. The other is that you are, indeed, Faith Ahya, or some aspect of hers. That woman and her family already hold a spark of that. All I intend to do is kindle it. We kindle our story, Lilia, or we get burned up by the blazing storm of someone else's."

"I'm not going to lie to people," Lilia said.

"You already deceived them," Gian said, munching her apple.

"This is different."

"We'll tell the stories they've already made up," Gian said. "It's not as if we'll make new ones."

"I'm going to burn up all those Tai Mora in Liona," Lilia said. "That will be story enough." But she heard the wisdom in Taigan's words. All her power came from these people. If things went wrong, and the Kai blamed the war on her...

"You're untrained, raw," Taigan said, "and after killing a few legionnaires who couldn't defend themselves and hurling yourself to the top of a wall, you've gotten supremely arrogant. Power is nothing without discipline. Power without discipline is short lived."

"All right," Lilia said. "But don't hurt anyone. I could bind you up in a bone tree forever."

"See how that transpires a second time," Taigan said coolly.

"What do you care what happens, Taigan?" Lilia said. "Why not go home to Saiduan on your own?" But that wasn't her real question. Her real question was why Taigan gave her any choice in her fate at all now. Why hadn't she bundled Lilia up in a sack and thrown her into a ship bound for Saiduan yet? What was she playing at?

"I do what I please," Taigan said, but there was a briskness to her tone that made Lilia wonder why she would be so defensive.

"It's at least seven more days to the harbor," Lilia said. "We should talk about what happens there."

"Ships arrive. Ships depart," Taigan said.

"Bone tree," Lilia said.

Taigan shrugged. "What is it you intend to do there? Burn them all up? There will be more than a few hundred legionnaires there with them. And the Tai Mora will be gifted. The legionnaires were not. You have won thus far on luck," Taigan said. "Best not forget that." She slunk off back to her tent.

Gian came up beside Lilia. She had finished her apple, and now asked, "May I take your hand?"

Lilia held out her hand. Gian took it. There was fear in her face. "What is it?" Lilia asked.

"Let's stay in Kuallina," Gian said. "We don't need to go to the harbor. Look how safe it is here! Food for everyone. Nice people. Freedom. My whole life, I just wanted this. Two people holding hands in the warmth of a fire. We can have our own warm house, our own–"

"The Tai Mora killed my mother," Lilia said.

"I don't want to be lonely anymore," Gian said. She raised her hands to Lilia's face. Lilia remembered, again, the other Gian, clearing a path with her weapon, shirtless, the corded muscles of her back moving just beneath her skin. The Gian who had died for her, for a greater cause than Lilia would ever understand. Did Lilia have that kind of resolve, to die for a cause, for what she believed was right, even when others called her mad for it?

"Can I kiss you?" Lilia said, and her voice trembled when she said it, because she knew she wanted to kiss the woman for all the wrong reasons – for who she could be, not who she was, and for a life she dreamed about, not one they would have.

Gian kissed her. Her mouth was warm and soft.

"Let's stay here telling stories," Gian murmured. "We'll build a life here, just the two of us. I can plant a garden, grow big tomatoes and squash and–"

Lilia saw her mother's terribly twisted body mounted on the top of the Tai Mora mirror, saw her bursting into a thousand fractured pieces when she destroyed it.

"I'm sorry," Lilia said, "But I don't have any hold on you. You can do what you want."

"Do you want me to stay?"

"Yes," but when the words bubbled out, it all felt very selfish. She liked the way Gian looked at her. She liked that Gian seemed to need her. Gian wanted her.

Her feelings were terribly tangled up, because if Lilia asked herself what *she* wanted, she wasn't sure anymore. Maybe all she wanted was to go back to the beginning of it all, and refuse to go through the tear in the world, and fall on the Kai's willowthorn sword. Maybe the world where she did that would be a better place.

"All right then," Lilia said, "but you must be with me to the end. Promise me that. No matter what happens."

"I promise," Gian said. "To the end."

10

The way back to Oma's Temple was swift. Ahkio and
Caisa went by Line. The stories from Liona would spread.
They would get worse when people found out he'd sent
some scullery drudge from Dorinah to the harbor to help
with defenses. An omajista's place was there, at their
most vulnerable point, but it would make her look just
like the divine thing she said she was, and that worried
him.

When he arrived, Ora Una, the gatekeeper, told him
the Tai Mora emissary was in the garden. Ahkio crossed
the foyer with Caisa to the entrance to the back garden.
His stride was longer, and she skipped to keep up.

Ahkio followed the winding path through the garden.
Most of the greenery was still dormant, waiting for the
first kiss of spring. Caisa hurried beside him, her breath
crystallizing in the cool mid-morning air. A mist had
descended, and still clung to the bases of the trees. The
central fountain, its centerpiece a massive three-pronged
claw that mirrored the shape of the temple, had been
drained. It stood still and silent, its crown lost to the mist.

"Is this some emissary from the south?" Caisa said,
rubbing her shoulders. He realized only then that he had
given her no indication of who the emissary was.

Ahkio rounded the fountain and went up a broad set

of stone steps to a great living structure of bowed bonsa saplings draped in withered wisteria. A slim figure stood beneath it, gazing out toward the great chasm that held the Fire River in its mouth.

"Hello," Ahkio said.

The figure turned. She was a slight woman with a broad grin. Her dark hair was cut strangely, as if hacked with a hatchet. She wore a long blue coat of what looked like wool and dyed fireweed cord.

"You must be the Kai," the emissary said. "I know your face. I am Hofsha Sorek."

Caisa made a sound behind him. Ahkio turned. Caisa had stopped at the base of the steps, hand on the hilt of her weapon.

He glanced back at Hofsha. Hofsha's grin had faded. "Do the two of you know each other?" Ahkio asked.

"I have known this little boy since he was a pup," Hofsha said.

"You've mistaken Caisa for someone else, then. Caisa is a woman, not a boy."

"Not where I'm from," Hofsha said. "Where I'm from you get a pronoun at birth and you keep it, like a civilized person."

"How does she know you, Caisa?"

Caisa's mouth moved, but no sound came out.

"Caisa?" Ahkio said.

Ahkio felt a chill. *I wasn't sure she was on our side*, Liaro had said, back when the council house in Raona had burned. But Caisa had hacked apart the man who had wanted to take Ahkio's life. She stood by him with Liaro when he was ill and brought him to Kuallina. Was she really Tai Mora or some Tai Mora's twin?

"Wait for me inside, Caisa," Ahkio said.

"I can explain," Caisa said. "You don't want to be alone with her!"

"I suspect Hofsha isn't here for murder," Ahkio said. "We'll speak later."

Caisa ran down the steps and through the garden.

Ahkio regarded Hofsha. "She's one of yours, then? How long ago did you put her here?"

"Not at all," Hofsha said. "He's a runaway from our parajista ranks. We sent the hounds after him, but had very little luck. Now I know why."

"Hounds?"

"It's how we retrieve our people," Hofsha said. "Deserters, and the like."

"I expect you have a lot of those."

"Less than you think." Hofsha smiled.

Ahkio rose to the bait, and came up the rest of the steps. He stood beside her, his elbow placed a few inches from hers. "You come here alone, ungifted, to parley?"

"My gift is not with the satellites," Hofsha said, stirring her fingers in the air. "My gift is with people. Moving them. Managing them. Mitigating harm to them."

"What do you need here that you can get from me without blood?"

"A peaceful surrender," Hofsha said. "I've come here to save you from a very prolonged death by starvation and disease. I've seen it happen to a hundred and twenty-seven countries across three worlds. My Empress, my Kai, always gets what she wants. It's up to you to decide in what way it's delivered to her."

"You haven't fought us before."

Hofsha patted the railing. "I'm afraid we need your temples."

A fist of fear squeezed Ahkio's heart. The heart of Oma's seat. The riddle of the temples.

"What would you need the temples for?" Ahkio asked.

"My Empress is weary, she will be the first to admit, but also merciful. It doesn't please us to kill so many. We'll take the temples, and you'll all keep your lives."

"What will you do with the temples, Hofsha?"

"What do you care, as long as you have your lives? I promise you, Kai, I am offering you a way out of madness and bloodshed. So much you can't even fathom it. What do you have left here? Twenty thousand people? Thirty thousand? Hardly a drop in a pond. The Dhai left in this world just barely register as a people."

"What else?" He remembered Kirana killing herself before her shadow could do it, ensuring he ascended to Kai before her shadow moved in. It was why she waited until he was safely inside Oma's Temple before perishing. Did they know how that worked yet? Or would that wait until they'd already come in and discovered that the new Kirana had to be Kai to unlock the temple's heart? Would they ask him to open the way for her? And when they activated the temples to do... whatever they did, what would happen to the rest of the world? The world broke when Oma rose. Ahkio suspected the temples played a large part in that.

"Oh, there's one more thing," Hofsha said, "but it's a trifle. There's a woman we're looking for. I believe you know her. Yisaoh Alais Garika. If you could assist us in finding her, we'd think most kindly of you."

"If I had any idea about where to find Yisaoh, I'd happily tell you where she was." Right up until Ahkio said it aloud, he believed it. But he was not that man.

"Well, it will be appreciated. What do you say to our offer, Kai? It's been some time since I came to the leader of a country with such a fine offer. It's usually very bad news."

"What are the usual terms?"

"She lets a lover, a child, live. Maybe spares a few dozen close kin, all exiled."

"And the rest?"

"The rest die," Hofsha said.

"And these people you speak to, they agree to that? They give up the lives of their entire countries to save a few dozen close kin?"

"The first few didn't," she said, "the others learned. You know what choice to make."

"I know what choice you'd like me to make, and they are entirely different things."

Hofsha exhaled, sending out a puff of breath into the air. She seemed to marvel at it as it dissipated. "Shall I tell you a little story, Kai?"

"I'm not fond of stories."

"That's not what I heard. I heard you have a love of a fine tale from *The Book of Oma*. That's what it's called here, isn't it? Oma's Book. Ours is *The Book of Dhai*."

"Why spare me?" he said. "You sent people here to kill many others, and you're asking after Yisaoh, but you haven't killed me. Why?"

"I'm only telling you what my Empress bid." She pulled something from the deep pocket of her coat – a soft, floppy hat. She pulled it on. If not for the dark color, and her somber attire, and the substance of her message, it might look ridiculous.

"Good day, Kai. I wish you the best." She trotted down the steps, paused at the bottom, and looked back. "I'll say this. I've watched a good many people die in my time, and seen a lot of lovely places burn. I'd hate to see you gutted out here, and all these lovely gardens turned to dust." She began to whistle.

Ahkio watched until the mist swallowed her.

In the temples, they taught a class each year on strategy and tactics, mostly based on records of the final battles the Dhai fought with the Saiduan. Those fights were bitter ones. The Dhai ate one another not merely as a show of reverence, but as a means of survival.

They had been forced to do any number of terrified and desperate things, at the end, because they knew their fate. They would be routed, and their children turned into slaves. It was a known end. They fought hard because they knew there was no other alternative they could live with.

Ahkio went to the rail and listened to the eerie murmuring of the river below, made alien in its cadence

by the fog. The Tai Mora were like that. Some distorted
version of themselves. Not real people. Not truly Dhai.
If they were Dhai, they would not propose to slaughter
them all in their beds.

Ahkio left the rail and headed back to the temple,
in search of Liaro. Not for counsel, but for the comfort
of one known. He wanted someone to take him into
his arms and tell him there was some other choice not
constructed by a foreign army, even if he was too old to
believe in children's stories.

11

Lilia had smelled the sea for much of her childhood, but never set foot in it. The great rocky spur of land she grew up on had no safe path to the sea, so she had settled for viewing it from afar. As she came over the low rise of scrubland and saw the vast gates of Asona Harbor, she realized she was not likely to set foot in it now, either. The gates were easily the same height as the walls of Liona, maybe higher. She told herself that was all right. Revenge did not require a dip in the sea.

Lilia, Gian and Taigan had left the refugees ensconced safely at Kuallina and kept on northward to the harbor where they were met by Mohrai's cousin, Alhina, and two of her male relatives, both smart-looking men who did not go so far as to carry weapons, but who held themselves like people who would not be afraid to stand between Alhina and an aggressor. Alhina was a short, plump woman with a kind young face that put Lilia in mind of Kalinda Lasa, which made Lilia feel far more kindly toward her than she probably should have. The day was cool, and, as they trekked along the road, Lilia saw that spring had indeed come to Dhai in full force now. Many plants stayed green during the winter, but those that went dormant had begun to unfurl, revealing new green shoots and tender leaves and spines.

Now they drew up their mounts short. Ahead of them, a sea of floxflass covered the road.

"Curse this spring," Alhina said. She took a long drink from a flask at her hip.

Lilia glanced at Taigan. "I'll race you," she said.

"I will win," Taigan said.

Lilia urged her bear into a sprint across the floxflass field, and raised her fist high as she called on Oma. All around, her, the field of floxflass burned, sending sickly-sweet smoke into the air. Taigan galloped past her, murmuring words of encouragement in Saiduan to her bear. The sanisi gained the lead, and where she pointed her fingers out across the teeming sea of floxflass, the little tendrils burst into flame.

They dashed madly together for nearly a mile, burning and urging their bears on. At the end of the floxflass sea, Lilia reined in her bear and turned to look back at the scorched path, and she laughed.

Taigan pulled up beside her, grinning. "You are so easily amused," Taigan said.

"I cleaned pots my whole life," Lilia said.

"Fair point."

Lilia gazed up into the great trees standing in matted clumps amid the farmland all around them. "The trees were grander," she said.

"More dangerous."

"Grander," Lilia said. "I'll race you back!" She galloped back to meet their party.

Alhina and her male escorts looked at her askance when she arrived, she and her bear covered in char from the floxflass, but that just made Lilia grin harder. As she fell back into the procession with them, she coughed. It turned into a wheezing hack.

Gian moved her mount closer. "Do you need your mahuan?"

Lilia shook her head. She'd had a fit the night before, too, without it being triggered by the usual things –

frights, too much exercise. She suspected she was more exhausted than she felt. Sometimes, after holding Oma beneath her skin for hours, she felt invincible. The letdown when she finally released it was starting to become more pronounced.

Taigan finally caught up to her, and fell in beside her. "Take it anyhow," Taigan said.

"You aren't my mother."

"Stop acting like a child who needs one, then," Taigan said. "You natter like a bird."

"You fuss like a hen."

"You wheeze like a dying wren."

"You scheme like a raven."

Taigan puffed out her chest. "Thank you."

Lilia motioned to Gian for the powder. Gian added it to a small water bladder and handed it over. It took several minutes more of silent riding before the powder began to take effect. The constriction eased. All this power, and what did it get her? It didn't fix her labored breathing. And it wouldn't fix her leg or her hand, unless she chopped them off and had Taigan regrow them. Power over everything, the whole world, but not herself.

"The world has a bad sense of humor," Lilia said.

"I often think the same," Taigan said.

"Your body doesn't fail you."

Taigan laughed. "My body does what it pleases."

Lilia continued to drink and watched the harbor gates as they approached. The road here should have been bustling with traffic to and from the harbor. Numerous public houses lined the road, mostly eateries and way houses. She saw two tea houses with broad green awnings. The floxflass on the road must have grown up overnight. No stretch of road this vital would have been left unattended longer than that.

"Does your family live on the docks?" Lilia asked Alhina. She was not much good at small talk, but suspected talking about much of anything related to herself would become problematic quickly.

"Usually," Alhina said. She took another nip from her flask. "But we've moved to the gates. There are storage and living quarters inside the gatehouses, and all along the inside."

"How far do the gates go? To the cliffs?" Gian asked.

"Yes, they span the entirety of the harbor. Faith Ahya and Hahko anticipated raids from Saiduan and Dorinah. It was among the first structures they built."

Taigan said, "And you're running patrols along the cliffs?"

"Of course," Alhina said. "We have six squads patrolling the west where the wall ends and the black cliffs begin, and two more in the east, which is less ground to cover. It's not as far from here to the mountains, going east."

"Jistas with them?" Taigan asked.

"Each squad is eight militia, with three jistas. A coterie."

"One of each type?" Gian asked. "Is that what that means?"

"Yes," Lilia said, glad to show she knew something.

"Let's get up onto the top of the wall," Taigan said. "I'm eager to see how this looks from another vantage."

Lilia gazed at the massive, twisted wall in the distance, blocking off the view from the sea. She was very interested as well, but for a different reason.

She wanted to see the people she intended to destroy.

Taigan came up the steps onto the great harbor wall just behind Lilia. The warm wind from the Haraeo Sea hit Taigan square in the face. She smelled the changing season in the wind. It was the same wind that had blown across Saiduan. She tasted salt and something bitter, and memorable – the acidic tang of the red tide, the kelp the Tai Mora had brought with them to assault living walls. She came up to the heavy rail with Lilia, and put her hands on the massive tirajista-trained wood. It was not dead. She saw greenery winding up the outside of it.

"What's at the core of this wall?" Taigan asked. "It's all living, like this?"

"The gates are," Alhina said. "I think the wall was trained over a stone core."

"Dead stone?"

"Is there another kind?"

"Sometimes," Taigan said. She ignored the girl's dubious look.

Two great piers jutted out over the water for a thousand feet into the surging sea, a necessary thing for a harbor when the pull of the moons resulted in extreme tides that swept the water out for miles. She had heard of families swept away by the force of the tides in little coastal towns in Saiduan. Whole villages were sometimes swallowed when the fractious heavens changed the ebb and flow of the tides.

For all the Dhai's cowardice and unreadiness for war, they did have two very good defenses. What concerned her was that they relied on them so completely, to the detriment of their army, the construction of their cities, even the ways they organized themselves. Without a hierarchical structure to amass and order armies, they would be little better than a mob with pointed sticks and a few uncoordinated parajistas blowing around clouds before being wrapped in the breath of some jista on the other side. The Tai Mora would be coordinated... like their ships.

She stared out at the ships clotting the harbor. They barricaded the bowl of the blue bay. It was nothing like the number she'd seen at Aaraduan. These were fifty across and three deep, hardly a massive force. But Dhai had no navy, and only one harbor. That made fifty more than enough. What puzzled her was that the Tai Mora had not yet deployed anything against the gates. What were they waiting for? She saw bubbling red mist along the front line, and suspected they already had sufficient omajista barricades up to protect themselves from a gifted attack.

"Have they parleyed with your Kai?" Taigan asked.

"They sent an emissary," Alhina said. "That's why the Kai went to the temple first."

"Is that usual?" Lilia asked Taigan, "for them to talk first?"

"They did with us. In the beginning."

"They stopped?"

Taigan snorted. "They wanted us to deliver tribute in bodies. If we were going to give them bodies, bird, we'd make them fight for them."

"The Kai will not give them bodies," Lilia said.

"Then we best prepare," Taigan said. "You see the omajista barricade?"

"I see it."

Alhina stepped to the rail and squinted out at the ships. "What sorts of jistas do they have out there?"

"All of them," Taigan said. "If they've come at you the way they did us, they'll have eight coteries on every ship."

"Twenty-four jistas on every ship?" Lilia said, as if Taigan had told her she could lay eggs.

"You'll need to empty out the senior Oras from every temple," Taigan said, "and deploy them here. You think your Kai will give leave for that? You think they'll obey if he does?"

"Why wouldn't they?" Lilia said.

"Under the Kai? After fighting a civil war?"

"It wasn't like that at all," Alhina said. "I was here. You weren't."

"People died," Taigan said. "I thought you took that seriously. We certainly take death seriously in Saiduan."

"We are not like Saiduan."

"I'm sure you take great comfort in saying that," Taigan said. "The reality is that if that man has any hint of illegitimacy about him, if even one senior leader does not respect him, you are lost. You may be lost regardless, but it will certainly happen much faster."

"Let's speak to the Kai about it," Lilia said.

"In my experience, young men with power don't take kindly to advice."

"This is Dhai."

"Men are the same everywhere."

"It's a good thing there are a lot of women here, then."

Taigan grimaced. Dhai pronouns were cumbersome things; too many to remember, and trying to use their ungendered pronoun was uncomfortable. Ataisa was not ungendered, it was a gender in and of itself. Stripping away gendered markers in every conversation still grated. There were three types of people as far as Taigan was concerned, and what she defaulted to in any one anecdote depended upon which anecdote it was. Dhai people never understood the nuance.

"Let me take you to my cousin Mohrai," Alhina said. "We can address this with her."

Taigan waved at them. "You go. I want to watch the boats."

"For what?" Lilia said.

"For myself."

Taigan leaned out over the rail after they left. She gazed at row after row of ships. What bothered her was why they had come to Dhai at all. Why not selectively murder the few key people who were the doubles of those on the other side, and simply turn Saiduan into their new home? Why come down to Grania at all? What was there to gain here? People called Taigan monstrous, often, and she had done terrible things. She recalled smashing open the face of the woman who trained her, and flaying men alive for cheating her. She had destroyed people in every way they could be destroyed, but she always did it with purpose. These people were, if nothing else, calculated in the way they attacked. So why now?

She heard a scuffle behind her, and looked back to see Lilia limping toward her.

"Bored already?" Taigan asked.

"Mohrai is busy. I sent Gian down to eat while we wait for Mohrai."

"I'm sure she depleted much of her stores on the way here," Taigan said.

"It's like she's storing up for winter," Lilia said.

"Perhaps she's the smartest of us all."

Lilia came to the parapet. Put her arms on the wall. "I was thinking, Taigan."

"Always dangerous."

"If they wanted to destroy us, we'd be dead now. They've come for something here, haven't they? Something they don't want to burn down or risk being lost."

Taigan smirked at that. Yes, this was the same little girl who played strategy games in the woods, after all. She wished she'd had time to make her some great general, an asset to Saiduan. Now she wasn't sure what she was doing with this girl. Perhaps prolonging the inevitable. Soon Maralah would do more than just send notes that Taigan refused to answer. Soon, she would use the ward. She would call Taigan back, and there was nothing she could do to stop that when the time came.

"Oh! Taigan!" Lilia held up her arms, and Taigan saw little creatures scurrying up her shoulders and nuzzling her neck. They were baby tree gliders. Taigan saw their nest now, burrowed into the living wall. Lilia laughed and snatched at the little creatures, trying to pat their tiny heads, but they were fast, furiously fast.

Taigan regarded her a long moment while dozens of baby tree gliders scurried across her shoulders and then back down her arms. Several leapt from her head and rushed back into the nest. She still had two of them perched in her palm. She cooed at them.

"They're so beautiful," Lilia said. "See how cute they are?" She pressed her face closer to her final two friends, and they leapt from her palm and ran back to the nest with the others. She laughed again, a sound so lovely

Taigan forgot for a moment she was ugly and so very broken in so many ways.

"How long did it take you to figure that out?" Taigan asked. "About the Tai Mora."

Lilia's smile faded, but did not disappear. Taigan suspected she enjoyed her strategy for revenge almost as much as the tree gliders. "I considered it on the way here. But when I saw the boats... I knew."

"Not a fool bird," Taigan said.

"You think the Kai knows?"

"I think the Kai still believes he can talk his way out of this."

"Surely not."

"You watch him. Remember he'll do whatever it takes to avoid bloodshed. If you know that about him, you know his weakness."

"He didn't order us killed or turned back," Lilia said. "He could have."

"He wants to preserve who you are."

"He wants to save this idea he has of himself." Lilia's jaw firmed. "But the ideas we have of ourselves are foolish. He'll learn that."

"Indeed he will."

Taigan wondered, for the first time, if she was helping to make a savior or a monster.

She had such a plain, serious face. Taigan still worried about Gian's influence. A handsome woman like Gian, raised a dajian, would be drawn to power like a moth to claw lilies. Taigan suspected Gian had fucked the wrong person in Dorinah, or perhaps the right one, and it had all gone bad. But a Dhai this young wouldn't see a path to power through fucking. The older ones, perhaps, used sex and kinship to form strong ties. But not like Dorinahs did. Not like the Saiduan.

Such a peculiar little country, Dhai. It would be a shame to see it burn.

12

Harajan bordered an underground sea. Tactically, structurally, that seemed like a terrible idea, but it was another of the old holds built by the Talamynii, maintained by the Dhai, and inherited by the Saiduan. The Talamynii had an eye for making the illogical a reality. One level below the hold was a vast glass and iron ballroom jutting into the sea, twisted with still-living plant matter, suffused with some long-standing, and long-forgotten, parajista hex that kept the glass walls intact after these many thousands of years.

Instead of darkness, the view from the ballroom was luminous. Tens of thousands of bioluminescent creatures drifted lazily through the sea, casting an eerie light on those within. Maralah stood close to the glass. The smell of dust and damp was strong. No slave had been down here to polish it up for a party in at least ten years. Maralah remembered attending only one gala here, for Alaar's predecessor, Patron Osoraan. It was a riotous, drunken affair made even stranger with a variety of imported hallucinogens tucked away into select dishes. One man died, bashing his head repeatedly into the glass wall. Two women tore the skin from their own faces, and best Maralah could remember, there was a great deal of fucking – the mad kind, not the fun kind. If she inhaled deeply now, she could almost believe she smelled the incense that had suffused the space that night, watering her eyes, muddying her head.

Driaa was her only company now. Ze rocked back on hir heels, sipping thoughtfully from a flask of aatai, hir face lit garishly by the blue and white lights from the creatures in the sea beyond the glass. Ze passed the leather flask to Maralah.

Maralah drank, trying to keep the silence, but knew Driaa had not asked her down here for some sultry assignation. No, this was the type of place used by those who wanted to talk about dangerous politics.

"You've spent your whole life propping up weak men," Driaa said, finally. "How much longer are you going to wait to take the seat while Morsaar muddles about making cakes?"

The aatai burned Maralah's tongue. She coughed. Did Driaa brew it hirself? It wouldn't surprise her. Food stores in Harajan were grim. The last dog-sled caravan had been weeks ago, and half empty. Tai Mora scouting parties had slaughtered six of the eight teams. "I will be the woman who destroyed us," she said. "No matter it was the decisions of others that brought us to this place. No matter that Alaar was the wrong man to lead a war. Our destruction will be heaped on my shoulders if I take the seat now. They won't see we lasted five years longer than we would have with Alaar's successor. We wouldn't be here if not for me. We'd be singing to Lord Sina. But history won't paint it that way."

"What do you care for the books?" Driaa said. Ze took back the flask, and gestured at the dancing sea creatures. "You think anyone remembers who built this? What's their name? It's more likely no one will remember you or me or anyone but Rajavaa anyway. They'll write the story the way they want to remember it. Nothing you do now changes the story. That's for them to decide. You're here to act."

"I wish I hadn't sent Kadaan on that fool's errand. I could use him now."

"Couldn't we all?"

"He loved that Dhai boy."

"Love is not a bad thing, especially now."

Maralah hesitated. Was this an assignation after all? "Soft words," she said. She almost growled it. She was not so far gone that she would fuck another sanisi to pass the time. Too many politics in that.

"I was a different ataisa in training, Maralah. I believed we must be hard, and ruthless. We must gut them before they gut us. Now I wonder if something was lost in all that gutting."

"Is that so?"

"When I was very young, still living in Tordin–"

"I hope you don't tell many people that story." No one liked foreigners and slaves becoming sanisi. They had that in common, she and Driaa – Maralah once enslaved by an indebted father, Driaa clearly of foreign parentage.

"My father claimed me, yes," Driaa said, "and brought me back to Saiduan with him. Got me the papers and everything, or I wouldn't be here, would I? There was... bad business in Tordin in those days. My mother was a bit of a rogue. Wild. Not very popular with Saradyn. She and her people were killed. My father took me away from that."

"Becoming a sanisi was easier than staying with your father?"

Driaa made a face. "My father wanted me to be many things I'm not. But I saw what Saradyn did to my mother's people, and when you're six years old... you can't fight. I wanted to fight because of what I saw Saradyn do to the people I loved. Isn't that why we fight? For those we love?"

"I fear I just don't know how to stop. If it wasn't the Tai Mora, who would we fight? Ourselves? The Dhai? The Dorinah? Always another face, always the same face."

"You have, perhaps, had too much to drink."

"Not nearly enough," Maralah said, but she did not reach for the flask. She remembered fucking on this floor. How many people? A time best left forgotten, like her five years of servitude.

Driaa shrugged and took another drink. "I hold my liquor better."

"Is that an ataisa trait?"

"No more than your outpouring of nurturance is a female one," Driaa said.

Maralah snorted at that. She'd had a daughter once who'd said something similar, in precisely the same sarcastic tone. "Sometimes I wonder why we bother persevering at all."

"Well. It matters to me. It matters who I follow."

"That's a discussion for another time."

"If you don't take the seat, Maralah, someone else will. Others will be consolidating power."

"Have you been contacted by other parties?"

Ze shrugged. "I'm a sanisi. You know there are always warring factions."

"Who?"

"Just know this, Maralah. If you move, I am with you. If you do not... When Rajavaa dies, things may be very bad. No one dares now because of the loyalty of the army. But without Rajavaa—"

"I know," Maralah said.

Driaa tried to give her the flask again. Maralah shook her head.

"I best get back," Driaa said.

Maralah did not answer. Driaa shifted hir weight, almost imperceptibly. "You should have the seat," ze said, and then ze was walking lightly away, back into the dim corridors.

Maralah lingered in the space, though she would have preferred to be first to leave. Instead, she found herself stuck with far too many thoughts and an unclear plan of action. As she watched the creatures beyond the glass, a hulking form moved through the darkness, glowing softly blue, brighter and brighter until she could see its vast head, as big as a doorway. It fixed her with one of its eight massive eyes, each the size and shape of her fist, as it swam lazily past the tank. It was free to swim on, unencumbered, but the only thing that made it possible to stand here was to create a prison for the observers. Of all the things the gifted could build with their brilliant powers, they chose this decadent room, spying into the sea. Perhaps, in some other age, it was an observatory, an enclave for research and advancement in the study of obscure fauna. Alaar would have used it for that purpose, certainly. But that peaceful, prosperous dream was over now.

She needed Rajavaa – the man of war – whole, no matter the cost. She needed him put back together before her people turned on her, and the false dream that she'd brought with her, only to discard as war devoured them.

As a child, she yearned for control over the petty wars and local government squabbles that rolled through her village. Now that she ostensibly controlled it all, she had never felt so out of control. Huge forces moved around her, threatening to swallow far more than just a village.

She tugged at the threads of the ward that bound Taigan to her, murmuring a litany, and activated the ward she'd seared into his flesh the day he betrayed Alaar. A simple ward, sent into fiery motion with the barest hint of Sina's breath, was all she had now in its decline. No more waiting on messages, hoping for clear harbors. Driaa's message had been very blunt:

Put this house in order, or someone else will.

She called Taigan home.

13

The Oras confronted Ahkio as he stepped back into the banquet hall from the gardens. He came up short. The air was heavy, like milk. He wore no weapon, and he was alone. He took a deep breath and looked into their faces. There were six of them, all his most trusted Oras – Shanigan the mathematics teacher, Elder Ora Masura of Tira's temple, his third cousins Naori and Jakobi, Ohanni the dancing teacher, and a young novice, newly raised, named Silafa Emiri Pana, who wasn't much older than he was.

The heavy air, and the look on their faces, gave him pause. "Go ahead then," Ahkio said. "I hope you're prepared for the consequences." He braced himself for a gifted assault.

Shanigan shook his balding head, looking confused. "We're here about Ora Almeysia," he said.

Ahkio let out a breath. "What about her?"

"We want to know what happened to her," Jakobi said. Her voice squeaked when she said it, and Naori gave her a look, as if her fear had endangered their cause.

"That's something you should ask Nasaka," Ahkio said.

"We have," Masura said. She had, of course, been drinking, but she was not as yet drunk, best Ahkio could tell.

"We found her body in the Fire River while you were in Kuallina," Jakobi blurted. "She was killed by the gifted arts. A murder after—"

"After all that death in Raona," little Ohanni said.

There was a long silence. All but Masura had fought beside him there.

"Come upstairs," Ahkio said. "We need privacy."

The seven of them met in the Assembly Chamber. Ahkio asked after Caisa, but no one could find her. He worried that she had run, but pursuing her now when he had this chance to rally these Oras would be foolish.

After ensuring the door was closed to the hall and his own chambers, Ahkio faced the six of them at the broad table and said, "I mean to exile Nasaka, but I need a solid reason. We all know she took Almeysia into her custody, and while we were in Raona she worked here against me. I can't tell you how I know that. I have no proof of it. But if we are going to root her out and any other against us here in the temple, I need your help."

"The emissary?" Ohanni asked. "If there's peace with the shadow people maybe this won't be necessary."

"They aren't offering peace," Ahkio said. "They're offering to accept our surrender. That isn't the same thing."

Masura stood. "I'm sorry, Kai, I can't be part of this meeting."

"Why?"

"I just cannot," she said, and stumbled from the room.

The others looked after her. "Are you all so fearful of Nasaka?" he asked.

Jakobi fidgeted. "She is a powerful Ora."

"We fought Tai Mora," Ahkio said. "She's no more terrifying."

"There's legal precedent," Shanigan said. "Etena, your aunt, was exiled."

"Can we prove Nasaka is mad?" Ohanni asked.

"I intend to find a way," Ahkio said. "I'll speak to

Ora Masura. But can I rely on all of you for this? We've united the country, but the Oras are still divided. As long as Nasaka is here there will be more bodies, more secrets."

A knock sounded on the door.

Caisa peeked her head in. "Apologies, Kai, I thought–"

"No, let's speak," Ahkio said. "Excuse me," he told the room. "Caisa has some information for me about our visitors."

He met Caisa in the hall. She made to speak there, but he shook his head and brought her into one of the libraries.

"You didn't run," Ahkio said.

"Where would I go?" Caisa said.

Ahkio sat beside her on a hard yellow adenoak chair. The tables at the center of the room were piled with books and papers about governance. He moved toward the papers, wondering if Nasaka was ahead of him again. Was she going to figure out how to exile Ahkio now, after working so hard to get him in the seat? Her motives were inscrutable. She was always ten steps ahead. He rounded on Caisa.

"So how did you know Hofsha, when you lived among them?"

Caisa's face was wet. Her hands were clasped so tightly he wondered she didn't draw blood. "I served her. There were a lot of us. I wasn't even sure she'd know me."

"Are you hers?"

She raised her voice. "Did it look like it, Kai? Would I have killed those men, that man you couldn't kill in Raona, if I had chosen that side? I've been here four years, Kai. I don't know why I could suddenly come over. The wink stays open sometimes, after they leave. I snuck through. It was a long time ago. I've always been yours."

"I need information about them."

"I don't have much," Caisa said. "I wasn't anyone

important. It's why they didn't miss me."

"Who leads them?"

"She isn't your real sister," Caisa said. "But she has your face, yes. You knew that though, didn't you?"

His gut roiled. He remembered his sister on her death bed, reaching for him. She had died so she could choose her heir, but by dying she made it possible for her shadow to come over, and her twin was no less than the empress of the Tai Mora. He was going to have to fight his own sister. Soon.

What are you willing to sacrifice…?

"Gaiso is one of her commanders," Caisa said. "She leads the parajistas. I've met Lohin, too. She doesn't like Lohin much."

"She never did," Ahkio said.

"She isn't your Kirana," Caisa said.

"What else?" He needed to forget about the betrayal and squeeze her for information. "How large is her army?"

Caisa looked into her lap again. "Her army is the whole world, Kai. They will come here. They won't stop. Their world… our world is dying."

"Liaro thought you might not be ours, did you know that?" he said. He was angry now, and letting it rule his speech. He tried to rein it in, but his fear of Nasaka and the emissary was getting the best of him.

"Oma," she pressed her hands to her face. "Liaro."

"You put us all in danger."

"I chose my side, Kai. I'm sorry I didn't do it the way you wanted, or do it bravely. Hofsha hates me. If I was some spy, you think I'd have run off?"

"I think it best you're reassigned to another temple," he said, even as his gut told him that was a terrible idea. He had six – no, five – Oras in the Assembly Chamber he could maybe count on to subvert Nasaka. He needed Caisa.

"Kai–"

"Elder Ora Naldri will be happy to take you. You can continue your studies. We'll need good parajistas on the front lines at the harbor, when that time comes."

"Please don't do this. I'm yours. I promise–"

"That's all, Caisa." He pointed to the hall.

"Please, Kai... Ahkio, please–"

"I have too many knives in my back," he said. "I can't risk another."

"Are you going to tell Liaro?"

"Is there anything I don't tell Liaro?"

"Kai? Hofsha would have killed me."

"I know," Ahkio said. "That's what makes us different. That's why we'll win."

"The good people don't always win, Kai."

"I know," he said. He thought of Nasaka.

After dismissing his arguing coterie of Oras from the Assembly Chamber, no closer to a legal solution for his Nasaka problem, Ahkio found Liaro in the bathing room beneath the temple. Ahkio was still exhausted from his ordeal in the heart of the temple. He felt like an old man. The bathing room was relatively quiet. Two small novices shrieked and splashed at the other side of the broad room, but Liaro had a steaming little round pool all to himself. He read over the lip of the pool, some expensive book that Ahkio suspected would be difficult to replace if it fell into the water. That's the least of my problems, Ahkio thought dully. Steam made a misty blanket across the surface of the water. The whole room was dim, lit by bioluminescent plants and great semi-sentient water lily spiders that glowed blue every time they puffed out their forms in the depths of the pools, filtering the water with every breath.

"You look especially lovely," Liaro said, raising his head from the book.

Ahkio pulled off his clothes and sank into the water beside him. "And you're especially complimentary. I wonder what you've done lately to offend someone," he said. "You didn't tell me about Almeysia's body."

"Ah, that," Liaro said. He closed the book and pushed it far from the edge of the pool. Ahkio glanced at the title. It was a Dorinah romance. "It's in the notes I made while you were in Liona. I can put them on your desk, Kai, like a good little sparrow."

"I asked you to stay here because I trust you."

"And I'm glad you trust me, after I hauled you half dead out of the bottom of the temple. You know how stupid that was?

"You've only told me twenty times."

"What did their emissary say?"

"War's coming if I answer too quickly," he said.

"Lovely. Lovely little time we're having here." Liaro rested his elbows on the stone rim of the pool behind him. He was thinner than he had been a month ago, his face haggard. Ahkio saw the scars on his torso from that day in Raona when he'd been wounded, tripping and falling on his own weapon. Ahkio might have poked fun at him about it, but he was tired. As tired as Liaro looked.

"Do you have any good news, then?" Ahkio asked.

"Well, everyone loves me," he said, "so it's been easy to ask around about vacant Ora positions being filled. With so many gone running around the clans playing at fighting with us, it's opened up a lot of seats."

"Nasaka's council?"

"Elder Ora Gaiso was replaced by a person named Soruza Morak Sorai. Have you heard of them?"

"Sorai," Ahkio muttered. Liaro was using the ungendered Dhai pronoun in reference to Soruza, which narrowed down the number of people it could be. Ahkio went through the list of Mohrai's kin in his head. Soruza, ungendered, an Ora – sibling to Mohrai's grandmother? "Jista from…?"

"Temple of Tira," Liaro said. "One of Elder Ora Masura's."

Ahkio rolled that over. Was Masura his or Nasaka's or just trying to stay uninvolved? He needed to find out, and soon.

"A good deal of your mother's former lovers seem to like you," Liaro said.

"I'd call it jealousy, but you know where you stand in my heart."

"The left ventricle?"

Ahkio made an expression that felt more like a grimace than a smile, and let the silence stretch. "I'm going to exile Nasaka. I've put things in motion."

"That's... bold. Have you spoken to her since you got back?"

"No, and I intend to avoid her awhile longer. Her star is descendent, Liaro. If I'm going to move, I must do it now, before this all goes to Sina's heart. When I reject that emissary's offer, we'll be going to war. I want to delay my final answer to her as long as possible. That gives us time to move against Nasaka, clean up any of her appointments, and get the temples in order so we're strong enough to face the Tai Mora. And I need to... visit the basements again."

"No," Liaro said. He tone was deadly serious.

"You don't have to come."

"Don't do that again. I won't go through that shit again," Liaro said. "You were dead, Ahkio. Barely breathing. A week you lay in a bed. I won't pull you out again. Whatever's down there is mad, and it probably killed your sister. What if pitting herself against that thing is what killed her?"

"It wasn't."

"How do you *know*?"

"Is everything all right, Liaro?"

"It's funny, being cousin to the Kai, you know?" he said bitterly. "You're never sure if someone's affection is for you, or for the Kai. It's like you're the Kai-by-proxy. I'm the dog-faced Kai with the better sense of humor."

"Is that so horrible?"

Liaro flicked water at him. Ahkio forced something more like a smile this time. The novices on the other side of the room had fallen into a panting, giggling embrace. Ahkio couldn't help but watch them, and long for that kind of carefree afternoon.

"I can't lose you, Liaro."

Liaro shook his head. "You won't, I just... this is too big for me, all right? I'm not... some smart hero. I'm just a smart-talking day laborer. That's all. I wanted a bed full of friends and a drink in my hand. I don't want this."

"I don't either. But this is what we have."

The novices helped each other out of the pool and scurried off to the changing room. Two blue-lit waterlily spiders surfaced at the center of the pool, expelling their bladders of filtered water, and resubmerged.

Liaro raised himself out of the pool. He mussed Ahkio's hair and picked up the Dorinah romance. "I'll go look in on Soruza for you," he said, "and tell Caisa to set up a meeting with them tomorrow. As for this thing with Nasaka, and the basements... let's talk about it later, all right? Preferably with a drink and some bad poetry."

Ahkio almost told him, then stopped. Let Caisa tell him. She had at least a week before Ahkio finalized her transfer to Para's temple. "I'll be a few more minutes," Ahkio said.

Liaro nodded. "You should have given them your clothes," he said. "They're going to get wet." He walked back to the changing rooms.

But Ahkio wasn't really listening. He was watching the water lily spiders puffing their way through the water, content in the near stillness of the bathing house. Ahkio lingered there for another half an hour or more, watching the plants surface and dive, surface and dive, over and over again, the program for their behavior written into them from the time they were little seedling embryos growing on their parent's back. They knew nothing else, no other way to conduct themselves. If Ahkio drained the water from the bathing house, they would flop around on the floor of it until all the water evaporated, and they would die. They could not rewrite what they were.

He wondered if the world was like that, and the satellites in the sky, running some cosmic program that they were all fated to play out from birth, something Oma infused them with. So the Dhai came around and around and around again, killing other people, killing themselves, a long, unending cycle of violence and renewal.

It wouldn't stop until someone drained the pool.

Who would move first, he wondered, him or Nasaka?

He knew whose hand would be deadlier.

14

Spring in the mountains, like something Zezili had read about as a child – the smell of tree lupins and honeysuckle, wafting on a wind that carried with it the stink of her little army. She got a warm week of that, and then they descended into the Tordinian lowlands on the other side of the pass, hurrying just ahead of a pack of strange animals Zezili had no name for.

The animals sprang on them their first night in the cold, foggy bottomlands, an attack so fast Zezili didn't have time to pull up her trousers from the pit she was pissing in. She ran into camp with sword in hand, naked ass bared to the cold air. She hacked and slashed. Her blade found purchase. Slid home into some scaly backside. A yelp. Howling.

Zezili pulled her blade from what looked to be a giant scorpion dog. She had no other name for it. She grimaced and wiped the violet blood on her boot, hoping it wasn't anything poisonous. Rhea's tears, how did anyone put up with living in such a vile place?

The dogs took two of her women, and badly mauled another, so savagely Zezili suspected she'd die of the wounds. But leaving her there would be bad for morale, and sending her back with a couple of others would mean losing three women instead of one. So they pushed on, carrying her at the back of the train on a muddy litter.

"We're leaving the lowlands," Jasoi said from her mount at Zezili's side.

Zezili glanced over at her. The fog was lifting. Jasoi's expression was, as ever, blasé. She was smeared in scorpion dog blood from head to foot. The first slash of open water they found, Zezili wanted a dunk, no matter how cold. Her skin itched.

"You all right with being in Tordin?" Zezili asked. She'd asked before they started, but suspected the answer she might give in Dorinah would be different than one back on the turf of the place she'd grown up.

"Saradyn burned down my mother's farm," Jasoi said. "I've got no quarrel with burning down a few of his."

"Going to be more than a few farms."

Jasoi spit. She was chewing on some bit of bonsa sap. "Better than gutting chattel."

"Yes, the dajians were a nasty business."

"You think she's going to kill the rest? Have someone else do it, now we're gone?"

"I don't know," Zezili said. "I'm not sure our... agreement with the Tai Mora is still on."

"You fuck that up?"

"As much as it could be fucked up, yeah."

"Tordin's different from every place else," Jasoi said, dismissing the other conversation as if she knew it to be as potentially fraught as Zezili did. Jasoi was a woman of simple pleasures, but she was not stupid. "Wild here, kind of like in Dhai. Lot of jungle, bands of thieves. They'll skin you as soon as look at you. Most are refugees from the fighting. Civil war, all the time."

"All the time?"

Jasoi shrugged. "Long as I can remember. The Empress's cousin, Penelodyn, ruled here for a while before the Thief Queen unseated her. And after that it all started falling to pieces. Saradyn's trying to bring everybody together again under a sword. Side with the guy with the biggest stick, you know?"

Zezili cleaned her weapon and sheathed it. She urged the bear forward and called up at Storm, "You going to put better scouts ahead? I don't want any more surprise dogs!"

Storm glanced back. "I thought you'd be pleased at the chance to show your skills."

"Fuck you, Storm."

"I sent a boy up."

"A boy? Is that a joke?"

"He's fast. Good eyes."

"That's soft, Storm."

"Just practical. The clearing's ahead, another mile."

Zezili slapped her dog, and the animal trundled on ahead of Jasoi and the half dozen legionnaires between her and Storm.

Storm rode at the head of the group, something Zezili would not have done herself. Any kid with a bow could loose a bolt in her throat. But Storm swayed on ahead with apparent ease. He had even loosened his collar and taken off his greaves.

"Think they'll take us both out together?" Zezili said as she came up beside him.

"Who, bandits? Saradyn's men? No, not a group this size."

"I've learned caution."

"I can see that in your face." There was no sarcasm in his voice, but Zezili flinched.

"We should have a clear view of the crater from this clearing," he said. "Should be an old temple to Rhea here, the Empress says. Our first landmark on the map. If this is it, we're only a week or so away from the site she's sending us to."

As the trees thinned, Zezili saw a massive mound jutting out of the clearing ahead. She was a little surprised they hadn't seen it before now, but the tree cover was thick. If the trees were two hundred feet tall, the mound was easily three hundred, a conical tower of soil covered in thorny vines and twisted saplings with yellowing leaves. When they broke into the clearing Zezili saw heaps of bones peeking up from the crawling vines. She stopped her animal at the edge of the clearing, and held up a hand for Storm to stop.

"You think there's some beast out here?" Storm said.

"We'd have drawn its attention before now," Zezili said, "unless that boy runner of yours was already eaten. You think he went up that?"

"Around, maybe," Storm said. "He's to scout, not explore."

Storm put his fingers to his lips and whistled for the runner. Zezili waited with him while the dogs and bodies behind her snuffled and shifted. Zezili was glad most of them couldn't see the bones.

Storm whistled again. Zezili saw movement ahead of her, to her left, and gripped the hilt of her sword. Another flash of movement, then a bob of dark hair. Not some creature, but a boy with his hair shorn monstrously short. He wore dark colors, and was wiry as a bonsa sapling. She saw a bit of hard strength in his face that she didn't like. He had the audacity to meet her gaze for a short moment before looking quickly away.

"Any monster out there?" Storm said. "Or worse? Another woman like Syre Zezili, perhaps?"

The boy shook his head. Young man, really. Twenty or so, if Zezili guessed right. "No sign of people ahead, for at least the next half mile. Biggest wildlife is a couple hundred pounds, some boar, long-necked herbivores–"

"Long-necked what?" Zezili said.

"Animals," he said, "that eat grass."

"Like range deer?"

"Bigger, and striped, not spotted. Sorry, I don't know the name."

Zezili pointed to the mound. "Scout up that next," she said. "Should be our landmark."

Storm frowned, scrunching up his scraggly beard. He

had the decency to continue having his mane of hair done each morning while on the march, at least. "I can confirm it's the same as what's on the map," Storm said.

"He'll have a better view of what's ahead," Zezili said. "No more surprises."

The young man's throat bobbed. He glanced at Storm.

"Don't look at him," Zezili said. "We're both leading this charge. Get your skinny ass up the mount."

"Go on, child," Storm said.

The young man crept to the edge of the clearing and trod slowly across the tangles of yellowed bones.

Zezili leaned forward. She realized she wanted to tear the tunic from him, and watch him navigate the gauntlet naked. A perverse pleasure, she knew. But her pleasures were fewer and fewer these days. What she could not control, she wanted to punish. It was an instinct that served her well in Dorinah. Outside of it, she realized, it meant punishing everything, everyone – the world; the sky.

Zezili admitted she was surprised when he got to the base of the mound unscathed. He kicked at the loose soil and began to pull himself up, gripping vines and dying saplings for leverage. After a few feet, one of the saplings he grabbed tore away. He yanked it from the soil, and as it tumbled free Zezili saw the roots of the sapling were tangled around something that looked distinctly like a hunk of flesh of some kind. Animal or human, she didn't know. She rubbed her eyes. It had been a long ride.

The boy climbed higher. Below him, the sapling and whatever it had rooted itself to tumbled into the wash of bones and vegetation below. Zezili saw the detritus tremble. She squinted. It continued to waver; a sea of bone. She saw ripples move out across the pile.

"Storm..." she said, pointing.

"I see it," Storm said. "Come down, boy!"

"Don't!" Zezili said. "He's making progress."

Storm slid off his bear with a grunt. He strode to the

edge of the bone sea. "Come back!" he yelled. "Don't go further!"

"There are stairs further up!" the young man called. "I can see steps built into the tower here."

"Come down!"

The young man swung further up the mound. Gripped what Zezili supposed he meant by "steps." From this distance, there were indeed some kind of patterned protrusions on the outside of the mound, but to Zezili they looked like teeth.

Zezili didn't get off her dog, but she edged it forward to get a better look. The boy was at least thirty feet up, climbing with some regularity. Zezili saw bits of stone and loose soil tumble down the edge of the mound as he ascended. His fingers dug into the irregular grooves.

Then the soil began to fall faster, and the falling stones grew larger. Zezili recoiled. The entire mound trembled.

"Get off there!" Storm yelled.

Zezili drew her dog back.

A massive moaning broke across the clearing, as if the world had cracked open.

The young man yelled, and held on. Great, fleshy tendrils erupted from the mound, a thousand snaking arms of tuberous tentacles. The boy screamed and let go. He slid four feet toward the bone yard before the tentacles caught him.

The fleshy tentacle shook him like a doll, so violently Zezili thought he would come apart. Zezili heard the cracking of his spine.

"Retreat!" Storm yelled at the women behind them. "About face and forward!"

They were all too eager to obey. Zezili heard the jingle of tack, the babble of muttered prayers.

Storm lunged back onto his bear, sliding his substantial girth into the saddle. He brought his mount around. He galloped ahead to catch up with the tail end of their force.

Zezili gazed back a moment longer at the seething mound. The tentacles began to retract back into the soil. They took the boy's broken body with them. Zezili watched as the tentacled thing folded it into the maw of the giant semi-sentient flesh-eating plant. The horror gripped her then. She gagged. Yelled at her dog.

She followed the retreating tail of their force. Storm forged on ahead to take the lead, but Zezili remained at the rear, looking constantly over her shoulder for some massive tentacle to come curling up from the undergrowth.

They had no tracker for the Tordinian woodland. Jasoi had left the place as a girl. What did she know? Foolish, to bring women to a place as wild and contaminated as Dhai. No infrastructure. No order. No law.

An hour before dusk, Storm had them burn out a clearing and pitch camp. The Empress's Seekers were well gone, run out or destroyed by the Empress herself, so they worked with foreign tirajistas and parajistas from the island country of Sebastyn, a rocky shore much fought over by Dorinah and Saiduan. They enjoyed a negotiated peace now, one that had the Sebastyn collective agree to hand over a dozen jistas as a sign of goodwill and friendship.

The Sebastyns were mostly short and dark, with a couple of exceptions. Zezili had yet to learn their names. It felt like an inordinate amount of work. She had spent much of her time drinking and sleeping. It worried her that the Empress had placed her trust in whatever needed to happen to wake her sleeping weapon into the hands of these foreigners.

Storm's pages put together Storm and Zezili's tents. Zezili yelled at one of the jistas to come over and burn out a tendril that looked like it was moving again, then sat down and started untangling her armor. After the tents were up and darkness descended, Storm invited Zezili over to his fire. Zezili saw Storm's second there, and Jasoi, and even the youngest page, a girl Zezili had taken to calling "runt" because she had some kind of mangled walk.

Zezili was already a little drunk, but she shuffled over. Drinking alone got old, and in the right light, Storm's second looked a little boyish.

"What did you think of that... thing today?" Jasoi asked. Her eyes were bright, and her cup was nearly empty.

"I think we need some help," Zezili said, "or we're all going to get eaten out here."

"It tells us we're on the right track," Storm said, "and we have the jistas."

"Jistas traveling at the center of the group," Zezili said. "They aren't going to be much help if something surprises us again."

Storm grunted. "That surprise could have been avoided."

"That so?" Zezili said. "You'd rather I took you and Jasoi up there, so it was our bodies getting eaten by worms?"

"Just a waste, is all," Storm said. "We didn't need to scout that view."

Zezili leaned forward. "Every one of us is here to be ground to death for one purpose. To wake up whatever the Empress has huddled up here. That's it. And we'll fall for it, every one of us. There's no waste in that. That's precisely why we're here. If we took a load of apples with us, and ate them, would you say they were a waste for being eaten? No. That's their purpose. There's no waste. Same with you or me."

"You always were a cold bird, Zezili," Storm said.

"You should have romanced proper," Jasoi said. "A nice warm woman."

Zezili glared at her. Jasoi hiccupped, and covered her mouth.

"I have a husband," Zezili said.

"Husbands are sufficient for children," Storm's second, a lean woman named Haloria, said warmly; a little smugly, "but love is only for equals. Love is something only a woman can bring you." She said it like she was reciting from *The Book of Rhea*.

"You making me an offer?"

Haloria guffawed. "I know some good girls who could warm that soul."

"It's not my soul needs warming," Zezili said. "It's up to the task." She didn't like the way the conversation was going. She stood. "Long day tomorrow."

"Yes, Syre," Storm said.

Zezili narrowed her eyes. Was the mocking worth a scene? She wasn't certain. She was tired. She stepped to her tent and kicked out her fire. Inside, she pulled on a heavier coat and kicked into her bedroll. For a time, she sat awake listening to the noise of the camp; laughter and murmured prayers, the singsong voices of recited stories, the dark whispers of the day's fears. The Empress had put her in charge of all of it, all of these lives, again, though she had watched half her women burned to death by some mad omajista, and declared her own life forfeit. The Empress liked to move them all around, just to see how far she could push them.

And she can push me far, Zezili thought, all the way to Tordin. She closed her eyes and saw, again, the runner's body broken, his meaty suit of humanity yanked into the boiling mound. She imagined the Empress was that alien, unknowable thing, devouring all she touched, scattering bones at her feet.

We are not wasted, she had told Storm, and that was true, perhaps. They were no more wasted than those bones. It was their fate, to become bones fed to the ravenous beast that was their Empress.

Or to feed the Empress her own bones, in the end.

Whatever way it went, Zezili didn't much like it.

15

Saradyn of Lind, King of Tordin, woke from a dream of ghosts. The ghosts had trailed after him from his dreams and stood over him, pale in the way of Dorinahs, bloodless – all ghosts looked like Dorinahs, in the dark. He gazed through their misty forms to the dogs lying deep in their slumber at the mouth of his tent.

"Saradyn," the ghosts murmured.

Saradyn turned his back to the ghosts, and slept.

He woke at dawn and pulled on his boots and coat, scratched at his bearded face, and rinsed his mouth. The ghosts were gone.

The dogs rose with him, two perpetually adolescent runts he called Dayns and Sloe. Their heads just reached his shoulder. He had tended their birth himself, and raised them from pups when their mother saw fit to eat them. They were a useful size – large enough to be intimidating, but small enough to sleep inside his tent.

He stepped outside onto frozen ground. The air was chill. The dogs followed. His men emerged bleary eyed from the thin folds of their own tents, and huddled around cook fires. These men had been with him from the beginning, and later, brought their sons into his service. They camped now at the base of the Tongue Mountains, toothy protrusions raking the sky along

Saradyn's peripheral vision. Dawn tore the sky like the remnants of a red dress. The woods of old pine were rimmed in frost, but the day promised to warm as the suns rose. Para's milky blue light already touched the treetops. Laine's sons had not blessed him with the magic to control the wind, raise the dead, or bend living things to his will. What the satellites bestowed on him was darker, a curse more than a gift – from Laine himself to remind him of his sins – and the sins of others. He could see ghosts.

As the dogs took in the measure of the camp, Saradyn took in the day's news and gossip. There was talk among his runners that Natanial Thorne had crossed back over the Mundin Mountains and into northern Tordin the day before. What he had been doing in Aaldia, Saradyn could only guess. Saradyn had sent a runner up that way to confirm. Rumors were already coming out of Dorinah about cats and assassins and the rising of Laine's Eye, but Saradyn had no time for rumor until Natanial confirmed it. There were troublemakers in Saradyn's own tenuous kingdom in the one Tordinian province that had sided with his enemy in the old days. Fools, all. Educated by witches and girls.

Tanays, Saradyn's second, gestured to him from a nearby fire. He and his ghost. The ghost was always at Tanays' shoulder; a small, hunched figure with big, dark eyes. She did not speak. Only watched. It was a fitting place for her to end her days. Saradyn had known that ghost in life. Tanays' daughter.

Saradyn squatted next to Tanays. He shifted purposefully into the ghost, so their images merged. Her form flickered, faded, and reappeared at Tanays' opposite elbow. Saradyn had learned long ago he could not banish the ghosts Laine forced him to see, only antagonize them. Best they had ghosts, though. The ones who did not… they were the truly dangerous ones.

"We received more information last night," Tanays

said. "The rabble out of Old Galind is a group of the Thief Queen's lot."

"Thought I'd killed them all," Saradyn said. His circle was one of the last to hold to the Thief Queen's old moniker – Quilliam of the Mountain Fortress; Quill of Galind; Quill the Thief Queen. He supposed he was one of the few old enough to remember she had a real name once before she tried to take his power and he killed her for it.

Tanays leaned over the fire pan and pushed a sizzling slab of boar bacon with a charred stick. Above his peppered-gray beard, lines etched the corners of his eyes. He kept his brow perpetually furrowed. He was always squinting.

"I'm assuming this group of rebels wants autonomy," Saradyn said.

"They want to call themselves Rohandar," Tanays said, "after some dead city."

"Just what Tordin needs," Saradyn said. "Another country."

"That's their thought."

"Let's sweep the village of dissidents, then," Saradyn said.

"I haven't told you everything," Tanays said.

"Sweep it clean. I don't want it butchered completely." He liked Tanays, but Tanays had always been too hesitant, too willing to sit on his heels and let events run their course. Saradyn had not gotten this far by sitting back from the fray. Tordin had been in disarray since the murder of the Empress of Dorinah's sister, Penelodyn, twenty years before when she was burned out by the Thief Queen. Saradyn had taken full advantage of the chaos. Now the whole region was nearly his, from the northern mountains to the southern sea. Nearly.

Saradyn gazed out at the camp and saw a cluster of figures at the edge of the trees, insubstantial, like fog. He whistled to Dayns and Sloe. The dogs loped toward him.

"See," he said, and pointed to the tree line. The dogs galloped through the camp. They smashed through the line of hazy figures. The dogs did not howl, and did not bark.

So the figures were just ghosts. The older he became, the wider his influence, the more invaluable the dogs. They had saved his life more times than his own men. They had often saved him from his own men. The dogs always knew who to fear, and who was just some wandering specter broken loose from Laine's sons in the sky.

Saradyn whistled the dogs back. He looked down at Tanays.

"We run a sweep," Saradyn said. "Tordin has just one ruler."

They went house to house. They dragged men from their beds, from closets, from lofts, from stone cellars. They gathered the men in the big wooden church at the center of town. Saradyn wanted every drop of blood dedicated to Laine.

"Keep your heads high," he told his men before they swept the town for insurgents. And they did. They left the women – crying or defiant or fighting – untouched in their homes, left the children screaming, but took every boy over ten. They interrogated them, one by one. They took them into church boxes, alcoves. They left the priest unscathed, and did not even touch his fingers. Saradyn knelt before the old man and asked for absolution from Laine, and the priest gave it, though his voice trembled and his hands shook.

Saradyn had not underestimated the women of northern Tordin. After asking that they remain untouched, he was not surprised when they marched out of their houses and tried to storm the church.

Saradyn had his men open the big doors. They cleared the stairs with a smattering of arrows. He grabbed up the village headwoman's eldest son and dragged him onto the stair. Tanays was just behind them, and a half dozen of his best fighters. Dayns and Sloe paced the lip of the lower stairs, hackles raised, growling at the mob of women.

"We come to do no violence," Saradyn told them. "Any violence done will be in response to your actions. Go back to your houses, or you'll see death on these steps."

The women screamed at him. Surged forward. Saradyn cut the boy's throat. He pushed the gurgling body down the steps, and called behind him, without taking his eyes from the women – "Give me someone they care about!"

He saw a hundred screaming ghosts at the women's shoulders – dead children, bloody babies with dark lips, and the ghosts of their own pasts; old women and matrons in their youth, all paths open to them, before their roads grew shorter, before pregnancies and abortions, nursing, husbands, obligation, sacrifice; before binding their blood to another and giving over their passions for it.

Saradyn stared out at their ghosts and said, "Go back to your houses. I don't want to threaten your children, but your children have threatened my rule. You are good women. Good mothers. It's your hand that keeps me here or keeps me away. Don't teach your boys defiance. Don't teach your girls swordplay. That only brings more violence here."

The ghosts stirred.

"You're a fool!" one of the women cried.

"Maybe so," Saradyn said, "but it's not my children bleeding on these steps."

The surge of women heaved a collective breath. Saradyn watched the ghosts. The ghosts wailed and thrashed. Flickered. Two women near the back of the mob turned away.

"This is your power," Saradyn said. "Stay here, and

you condemn me and my men to stay with you. Go home, and we finish and go our way. Keep weapons out of your children's hands, and you need not see my face again. I'm here to unite this country, not destroy it."

A few more women broke away. Then others. Slowly, in small groups. They dropped their stones, smoothed at their hair. Their children clung to their apron strings.

Saradyn did not turn his back until the ghosts of those left had ceased to scream, and whispered to themselves instead. When he turned, Tanays was watching him.

"I never pegged you as a man who knows how to talk to women."

"I talk to them like men," Saradyn said, "men who are bound to their bodies. But I know where women belong in my country, and it's not in public spaces. They know it, too. It's why they listen to me."

"Now?"

"Now I find my troublemakers, and show them Laine's mercy."

Saradyn sat in on a half dozen interrogations. He took the fingers off a boy of twelve whose father would not speak.

The old man burst into tears. He clutched at his screaming boy. The two had a stir of ghosts around them, misty figures – sobbing torsos, women with streaming hair.

Saradyn did not look at either of them, but at the lonely fingers lying on Laine's altar. His ax had made a deep groove in the silver-painted wood.

Tanays sat on the steps just below Saradyn, speaking with a hysterical young boy who was spilling names and wild stories.

Saradyn set his ax on the altar and pulled the old man away from his son. "Tell me where the troublemakers are," Saradyn said. "End this."

The man collapsed in front of Saradyn. His hair was a white tangle. Red dust filled the seams of his face. "Liege, they don't mean harm. Not one of them. They're just girls. Young. They don't know better." His big hands clung to Saradyn's trousers.

Tanays pulled a pipe out of his long coat, lit it with a scorch pod. The pod was one of the few precious Dhai resources that made it through the blockade of Dhai's harbor. "Down here, Saradyn," Tanays said.

Saradyn shook the old man off. He stepped around the bloody pool growing around the boy's fingerless hand. The boy lay slumped against the altar. Saradyn's surgeon attended him.

"Who?" Saradyn asked, crouching next to Tanays and the boy.

"Rosh started it," the boy bawled. He was very young, younger than ten. He'd likely lied about his age when they swept the houses.

"Where can I find Rosh?"

The boy pointed with his good hand. A misty halo rode his right shoulder, the beginnings of a face.

Saradyn looked over at the pews where a group of boys huddled.

"Which one, boy?" Tanays said.

The boy wiped his face with his grubby remaining hand. He scrambled to his feet and turned on the other boys waiting in the pews. They stared at him. A stir of jeers started.

Pol pointed to a skinny youth at the center of the bunch. Saradyn took the youth for a boy, at first – narrow and smooth cheeked, with big, dark eyes and cropped dark hair the color of old blood.

Saradyn told the youth to stand up. "You're being accused," Saradyn said.

The youth glared at him. He expected more fear. But then he saw the ghosts, and decided she was female. The ghosts were as defiant as she – two boyish figures and the torso of a deathly pale woman with a halo of black hair. They were mute ghosts, and static.

"He's a stupid boy," she said. "You listen to fool boys?"

"Stand up, Rosh," Saradyn said.

The girl stood, though he couldn't mark her as a girl, even knowing it, looking for it because of her ghosts. She was the sort of androgyne who had passed through his army in the old days. These days, he tried to pick them out and send them home. He couldn't grow a country with half its women fucking about in the army instead of having babies at home.

"There are worse things we can do, to a girl," Saradyn said.

She spat at him. "It's no different, no matter who you do it to."

Saradyn hauled her out by the collar. She struck at him. He twisted her arm behind her and pushed her against the altar. "We need to know the rest of your little band of dissidents," Saradyn said. "You ran with the Thief Queen? You don't look old enough."

"My mother did."

"And where's she?"

"Dead, fuck you," the girl said.

Saradyn gripped her cropped hair, and smashed her head on the altar. "Again?"

"Dead," she gasped. Blood dripped from her mouth.

The old man was gripping his son's arm at the behest of the surgeon.

"You brought all this on us!" the old man cried at the girl. The misty faces around him contorted. "You brought the hound up from the south, you fool!"

"Who else?" Saradyn leaned into the girl and murmured in her ear. She kicked back at him, and nearly caught him in the groin. One of his men stepped in and helped keep her still.

"You can't scare me," she said. Her ghosts hovered around the altar. They stared stoically back at Saradyn.

"You'd prefer I give you over to my men?" Saradyn said.

"What? Fucking me? Fucking doesn't scare me, you old fool. I'll still be here. I'll just be more pissed off."

The ghost with the black hair moved. She hissed. Perhaps that was her mother's ghost.

"How many parts need to be here," Saradyn said, "and still keep you speaking? Not many." Saradyn released her into the hold of the other men at the altar. "Bind her and take her with us."

They took a handful of the village boys as well, the midwife's son, the headwoman's youngest, and an assortment of her cousins. The boys were sworn to Saradyn and to Laine. Saradyn left two dozen of his fighters in residence to root out the rest of Rosh's rebels.

The remaining men trudged back south with Saradyn. They camped that night with a double guard. Errant villagers had been known to come after their kin.

Saradyn sat in his tent with the dogs and broke open his old copy of Penelodyn's *On Governance*. He'd had all of her work translated from the original Dorinah. His copy was dog-eared, the spine broken twice. He followed the writing with his finger, mouthing the words.

Tanays' voice came from without. "Permission to enter?"

"Enter," Saradyn said.

Tanays ducked in. He knelt back on his heels across from Saradyn. His ghost tailed him, a pace behind. She was clasping and unclasping her hands. A new affectation. Saradyn did not often see her move. She was usually a static ghost.

Sloe nudged his big nose toward Tanays. Tanays scratched the dog's ears.

"Any trouble?" Saradyn asked.

"That girl isn't easy dealing."

"The men will soften her up."

"Not really."

"Nothing worse than a talkative woman," Saradyn said.

"No man would believe you married," Tanays said.

"But they might believe she's dead."

Tanays did not look at him. He kept scratching behind Sloe's ears. The dog wagged his enormous tail, nearly tumbling over the lantern. Saradyn pulled the lantern out of the way.

"You're too hard on that girl, I think," Tanays said. "She might be more useful if you turned her. Try kindness. Convince her of your vision as you convinced us. Any girl who leads a rebellion is–"

"Too much like the Thief Queen," Saradyn said. "I knew Quill before she was Queen. And she was just like that girl. Dirty, foul-mouthed, promiscuous, following no god but her own black conscience."

"She's dangerous because there's no place for her," Tanays said.

Saradyn closed his book. He felt a stirring of anger, a tightening in his chest. He had run with Tanays for over twenty years, and the man had only gotten softer with age. Since Tanays' daughter's death, he'd seen her in every ragged girl they tracked down, every girlish boy who'd tried to join their ranks because of some foolish peasant story about the Thief Queen.

The ghost at Tanays' elbow stared forlornly at Saradyn.

"There's no place for women here," Saradyn said. "She'll bleed and get pregnant, and then we'll have squalling pups to deal out. She'll make jealousy in–"

"You know as well as I about jealousy in the ranks. That Morran boy–"

"Is too pretty for his own good," Saradyn said. "I have him set for the next scout. I'd toss him out altogether if he wasn't our best archer."

"My point–"

Saradyn eyed him sharply. "Have you forgotten what I've done for this title? This vision? A united Tordin. No one comes in the way of it. Not women. Not my own wife. Not my own children."

"Must they all pay for your mistakes?"

"Get out," Saradyn said.

Tanays bowed and left him.

Saradyn glared at Sloe, who looked mournfully after Tanays and his big-eyed ghost. Sloe's tail thumped.

"Be still," Saradyn said.

The dog whined.

Saradyn and his company arrived at his seat in Gasira eight days later. Itague, his steward at the Gasiran hold, met him just inside the gate. Itague was a big man, heavily bearded. He took Saradyn into a meaty embrace and kissed the backs of his hands.

"You brought those dissidents to heel?" Itague asked. A twisting morass of ghostly figures contorted just behind him – a woman screaming, a blind old man with hands like claws, three boys with bloody faces.

"That's yet to see," Saradyn said. "Has Thorne arrived? I heard word of him in the north."

They started together up the curve of the outer stair and into the hold. Inside was little warmer than without. Saradyn's dogs trod behind him. Their nails clicked on the stone.

"Natanial Thorne came in just this morning from Aaldia," Itague said, "carrying a motley bunch with him. Don't know where he picks them."

"Hostages?"

"I assumed."

"Tell him I want him in my quarters."

Saradyn went up to his quarters and unbolted the big iron banded door. He sent the dogs in. Some drudge had lit the hearth and lantern above the bed. Saradyn saw furtive shapes near the slit window, and another in the chair amid a stir of shadows.

Dayns and Sloe paced the room. Sloe snuffled under the bed, and nosed open the wardrobe. Dayns went straight to the figures at the fire. He paused at the far chair. His hackles rose. A low growl came from deep in his throat. Sloe bounded over and paced in a wide circle around the chair, whining.

Saradyn shut the door and whistled the dogs away. Dayns shook off his stance and settled in front of the fire. Sloe lolled beside him. The big dogs took up all the space in front of the hearth, blocking the heat.

Saradyn yanked a knife from his hip and threw it at the chair. The knife buried itself in the leather arm of the seat. The figure sitting there didn't flinch. Saradyn grunted and began unbuckling his leather armor.

"You're tardy," Saradyn said, "by a large margin. I should murder you for it."

"Don't you have a boy to help you with all that dressing and undressing?" Natanial asked. His voice was a quiet rumble. He pulled the dagger from the arm of the chair and regarded it. "You keep your blade far too dull," he said. "Blunt instrument." He sat with one leg hooked over the other. He rolled a lump of sen between thumb and forefinger, staining his hands crimson. The hands had been the first thing Saradyn noticed about Natanial, after his lack of substantial ghosts. The shadows that rode Natanial's shoulders were just that – voiceless patches of darkness without solid form. They carried no names, no faces, no past. Natanial was the only man he'd met whose ghosts had no faces, as if Natanial had never marked them in life. He wasn't a man to hang onto his regrets. Saradyn appreciated that.

"A blunt knife to the eye is as effective," Saradyn said, "if thrown with enough force."

Natanial shrugged. "Surely you have more experience with such things than I."

Foul-mouthed little sarcastic shit, that one. Saradyn pulled off his stiff, dirty tunic and tossed it next to his bed. He washed himself with cloth and water from the basin near the wardrobe. He watched Natanial's figure in the polished bronze above the basin.

Natanial was long and lean, his face the rugged,

angular cast of some handsome house. Natanial's face and form were nearly as valuable as his wit. Nearly. Saradyn would have dismissed the man for looks alone if not for his shadows. Saradyn didn't trust beauty, but it roused him. Natanial's mix of beauty and arrogance never failed to stir him.

"Tell me of Dorinah," Saradyn said. He pulled a clean black tunic from his wardrobe, "and this dalliance in Aaldia."

"You look as if you need help," Natanial said.

Saradyn recognized the invitation. He tugged open his trousers and let his cock free. He sat on the chair opposite Natanial, spread his legs, and met Natanial's look, daring him to act.

"The sinajista you wanted me to kill is dead," Natanial said. His gaze moved lazily to Saradyn's groin. "But one of their effeminates stumbled in just after I finished the sinajista. He's the husband of Captain General Zezili Hasaria." Natanial rose from his seat.

Saradyn leaned back in his chair. Natanial sat on the edge and took Saradyn's cock in his hand. He gently pulled his foreskin back and circled the tip with his thumb.

Saradyn grunted.

"He can open doors," Natanial said. His fingers tightened around Saradyn's cock and began to work, quickly and nimbly.

Saradyn imagined taking every woman in that little festering village, imagined their faces rapt with desire. He grunted again. Dayns barked, but he was too far gone now to care for them. He wanted to fuck everyone who opposed him, and have them thank him for it.

"He tore open a door in front of us," Natanial said. His voice sounded very distant. Saradyn's mind was filled with Rosh, and the Thief Queen before her. Laine's ass, why had he not murdered them both sooner? "We fell into it," Natanial said. "That's what took so long. He transported us to Aaldia."

Saradyn leaned forward. His hands tightened on the chair. The Thief Queen with her thick legs and sharpened teeth, the hands that found his throat, and when she bit that hunk from his leg when he first caught her–

Saradyn came. He expelled a long breath and shook himself back into the room, as if awaking from a dream. His body trembled as he stuffed himself back into his trousers, trying to catch at the end of Natanial's last words. "Our Aaldia?"

The dogs whined and came over to lick up the mess on the floor.

Natanial got up and fell back into his seat opposite. He shrugged. "I knew you'd be able to tell if we weren't in the right world," Natanial said. "And you've said nothing, so I assume I'm still here."

Saradyn's gaze moved, unconsciously, to the faceless ghosts that followed Natanial. Yes, he was real. All of those with ghosts were of this world, his world, stringing their pasts along behind them. Those without ghosts, without a past... those were the ones he killed on sight. Those were the travelers. The interlopers.

Sloe finished licking the floor and rested his head on Saradyn's armrest. Saradyn scratched Sloe's ears. "Interesting." He patted Sloe's rump. The dog raised his head. "Find dinner," he said.

Sloe rose and padded to the door. He grabbed the rope affixed to the handle and pulled the door open. He went into the hall.

"The sinajista you had me kill talked," Natanial said. "The Empress has killed off her dajians at the behest of the Tai Mora and sent troops to Tordin."

"To what purpose? There's no gain for her."

"Knowing the mind of a monarch is your specialty. I just kill them."

"And fuck them," Saradyn said.

Natanial shrugged. "I enjoy my work." He held up his

hands and began counting off with his long fingers. "No dajians. Fewer legionnaires. And she has just increased her people's child tax, so they must have five children instead of four to avoid it. I think the Empress has some bloody plan in the works."

The door opened. Sloe padded in ahead of a little drudge who trailed wispy blue-clad figures with static faces.

"Thorne, join me for dinner?"

Natanial stood. "Alas, no. I have an appointment."

Saradyn felt a jolt of disappointment, and perhaps jealousy. Natanial provided many useful distractions.

The drudge set the tray on the table between them. A decanter of dark wine, a half loaf of rye bread, red meat in a heavy sauce, and salted hasaen tubers. She bowed her head and retreated.

"Collect your due with Itague," Saradyn said. He went to his desk and wrote out a receipt, stamped it, and handed it over to Natanial. He waved him away.

"This includes–" Natanial began.

Saradyn grimaced. "You're little better than a whore."

"I'm a *preferred* whore," Natanial said.

Saradyn wrote out another receipt.

Natanial bowed.

Saradyn sat and ate in silence. After, he went and met with Itague and Tanays, and discussed matters of the hold. He approved the appointment of a new tax minister to the province of Concordyns to replace the one dipping too deeply into its tax coffers. Itague reminded him of an inspection appointment of the garrison. They had taken on another dozen boys in his absence. Saradyn told him to enlist the boys he'd brought back from the village.

"What about the girl?" Itague said.

"Rosh," Tanays said.

"Hang her in the square," Saradyn said.

Saradyn parted company with Itague sometime after midnight, after a briefing about happenings in the hold.

His dogs followed after him and paced at the end of the bed before lying at the foot of it. Saradyn sat awake reading for a time until the clotted shadows in the corners of the room began to converge.

Murmuring figures drew away from the curtains and slid along the floor. Saradyn read aloud, to drown out the whispering voices. As night deepened, the shadows began to solidify. He had picked the room for its ghosts. They were few and reasonably static. A wispy crying girl in the corner by the door, and a dead woman beneath the window who was never more than an outline. But as he grew more tired, his own ghosts began to leak into the room, and then he had to shut the book and kick off his boots.

He slid into bed and reached for the light. It was the worst time of the night, that moment just before he put out his light. Just before darkness took away most of the ghosts' features, and drowned them in blackness. Some nights he fell to bed before the shadows came, before the ghosts leaked out. Some nights, he slept in silence. He had sacrificed many to unite his country. They would not let him forget.

His candle snuffer came down. He heard children playing on the other side of his bed. Familiar voices.

The light went out.

He pulled the comforter over his head, to drown out the noise of his children.

16

Lilia stepped into the meeting room atop the harbor gate's eastern tower as if stepping into a battle. Plump, curly haired Mohrai was there with another young woman, and two older people Lilia did not recognize.

Taigan came in beside Lilia, but she had left Gian in the opposite tower where Mohrai's family had given them rooms.

"I'm Lilia Sona," Lilia said. "The Kai has sent me to help oversee the conflict here."

Mohrai and the older woman exchanged a look.

The younger woman stepped forward. She was slender, all arms and legs. She looked like a heron. "I'm Ora Harina. Ora Nasaka of Oma's Temple sent me to oversee this venture."

"Parajista?" Taigan asked.

"Sinajista," Harina said.

Taigan grimaced. "Your Ora was sure to send someone expendable. That's lovely."

"Let's be civil, Taigan," Lilia said. She wished she spoke Saiduan, then, so she could be clearer without being even more rude in front of these people. If the harbor was about pieces on the board, so was this room. All of these people wanted something beyond just surviving this siege, and if she didn't figure that out, they weren't going to get far. She saw them all now as possible allies and adversaries in her revenge.

"And you're the clan leader?" Lilia asked the older woman.

"Yes, I'm Hona Fasa Sorai," the woman said. Her gray curls were knotted away from her face with blue ribbons, a touch even more extravagant than her daughter Mohrai's coiffed hair. "And you've met my daughter Mohrai. And this man is Elder Ora Naldri of Para's temple."

"Yes, I think I've seen him before," Lilia said, the memory kindling. Naldri, the great barrel of a man, with the meaty fists and shoulders that always seemed ready to burst from his tunic. She never understood why he didn't have one tailored to fit him properly. "This woman with me is Taigan. She is a sanisi, and my mentor in many things."

She saw Naldri's heavy white brows rise at that, but decided not to clarify in exactly what ways this Saiduan person had come to act as more a mentor to her than anyone in Dhai.

Lilia approached the broad round table. The table itself, like the table in the Assembly Chamber of Oma's Temple, was embedded with a mosaic map. This one was of Clan Sorai, from the southern border where it met Clan Adama to the jutting piers of the harbor. She saw the long thread of the obsidian cliffs that ringed the coast stretching from the eastern mountains that separated them from Dorinah, and all the way west, to the woodlands. It was a perfect barrier to keep what came from the sea in the sea.

She saw yellow rings set along the harbor. She counted fifty, the same number as the boats. Blue rings along the gates. Blue, green, and violet rings – set further apart – along the black coast.

"These are the jista groups?" Lilia asked, pointing at the rings.

Naldri nodded. "I committed a dozen of our best parajistas to this effort."

"How many on the wall at any time?"

"I think–" Mohrai said.

"The Kai asked her here," Hona said.

Naldri cleared his throat, and rolled his meaty shoulders, as if from long habit. "Six are at the wall. They work in shifts."

"How long are the shifts? An hour? Twelve hours? How many are up there at any one time?"

"Three," he said.

"So," Lilia said, pointing to the boats, "if there is an omajista and three parajistas on each of these boats, and they decide, this instant, to send a blast of air at us to knock down these gates, those two jistas will counter it?"

Hona said, "We don't expect–"

"I have been there," Lilia said. She did not have height, or age. She did not have a reputation. But she had been there, and she was an omajista, and that made her uniquely suited to be here. But they needed to see it. "I've seen the army that waits for us. And as an omajista, I know what they can do if they have a mind to."

"We don't have the resources–" Hona began.

"Then you should open the gates," Lilia said. "Because we are already done."

"If we are discussing an assault as opposed to a defense," Hona said, "we should consult Ghrasia Madah."

"She is busy," Lilia said. "I've been tasked with this issue by the Kai. Or was that not clear?"

"Now wait–" Mohrai said.

Taigan shifted toward her, grinned wolfishly. Mohrai seemed to reconsider.

Lilia looked for the heaps of rings on the table, and found the store near Naldri. She shuffled over to him, dragging her twisted leg behind her, and ignored the stares. Let them look.

Lilia took up the rings and began to place teams of jistas along the wall, and the coast. "We need a wall of air up now, maintained by a parajista permanently posted to these gates. There needs to be a dozen up there, at least. We have three omajistas here now, as well – me, Taigan, and Tulana, my Seeker. One of us needs to be up there too, at all times."

"We don't know what they're waiting for," Hona said. "They could attack tomorrow, or not at all."

"If you think they will not attack at all," Lilia said, "if the Kai thought they would not attack at all, he would not have sent me here. None of us would be here."

"You'd be out fucking, likely," Taigan said.

"You're being rude," Lilia said. She did not like Taigan's smirk. Taigan could offer help, but she wasn't, as usual. She preferred to laugh at them, at the futility of it all. That angered her; Lilia felt a trembling seam of Oma's power flitter beneath her skin, and took a breath to calm herself. Anger would win her no allies, and she needed allies.

She began again. "We'll need more than the parajistas at Para's Temple, of course. I don't know how you go about summoning more militia, but we'll need more of that, too."

Hona crossed her arms. "We're coming up on planting season. The more bodies I pull out of the clans, the less likely we are to be able to feed ourselves in two months."

"Dhai has stores, surely?" Lilia said.

"One year," Hona said. She pushed one of her blue ribbons behind her ear. Lilia thought it must be distracting, to have all those things in one's hair. "But that's people living on nothing but rice and woodland foraging. Those aren't going to be people who can fight."

"I expect many will find they can fight just fine when it's their homes burning," Lilia said.

Taigan sighed. "You will lose this way."

"Taigan, you're–"

"No." She shook her head. "You are thinking this is a fair battle. But you have no navy, and two of their legions number more than your entire population. If you want to win, it won't be a clean fight."

Lilia stared at the lines of rings in the harbor. "Have any of you thought of anything clever, then?"

Mohrai snorted. "These are classic battle tactics."

Lilia glanced over at Hasina. "Boats burn," she said.

"Well, sure," Hasina said.

"And parajistas can hold their breath a long time, can't they?" Lilia asked Naldri.

"Of course, it's a matter of the Litany of–"

"Then I have a way we can surprise them."

"There's still a chance they won't attack," Hona said. "If we provoke them, it could undo a more peaceful solution the Kai has planned."

"If the Kai intended peace, he would not have sent you two omajistas, one of them a sanisi," Lilia said. "If we are going to succeed, we must play the aggressor."

"I find it abhorrent, the idea of fighting a foe who's not shown us any aggression," Naldri said.

"I have seen their aggression. I'm comfortable striking first," Lilia said. "I'd try to burn those boats myself, but they'd see a wave of bloody mist coming at them. What they won't see are parajista swimmers lobbing sinajista-trained fire bursts onto their decks."

"That's bold," Taigan said.

"We are bold, or we are buried," Lilia said. "Do you have a better idea?"

"I intend to take up farming," Taigan said. "Perhaps a wood carving profession of some kind."

"A little late for a change," Lilia said.

"You'd be surprised," Taigan said. "I once knew an alewife who became a painter."

"Could we please discuss this?" Hasina said. "First, we do not have the sinajistas here who can do that. The sort of pattern we'd have to make for... what, fifty boats? That's not an easy task with Sina descendent. The nearest sinajista I know with the sensitivity to do that is at least four days away, and it will take her another week to complete all those. You'll have to have a parajista on hand while she makes them to knot them into an air pouch, as well, if you want the parajistas to throw them. Jistas who must work together to complete a task like this… that takes time. It's not something you wave your hand at."

"Then I'll rely on you," Lilia said, "to make sure it's done."

Hasina pursed her mouth, and glanced at Hona. Hona gave a slight nod.

"I could walk away from here," Lilia said. "Any of us could. But we're not. So let's do something they won't expect. These people destroyed Saiduan. And Taigan is right – they are better fighters, and there are more of them. They will expect us to…" She hesitated. The Tai Mora would know their tactics, wouldn't they? They were the same people the Dhai learned them from.

"We can't use anything we learned in the temples, can we, Taigan?" she asked.

Taigan shrugged. "Just know they learned the same."

"What advantage do we have, then?" Mohrai said.

"None," Taigan said.

Lilia sighed. "Taigan –"

"None save this," Taigan said. "You are fighting an enemy with your faces, and some twisted version of your culture. You know their minds better than we did."

"No," Lilia said. "They might as well be from some foreign star, Taigan. They are nothing like us."

Taigan cocked her head at Lilia. Lilia felt the weight of her stare; amusement more than accusation.

"You know what I mean," Lilia said.

"How old are you?" Hasina asked.

"Does that matter?" Lilia said.

"Sometimes it does," Mohrai said. "You hardly look

twelve, if a day."

"If I had not reached the age of consent, I would not be here," Lilia said. "I'll be eighteen in the winter. I have not been a child for some time."

"If I was on fire and a child offered a bucket of water, I'd take it," Taigan said. "Wouldn't you?"

Hasina tapped the new line of colored rings along the map of the gates with her long, bony finger. "We'll take the bucket," she said.

17

Nasaka thought she knew the basements of Oma's Temple as well as its Kais. But no more. And that frustrated her, to run a country where anyone in it knew something she did not. Ahkio's foray into the basements, running after whatever it was Kirana had risked her life to cover up, had not gone unnoticed, nor had his secret councils with his closest Oras. But Nasaka knew something more of the matters than Kirana suspected. She knew Etena had been feeding Kirana information for years, from exile. Etena knew things about this temple that would turn the tide of the war.

What she didn't know was where they'd hidden Etena.

But she knew someone who did.

Nasaka strolled down to the second level of the basements, through a little-used door for which she had the only key, and walked down a short corridor. Just four doors. Four cells. The only holding cells in the entire temple.

Nasaka pushed open the storage room door. Meyna lay on the floor, huffing and hacking. She had picked up some bronchial infection that left her hocking great gobs of snot. Her face was a mess. Her child was, blessedly, quiet; it clung to her breast with great, plump hands.

Nasaka thought it kind to keep the child with her, for a time. Using the child as a means to break her would work better if she was well attached to it, and that often took time. Months, it turned out.

"And how are you today?" Nasaka asked.

"Go fuck yourself," Meyna said.

"You sound like a seafaring Tordinian this morning." Every morning, in truth. Nasaka understood what Ahkio had seen in her, despite her politically unsuitable upbringing. Meyna had borne a child here on a cold floor strewn with straw, alone. Nasaka left no one to watch over her down here, and the birth happened overnight, between her evening feeding and when Elaiko returned in the morning with breakfast. Elaiko said she was shocked at the amount of blood and afterbirth. Nasaka sometimes forgot how young Elaiko was.

The whole thing reminded Nasaka of her own three days in a bloody childbed, so racked with exhaustion and cramped with fear and pain that she thought she would die. Birth was an unending torment. She admitted something in her admired Meyna's stubborn will and significant health.

"And you're a nattering old crow," Meyna said. Her tone was haughty, but she pulled the child closer.

"Are you ready to assist me?"

"I'm not doing anything for you."

"You may not have a choice, soon." Nasaka leaned in the doorway. "You and that child put the Kai, and this country, at risk. Unless you want exile, or death, the option I offer is your only choice."

Meyna slowly drew the child from her lap and set it into a cushion of straw. It stirred, but did not wake. Nasaka watched it. Ahkio's child, no doubt. Nasaka saw her own face in the child's, the bold nose and broad cheeks. It mattered little, of course, who a child's father was in Dhai. Descent ran through the mother's side, always. Who Meyna chose to bring to bed was of little consequence. Men married for economic stability, and a desire for love, children, companionship. Who actually fathered a child didn't often come into argument.

Not unless the child's father was the Kai.

"So what are we going to do with you, then?" Nasaka asked.

Meyna stood. Nasaka watched her, waiting.

"This won't end well," Meyna said.

"Not for you, no," Nasaka said. "But I might spare the child."

"You wouldn't harm me. Ahkio will find out. What will happen then?"

"What makes you think it wasn't Ahkio who had you put here?"

Meyna laughed. She threw her head back when she did it, a petty bit of theater that might have fooled a younger woman. But Nasaka saw the fear in her eyes and the slight tremor in her jaw. Meyna was good at games, for a young woman. But they were all games Nasaka had played for far longer, and with much more success.

"Ahkio is just a boy," Meyna said, "and only you would tell me to go find his mad Aunt Etena to take his seat." She stepped forward. "I wonder, Ora Nasaka... what changed? You wanted him to be Kai so badly, but now you want to give it to someone else? Why? Because of me? My child?"

Nasaka called on Sina; recited the Litany of Breath to call a glimmer of Sina's power beneath her skin. It was difficult to draw on, now that Sina was descendent, but she noted a subtle shift in the amount she could pull. Sina would come around again, very soon. Nasaka trembled, just a little, in anticipation.

Meyna kept walking toward her as she spoke. "I bound him to me," she said. "He'll walk through fire for me, if I ask it."

Nasaka bound the violet mist of Sina into a simple

knot, and absently waved her hand, tossing the bundle of violet energy into the straw bundle.

Meyna leapt at her.

Nasaka side-stepped her neatly. Caught her by the wrist. Twisted her arm back, pushed her head down. Then she let out her breath, and the violet burst of Sina's energy exploded. The straw ignited.

The baby cried.

Meyna yelled.

Nasaka released her. Meyna ran to the child, pulling it from the flaming straw. She wrapped the child in her arms and kicked at the flames, throwing bits of burning straw into the air. Nasaka watched it all from the doorway. The child was screaming, screaming, far more than the fire warranted. Fear, not pain.

Meyna pressed herself into a corner. The air was filled with the smell of burnt straw. Nasaka saw a few errant embers, but didn't care much for them. There was only so much straw in the room, and certainly not enough to kill Meyna and her child if it all burned up.

"Don't think I'm as stupid as he is," Nasaka said. "I've been running this country longer than you've been alive, and I'll go on doing it long after you're dead."

Meyna's eyes filled, but instead of a sob, she grimaced. The child would not stop screaming. It was starting to rattle Nasaka's nerves. She stepped out of the cell.

"Ora Nasaka!"

Nasaka hesitated; left the door open a few inches.

Meyna remained in the corner, showing her teeth. The child screamed. Meyna shouted over it. "You don't deserve this country," Meyna said. "Neither did Etena."

"Nor do you," Nasaka said. "Ahkio may not have seen through your ploy, but I did. You hoped to set a precedent. Hoped that child would be a way to a seat upstairs. But you will always be a mewling, insignificant little brat from Clan Mutao. A Mutao who will die here, alone and unremembered, unless you do as I say."

"Worse people have tried to make me do what they willed," Meyna said. "You won't have better luck. My mother said Etena cast herself into Mount Ahya."

"Where is your mother?"

Meyna pulled her child closer. Then, "Give me a bath. Give me a bath, and I'll tell you. It won't matter if you find my mother anyway. She'll never give up Etena."

Nasaka nodded. "Fair trade, then," she said. "I may even give you a clean skirt."

Meyna stared into her child's face.

Sugar won more often than salt. Nasaka had forgotten that. "I'll bring you a blanket *and* clean clothes," Nasaka said smoothly. "You never did get on with your family, did you? What does it matter if I know where she is?"

"Bring a map," Meyna said.

Nasaka shut the door.

Elaiko stood outside, hands in the deep pockets of her tunic. "Should I make some tea?" she asked.

"That would be lovely," Nasaka said.

Meyna yelled after them, "My mother will never give Etena up! Not for my life! Not for my child's! Do you hear that?"

They started back up through the corridor. There were other rooms here Nasaka had set aside for prisoner interrogations, her own semi-secret gaol, but when she brought in Meyna she had them cleared out, including Almeysia. She had found out enough about Almeysia to know that the one they had wasn't theirs anyway. She was some agent of the Tai Mora's, sent here for a dark purpose that Nasaka still wasn't certain about. Almeysia would not speak for sugar or salt.

Only six people knew Meyna was here, and that was three too many for Nasaka's comfort. Already the temple was taking sides – her against Ahkio. But she was not fool enough to move her hand until she had Etena. Ahkio should have just let her be, but things were too far gone now. She needed someone she controlled who could get into those basements. Ahkio was turning into something else. If she could not control him, she could not protect him. She mourned that.

"Has there been progress on Yisaoh?" Elaiko asked. "I know you had someone looking for her."

"Too inquisitive for your own good."

"Just looking to stay on top of things. We've had... some unfortunate incidents in Garika. And they are not improving."

"I'm aware."

"Of course."

Nasaka kept the silence as they ascended into the upper tiers of the temple. Two barred and sealed doors – sealed by both sinajista and tirajista traps, just in case. Nasaka had always appreciated Elaiko's silence. She had a gift for understanding when it was appropriate to speak, and when it was not, a virtue Nasaka did not often find in young people.

They walked up into the hall outside the bath house, one story below the temple proper, and five floors above the gaol.

"I have an errand," Nasaka said. "Meet me in my study. An hour, perhaps. After your prayers."

"Of course. I'll bring the tea."

It did help that Elaiko could make a very good cup of tea.

Nasaka crossed through the Temple of Oma, and started up the grand stairway. Nasaka went up five flights to the guest quarters. Most guests were kept on the second and third floors; only Dhai were permitted up further. But in this instance, well... Nasaka supposed her guest more or less counted.

She knocked on a banded door of amber wood.

"Do enter!"

Nasaka pushed open the door.

A slim young woman stood silhouetted in the great window looking out over the brilliant green expanse of the Pana Woodlands. Her hair was chopped and crimped into some odd Dorinah style, as if attacked with a razor and burnt. Her grin split her face.

"Greetings, Ora Nasaka, on this fine morning!"

"Good morning, Sai Hofsha," Nasaka said. "I'm sorry this has all taken so much longer than you anticipated."

It still unnerved her, how much Tai Mora like Hofsha looked like Nasaka's own people. Clearly, their manners and postures were foreign, but in profile, at first glance, Hofsha could have been some Sorila businesswoman come to talk about tariffs.

Hofsha's grin never wavered. "That's no matter," she said. "I'm sure he'll come to his senses in time. They always do. Generally." She gestured back to the window. "Has that woodland always been so dangerous?"

"It's the world Faith Ahya and Hahko recorded when they first crossed over from Dorinah," Nasaka said. "It has not changed much in all that time."

"We burned ours out," Hofsha said.

"I expected no less."

Hofsha picked up a hat from the bed. "Come, give me a tour of the temple," she said. "My Kai has asked me to begin assigning quarters for her people. It won't be long now."

18

Ahkio told no one when he went to visit the heart of the temple again, despite the known danger. Liaro had told him the stone was broken, so what was the harm? After two weeks in the temple, watching Hofsha stride about the grounds as if she already owned the place, he was running out of reasons to put her off. A few days before, he had seen Nasaka escorting Hofsha around the temple, showing her every room like she was a loved and respected guest. He spent most of his days talking over paper, and he was tired of his own inaction. He needed the temple keeper's advice. He needed to know what had happened to Almeysia. He needed to understand Nasaka's plan for the temple, and how he would subvert it, and his Oras were too often bickering with one another to provide him many answers.

He waited until he had sent Liaro on various errands, and Caisa was safely off at the Temple of Para. The only one who questioned where he was on occasion was Masura, who had taken up residence in the temple sometime after his ascension and had simply never left. When he asked Una why she tarried here, Una admitted that Masura had stepped down in all but name from her duties as Elder Ora of the Temple of Tira. He heard little from the harbor in all that time. Mohrai sent a missive that Lilia and the sanisi had arrived at the harbor and discussed strategy, but gave no details. He suspected that was prudent. Not even he knew how many in the temple were trustworthy. They were engaged in delay just as he was. Delaying the inevitable.

He visited the heart of the temple the second time in the midafternoon as a heavy thunderstorm rolled in over the plateau. Novices and drudges rushed throughout the temple, shuttering windows and doors against the storm's incursion.

Ahkio moved from this eerie darkness to the black basements, and put his hand on the stone for the second time in the flickering light of a flame fly lantern. As Liaro had said, the stone was broken. Ahkio examined it, wondering what it was he hoped to find. Whatever ward Almeysia had set on the stone must have done this damage, but to what end? To silence the keeper? To keep him from going through?

He raised his hand to the mark on the stone, just to be sure it was inactive, and–

–And he fell through the stone, or through time, or into the seams between worlds, and there he was again, standing in the brilliantly lit room, unstuck in time.

He had thought to find it ruined, or mired in darkness. But it was still broad daylight. The sky had not moved. The moon remained, and the double suns rode over the tongues of the mountains. He stood at the center of the room and waited for the keeper to appear. The whirling lighted numerals were gone now, though.

And so was the keeper.

He shivered. It seemed he wasn't the only one playing with forces he didn't understand.

Ahkio explored the room, poking at the large pieces of furniture, the end tables and desks. He half expected he would be able to pass his hands through them as he had through her, but they were solid. He rifled through what looked like large desks, but they contained no papers.

He called for the temple keeper, but received no answer. He began to feel vaguely alarmed, as if he trespassed on some sacred space. And perhaps he did. He found a set of double doors on the far side of the room, and tried to open them, but they were locked.

"Keeper?" Ahkio called, again.

Something wavered at the corner of his vision. He turned, but it blinked out. "Keeper?"

Nothing.

Ahkio tapped the walls, looking for some other way in or out. How did the keeper come and go? What was she, really?

"I want to speak to you again," Ahkio said. "I have more questions this time. I have–"

The floor beneath him rumbled softly. Ahkio froze. He gazed out the great windows. Something flickered in the sky there, a flashing star. He walked to the windows and found a faint trace of lettering there, as if someone had pressed their fingers to the pane and written letters. It was in the Kai cipher. But how did a ghost write on a window?

The same way a ghost became unstuck in time, perhaps.

He had been writing in the Kai cipher for so long that he was able to work it out in his head:

The Guide will show you to the engines at the heart of the temples. We will deliver the Guide. But you must lead the army. Now go. She is coming for you.

A chill rose in the room. The floor rumbled again. The light went out.

He woke suddenly on the floor next to the stone. He was sweating heavily. He stared up at the stone, and it was then he heard a noise, the sound of feet scuffling across the floor. Someone else in the basements. He shuttered the lantern and lay still on the floor, breathing softly. How long had he been out this time?

He lay that way for an hour or more, listening to someone stumbling around in the darkness. He saw the light swinging somewhere in the tangle of the roots that made up this final basement of the temple, but it was far off, indistinct. Even when it was well gone, when he heard nothing else, he lay there in the dark for a long time after.

She is coming, the keeper had said, but he didn't know if she meant Kirana, or Nasaka, or Hofsha, or any number of other people he didn't know about. Ahkio had spent a long time trying to avoid doing what he knew he needed to do, but it was time.

He stumbled upstairs into the light, and asked what day it was. The novice he asked looked at him as if he were mad, but told him. She gave him a date that must have been wrong – the date she gave was the day *before* he had entered the basements. And it was clearly evening, not the middle of the day.

"Are you… sure?" he asked.

She cocked her head at him. "Are you all right?"

"Fine," he said. He went to the scullery and asked a drudge. He found Shanigan in the banquet hall and asked the date. They all gave him the same date. He sat down next to Shanigan then, suddenly dizzy.

"What is it?" Shanigan said.

"We had a meeting today," Ahkio said. "You called me a fool boy."

Shanigan laughed. "That meeting is in a few hours," he said. "I thought you said you were going to rest upstairs? Why would I call you a fool? No, wait. I can think of several reasons."

Ahkio tried to work out why he would have gone back, and a terrible fear came over him. What if he wasn't in the right world at all? What if he hadn't gone through time, but he'd gone… somewhere else? Where was the "he" from the day before? He gazed at the staircase. Was he still up there, in bed? Were there two of him now?

He sprinted upstairs and burst in on Liaro. He was in a dance class with Ohanni. The whole class startled at his appearance.

"Liaro!" Ahkio said, breathless. He called him away into the hall. Liaro looked just the same way he had the day before. He asked him question after question. "Do I look the same? Are there two of me here? Who is Kai? Is Nasaka alive? What day is it, really? Who teaches mathematics?"

"What in Sina's name is going on?" Liaro said. "What did–" He came up short. Frowned. "You went down there again."

"I didn't lose time," Ahkio said. "I... I don't know what I did."

"You're going mad," Liaro said.

"I have an extra day, but... nothing of importance happened, not really. Why would I get an extra day that isn't important? Why would–"

"Because this is all mad," Liaro said firmly. "Ora Nasaka warned me–"

"When did you talk to Nasaka?"

"Who do you think is talking to Ora Nasaka for you now that you threw Caisa out? I don't care who she was, she was your ally – an ally to both of us – and that leaves me to ferry your little orders to Ora Nasaka while you avoid her."

Ahkio turned away from him and ran up two flights of stairs to the Assembly Chamber. He was out of breath by the time he reached his own quarters. He flung the doors open.

The room was empty, but the bed was unmade, as if he had indeed been sleeping in it. He walked to the side of the bed and pressed his hand to the sheets. They were still warm. He shivered.

He had moved, somehow, between one time and the next.

Liaro came into the room behind him, swearing and huffing. "What's going on?"

"I'm not here," Ahkio said.

"You aren't making sense."

"I have extra time," he said. "Why was I given extra time? Why did I jump from one day to another and back again?"

"Maybe it means nothing, Ahkio. It's not all signs and portents. The sky is in chaos. There are people from other worlds running around. Everything is mad and means nothing."

"No," Ahkio said firmly. "It's time." He turned to head back downstairs.

"Where are you going?"

"To Hofsha. Call Ora Jakobi and Ora Naori. Have them meet me in the foyer."

"No, wait–"

But Ahkio did not wait. He needed to put her out of the temple. She wasn't going to walk around like she owned it any longer. He had delayed enough. The longer she was here, the longer she and Nasaka schemed. The one thing he had not done the day before was finish things with Hofsha. He had let her stay here, continuing her long and oppressive occupation of their temple. Now was his chance to act.

He asked for and found Hofsha in the Sanctuary. The evening was warm. The light of the moons glittered against his skin. He moved as if he were in some dream. A day repeated. He had spent this day doing nothing but arguing over paper. He had spent the night alone while Liaro went out with Ohanni. A wasted day. He would not waste it again.

Hofsha raised her head when he entered. "Kai," she said, as he crossed the broad room. Her smile was large and ungainly, if only because it showed so many teeth. It put him in mind of the posturing of some predator.

"I've come with a response to your offer."

"So soon? I've enjoyed the hospitality of your temple the last two weeks. We can wait a while longer."

"Your boats block our harbor. It gave the impression you would like a quick resolution."

She returned the book she held to the shelf. He made note of it – she was in the section containing the epic romances, the great early stories of Faith Ahya and Hahko forging their way across the wilderness from Dorinah to Dhai. They were operatic tales of alliances and betrayals, hardship and the tornadic nature of love.

"Where is Ora Nasaka?" she asked. The smile remained. Her tone was light.

"I fear you may have been mistaken about Nasaka's role in this country," Ahkio said. "She is my religious and political advisor. To that end, I'm happy to listen to her counsel on all matters. But at day's end, I must be the one to speak for Dhai."

"Of course," Hofsha said. She folded her hands in front of her.

He squared his stance, but did not take a step back. "I appreciate your own Kai's... your... Empress? Well, I appreciate that she took the time to make this offer. We've been happy to host you. Unfortunately, I'll need you to tell her–"

Hofsha raised a hand. Her smile was less boisterous now. She showed no teeth. "Before you continue, I urge you to remember our ships lie ready." She leaned over, and picked up the cage of birds. She set them on the table beside her. The birds twittered madly, fluttering their little wings, hurling themselves at the cage.

"I remember."

She folded her hands again, standing just behind the cage so he had to look past it to see her. "Very well."

He hesitated. The droop of her shoulders, the look of resignation, surprised him. "How many others have you made this offer to?"

"A few."

"And how many take it?"

"Not enough," Hofsha said. The birds rattled the cage.

"You know, then, that I must refuse."

"Perhaps you should speak to Ora Nasaka again," Hofsha said. "I could stay another day or two–"

"I'm afraid that's my final word, Hofsha. Now you will leave peaceably."

She reached for her hat on the table, a broad-brimmed thing that Ahkio had only ever seen Aaldians wear. She ran her fingers over the brim.

"Spring is here," Hofsha said, "and that's not so bad, is it? You'll be dead before you have to see another winter." She put on her hat, and took up the cage with the other hand.

"What are those for?" he asked.

"Oh, these?" she held the cage aloft, smiled brightly. "I love birds. I love to cage them, you see, because when you first do it, they fight so terribly hard. They are so alive, so defiant. I measure how long it takes for them to lose their spirit. To stop fighting. To resign themselves to their fate."

"And how long does that take?"

"It depends," she said.

"I'm sure there are some who never give up," he said.

"Oh no," she said. "They all give up, eventually. They are all in a cage, you see. There is no way out." She touched the brim of her hat and strode to the door, swinging the cage.

"Hofsha?"

She paused, hand on the door. "Kai?" Hopeful.

"What were you looking for in Saiduan?"

She grinned. "A very good question, isn't it?"

Hofsha opened the doors, and left him.

Ahkio stood alone in the Sanctuary for a long time, wondering what would happen on the day Nasaka decided he wasn't worth saving anymore, either. Would she burn the temple down around them?

The door opened, and, as if thinking summoned her, Nasaka entered. "Was that Hofsha I saw in the foyer? Tell me you didn't speak a word without me. Tell me you had the sense to call on Ghrasia and Mohrai first."

"It will take time for Hofsha to—"

"No it won't, you fool," Nasaka said. "You're lucky Liaro came for me. They open tears between worlds to send messages. That invasion is going to start. There's no time to warn the harbor. They could be inundated as we speak."

"How do you know that, Nasaka? How do you know how they communicate?" He knew, though. He had always known.

"The invasion has been primed for just this moment. All she waited on was your refusal."

He pushed past her and into the hall.

"Where are you going?" she asked.

"We need strong lines of supply," Ahkio said. "You'll be stepping down as my political and religious advisor. I'll be appointing Ora Shanigan."

"What?"

"You're confined to your quarters," Ahkio said, "until further notice."

Nasaka barked out a laugh. "And who will hold me?"

Ahkio peered further down the corridor where Jakobi and Naori waited. He called for them, and turned back to Nasaka. He had thought he would need their help to escort Hofsha out. It was a bitter irony that it was not Hofsha he had to use force against.

"We'll start with Ora Jakobi and Ora Naori," Ahkio said. "I have no problem using the gifted arts against a woman who refuses my order."

"You're very lucky my star is in decline," Nasaka said, low. "You have committed us to war."

"No," Ahkio said. "You did that when you betrayed this country."

19

Lilia sat in a tiny room nestled in the harbor's eastern gate, rubbing her twisted foot. The stairs were laborious, never-ending. Everyone wanted to meet on every which floor, without a care that it took her three times as long to navigate them as everyone else. She grimaced and bore it, but the pain was getting worse. It was one of those days when the idea of Taigan cutting off her leg and taking a year to regrow it didn't sound so bad. She had spent two weeks at the harbor wall arguing with people about how to execute what she thought was a very simple plan, but it turned out she was better at coming up with plans than convincing people to follow them.

Lilia had taken the Line to Kuallina twice in that time to check on the refugees. They were having trouble finding places in the clans for them. No one wanted them, even the smaller family groups. She spent endless hours arguing with Gorosa Malia Osono, the head of the hold, about his efforts to place the refugees. His attitude was no better than that of the Kai. She could feel his disdain for them, and for her.

Lilia tried to keep their spirits up. Eventually, if every clan took in a few, they could blend seamlessly in with the rest of Dhai. It would just... take time. Time, she admitted, that Dhai did not have. What were the Tai Mora waiting for? How much longer before they moved?

Dusk had fallen. She had left Taigan and Gian to eat downstairs, and climbed back up here hungry. It was preferable to the company that met in the dining hall. One of the things she liked, living in Oma's Temple, was being invisible. Hardly anyone noticed her but Roh. Even when she routed someone at a strategy game, she was so unremarkable otherwise, it never drew their ire. But perhaps, as Taigan said, that invisibility had been her mother's gift to her, seared into her flesh with the ward Taigan had later removed.

Pain still shot up her twisted leg. She winced and lay back on the bed. There was just one narrow window. From there she could see the misty green lights of the Tai Mora lanterns stretching across the water as they lit them, one by one. It was beautiful, really, this view of the enemy. The sound of the water and bobbing of the lights put her to sleep every night.

The door opened, and Gian entered. She had found more suitable clothes – a long clean blue tunic stitched in silver and bright red trousers that fit her remarkably well after she tailored them to her own frame.

"Rice?" Gian asked. She pulled a sticky rice ball from her tunic pocket.

Lilia shook her head. Her stomach growled.

"I can hear that," Gian said. She sat next to Lilia on the bed. "I worry when you sit up here alone."

"I don't like people very much." It was the voices she couldn't stand. People speaking in loud voices about things they didn't understand, making what sounded like factual assertions about the enemy – about who they were, where they came from – that were utter nonsense. She wondered that the Kai hadn't done a better job telling people about the enemy. But how to give people that message without causing panic? That was a challenge, wasn't it?

"I can handle the people," Gian said, "if you like. I don't mind talking to people."

"Is that what you did in Dorinah?"

Gian began to eat the rice ball.

Lilia folded her hands across her stomach, and let the silence stretch.

"I refused to go to the Seekers," Gian said. "Is that what you wanted to hear? Some terrible story about my life?"

Lilia pushed herself up on her elbows. "Of course you're gifted, just like–" Like my Gian, she wanted to say, but that was unfair. "You're a parajista?"

"That's a good guess. That's what they said. I don't notice much of anything. I can't do the things you can do... it's just... I'm aware of Para. I can see the blue mist, sometimes. But that's all."

"Why didn't you go into training?"

"Do you know how dajian jistas are treated, among the Seekers? No, you wouldn't. We burn out very quickly. They use us at the front lines, like dogs. They'd rather risk us than each other."

"So you–"

"I killed a woman," Gian said. She didn't look at Lilia, but she had ceased eating.

Lilia moved closer. "May I hug you, Gian? Do you need comfort?"

Gian shook her head. She wiped her face with her sleeve. "That's what happened. That's all. I ran away to Daorian. They didn't know who I was, so I got sold into the scullery without being tested. But someone found out, the daughter to the Empress's secretary. She had me thrown onto a cart and dumped at that camp."

"I'm sorry," Lilia said. She thought of Kalinda teaching the first Gian how to pull on Para in secret, so she didn't have to join the temples. Different worlds, different lives, but far too many parallels. It was the parallels that bothered Lilia. How could two places be so different, but its people so much the same?

"I'm tired of talking about terrible things," Gian said. "All we ever do is talk about terrible things, did you know that? Weeks of terrible things."

"With Emlee, we didn't."

"I miss Emlee," Gian said. "Do you think that rumor is true, that she came in with the last of the refugees?"

"We'll look for her at Kuallina after things here are done."

Gian looked out across the water at the green lights. "What are they waiting for?"

"Orders," Lilia said. "Mohrai is finally sending swimmers out in the morning to do reconnaissance."

"Swimmers?"

"It was something I worked out with Elder Ora Naldri," Lilia said. She had kept quiet about her idea outside the campaign room, mostly because she wasn't sure anyone was going to do anything with it after all. "I asked him if parajistas ever used Para to breathe longer. He said yes – they just make this bubble of air around their bodies. It doesn't last long, but long enough to make it from the black cliffs to the ships and back."

"What then?"

Lilia swung her feet off the bed. Her leg still throbbed, but she noticed it less now. She pulled over the strategy board she kept near her bed, the one she had lined with stone markers to represent the ships, and sticks for the gates.

"Sinajistas can create these tangled bursts of energy with Para, like a packet of flame, and they go off when the jista says so. They're hard to make, and they can't be very large. It takes a lot of effort to make them with Sina descendent, and Elder Ora Naldri only has one sinajista strong enough to make them, but I've seen them work. I think they could set fire to the ships."

"Couldn't they put them out with Para?"

"The parajistas are going to put wards on them, so

they're immune to parajistas."

"Omajistas?"

"That's what me and Taigan are for."

Gian regarded the board. "Conflict is complicated, with jistas."

"It's like anything else," Lilia said. "You have to think ahead of your opponent."

Gian jabbed a finger at the stone markers. "They aren't going to expect us to attack them first?"

"They think we're going to wait, the way we've been doing. That's our advantage. They think we're pacifists."

"Aren't we?"

Lilia frowned. "I still have to convince some people. They don't want to listen. They think there's a peaceful solution. But I've been there, Gian. I've seen the army. I know."

Gian reached for her hand, hesitated. "May I hold your hand?"

Lilia nodded.

Gian took her clawed hand into her warm, calloused one. "We'll win with you here. You're the smartest, the most powerful–"

Lilia felt heat rising on her face. She pulled her hand away. "You don't have to flatter me. I'm not some special person."

"You're brave."

"It's not brave to send other people off to die," Lilia said. "Those parajistas are brave. Ghrasia is brave."

"Can I… that's… would you mind if I… Lilia, I would like to kiss you."

"Yes," Lilia said.

Gian leaned into her, and for a long, lovely moment, Lilia allowed herself to imagine it was the other Gian pressing her lips to hers.

"I need you," Lilia said, "your hands on me. Please touch me, take me away from here. Do you consent?"

Gian needed nothing else. She pulled at Lilia's tunic

and pressed her back onto the bed. Her hot mouth found Lilia's breast, and every part of Lilia seemed to light up like the boats on the water. A warm, desperate desire flushed through her whole body. She yanked at Gian's clothes. Her long black hair tickled Lilia's face.

"Gian," Lilia said, and she remembered the way Gian's body had moved in the woodlands – shirtless Gian, swinging her machete. Gian, who had massaged her cramping legs and feet. Gian, who had told her, wounded and delirious, that she loved her.

Gian tugged off Lilia's trousers and pressed her lips between Lilia's legs. Lilia gasped.

The boats. The lights in the boats.

The only light came now from the moons and boats, and the sickly green glow of them suffused Lilia's room. The lights were different, though. They blinked on and off, as if someone were shuttering and unshuttering the lanterns.

Lilia gasped. She cupped Gian's head with her good hand, tangling her fingers in her hair. "Please!" She wasn't even sure what she was asking, but Gian pulled her hips closer.

The lights in the harbor went out.

Lilia squeezed her eyes shut. She released Gian's hair and gripped the sheets, cried out.

The door banged open.

Lilia jerked away from Gian. Gian raised her head. Lilia resisted the urge to drag her closer. Her heart was pounding loudly now, with more than just desire.

"Lilia–" Taigan strode in. She hesitated a half moment, frowning at the two of them. "Get dressed," Taigan said. She took Lilia's clothes off the floor and threw them at her.

"You're rude," Lilia said.

"I hope you've had a pleasant evening," Taigan said. "The ships just docked at the piers."

Gian wiped her mouth on the sheets and pulled on

her tunic. "The Tai Mora ships?"

"Are there any other ships?" Taigan snapped.

Lilia pulled on her linen undergarments, and her trousers. "Why are they attacking now?" She was trembling, a terrible mix of emotions.

"If I knew that, I'd be King of the Dhai."

"We don't have a king."

"Maybe you should. Mohrai wants you on the wall. They've called all the parajistas, too. The Seekers will meet you there. Hurry."

20

It was a good day for an invasion.

"Tear it open," Kirana said.

She stood on a broad wooden walkway erected for just this purpose – to help propel her army over the swamp and through the gate as quickly as possible, before it closed. In the other world, the new world, there was a lake where she stood. On this side her people had filled it in long before, but as the climate changed with the blazing star, the glaciers on the surrounding mountains had sloughed off and turned the lowlands into a tepid swamp.

The mirror was broken. Every good commander had two or three alternate plans, but this was the one she liked the least. With Saiduan all but routed, its libraries sacked, she needed to turn her attention to the next phase of their invasion – cross over into the now weakened Dorinah, the country with the softest and largest rent between her world and the next. She could take out Dorinah and get her people safely established there, just in time for planting season. That gave her the summer to continue to hammer at Dhai, though she expected it would not take that long, not unless they figured out what she wanted there before she had it.

Across the swampy marsh, Yisaoh watched them from

atop a great white bear. She wore a massive brown cap, her hair twisted around its base in black braids, knotted in tiny beads and bells. She was the most extraordinary person Kirana had ever seen, and she suspected now, even preparing to cross into another world, that Yisaoh would remain so. Her heart ached, and for a wild moment she wished she had permitted their children to watch. But the children were very young, and the outcome of this breach was uncertain. Kirana could lose half her army if the gate collapsed while they were still in transit. She had lost countless thousands to failed gates in the early days of the war. It's why she had devoted so much time to the mirror. Another failed endeavor.

"On my command," Gaiso, Kirana's parajista company general, said. She was a plump woman with broad hands and features. It had been a boon her shadow was already killed in some petty skirmish on the other side. Kirana hadn't wanted to settle for the second.

Kirana braced herself. Those unfamiliar with tearing open the way between worlds often thought the end of the line was a safer place to be, but she knew better. As the first one through, right up alongside the omajistas who opened the thing, she could get herself clear of any blowback. Sometimes when the way opened it imploded, yes – but an implosion didn't affect those who had already gone through. If she ended up in the wrong world, well – that's why she only stepped through next to an omajista. Her own skills with the dark star didn't bend in that direction, much to her frustration.

Fourteen omajistas raised their hands. All around the field, for as far as Kirana could see, were cart after cart of jars filled with blood. When the omajistas said what they had brought was not sufficient, Kirana had killed another fourteen of her own people, drawn by lot, and piled their bodies, too, at the edge of the swamp. It was amazing what a person would put up with, when freedom from certain death was so close. Many turned on comrades, men and women they had fought with most of their lives.

The jars burst. Kirana stood her ground. Did not close her eyes. Did not cover her ears. This was the greatest expenditure they had ever made, and she had to be present and aware. Because they would end up in a lake, she'd had to remove her armor. Behind her, the twenty thousand troops she intended to bring with her were a nearly nude bunch, scratching at the dark seeds of the weapons in their wrists.

The air shuddered. A great weight descended on them, and something more – wind. A wind so hot and sudden Kirana caught her breath.

A black storm of blood poured into the sky from the shattered jars, a wave so mortifying that Kirana had woken screaming for three months after seeing her first. Now it looked like freedom to her. Promise.

It looked like survival.

The bloody gate coagulated ahead of her. She felt the soft crimson mist against her face. Her ears popped. The blood folded in on itself, as if devouring its own substance from the inside out. A seam opened in the world, a massive tear. Kirana saw a cold blue lake shining before her on the other side. Dark trees. Low mountains.

Gaiso barked at her parajistas. The wind kicked up again. The lake ahead of them on the other side rippled, then went still.

"It's solid," Gaiso said, and stepped through the tear in the worlds and onto the invisible bridge of air now riding the surface of the lake.

Kirana could not see work done by parajistas – she was a tirajista with some sensitivity to Oma – but if Gaiso said it was good, she trusted it.

She wanted to say something hopeful or inspiring, but her feet were already moving. She didn't even look up at the black, toxic star in her sky. Only when she stepped onto the hard surface above the glassy lake did she look back once, at Yisaoh. But the angle was all wrong – Kirana could no longer see her. And she needed to move, move, move because her army was coming behind her, and the longer they were on the bridge, the more vulnerable they were.

"Fan out," Gaiso said to her parajistas, and as they came through, the hundred parajistas leaped out across the water, skipping on it like stones, to take scouting positions along the perimeter of the lake.

Kirana did not release her weapon, but she stayed at the center of the next wave, a mixed contingent of tirajistas and regular infantry. The scouts said the area was clear. With the Empress's Seekers scattered to the winds and most of the country's publicly owned Dhai slaves dead, there was little to impede their progress.

As they marched across the lake, Kirana's stomach churned. She tried to look straight ahead. She couldn't swim, and losing the bridge would be embarrassing at best – deadly at worst.

Gaiso glanced over at her. "Not seeing any movement."

"It's quiet here this time of year," Kirana said. "I'll be confident when the whole army's through, though."

"She's not a fool," Gaiso said.

Kirana made a pinched motion with her hand. She had no interest in discussing the Empress of Dorinah within hearing of half her army. She was well aware the Empress wasn't a fool. If she had given over her Seekers and the dajians so easily, it meant she was confident she had something else she could use against them. Something far worse.

The Empress had sent a company to Tordin. For whatever purpose she sent them there, it left her even more vulnerable. And unlike tiny little Dhai, Dorinah had enough land to support a vast number of Kirana's people. If the end came in the next few months instead of the next year, she'd have at least saved this many. It was a risk to move now, but far riskier to wait.

Kirana jumped from the bridge of air onto dry land, and resisted the urge to kiss it.

The tirajistas closed ranks. Kirana moved further up the shoreline to wait for the mounts and supply carts.

Her infantry commander's squire, Lohin, met her on the low rise. "The squad's about done with the way house," he said, motioning to the squat little building on the opposite shore. "Should be cleared out shortly." Lohin was a mean-faced little man, wiry and stooped. She was not particularly taken with his talent on the field, but he was Yisaoh's brother, and she'd promised Yisaoh she'd get him to the other side, one way or another.

"I'll wait for your mother's all clear on that," Kirana said.

Lohin's jaw hardened, but he only pressed thumb to forehead and trudged back down the path. She imagined it would not be so terrible, to serve as squire to one's mother, but Lohin resented every hand she offered him. He didn't even have the good sense to thank her for getting him across. Kirana watched his back, wondering if she should tell him the murder of his shadow had been accidental, and if it'd been up to her, she'd have continued to leave that particular death up to chance until the bitter end.

But here they were.

When she heard the all-clear for the way house, Kirana made her way there, where her pages were already mopping up the blood and pushing together the inn tables. Six bodies were stacked outside.

The infantry commander, Rasina, stood just inside the door, arms crossed. "Got someone for you to see," she said.

Kirana gestured at the pile of bodies. "That not all of them?"

Rasina laughed. She was a long, lean woman – Lohin's mother through marriage, not birth – and she had a warmer face. "Sure isn't," she said, and gestured Kirana upstairs.

Kirana's wrist itched. Her everpine weapon already tasted her unease. "You going to give me a hint?" Kirana said, trying to keep her tone light. She had had enough horrible things happen in this horrible war to last eight lifetimes.

Rasina glanced back. Grinned. She came to the top of the stairs and opened a guestroom door wide. The air inside was heavy. Two parajistas and an omajista stood in the room, their specialties clear from the symbols on their collars.

A woman lay prone in the bed, arms held stiffly at her sides, obviously bound by the jistas. It took only half a breath for Kirana to recognize her.

"Oma's eye," Kirana said. She grinned now too, and met Rasina's merry look. "This is the happiest coincidence of the war."

"Isn't it, though?" Rasina said.

Kirana bent over the bed. It was the same woman, aged ten years from the one Kirana had fused with her mirror on the other side, but easily recognizable.

"Nava Sona," Kirana said. "You have no idea how pleased I am to find you here."

21

Lilia climbed the stairs up the great harbor wall, dragging her foot behind her, trying to make up the difference in speed by pulling herself hand over hand on the rail. Her breath came hard and fast, and she found herself wheezing. She had to slow down, though wave after wave of militia pushed past her, like she was just a drudge again, some spectator caught on the stairwell.

When she reached the top, it was still dark, but the moons were out, and they bathed the world in a pale white glow. All along the piers, dark, chitinous figures were pouring out of the boats.

"Parajistas!" Lilia huffed. She coughed, then – "Where's Ora Naldri?" "Not on the wall yet!" a young parajista called from her place at the parapet.

"Do you have the barricade up?" She leaned over, trying to catch her breath. She needed to let it go. Not think about it. Just breathe.

"It's up – but I can see Para's breath around their boats. They're going to deploy something!"

Taigan was at the other end of the wall, barking at two young parajistas just roused from sleep to join the two on watch at the wall.

"We need to double that barricade, Taigan!" Lilia called.

"They're too raw to act quickly," Taigan said, and Lilia recognized a Saiduan curse.

Lilia limped down the opposite side of the wall to see how many people they had on it. Forty militia, crowded up to the front of the battlements with their bows.

"Stand three paces from the wall!" Lilia said. Her chest hurt, but she had a thread of breath again. The parajistas were getting lost in the muddle of bodies. "Let the parajistas get line of sight!" She spoke as loud as she could, but to these people, she was just a little shouting person. She was no one of consequence.

"Mohrai!" she called. She continued down the wall, breathing deeply, until she found Mohrai, shouting orders for the militia to prepare the first volley.

"Give the parajistas line of sight," Lilia said. "They can't attack what they can't see. Three paces from the wall."

Mohrai frowned. Turned back to the militia, shouted, "Three steps back and hold!"

The line of militia obeyed, as if Mohrai wielded her own bit of magic. Lilia paused a moment more to rally her ragged breath, then called – "Parajistas!" and she started back down the line of the wall again, shouting, "Make sure that barrier ends at the top of the wall! Top of the wall! Make sure this volley can get through! Mohrai is sending a volley!"

Her throat was already hoarse. Though strategy on paper was all very well, limping and shouting along the wall was not the best place for her. She needed her mahuan powder. If not now, then very soon.

One of the parajistas broke away. She was a young woman, a few years older than Lilia, and though Lilia could not see the blue waves of power she manipulated, she recognized the slack face, the lack of concentration. The woman stepped away from the parapet, trembling.

Lilia yelled, "Step up!" right at her face, though Lilia was a head shorter.

The parajista cringed. "There are too many of them," she said. She bolted.

Lilia staggered after her, and nearly collided with a member of the militia. A spit and hiss came from the harbor, and a blister of red breath penetrated their defenses. Lilia fell back, but the tangle of mist collided with the militia member and the three behind her. Their clothes smoked and flamed. Their skin blistered. Screams.

The line of parajistas wavered. Lilia yelled at them again to hold. She skirted past the dying militia and forged after the parajista who had fled the ranks. The woman reached the stairs and plunged down them, far too fast for Lilia to follow.

Lilia crumpled by the entrance to the stairs, gasping like a dying fish. She saw another wave of red mesh slip through their shoddy defenses, but did not have the breath to even warn them. The red wave engulfed two parajistas. They flailed and vomited, their skin sloughing off as if soaked in acid.

Naldri came up the steps behind Lilia, out of breath. He gaped, staring at the bodies, and Lilia, and the quavering line of parajistas. He yelled below, calling for a doctor, and headed out to the line of parajistas, shouting at them to hold their ground.

"There's a tide!" one of the parajistas yelled. "Plant matter of some kind, crawling up the coast!"

A half dozen militia crowded forward at the parapet.

Lilia watched them as if from a great height, listening to the rasping of her own breath.

Then there were two doctors on the wall, an apprentice snapping her fingers at Lilia, Lilia mouthing "mahuan," and then Gian was there, and there was more shouting, and another red sliver darting through the parajistas' barrier, setting an entire line of militia on fire.

Gian argued with the apprentice. Pulled out the mahuan from her pocket. How did she think to carry it everywhere? She tipped it into the apprentice's water bag, shook it, and poured it into Lilia's mouth.

Lilia was so starved of air that stopping to drink felt like drowning. She coughed and sputtered. Naldri came up behind her, calling for the parajistas, but it was all a jumble. Now they had Naldri and Mohrai, at the far end, yelling at them. Disparate orders. Fear. The lines were falling, one by one.

The apprentice ran off to tend the next felled parajista, or militia. Two dozen bodies littered the parapet.

Gian kept Lilia drinking until she spit it into her lap and pushed her away. Lilia tried to get up, stumbled, fell into Gian, and Gian held her up. She smelled of sex and lavender. Lilia clung to her a moment longer.

Her breath came better now, enough to find her feet, but she was delicate, she knew. "Go below," Lilia said.

"We should both go," Gian said. "There's nothing you can do here. This is for Mohrai and Ora Naldri."

A cry came from further down the wall. Lilia saw a snarl of red mist engulf another parajista.

"Go below," Lilia said. She pulled her hands away. "Now, Gian."

Gian's expression was pained, but she went, looking behind her twice, three times, before she disappeared down the stairwell.

Lilia saw the remaining parajistas, trembling and sweating, their concentration breaking. It was too much – for her and them – to watch this horror.

She limped across the parapet, dragging her bad leg. She sucked at Oma's breath, pulled it fast and deep. In that glorious, blinding moment she could take a real, full breath of air. Her lungs opened, like she was perfect and powerful. And in that giddy first blush of total power she wanted to burn the whole world down, just because she could.

Below them, the red algae tide deployed twenty minutes earlier had reached the hem of the gate. Red flesh bloomed up the outside of the gates.

The parajistas were stepping back, making more sounds of distress. Dhai did not have the stomachs for fighting. Taigan had told her that again and again, and she hadn't listened.

"Burn it out!" she yelled. But they had no sinajistas on the wall yet to burn the algae tide. They had only her – raw and untrained.

Lilia let loose the burning breath of Oma. She drew deep and pushed the breath from her body out onto the gate, tangling it into intricate flaming trefoils with long tails. The massive clouds of mist met the red algae and burst into roaring flame. Just as she let go of Oma, she saw the answering tide of omajistas on the other side.

A solid wall of red mist formed ahead of the ships and moved toward the gates at an astonishing speed.

"Parajistas! Wall!" Naldri ran down the lines of parajistas again, rallying them.

Lilia had no idea what was contained in that red wall launched by the Tai Mora, and would not know until it burst upon them. Fire, choking smoke, pestilence, or something else? She didn't know everything Oma could do. She had no idea how to counter it.

What if she could build anything she imagined? She brought up her fist, and watched a ball of red mist curl up and away from her skin. She was brimming with Oma, soaked in it like bread left in water.

She could not see if her parajistas had succeeded in forming a wall. She could not see its chinks, its holes, its weaknesses.

"Is it up?" she called to Naldri. He wrung his hands. She realized that no matter how well she planned, the best strategy in the world was nothing if she had no people on the ground who knew how to carry it out. They had not trusted her.

The wall of red was just a hundred paces away.

Lilia spread her arms and opened her mouth and

gasped as the star filled her lungs and suffused her skin. Push it out, push it out... push it out... She expelled the breath from her lungs, forcing it out through her body, like vomiting some great formless monster. She had no litany for what she wanted, only will.

Turn it away. Push it back.

The power left her and roiled out across the parapet. She took a breath, but instead of air, drew Oma. She choked.

"Lilia!"

Oma's breath entangled her. She saw great streamers roiling into her body, taking form only as it touched her bare skin. She tried to scream. But there was nothing. She fell.

Taigan was running toward her. "Fool!" Taigan yelled.

Her vision swam.

The world exploded.

Taigan saw what was going to happen the moment Lilia stepped out onto the parapet, gasping like a drowning swimmer. A massive bubble of misty red breath suffused Lilia's form. It whirled madly around her, licking and twisting like some hungry ghost.

"Release it!" Taigan yelled. She bolted forward–

–and saw the wave of Oma's breath hurling toward them from the sea.

She had to choose – cut Lilia off from her source, or save every person on the wall, including herself, from the Tai Mora assault.

It was an easy decision. Taigan had been making it her entire life.

Taigan called the Song of Davaar, and drew deep and fiercely, so much so quickly that the ends of her fingers ached. She twisted her strings into an intricate netted trap and pushed the woven snare of Oma's breath over the parapet. Released it.

Taigan ran toward Lilia, muttering the song that

would cut her from Oma's grip. Arrogant, foolish, mad
– all that and–

–a rush of hot air took her off her feet. She heard a
heavy whumping, as if a forest of trees fell in unison.
The air shuddered and contracted.

Taigan spun through air heavy as spoilt milk. She
pulled Oma to break her fall. Oma eluded her. How
could one trust a god so impermanent, so intemperate?

Taigan hit the parapet hard. Her left shoulder bore the
brunt of her fall. The bone snapped in two and thrust
up through the flesh of her arm, opening her cheek. Her
fingers crunched.

She hissed. Heard another great wallop as the tangled
palisade defense she had built collided with the offense
the Tai Mora had thrown. The air juddered. The whole
gate trembled. She bit through her pain and pushed
herself over. She saw a great snarled light just over the
parapet – her concoction warring with theirs.

Her fingers were unresponsive. As she tried to stand,
she felt a sharp pain in her back, and crumpled again.
She had broken something vital.

She reached for Oma and caught a breath. She began
to reknit herself. Flesh hissed. Burned. She pieced her
spine back together first, then pushed up again and
limped toward Lilia while spinning the intricate whorls
of Oma's breath to yank back and reknit her bones and
flesh.

Lilia lay at the center of a massive charred ruin. The
explosion had taken off the rear half of the parapet and
half the parajistas on the wall. The edges of the splintered
wood were still smoking.

Taigan found Lilia blistered, her clothes blackened
tatters, most of her hair gone.

She edged closer, rubbing at her own burning arm as
the bone restored itself.

"Lilia?"

No response.

Taigan knew what she would find, but tried anyway.

She pulled on Oma, and began to compose a song for a constricting mist that would kill the girl.

The ward on her back did not burn. Nothing compelled Taigan not to kill this girl.

There was nothing to say Lilia was uncommon at all.

Taigan dropped her hold on Oma. Sighed. She hoped Lilia was dead, or perhaps would die. It wasn't too late for that.

A boom behind her shattered her reverie. She ducked. The battling songs that bound Oma's breath had burst apart, their fight exhausted. Taigan saw the blooming mist of another Tai Mora attack engulfing the skies over the boats.

She gazed once more at Lilia.

Broken little girl, worse than nothing, now. Worse than what she had been even when Taigan found her. Because when Taigan first found Lilia, there was still the potential she could be powerful.

Now she was a burn out. She would never draw on Oma again.

Taigan stepped away.

"Sanisi?" the leader of the parajistas called to her. He limped over, clutching at a wound from a fragment of broken wood. "Where are you going? What's happened to Lilia?"

Taigan shrugged. "That's none of my concern." In truth, Taigan was going down to find a doctor, though she could hardly admit that even to herself.

Then her knees buckled. She cried out, and fell.

A searing pain set her spine on fire. She arched her back. The pain was worse than falling, worse than knitting herself together again.

Maralah's ward.

Maralah calling her home.

The pain receded, but only just. The compulsion held. The ward only burned softly now, like a fingertip pressed to a hot teacup. Taigan shuffled to her feet. Sweat poured down her face. She should have gone a long time ago, yes. These people were foolish. This battle was lost long before it started. Now she had no omajistas at all, nothing to show for over a year of hacking across this blighted place.

"Wait, sanisi. Who will help us?"

"I suspect you'll save yourselves," Taigan said. "Or perish. It doesn't concern me."

Taigan turned away. Her spine still ached. Home, home, but what was that anymore, but a burning brand and a woman with a leash? She began the long climb down the wall.

She would miss the scullery girl.

22

Ahkio called in the clan leaders for aid the moment Hofsha left the temple. Endurance was the only way he could think of the war. Enduring a siege. Enduring an incursion. Enduring, not fighting. Not strangling his own sister with his own two hands.

Who would he be, then?

Just eight hours after Hofsha fled with her birds, Ahkio sat with Clan Leader Isailia, Tir's replacement as leader of Clan Garika. She had responded swiftly to his summons, the first of the clan leaders to make time for a meeting since he brought them together in Raona.

Ahkio was not a strong reader, but he excelled at numbers, and he could not make the numbers she brought with her work.

"Rice," Ahkio said. Isailia sat in the chair opposite him in the Kai study, hands clasped firmly in her lap.

"We have paid our tithe to the community stores in full," Isailia said. "I'm sure you know that we would help more if we could, but we are not the rice producers they are in, perhaps, Clan Adama or Alia. We have less to spare."

"Ghrasia has given me figures for the number of militia we've had to call up – a twenty percent increase from all clans. Someone must feed them."

"That's what the community stores are for."

"This is an unprecedented time–"

"Kai, each clan must look after its own borders first. I can't spare what we simply do not have. I thought I explained this fully in my letters. We cannot–"

"And I've summoned you here because though you can pen a letter, you obviously haven't been reading mine," he said, and his tone was sharper than he intended. She stiffened. He had some concern about putting her on the defensive. He worried his own fear filled his voice.

"Kai," she said, gazing at the portraits above him. "We've had at least a dozen families flee Garika for the woodlands in the last week. One of our bakers simply closed up her storefront and left with all dozen members of her family. That is not an insignificant number. We've all heard about the harbor. There is… concern about the ability of the Dhai state to combat this threat."

"There is no Dhai state," Ahkio said. "There's all of us working together, or dying together."

"We may die regardless. I've spoken to several clan leaders, and they agree it's best if we retreat into the temples."

"Which clan leaders?"

"I… some leaders."

"Who? Badu? Adama? I didn't spend a year uniting us with a single purpose just to see us break apart at the first sign of trouble."

"I'm sorry, with Ora Nasaka telling us one thing, and you another–"

Ahkio leaned forward. "And what is Nasaka telling you?"

"She says to prepare to welcome these people to Dhai as kin. But you're telling us to prepare to fight them. It's all very… confusing, Kai."

"I can tell you now that the Tai Mora emissary has been escorted from Dhai, and we have turned down their offer of a politic welcome."

"But... why? That goes against everything–"

"I sought a peaceful solution," Ahkio said. "They are not here to be peaceful, whatever Nasaka is telling the clan leaders."

"You'll pardon, Kai, but when the Kai and his religious and political advisor cannot even agree–"

"Nasaka does not speak for me. She speaks for herself. I'll be ensuring that is communicated more effectively in the future. In the meantime, we need those rice stores."

"I cannot–"

"I replaced your predecessor," Ahkio said. "I can replace you just as easily. What's your decision, Isailia?"

"Threats are hardly–"

"Promises." He stood. She shrank back, just a little, which startled him. He had never thought of himself as an imposing person. "Every word I speak now is no longer a request. It is a directive meant to ensure our survival."

"We aren't a tyranny."

"No, we're a cooperative. And you're being less than cooperative."

Isailia smoothed her tunic. "I resign my position," she said. "I am not suited for war."

"None of us are," Ahkio said. "We must make ourselves so."

"No," she said. "I reject that."

"Reject it or not, it is coming."

"Ghrasia Madah speaks well of you in the clans," she said. "Ghrasia says you won't try and make us into what we are not. But this fight... calling up more militia, murdering people at our gates... It is defensive, yes, but it will change us. I don't want to be the people our ancestors were."

"Isailia–"

"That is all," she said. She turned abruptly and hurried from the room.

Ahkio rested his hands on the desk. Somewhere in the conversation, or perhaps in her appointment, he had misstepped. She would go home and speak of this meeting, and her family would flee with all the rest.

"Kai?" A plump novice entered. She had a scrunched little face, as if she had sucked all day on a lemon. "I'm Pasinu Hasva Sorai, Ora Nasaka's new apprentice."

"Where's Elaiko?"

"She's been put on an errand, some time ago."

"Is that... so?"

"Ora Nasaka has asked that you dine with her in her rooms this evening, as she is, of course, confined to quarters. Can I relay your response?"

"How are you related to the Catori?" Ahkio asked.

Pasinu did not even stumble. "I am her near-cousin, on her third mother's side."

"Of course," Ahkio said. "Tell Nasaka I will meet her."

"Pardon, Kai, isn't it very rude not to use Ora Nasaka's title?"

"It is," Ahkio said.

"I see," Pasinu said. She pressed thumb to forehead. "I'll tell Ora Nasaka you accepted. Good day."

Ahkio mulled over this new piece of information. He had just started to get used to Elaiko. What new game was Nasaka playing? Game upon game. All information and none. What had she sent Elaiko to do? He had her confined, now he just needed legal precedent to exile her. But from where? Who had the information he needed to do that?

Assemble your allies and go to battle – with affection and politics or swords and ships – what was the difference? It occurred to him that Nasaka had been playing the Tai Mora's game for a good long while, and, though he was running to catch up, he was not going to be fast enough.

He sat alone in the Kai quarters, going over correspondence. A novice entered, popping only her head in, ducking back a little when he looked up.

"You can come in," he said.

"Farosi is in the study. He has some news about the errand you sent him on."

"Ask him in."

She ducked out, and Farosi came in. He was a lean man, beardless, with short dark hair and a perpetual squint.

"Would you like tea?"

Farosi shook his head. "I had some news about Yisaoh."

"You found her?"

"Just news of her. There are reports putting her in the woodland. The same as her two missing brothers, Rhin and Hadaoh, their wife Meyna, and the child. You should know, Kai, that Ora Nasaka had people looking for Yisaoh as well."

"I could have guessed as much," Ahkio said. "The woodland is bigger than Dhai. Do you have any idea *where*?"

"I've sent two of my people out there to scout," he said. "Ora Naldri was kind enough to lend us a parajista, before he went to the harbor."

"You didn't tell Ora Naldri who you were looking for?"

"No. Only the two militia know. No disrespect meant, Kai, but I don't trust Oras. Not after all the blood that's been spilled here. She'll know you intend to meet her personally, at a time and place of her choosing," he said. "But Kai, with the blood between you–"

"I need to get to her before someone else does," he said. "She may not trust that, but if she waits long enough, she'll find out the truth of it. Anything else?"

"That's all, Kai."

Ahkio stifled his annoyance. The man could have sent that in a letter. "Thank you."

It wasn't until Farosi closed the door that Ahkio

realized he might have been lingering in the hopes of sitting down to dinner with him. But Ahkio was too exhausted for social niceties. He hardly understood what they looked like anymore.

Ahkio lay in bed, wide awake, while Liaro snored. He imagined the harbor on fire, and Tai Mora flooding up the coast. Twelve hours ago, he had sent word to Para's temple to send every parajista they had to the wall, and started the Kuallina militia marching there. But they had had no word back from either, and nothing from the harbor. Every time he thought he could remove Nasaka from the temple, there was some new crisis. He was starting to suspect they were her doing.

Sitting in the dark, he found that he missed Ghrasia. Sina take him, he still missed Meyna. Liaro's snoring intensified. He babbled something in his sleep. Ahkio nudged him with his foot.

"Sina take you," Liaro muttered, and shifted positions, pulling the comforter with him.

Ahkio lay exposed in the cool air, staring out the big windows at the plateau and sweeping woodland beyond, all of it lit by the pearly white glow of the triple moons. It was mesmerizing to sit up and watch them move across the sky.

"Nasaka has done enough terrible things that someone must be willing to speak up about it," Ahkio said.

Liaro snuffled. "Keeps people up at night. Exile her for it myself."

"Should we–"

"I'm asleep."

"What should we do about–"

"Sleep," Liaro said.

Ahkio got out of bed and began to dress. He knew who had the information he wanted. She had walked out on him because of it. "I need to run an errand."

Liaro mumbled an acknowledgement. Ahkio walked two flights down to the guest rooms and opened Masura's door.

"Elder Ora Masura?" he said. "It's Ahkio. Are you awake?"

"Hm?"

"Ahkio. I'm sorry it's late. I have a question."

"Come in, come in," Masura said.

The room was dim, so Ahkio took up the paper lantern on the bedside table and shook it. The flame flies stirred, giving off a warm light.

Masura sat up in bed, rubbing her eyes. She swung her legs over the edge of the bed, parting her robe; she was naked beneath, and her sex dangled free. She looked gaunt and terribly frail in the bad light. "Don't tell me you're having bad dreams," she said wryly.

"I want to know about the day Nasaka had her child," Ahkio said.

"That's old dead business."

"Who was the midwife?"

"Why come to me about this?"

"Because you're old enough to have known about it, and you don't care for Nasaka." And you loved my mother, he wanted to add, but did not. There were few people he'd trust enough to ask.

She sighed. "It was nearly twenty years ago. What does it matter?"

"Humor a foolish boy?"

She reached for a bottle at her bedside, uncorked it. She poured herself a drink, took a long swallow. "She was from Nasaka's clan, of course. Woman named... Orsala? Unissa? Something. I don't know. She was well known in the clan, though, in Saiz. Try there."

"And who attended my mother, that same week?"

"Ah, well." Masura took another drink. Narrowed her eyes. "Why is this important?"

"Do you remember, or not?"

"Of course I remember. I'm not that old." He didn't protest. "Javia went to childbed early, right after Nasaka.

They were both in the temple at the same time, so that Unissa... Unalina woman, she attended both. Yes, I remember that now. I remember thinking she looked quite young to have attended Nasaka's birth. Why did you want to know this?"

"I just needed a few questions answered. Thank you." He got up to leave.

Masura set her drink aside. "Ahkio, some advice."

"Of course."

"Let this lie. I suspect you know what you'll find if you dig."

"I already know who I am," he said. "Nasaka is a danger to me, and this country. She's betrayed us a hundred times. I don't know how to fight her, Masura. How does a man fight his own mother? A Dhai man? A peaceful man? How can I retain who I am while keeping this country safe?

"Ahkio, if you go after Ora Nasaka on this, trying to find some way to exile her, it will all come out. The whole country will know who birthed you. Do you understand? If you destroy Ora Nasaka, you destroy yourself."

"I don't know what else to do."

"I advise finding another route," Masura said. "Listen, Ahkio. Your mother exiled her sister Etena based on madness. The things Ora Nasaka has done in her life... are they not mad?

"They are."

"Then perhaps that is where the answer lies."

Madness. Was it that easy? It had been for Etena.

"Will you back me?" he asked. "I need you to back me, Ora Masura."

"Ahkio–"

"If she's exiled she can't hurt you."

Masura barked out a laugh. "Oh, I have heard that before. It's a lie."

"Back me for Javia," he said. "Back me on it for my

mother."

Masura's face crumpled. She nodded. "Ora Nasaka will kill me."

"She won't," Ahkio said. "She won't hurt anyone again."

Ahkio pressed himself against the doorway after he closed it, trying to get his head together. He would write up the papers tomorrow and call Ghrasia's militia to exile Nasaka for betrayal and madness. He had to do it now, before the chaos started. Before the harbor was breached. Before the Tai Mora came to her, ready to pay whatever debt it was they owed her.

He was Kai. He kept telling people he was. Javia had exiled her own sister for less.

He could certainly exile his own mother for the same.

23

Lilia woke, screaming, to fire.

Figures rushed around her. She heard a great rumbling in the distance, and tried to move her fingers. Her skin burned. Lilia rolled over and scratched her way forward. Her hands were blistered, covered in char. From the burned gate? Oras and militia ran madly around the parapet. Shrieking. A booming crash.

The gates shuddered. Lilia pulled herself up onto the edge of the parapet, and peered over. The Tai Mora ships had docked at the harbor, buoyed by the high tide. Hundreds of figures in chitinous blue and green armor flooded across the piers like shiny beetles, swarming the gates.

"Parajistas," Lilia huffed, but it hurt to breathe. She turned away and saw Naldri dead twenty feet up the walkway. A score of other bodies lay tangled across the top of the wall. The line of parajistas was long broken. Someone on the other side was shouting – Mohrai's voice, calling up the militia.

"Get off the wall!"

This came from someone further away, a woman dressed in the blue tunic and trousers of an Ora.

Lilia stared at the shimmering horde of invaders, and raised her fist. She drew a breath, and called on Oma.

Nothing happened.

She started coughing. Dropped her arm. She hacked and hacked, like hocking up some piece of her lung.

"Off the wall!" The Ora came toward her. "Are you hurt? I will carry you, if you permit it."

Lilia's vision swam. She did not recognize the Ora. "Where's Taigan?" she asked.

"We're retreating," the Ora said. "You're the last on the wall. I thought you were dead. May I take your arm?"

"Yes, all right."

The Ora looped a strong arm around her and hauled her down the steps just as a bubbling tide came over the lip of the parapet. Lilia glanced back and saw a great red algae swarm breach the wall.

The retreat from the harbor was a mad one, full of rushing bodies, shrieking, tears, sobs. Lilia navigated it all as though in some dream. She was ushered onto a cart with other injured. She fell back into a pile with the bloody, the bleeding, the maimed, and the newly dead.

She asked after Taigan, and Gian, but no one knew who she was speaking about. They had abandoned her up there on the wall. The betrayal hurt so badly she thought she might burst. She had lost Oma, and the worst had happened – her country invaded, her companions in retreat. Taigan had warned her about burning out. She tried to draw Oma again, and failed.

The other Dhai hushed her like she was some child. They did not know her. Lilia could get no answer about where they were going.

Her strength finally gave out. She collapsed in the back of the cart. From the rocking belly of the cart she watched the harbor gates burst open. A steely army of hundreds poured into the Asona Clan square and surrounding warehouses and shops. The square went up in moments, burning uncontrollably. In a quarter hour, the surrounding forest and grassland were on fire as well, sending choking clouds of smoke into the air.

Thick bands of smoke pushed forward ahead of the fire, low against the ground, as if some parajista manipulated their path. The smoke was a living thing, hot and cloying. Lilia saw the roiling blackness pursuing them, and knew she would not survive it. Her lungs still ached. Her skin was hot and painful. She tried to draw on Oma again, desperate. Burned out. It sounded final. Like death.

Cries came from the people around her – large family groups, traders; lost, screaming children picked up by strangers, their faces smeared in soot from the explosion at the gates. My explosion, Lilia thought. She closed her eyes, and the burning power of Oma filled her again.

She reached…

Nothing.

Lilia retched over the side of the cart.

Smoke rolled over a nearby creek. The smoke did not follow the curvature of the ground. There was clear air above the creek bed. As the smoke rose, a parajista barrier above it kept it from escaping.

The smoke chased them another mile. When Lilia could reach out her hand and touch it, she rolled out of the cart, and into the huffing legion of refugees. She could not raise her breath to shout, to urge them to keep low, but she tried anyway, calling until the smoke clogged her nostrils and she had to press her face to the ground to breathe.

She held the ground tight. People ran past her and over her, hacking and coughing. Lilia crawled toward the streambed, wheezing. Someone tripped over her, a small girl. Lilia grabbed her ankle, hissed, "Stay low. Stay against the ground."

The little girl trembled like ashy paper. She pressed herself against Lilia. She was only six or seven, far from the age of consent, so Lilia took her by the arm without asking, and told her to come along.

"My mothers–"

"They'll find you," Lilia lied, because in truth they ran through a death trap, like rats smoked out by poison.

Lilia tumbled into the streambed. She submerged her scorched, aching body. She lay her face in the mud and remained still. Beside her, the girl did the same, taking great gasping breaths of clean air while the black smoke moved over them like a shroud.

As Lilia watched the back of the girl's head, she was reminded of Nirata's granddaughter, Esau. Sliced in two when the portal between Dorinah and Dhai closed. A seared side of meat. Half a person. A needless death.

Lilia smoothed the girl's hair and held her tight, like calming a terrified rabbit. The girl's heart pounded harder than her own.

"What's your name?" Lilia asked.

"Tasia."

"We'll wait until the smoke is gone, then we'll follow after the others."

"But won't the Dorinahs come?"

Dorinah. Is that what everyone thought they were?

Tasia said, "There are so many of them. Why do they hate us?"

"I don't know," Lilia said, because though something more complex than hate fueled this invasion, she could not imagine killing something she did not hate – like those Dorinah legionnaires.

But the image of Esau flashed in front of her again; a little girl killed so one selfish, desperate person could get out of a terrible situation.

Was Lilia any better than the Tai Mora, in that moment?

She lay still in the creek bed. Tears rolled down her cheeks. The smoke moved past them. The air cleared.

Tasia poked her head up.

"Stay down," Lilia said. She shifted painfully up the edge of the creek bed and peeked over. Dozens of bodies littered the grassy plain. The fire still burned north of them – Asona on fire, and the woods blazing – but it would be some time before it caught up to them.

She gestured for Tasia to come up. Together they limped across the trampled grass. Lilia moved among the bodies, collecting food and a water sling, searching for other useful items. She found a large stone, and slipped it in her pocket.

"There are so many of them," Tasia said.

Lilia wasn't sure if she meant the bodies, or the Tai Mora.

"How will we fight them?" Tasia said, and there was a note of fear in the voice, a note that told Lilia the girl was about to start shrieking. Shrieking would put them both in danger. It was likely the Tai Mora would send scouts ahead of the main force. She would have.

"We must be clever," Lilia said. She came up short. There was a figure lying on the ground near the trees on the other side of the road, crawling on all fours, making terrible hacking sounds. It wore red armor shiny as any beetle's carapace.

"Stay here," Lilia told Tasia, and she crept toward the figure. She pulled the stone from her pocket and brandished it in her good hand.

The figure raised its head. The face was mostly covered in the flat planes of the helm. She saw two eyes, a hint of a chin. But it was not only the smoke that felled them. There was a crack in the helm at the back. She recognized the sap and residual peridium of a capsillium plant, all sticky and bubbling around a hole in the back of the helm. They must have stumbled into a mating plant, and gotten stuck with its pollinator.

Lilia raised the rock and smashed it into the open wound. The figure jerked. She hit it again, in the same place, and again, until blood spattered her arm and the helm was cracked even further. The armor wasn't metal, but chitin. Once cracked, it gave way easily around the wound.

She sat for a long moment over the prone body, trying to catch her breath. Then she gently pulled off the helmet. The face was twisted. Lilia regarded the helmet, remembering her ruse with Zezili on the other world.

"We need to bring this armor with us," Lilia said. "Can you help me take it off?"

"Is it dead?"

"Yes. Don't be afraid. If we take this armor we can fool them if they get too close. I can pretend I'm one of them."

"It's too big for you."

It sounded like an accusation. Lilia found herself irrationally angry. To survive an attack on the harbor, to botch it so badly, to lose her power, to crawl into a creek bed and escape certain death, and here was this child, seeing right through her, all her big and important ideas, fanned by Taigan's great expectations for her. Taigan, who had abandoned her on the wall. And where was Gian? When the end came, they all ran. They cared for her only so long as she was useful, one no better than the other. And this little girl knew. Knew the task Lilia had been given was far beyond her capabilities. She had no power now. Maybe she never had.

Lilia started to cry. She gripped the helmet and sobbed, a few choking huffs. It lasted half a minute, maybe more. Then she knelt next to the dead scout and started pulling off the armor, piece by awkward piece.

"Cleverness," she said aloud. "Not with swords."

Clever, like the Seekers had been, hiding from their Empress and the Tai Mora in plain sight.

Were the Seekers still bound to her? Taigan had created the ward, and she had bound it with her own hand. Lilia went very still, searching for some tenuous connection to the five Seekers. She found them fluttering at the edges of her consciousness, in the same place she reached for and did not find Oma; some bundled reserve of power tethering her to them. She closed her eyes and pulled at the lines of power. She knew no litany to draw them to her. But a ward, once set, could only be undone when the one who made it released it, or some very skilled jista understood the maker well enough to figure out how to untangle it.

"Mother."

Lilia opened her eyes. Tasia had hold of her charred tunic. "Mother" was often used as a polite term for an older woman. No one had ever called Lilia that before. She was just a girl, wasn't she? But in this little girl's eyes, she saw that those days were long past, her childhood wants and desires, so simple, really, for a mother and a home, buried here on the killing field.

"We're going to Kuallina, child," Lilia said. "But we must be quiet and keep to the woods. You understand?"

"My parents are going to Kuallina."

"There, see? We'll find them together."

But as they started off, Lilia found she could barely walk more than a hundred paces before she was out of breath and exhausted. She had to dump the idea of hiding in the armor. As the girl pointed out, Lilia was too small, and weak. They rested often, following the curve of the creek.

"Look out for a little plant here in the creek bed," Lilia said. "Its roots are round and pop above the surface. The stems are mostly brown right now, but they grow long and tall as my arm."

Putting Tasia on the hunt was a good idea. It kept her busy, even when Lilia was wheezing along the creek bed. It was an hour before Tasia clapped her hands and announced she'd found the plant – raw mahuan.

Lilia dug into the cold mud and pulled out the bulbous yellow roots. She washed them, broke them apart, and chewed them, careful not to swallow.

"I'm hungry," Tasia said.

"It's not food," Lilia said. "It's medicine."

Raw mahuan was dangerous, but so was dying here,

asphyxiated like a beached sea creature. She broke out sticky rice and dried yams from the stores she'd taken from the dead, and sat silently chewing the mahuan root while Tasia ate and poked at things in the creek.

The army caught up to them that night.

Lilia camped up in the welcoming arms of a bonsa tree, its great bows so broad and thick that she could wedge herself into them without fearing a fall. Even so, her newfound fear of heights prevented her from going up more than six paces. It was enough. Tasia fell asleep almost immediately, bunched up close to Lilia in the leafy canopy. Lilia envied her. She lay awake watching the first wave of the army coming up the road, hacking and burning vegetation as they went to clear the way. The landscape of Dhai itself was a good defense. If people had any sense they would flee to the edges of things instead of bunching up in the clan squares. But they would want to be together, wouldn't they? Together until the end.

The potent mahuan root opened her lungs. She took her first full breath in a day sometime in the darkest part of the night, her brain buzzing, hands trembling. Her body felt very light. She gazed at the stars through the breaks in the trees, and pretended to be a bird, flying faster and faster, until her vision swam and her head ached and she vomited bile and chewed more mahuan root.

Tasia woke her at the blushing blue of Para's dawn. "There are women down there," Tasia said.

Lilia peered through the branches and saw four figures in hooded coats picking among the snarling brambles of floxflass and morvern's drake.

Lilia reached for her ward again, thumbing at the snarls of power still hidden there.

The figure at the front raised its head, then the other three. One actually fell to their knees, keening, and that drew Lilia up short.

She stopped poking at the ward.

Tulana pulled back her hood and peered up at her. There was a twist to her mouth that Lilia thought was anger, but when she spoke, the strained tone was not anger, but pain.

"Please desist that meddling," Tulana said. "I'd hoped you were dead."

Lilia palmed a bit of mahuan root from the bag at her side, and started chewing. Took a long, full breath.

"Where are the others?"

"Dead," Tulana said. Flat tone.

"The Tai Mora?"

"You," Tulana said. "Taigan didn't teach you how to use that foul shit you seared into us, and this is what it gets you."

"That wasn't my intention."

"Well, someone was going to murder us eventually," Tulana said. "You. The Tai Mora. The Empress." She laughed hollowly. She seemed to relax, now, though, as she came up under Lilia's roost.

"I need to get down," Lilia said. Her voice sounded tremulous, even to her. She said it again, more strongly, "Help me down."

"Use your little powers," Tulana said.

"I can order you."

"You are loathsome."

"How many Dhai have you killed, Tulana? You and your Seekers?"

"You've got more blood on your hands than I, girl."

"You're wrong." Lilia felt the mahuan working on her aching, blistered body. She could barely feel any pain anymore, and breathing was like a dream, almost as lovely as when she could draw on Oma.

Tasia clung to her, trembling again. "Come and get the child," Lilia said, and Tulana reluctantly raised her arms.

Tasia gave Lilia a furtive look, but obeyed, far more trusting than Tulana. What would this little girl think, if she knew what Lilia was?

Lilia went down next. She asked for no help, and none moved to help her. She fell, stumbled to her hands and knees, and shuffled to her feet with great difficulty.

"Where did you come from?" Lilia asked.

"The Dhai from the clans, all the ones stretching from here to the harbor, are meeting at a large stronghold inland. Kuallina? That's where we were headed before… you called."

Lilia glanced at the faces of the remaining Seekers – mean-faced Voralyn with the streak of gray hair in the black; plump Amelia; and Laralyn, the youngest. They were missing the man, Sokai, the lean, wolfish one who went everywhere with Tulana, the one Lilia once saw her singing to.

She glanced back at Tulana. "I am sorry, again."

"There is no real regret," Tulana said, "and no forgiveness to be had, between master and slave."

"Did you tell your dajians that?"

"To make someone free into a slave is far worse than–"

"We bleed the same," Lilia said. "I gave you a choice, and you made it." Tasia clung to her frayed tunic. "Now which of you is a healer? Voralyn?" Lilia held out her blistered hands. Patches of her skin were weeping fluid. "Attend this, and then we must get back around the army to Kuallina."

"You intend to make a stand there?" Tulana said. Sarcastic, almost sneering. "That did not turn out well last time."

"We were unprepared. I have something else in mind." Lilia spit the wad of mahuan pulp, and snapped off another bit.

"Some fool plan," Tulana said. "You nearly killed us all last time."

"The plan I had would have worked," Lilia said, too sharply. "We never got a chance to use it. Something went wrong at the harbor. We should have had more time. But we didn't. So you can follow me, or die here.

The same as in Dorinah." She almost plucked at the wards again. Almost. The worn, exhausted look on Voralyn's face reminded her too much of Kalinda Lasa. When had she become a monster? She pressed her hand to Tasia's head.

Esau.

It had started with Esau, the little girl lost in the seams between things.

Now it was too late. There was no turning back. Someone had to fight the monsters.

Who better than a monster?

24

Ahkio sat with Nasaka in the Kai study. Or, rather, he stood, fingers pressed to the table, voice raised about lines of supply to the harbor, and Nasaka sat across from him, one leg bent over the other, expression unreadable.

It was his new assistant, one of his former students from Osono, Rimey, who ran in with the news, ran all the way across the Assembly Chamber, so Ahkio had time to stop his yelling before she blurted, "The harbor has fallen."

Nasaka did not even turn.

"Did Mohrai send a report?" Ahkio asked.

"Ora Hasina did," she said. "They're uncertain of casualties. When she sent word, they were fleeing."

"Where?" Ahkio asked.

"Kuallina," Nasaka said.

Ahkio raised his brows.

"It's the next logical holdout," she said. "The only other place with any defense. The temples are too small to hold the kinds of populations that must be evacuated, and Liona–"

"Enough," Ahkio said. "You have the letter?"

Rimey handed it over.

It was brief, maddeningly short on details:

Lines broke. Harbor walls breached. Retreating to Kuallina.

"Oma's breath," Ahkio said.

"We'll need to divert supplies to Kuallina," Nasaka said.

"Do it," he said. When she did not move, he raised his voice. "Go, Nasaka."

She rose slowly. "Of course, Kai." She sauntered out.

Rimey waited in the door, staring at him.

"What?" he said.

"There are other bad rumors. The drudges are saying–"

"I don't need rumors, Rimey. I need facts." She was younger than Caisa, smart, but moving her from Osono to Oma's Temple had proved a great adjustment for her. She wandered around with wide eyes and jumped at loud words.

"Kuallina is not ready for them. They can't hold that many refugees. They sent a message to Ora Una."

"She didn't see fit to tell me this?"

"I think she told Ora Nasaka."

"Of course she did." He wiped at his face. "All right. We're running out of time. Get me Liaro. We need to make another trip to the basements. I also need Ora Soruza. We'll need every Ora we have at Kuallina."

"But you said–"

"What did I say?" Too sharply, he knew, but he was tired.

"I'll get Liaro."

"And Ora Soruza. Have them meet me in the Sanctuary."

Ahkio put away his papers. Wasted time, all of it. He felt like that's all Nasaka wanted to do – waste his time. With so few details on the harbor, he craved a first-hand account. Information was scattered here, and too much of it filtered through Nasaka.

Liaro came up just as he was changing his clothes in the adjacent Kai quarters.

"You heard about the harbor?" Liaro asked.

"I did. Do you know any other details?"

"Only that it fell. A runner just came in by Lift from Kuallina with someone who was there."

"Mohrai?"

"No, I don't think so."

"Why didn't Rimey tell me that?"

"It just happened. As I was coming up I saw them in the Lift chamber and asked."

They plunged downstairs and intercepted the two people who had arrived by Lift, a member of the Kuallina militia who looked vaguely familiar and a soot-stained young woman with a badly burned arm wrapped in linen.

"This is the Kai," the militia member said.

"What's happened?" he asked, and felt a fool for it, because she was hurt and he had no manners.

"They brought down the harbor."

"The Tai Mora?"

"Yes. I'm the Catori's cousin, Alhina. I was on the wall when the lines broke."

"Did you provoke an attack?"

"No, we were still preparing our offensive."

"Offensive?"

"It's a long story."

"Where is everyone? Mohrai? What about the scullery girl, Lilia? Did she betray us? Was she theirs?"

"I'm sorry, Kai, I don't know very much. Mohrai is in Kuallina. We were some of the first to get there. The scullery girl, she… she died on the wall. It was a bloody mess, Kai. It was… it was awful. I never thought… I never imagined…"

"Have you heard anything of Liona?" he asked the militia member. "Can we divert some of the refugees there?"

"When we left there were reports coming in. Rumors, mostly. There's strife in Dorinah. Armies on the move. I'm sure someone will send a proper missive when they know more."

A proper missive, straight to Nasaka.

"Thank you both. Please, go down to the infirmary. They'll see to that arm. You can get something to eat in the kitchens."

Ahkio motioned Liaro back to the scullery stair to avoid accompanying them down. He could move faster.

"What are you planning?" Liaro asked.

"I need to get back down to the basements." He had gained back a day, once. Could he stop the invasion at the harbor? Warn them? He could get himself onto the wall and find a way...

"Ahkio, let's not get on this again. You said she told you she couldn't help you–"

"This is a special situation."

"I know you're desperate now, because you're relying on seers and mystics and hallucinations."

Ahkio rounded on him. "Stop with that. Do you have anything better to add? A great plan? A way to stop a massive Tai Mora army from crushing us? Because that's what's likely to happen. Everyone told me I couldn't stop this, and yes, they're right. With no one behind me, and Nasaka working against me, with us grabbing at each other's throats and my own people turning against me, they're right, we can't. But I'm not going to roll over and die here, Liaro. So will you help me, or stand here and make jokes?"

Liaro said nothing. The expression on his face was so hurt that Ahkio had to turn away. He continued down the stairs.

He met Ora Soruza in the Sanctuary – a tall, plump person with cropped curly hair and a squint. Ahkio told Soruza bluntly that they needed every parajista in the temple at Kuallina.

"Have you contacted Ora Naldri?" Soruza asked. "There are plenty of parajistas at Para's temple. We have only–"

"Ora Naldri is dead," Ahkio said. "The harbor has

fallen. I have no idea how many of those parajistas are still alive. If Kuallina is going to hold, it needs parajistas."

"Kai, we have only fifty full parajistas here. I'd prefer we kept at least half here, in case–"

"If the army gets to the temples, we're lost," Ahkio said. "Keep a dozen here, if that makes you feel better, but I can tell you now – they've broken the harbor. If Kuallina and Liona go, we're finished."

"We should really call the Ora council," Soruza said. "A full council meeting–"

"You mean you want to ask Nasaka," Ahkio said. "You should know that Nasaka is being stripped of her position, and won't be in this country much longer. I suggest you consider again what will happen if Kuallina falls, and send those Oras, or I will do it myself."

"Kai, strategy is not... perhaps if Ghrasia–"

"Ghrasia is not here," Ahkio said. "It's possible we lost a good many people at the harbor. Do you understand our position yet?"

Soruza nodded curtly. "I am beginning to appreciate it."

"Please, Soruza," he said. "That army will murder them all in Kuallina without reinforcements from us."

"All right," Soruza said.

"Thank you." Ahkio left the Sanctuary and went to Una's office. She was gone, but her assistant was there. He demanded the keys to the basements, which the boy handed over with wide eyes.

Liaro followed him silently down the steps to the warm bathing room, then along the broad corridor running to the second basement entrance. Down and down, like disappearing into the belly of the world.

As he stepped up to the door of the sixth basement, Liaro said, softly, "Please don't do this again."

Ahkio glanced back at him. Liaro's expression was pained, almost sick. "What's wrong?"

"You don't know how you looked when you touched

that stone," Liaro said. "You were dead. Like a stone corpse. Don't do it again, please. What if you don't come back this time?"

"Then Nasaka can burn the temples to the ground," Ahkio said. "I can stop the harbor."

"We can go away," Liaro said.

"What?"

"Evacuate the temples. We can go to Tordin or Aaldia or–"

"As refugees?" Ahkio said. "Have you seen how countries treat refugees? You've seen what we are in Dorinah. I won't see us be slaves again."

"If this is a war that can't be won–"

"I have to exhaust every possibility," Ahkio said. "Whatever this temple was made to do can turn these people back. We must understand it."

"You said it was broken."

"You can go back up, Liaro, but I need to put this to rest."

Ahkio opened the door.

On the other side, Nasaka and Una waited for him, sitting on one of the great roots, sharing the light of a flame fly lantern.

An icy knot of fear bloomed in Ahkio's gut. He did not cross the threshold.

"I've been very curious about what you've been up to down here," Nasaka said. "Ora Una suggested that I simply ask you directly. What do you think of that, Ahkio? Some direct conversation."

"We have nothing to speak about. Get out of here."

"The temple belongs to the Dhai," Nasaka said. "You're merely the Kai. And, as we have learned this last decade, the place of a Kai is very precarious."

"Are you threatening me now?"

"Not at all. I'm inviting you to show me to the center of this level, and demonstrate exactly what that stone does. You know, don't you? You've activated it."

"Do you have any idea what's happened in the harbor?"

"Yes," Nasaka said. "I predicted it. At every turn, I've tried to prevent this horror from happening, but you thwarted my advice again and again. Why? Because it came from me? Perhaps I should have put it into the lips of one you trust more."

"Get out of here before I remove you," Ahkio said. Facing her now, in the quiet of the basements, with only sour-faced Una and Liaro-who-had-fallen-on-his-own-sword, he knew he had little but words. He didn't even wear a weapon. Never had. Nasaka wore hers.

"And how do you intend to remove me?" Nasaka asked. "I'm curious to know because there's a strong rumor you do intend to do it. Do you mean to murder me in my bed?"

"No," Ahkio said. The harbor was burning. It was all ending, and she wanted to play this game? Let them speak plainly, then. "I mean to have you exiled."

"And lose what I know about what we face? No. You won't."

"We've reached a point in this conflict where having you here is dividing our country."

"What's your charge, Kai? You mean to move against me?" She laughed. "I've done nothing in violation of any law, whether in the Book or in the amended constitutions. If you want to retain some semblance of authority, you must exile me thoroughly and correctly, and you can't do that."

"I can," Ahkio said. "For madness."

"That does sound terrible indeed," Nasaka said. "What proof do you have of that?"

"I'm Kai. My word is proof, is it not?"

"Not before any clan leader."

"Was your word proof enough to exile Etena?"

Nasaka said nothing, so he barreled on. "You have played this game straight, that's true," he said. "You didn't go against many direct edicts, but you planted the seeds of ideas. You got the Kais to do what you wanted, my mother and Kirana. But Kirana only to an extent, right? Because Etena got to her first."

He was rambling now, clawing at something that might get her to unmask herself. But what did it matter, if she did that here? These witnesses were few. He found himself glancing at her sword again. Some darker part of his mind told him he was fighting for his life now that he had threatened to exile her. She would fight him to the death for that.

Nasaka picked up the lantern. She walked right up to Ahkio, and though she stood on the steps below him, with him gazing down at her, he felt as if she were some towering specter, bathed in the eerie, flickering light of the lamps.

"You know what's so ironic?" Nasaka said. "I put you into this seat to save you, but you've done nothing but make it into a seat of thorns. And there's no reason for it, is there? Etena abdicated, yes, when she ran off into the woodlands into exile. But she is by right of birth and gift the true Kai of this temple. I wonder what will happen if she returns, and declares herself Kai again? Perhaps it will be better for you. Let us lift this responsibility from your weary shoulders."

"The harbor is *burning*, Nasaka."

"There are a million worlds," Nasaka said. "The harbor is burning in some, and not in others. The Tai Mora want a gateway to those worlds, one not bought with blood. They came to me a decade ago, looking for it. You've found it, haven't you, Ahkio?"

"I knew you were theirs," Ahkio said, but his voice broke, because the betrayal was so deep, even for Nasaka.

"They murdered you in front of me," Nasaka said. "Pulled me through some rip in the world and laid you out and slaughtered you like some animal. They said they would do it to all of us, eventually."

"What did they offer you?"

"Your life, and mine, and a few others. All I could save. Ten years I've worked to ensure that some sliver of our people survives this onslaught, and you have undone it all."

"I won't bargain away the entire country just to save a handful of lives. That's how we're different."

"I've seen what they'll do here, Ahkio. Now, sometimes, I wonder – are you the Ahkio I think you are, or some darker version, some imposter they sent to undo all my plans and ensure our eradication? How many worlds are there? Maybe there are many of you, pulled here just to thwart me."

She took his wrist. He fought her. Slip and pivot. He fell back into Liaro. Liaro's hands came up and held him still.

"Don't fight, Ahkio. Please," Liaro said.

Ahkio twisted out of his grip, shocked, and fell down the stairs. He landed hard and lost his breath. Nasaka grabbed Ahkio's leg and yanked him back. Ahkio kicked her with his free leg and rolled up. He took her arm and tried to use her as leverage to get to his feet. She twisted, and for a moment they danced around one another, locking and breaking one another's grips. She had taught him a great deal about self-defense after he returned from the burning of his family in Dorinah.

Nasaka punched him in the kidney. The pain was sharp. He went down. She pressed her knee into the small of his back and yanked his left arm behind him, rotating it sharply. He hissed.

"You taught me to fight," he said. "Did you ever think it would be you I was fighting?"

"Yes," Nasaka said.

Ahkio tried to catch Liaro's gaze. Liaro hung back in the doorway, face pained.

"Liaro," Ahkio said.

"It's for the best," Liaro said.

Another betrayal. Another ally turned. "You're not even one of the Tai Mora, are you?" Ahkio said, and the pain now was more than just physical. "Just another petty liar. And for what?"

"You're on a dangerous path. You said yourself the harbor is burning–"

"Liaro, please–"

"Ora Una! Help me take him to the cells," Nasaka said. Ahkio howled.

25

The faces of Harajan were grown into every surface – from the cats' eyes hewn into either side of the broad round gates to the playful, puff-cheeked heads of slaves that made up the doorknobs of every room in the hold – even the slave quarters. The portraits in the walls were not mounted, but living things, trained to grow and renew themselves into just this pattern by some long-dead tirajista sorcerer. It had been weeks since Driaa brought Maralah word that the pass had opened up. The weather had broken the day before, and she looked forward to sparring outside with Driaa wearing far fewer cumbersome clothes than usual. With the weather broken and Taigan on the way, she almost felt hopeful.

Maralah passed portrait after portrait on her way through the blue-glowing corridors. The bioluminescent fungi lining the ceiling and edges of the walkway were nearly bright enough to read by, but they cast the portraits in grotesque shadows. She could not shake the feeling that perhaps some sinajista had captured the souls of the men and women and ataisa bearing these faces a thousand years ago and stored them here, a treasure trove of power held in reserve, for just such a time as this.

She let her fingers tarry over the portraits as she went,

but could sense nothing inside of them – no fiery, tingling essence of power. Sina was descendent, and though some mornings she woke quite certain she could feel it coming back into the world, most days her connection was just this – a tenuous flickering at the back of her mind.

The hurried footsteps ahead of her gave her pause. She expected the Tai Mora any day.

Rainaa, one of the Patron's slaves, rounded the corner, and nearly collided with her.

"Where are you off to?" Maralah asked, fearing the worst. If Rainaa had come, it meant Rajavaa was dead.

"Wraisau's boy sent me to find you," Rainaa said. "There's an army at the gates."

"Tai Mora?"

"I don't know."

Maralah pushed past her. "Where is Kovaas?"

"Western tower."

"Find Driaa and Morsaar and have them meet us there."

Maralah hurried toward the central keep and into the broad courtyard, still heaped with dirty snow. The sun was out, and she could hear dripping water. The kennel masters were exercising the animals, but there were no sanisi training in the yard. She thought that odd, but suspected many were already on the walls.

She scanned the top of the twisted ramparts. They pulsed with green and blue defenses – a misty, static barrier that could repel a fist or a blade equally. She saw two sanisi there, and counted six regular infantry. That was a few more infantry than usual, but if there was an army out there, it should have drawn gawkers. She drew the short blade at her hip, just in case.

Maralah gripped the puff-cheeked slaves' head of the doorknob leading up into the western tower, and stepped inside.

The interior was dark. She squinted, momentarily blinded by the abrupt change from the sunny, snow-white courtyard to dim tower. The air felt heavy. She swore.

A great weight thumped into her chest.

Maralah reeled, knocking back into something solid. Her ears popped. A great force squeezed her body rigid, capturing her arms against her sides. It yanked her into the room. The door slammed behind her.

She hung suspended several feet above the floor in the tower foyer, strung so tight it hurt to breathe. She tried to focus on the shadowy figures around her.

"Kill her?"

"Wait for Morsaar."

Bloody fuck, Maralah thought. He had moved faster than she anticipated. Army at the gates, indeed. She felt like a child.

She sucked in a shallow breath. "Patron," she wheezed. "My brother?"

She didn't know why she asked. She knew this song. She had sung it herself.

"Morsaar is Patron."

Maralah squinted again, and saw the speaker was an infantry man. But the sanisi? Who was the parajista who held her? What traitorous coward had turned?

"No one is Patron until I say so," Maralah growled.

The air around her contracted. She wheezed.

Her vision finally adjusted. She saw Driaa standing to the left of the infantryman, a neutral expression on hir face.

Maralah said, "This close to the end, you side with him?"

"I told you to take it while you could," Driaa said. "I did come to you first."

Maralah heard footsteps. She raised her head, straining to see if Morsaar would dare face her. But no, it was just more infantry, and two sanisi. All of them were covered in blood. Killing themselves. At least the Dhai had killed and eaten each other, and made some use of all that death. She would just be burned.

"The Patron wants her locked up," one of the men said.

Maralah felt a shiver of relief. Morsaar still wanted something from her.

"The Tai Mora," Maralah said. "Are they here?"

"Not yet," the man said, and she recognized him as a confidant of Morsaar's, "but soon enough. You think we didn't know how to get you to come running?"

"None of this matters," Maralah said.

"Shut her up," the man said.

The air constricting Maralah's chest grew heavier, tightening like a noose. She gasped. Her mouth filled with heavy air, thick as soup.

Black spots juddered across her vision.

Sina, she called. Sina, my star, my breath, where are you?

She felt a tremulous snarl of power in answer, and saw a little puff of violet mist.

Then blackness.

26

Saradyn stood inside the shadowy square as morning burned away the last of the frost, a week after returning from his sweep of the rebellious village, Mordid. He watched Rosh and her ghosts die at the noose. He waited only until her ghosts faded, and her feet had ceased to jerk. Then he turned away, pulled his hood up over his shaggy hair, and went back to the hold to inspect Natanial's hostage.

"He's been quiet," Itague said as he led Saradyn down the narrow stair into the tight corridors of the gaol. "The bitch-boy whined for water and a pot, but once he had it, got real still. Might be sick. He's skinny as a virgin."

Itague opened a broad door at the end of the corridor. Cold air and light seeped from a high barred window at the far end of the room. The cell was meant for the more important sorts of prisoners, nobility and high-ranking officers. The bed was big, set on plain wooden planking. The sheets were stained. There was a table, a chair, a handful of candles, and a low, bookless shelf. A boy lay curled on the bed, dressed all in Dorinah fashion. There were other figures in the room – a misty stir above the boy; a quivering old woman in one corner; an emaciated man hanging from a noose tied to the bars of the window.

Saradyn moved toward the figure on the bed. The

ghosts turned to watch him.

The boy looked up. He was filthy, unshaven. He had knotted the matted length of his hair back from his face. He had big brown eyes, sharp cheekbones, a strong chin, but his form was that of a child. He was thinnest in the hips, broader at the shoulders, a Dorinah deformity encouraged in men through the wearing of bindings that emphasized the inverted triangle of a man's form.

Behind the boy were female ghosts, a roiling stir of them – a freckled woman with a face like a dog, a woman's dark torso, the eyes of a bitter old woman with rotten teeth, and more, mostly disjointed, merging, bickering, a gaggle of oppressive faces.

Saradyn grimaced. He would not spend long in this boy's company. His brood of ghosts was maddening. Saradyn had no idea how the boy could live with them.

The boy pushed himself back against the wall. He still wore his binding, though it was as dirty and tattered as the rest of him.

"Does he speak Tordinian?" Saradyn asked Itague.

Itague juggled the keys. He was looking at the desk. "No, just Dorinah."

Saradyn went over his limited vocabulary of Dorinah. He could speak it, after a fashion. The words tasted bad on his tongue. "Husband, Hasaria?"

"Yes," the boy said. "She's my wife, she–" He broke into a long tirade, too fast for Saradyn to catch.

Saradyn held up a hand. "Slow," he said. "Explain."

"I don't know anything! She doesn't tell me anything. You're Saradyn, aren't you? I know you, I heard you were–"

He flitted off again into nattering.

Saradyn swore, turned to Itague. "Do they teach them to talk like women, too?"

Itague shrugged his big shoulders. "Never met no Dorinah man before. This what they make of us there, I'll burn every witch from here to the sea."

"Clean him up. Get him some proper clothes. Find me the historian. I want to have him ready some news for press."

"Think he'll be useful?"

"He's worth a fortune," Saradyn said. "Dorinah women take great pride in their men. They're given as prizes. To lose him is a great disgrace. She'll pay. It will fund our efforts to unite Tordin."

"Yes, sir," Itague said.

Saradyn pushed back into the foyer, and whistled for Dayns and Sloe.

The dogs followed Saradyn to the library just off the reception hall. He found a servant and asked for ale.

The historian arrived some time later, eyes downcast, nodding his too-big head and stirring his hand in the air, asking for tolerance for his truancy.

"May I sit, lord?" the historian asked.

"No, this will be short," Saradyn said. "I want you to rewrite the history of Galind."

The man's throat bobbed. "How would you like it changed, lord?"

"Bring me what's written. I'll decide from there."

"Lord, they are all rather short, written by Faytin Villiam during the time of the Thief Queen. I don't–"

"Then bring them to me. Don't presume to know my interests."

"Yes, lord."

"That is all."

"Yes, lord. Thank you, lord."

The historian crept from the room.

Saradyn had picked the man up outside a puppet show in Caratyd, where he sat with slate and chalk, writing blessings for children. He could recite a lot of epics, but Saradyn found himself increasingly dissatisfied with his ability to pen them. The histories of Saradyn's reign thus far were still the old ones written during the Thief Queen's time, which – when they spoke of him at all – ridiculed him as one of Penelodyn's lackeys, a poor guardian to the Thief Queen, and a disgrace to his home nation. They may not sing them aloud in his presence anymore, but he heard them outside every public house in the moments before he crossed their thresholds. He understood the importance of stories. He needed to be a heroic figure.

His best astronomers told him war was coming – the harbinger of Laine's wrath, Oma, was rising. It could destroy everything he had built, or usher in a new era of ascendance, where he was lord not only of Tordin, but all of Grania. Times of great change had to be seized, not squandered. And he needed someone to shape what he had done – an epic to be sung alongside Laine's praises.

Saradyn stepped to the heavy lectern that supported his massive copy of *The Book of Laine,* and frowned over the tattered pages. He would need to set a scribe to recopying it.

A knock at the door startled him. "Yes," he said.

Itague entered, carrying a letter with a broken seal. "Pardon, lord–"

"Why've you broken my letter?" Saradyn said.

"It was addressed to Tanays," Itague said. "It's a... report from the north."

"Why've you brought it to me?" Saradyn said, taking the paper.

"Tanays went cold as death when he read it. Told me to give it to you."

Saradyn peeled open the letter. It was from the temporary governor he'd put in charge of Mordid. Saradyn skimmed the text, and grunted. Reading was not his strongest suit, which frustrated him. He suspected he'd read something wrong. He shoved it back at Itague.

"What's this nonsense?"

"The governor says that girl ran away, back to Mordid. The dissident girl. Rosh."

"That's impossible," Saradyn said.

Itague shrugged. "Then that governor is mad, or someone is impersonating her. Rosh is alive, he says, back to leading those rogues against us."

Saradyn felt a cold chill creep up his spine. "I watched her die."

"Then she must be a ghost," Itague said, and laughed.

Saradyn did not.

Saradyn pushed out of the main hold and across the courtyard. The night was deep. He needed to leave for that little no-nothing settlement in the morning to search for Rosh – he didn't trust anyone else, as they didn't have his talents – but not before securing a bit of help. He stepped up into the apartments above the kennels. Saw light under the door at the end of the hall. He pushed the door open.

Natanial stood naked at the center of the room, illuminated by the crackling fire. He was still tossing away his tunic. He turned to Saradyn, his handsome face licked in shadows. Saradyn had seen Natanial naked on any number of occasions, but his body was still sometimes unsettling. He had the slender, wiry torso of some young, virile man – he could have been one of Laine's blessed sons. But nestled in the dark, wiry hair between his legs was not anything Saradyn would associate with a man. Saradyn assumed Natanial had been castrated, or suffered some injury that left him without balls or most of a cock, but never asked. There were some things, among men, one did not ask.

"What can I do for you?" Natanial said. He made no effort to cover himself, but sat down in a broad chair. He hooked one leg over the edge, baring his genitals. It was the confidence Saradyn appreciated most about him – the absolute fearlessness.

"I need you to come with me and kill a girl."

"Easy enough."

"I've already killed her once."

"Well, that is something."

"If people I kill start coming back to life, I don't need that getting out." He didn't believe resurrection was the miracle at work here, but he needed to be sure. With Laine's harbinger coming back to the world, any number of strange things could happen.

Natanial guffawed, but cut it short when Saradyn did not share his mirth.

"You're serious?"

"I am."

"I'll take care of it, then. Anything else?"

"Put some clothes on," Saradyn said.

"Whatever my glorious liege wishes," Natanial said, but he did not move from the chair. "I have a boon to request, though."

"Why should I grant it?"

"You'll turn the Dorinah man over to your wind witches," Natanial said. Not a question. It's what Saradyn did with all of the new jistas they uncovered. Still, it surprised him that Natanial knew Saradyn had no intention of ransoming the boy. Oh, he would collect a ransom, but he would not return him.

"You know the answer. He's raw, untrained. A danger to himself and others. You could have ended up in that dying world. You got lucky."

"And he will be a great asset," Natanial said. "A man who can so naturally open doors not across worlds, but across countries."

Saradyn said nothing. He suffered many fools under his command, but Natanial was not one of them.

"No one has been able to unite Tordin because of the geography," Natanial said. "The distances are not great, but moving armies through woods that spring up again half a season after you cut them, trundling over great hill monsters and through clusters of–"

"I'm aware of the issues around Tordin's lack of cohesive governance."

"I see how they train the jistas," Natanial said. "The boy is used to pain. He's learned to enjoy it. Those methods won't help him."

"You think you can turn him?"

"I think putting him into the hands of a woman is the last thing you should do right now."

"You think a Dorinah will be more loyal to his teacher than to me?"

"I can train him," Natanial said. "I know better teachers, with better methods."

"You question my methods?"

"Only for this boy."

"So he is a boy now?"

"I spent much time in his company," Natanial said. "It was often like speaking to a child. Grant me this and my next assignment for you is free."

"Any assignment?"

"Any save a monarch, yes. He'll still be yours, Saradyn. All I ask is that I help shape him. He still thinks you plan to ransom him to Zezili Hasaria."

A disturbing request from any man, a plea for one of his weapons. Saradyn understood treachery. He had been treacherous himself.

"Is this some lecherous thing?" Saradyn said.

Natanial laughed. "Would that it were," he said. "He's Dorinah."

As if that explained everything. But Saradyn had to take that into account. Dorinah men were a different breed, twisted and hobbled like chattel. To twist them further...

"How long?" Saradyn asked.

"Until the autumn."

"But you have my Aaldia assignment."

"I do. He'll come with me. What better test than seeing if he can open a door again for your most prized assassin?"

"You overly flatter yourself. I have less brazen assassins."

"But none so handsome," Natanial said.

"None so arrogant," Saradyn said.

"I can use him to open doors between here and Aaldia, here and Dorinah, here and into the bedroom of whatever petty lord in Tordin you want to die. When he's learned that, we can teach him to transport whole armies across this world, and it will be yours for the taking."

"You think my witches can't do this same thing?"

"To this boy? No. I do not."

Saradyn perceived no ill intention. If Natanial wanted him dead, he would have killed him long ago. If he worked for some other lord, Saradyn could have sniffed that out easily. But Natanial was no one, nothing – a man with a brutal past from some backwater village. No family, no lovers, no ties. If he cared for this boy – in whatever way he cared for him – that gave Saradyn leverage over him in a way that he had never had before. And to have an advantage over his assassin…

"Then take him," Saradyn said. "But I expect results. I want him to move an army by the end of summer, and the season is moving swiftly."

"Done," Natanial said.

Saradyn left him. In the hall, he whistled to Dayns and Sloe. They padded after him. Something about Natanial always unsettled and enraged him, but he found the idea of beating fear into him distasteful. Fear would see him lose that arrogant swagger, that perfect confidence. And fear, Saradyn knew, would make Natanial run. He was not a man to be bought or controlled on fear. Saradyn had not gotten as far as he had by misreading men.

Or whatever it was Natanial pretended to be.

27

Kirana's army swept through Dorinah like a plague. She likened it to a campaign she ran very early in the Great War, just before the toxic star entered the sky and everything went to Sina's maw. She needed blood, badly, to fuel the gates and find the missing omajistas the resistance was secreting away across a dozen worlds between hers and this one. She needed death in numbers she did not yet have an army large enough to mete out, so she relied on plague. Yisaoh worked at a field hospital in those days, and Kirana had her fold up the sheets and clothes and comforters of the dead, then donated them to the trading ships heading to the newly discovered northern continents.

Her army came in two weeks behind the plague, and bottled up blood to ship back to her omajistas. They took an entire northern continent like that. Later, she kept portions of every nation intact to swell the ranks of her army. Plague only worked on isolated populations.

Still, the memory of the villages of corpses in the north was strong as she walked the empty Dorinah towns. She had come upon them so unexpectedly the Empress hadn't had time to mobilize her legions.

She marched straight to Daorian, knowing that once the Empress's seat fell, there would be very little resistance. The upside to the Empress's absolute, unchanging dynasty was that it left very few powerful families in the field to take her place.

"Why so little resistance?" Gaiso asked several weeks into the campaign while they lay camped outside Ladiosyn. Kirana had called her four line commanders together – Gaiso, Madah, Monshara, Yivsa – and Lohin, her intelligence officer.

Lohin said, "She's sent two legions to Sebastyn on an unknown assignment. That's been verified. Without those, she has just two legions left inside the country that can move quickly enough to oppose us. One is already in place around Dorinah. If we can move quickly, we may reach it before the second. The eastern legion is behind us."

"Hoping to smash us against the walls of Daorian," Kirana said. "Not a bad idea. How are we doing with the dajians?" she asked Madah.

Madah was a slim young woman, and looked much like her mother Ghrasia. It had been easier to kill the Madah in this world than her mother, alas. Kirana had wanted to bring over her own Ghrasia. For now, the daughter would have to do. Circumstances were bound to change as the war progressed. They would get this world's Ghrasia eventually. It was only a matter of time.

"A few stragglers," Madah said, "but we're making progress." She made as if to say more, but firmed her mouth. She was a fast-talking woman most days, but she had taken up the habit in recent weeks of cutting herself off after a few sentences and pressing her finger to her mouth, as if urging herself to quiet.

"The farms?" Kirana asked Gaiso.

Gaiso pointed to three large homesteads marked on the map near the lake where they'd crossed over. "These three are being worked now, by our own people. We had six we needed to come through who were stopped at the gate. Somewhere there's six here that are still alive. So we've had to make do."

"Keep the farms untouched. I need every one assigned to our own people."

Gaiso said, "Bringing in a dozen at a time isn't enough to work a farm."

"Without the mirror, this is what we have. We need those farms producing." The mirror, her greatest triumph and greatest failure. She could have dumped an army big enough to colonize Saiduan in six hours if they'd had that mirror operational. Monshara had never given her a satisfactory answer about what had happened. She said only that she had been followed, and the mirror sabotaged. If they weren't so close to the end, she'd have killed Monshara for spite.

"Without dajians–" Madah began.

Kirana frowned at the map. She could bring all her people over, but that was worth nothing if they starved in three months. "Then we switch strategies," she said, remembering the shift she made after the plague left no one to join her army. "Let's save ten percent of every village we rout, to work the farms. Just make sure they're Dorinahs, not dajians."

Monshara shifted her weight. Kirana said, "You have any problem with this, Monshara?"

"Not at all," Monshara said. "She isn't my Empress."

"No, I am," Kirana said. "And it's a testament to my faith in you and your abilities that you're alive after your little fuck up."

Monshara bunched up her mouth into something very like a grimace. Outside the tent, it would have been.

"You know Yisaoh isn't among the dajians here," Gaiso said.

"Maybe, maybe not," Kirana said, "but the shadow of someone's lover or wife or husband or near-cousin certainly is. Eliminating these mirror images helps everyone. Are we decided, then?"

Lohin said. "There's the matter of Nava Sona."

"I'm saving her for Daorian," Kirana said. "That's the problem with shadows. She isn't nearly as well trained as our Nava was. Osoria says she tested with half the ability as our Nava. How that's possible, I don't know. But an omajista is an omajista, and I'm not going to dump her. Anything else?"

Silence. She liked silence. "Then let's get some sleep. Lohin, you stay."

The others left. Lohin waited patiently while she poured herself a drink. She sat in one of the field chairs. Her feet hurt from all the standing. The march to Daorian had been sixteen hours a day for three days straight. Now they rested before the final push, but even the resting was exhausting. She had pushed this army to its limit. Some had already deserted since crossing over. Now that they'd made the crossing to the new world safely, there was nothing binding them to her. She had pondered having them all warded to her, but the logistics of that were even more complicated than feeding upwards of a million new mouths in this country in six months.

"Have we found any more omajistas?" she asked.

"Just Nava," he said. "Nava says the Empress murdered all her Seekers months ago."

"What madness was that?"

"She says the Empress said it was at our order."

Kirana sipped her drink. "Interesting."

"It's possible she thought we'd infiltrated them?"

"No," Kirana said. "The Empress knew we were coming. This was about burning out the fields. She knew we'd look to the Seekers to increase our numbers. I need to know why those legions are in Sebastyn and Tordin, though. That's key."

"Still no progress on that."

"Then get progressing."

Lohin bowed stiffly and took his leave.

She stared after him. A man as point of contact for intelligence in Dorinah was not her first choice, but like

Madah, she'd had to make allowances for those who couldn't come over because their shadows lived. All this killing, and the physical rules of the seams between worlds still limited her options.

She took her cup with her and pushed outside her tent. She walked behind the stir of the army to the very edges of the camp. She climbed a slight rise and found a break in the trees. Kirana gazed up at the moons – the same moons as her world, mostly. Ahmur on her world had no tiara of satellites. She wondered where they had gone, on her side – fallen from the sky, in some other part of the world? Or had the diseased versions of her satellites gobbled them up on their entry into the world?

She drank. Questions for thinkers and stargazers. She was neither, really. She heard something behind her. The weapon at her wrist throbbed in answer, and partially extended. She turned.

"Empress?"

It was some infantry-level man, one of the foreign ones. She didn't recall ever having learned his name, though.

"Something I can do for you?" she said.

He bowed deeply, did not meet her gaze. "I saw you walk over here–"

"Out with it."

"I apologize, but there is something you should know… about Lohin."

"Is there now? I suspect you have little to share I don't know, but do entertain me."

"Of course," he said, bowing lower still. "Lohin has been keeping intelligence from you."

"Is that so?" It was not the first time she'd been approached by a member of the infantry hoping to win favor by outing one of her inner circle. "You could have taken this to your line commander."

"I could. But I could not guarantee it reached you."

"Well?"

"There is a legion just a few days behind us."

"I know that, soldier. So does anyone with ears. An entire legion is difficult to hide."

"It's not a legion of Dorinahs."

"What, did they hire mercenaries? How do you know what they're composed of?"

He glanced behind him. "Send another scout. Not one of Lohin's. I could go, but you won't believe me."

"And what's your name?"

"Marister, Empress."

"Marister. From what blighted place? I know that accent. Havasharia? Osadaina?"

"Osadaina," he said. He straightened. "I offered to join your army. I wasn't conscripted."

"It was conscription or death."

"That's how I know they're mercenaries," he said. "They speak my language."

"There is no Osadaina on this world," Kirana said. "You were mistaken."

"That's what I'm trying to tell you," he said. "If there's no Osadaina here, and you… killed or conscripted those of us on our world, where did the Dorinahs get *these* ones?"

"Fuck," Kirana said.

The other worlds were on the move.

28

"It's a small town," Zezili said, watching the wispy smoke of the village's fires waft over the dense woodland below them, "and we've got a lot of mouths to feed."

"It'll keep us until the supply line catches up," Storm said. He stood at the top of a low rise beside Zezili. The new runner told them the town was called Mordid, and had a massive church at the center and about three hundred residents. No fortifications to speak of. Her force was large enough that they likely knew the Dorinahs were nearby, even if they didn't anticipate an attack. After going south for over a week, they were turning east now, to the circular landmark indicated on Storm's maps. What exactly they were meant to uncover in it, Zezili still didn't know, but it looked like a graveyard to her, staring up at them from the map like a great glaring eye. Trouble was, they were short on supplies, their supply lines mired in the tangled wood. The little village would give them enough supplies for the final push.

"I'd like to burn it down," Zezili said of the little town. Destroying something would feel useful, at least. Weeks of traveling through mud, pulling thorny plants from her boots, scrubbing lice from her hair, was like some nightmare.

"And I'd like a new pup," Storm said. "But this is the

task. It's best you lead the charge into town. They have no defenses. Should be easy to get in and out."

"You don't want to lead it?"

"You know I cannot."

It took her a moment to remember. She'd gotten so used to him the last couple of weeks she'd forgotten he was a man. "Yeah, sorry."

"Men invest in armor, not weapons," he said. "And this, of course." He tapped his head.

Zezili called up forty of her women – which she thought might be a little much – and began the march down into the valley. She broke them into four groups, ten women across, who hacked at vegetation as they went. She came up with the left flank. Their instructions were to subdue and pillage, taking down as many runners as they could. The King of Tordin would know they had crossed the mountains soon enough. Zezili had to hope that the people the Empress had tasked them to find were going to make up for the fifty thousand men Saradyn was said to be able to call at will.

Her squad leaders communicated with whistles. In deep forest like this, it was more practical than semaphore. She drew her sword and called for the strike. Forty softly padding bears and dogs took off at a swift pace through the brambled woodland. Zezili saw three young women bolt from the edge of a nearby stream. She whistled and gestured for archers. Four arrows snarled toward the running women. Only one found its mark. The woman dropped.

They broke into the clearing outside the village. A few stragglers were still running for cover or breaking for the trees. Zezili shouted at the archers to take a woman hitching her cart to a mangy dog. They had smaller dogs here, yapping things no taller than Zezili's knee that snapped at her army's mounts. The bears made short order of them, but the dogs, including Zezili's, were more skittish about eating their own kind.

A vortex of air exploded on the other side of the village. Zezili saw six of the riders ahead of her tossed upward. They careened into the woods, landing on roofs, smacking into trees.

"Parajista!" she yelled. "Take it out!"

The archers at the back kindled flaming brands. Zezili didn't want the fire to spread too fast or they'd lose the supply stores, but she needed something to distract the jistas' concentration. A sloppy vortex like that in a nowhere village like this meant there weren't more than one or two, and they weren't very skilled. She had not expected a jista way out here. But she had contained a few on her own.

She whistled and gestured for a flanking fire. The arrows zipped off. "Let's clear out these supplies!" she said. Her women had gutted a few of the bolder villagers, but most lay in the dirt now, prostrating themselves. She wondered how often bandits came through here, or perhaps even the king himself, raiding like the petty lord he was.

The roofs around the vortex were aflame now. Zezili dismounted. She would be less of a target on foot. She kept her sword out and menaced forward, encountering no resistance. She grabbed the hair of one of the men on the ground, yanked his head back.

"Jasoi! Ask him where the meat is. We need rice, too."

Jasoi slid off her bear and snapped off something mushy in Tordinian.

The man babbled and pointed to a great building at the center of town that bore a shining eye on its face, not dissimilar to the eye of Rhea.

"Cellar's under the church," Jasoi said.

Zezili called for the nearest dozen of her women, leaving six behind to rummage through personal stores and ensure the pacified natives didn't get bold.

She pushed open the door of the church. A young girl knelt in front of a massive bronze edifice of some large jowled man in a wasp-waisted corset a lot like the one the Empress wore. His feet were not visible beneath his long flowing gown, and he had a strange, beatific expression on his face, as if he were taking a long-held shit while basking in the sun.

Jasoi asked the girl something.

The girl did not look startled at all, which Zezili thought odd, but people did all sorts of weird things while in religious ecstasy.

"Tell her we're not after more death," Zezili said. "Just the supplies."

"People like you always say that," the girl said, in heavily accented Dorinah.

Jasoi kept a hand on her weapon.

"You the parajista?" Zezili asked. If the air turned to mud, she could flatten herself on the ground and crawl under the pews, hoping to evade the girl's line of sight. Without line of sight, it was harder for jistas to hit what they were aiming for. She tensed, ready to drop.

"No," the girl said. She narrowed her eyes. "Is one of you Zezili Hasaria?"

Jasoi tensed, waiting for direction. Zezili scanned the rest of the church, looking for the trap. "We're just after supplies, girl," Zezili said. "We're happy to leave you intact."

"To starve, then?" the girl said. "You say you'll let us live, but the crops aren't even in the ground."

"Plenty of crawling stuff out there to sustain you."

"Zezili Hasaria?" the girl said, nodding. "Yes, that's you. I have word of your husband."

Zezili's heart clenched. "Who the fuck are you?"

"Rosh," she said. "And you're Zezili Hasaria. I know where to find your husband."

"Where is he?"

"South of here," Rosh said. "A week, in Gasira. It's a big stronghold, though. You have a lot of women here, but you won't be able to take it."

"We'll decide what we can and can't take," Zezili said. "How was he? Was he hurt?"

"Hurt? No, he was fine." Rosh's expression got sly. "I could take you there, if you like."

"Just tell me where he is," Zezili said.

"You want Saradyn dead? That's why you're here, isn't it, raiding this village? Well, I want to learn more about Saradyn too. I can take you there."

"Out of the goodness of your little roguish heart?" Zezili said.

"Hardly," Rosh said. "You get Gasira, and your husband. I just need… something else. Just some information. It won't harm you. I won't get in your way."

Zezili eyed Rosh. She stood with hands in pockets, spine straight, fully confident. Just a girl, yes, but Zezili had killed the Kai of the Dhai when she was her age, hadn't she? Saradyn must hate her to pieces. A ruckus came from the doors. Three legionnaires pushed in, Storm at their head.

"Decided to make a showing of it?" Zezili asked.

"There was little resistance," Storm said. "Most are fled by now. Who's this, some priest? Does she know where the cellar is?"

"She knows where Saradyn is," Zezili said. "And my husband."

"What does your husband have to do with this campaign?"

Zezili motioned him over. "A word. Jasoi, you and the others find the cellar. Rosh, you show them? Some good faith, yes?"

Rosh jerked her head toward the rear of the church.

Storm folded his arms. "We can't go marching to take some fortified hold for no reason. We don't have the women for it."

"I can take Anavha back."

"Listen to yourself," Storm said. "What, is he dying?"

"Held hostage, most likely."

"He's worth more to them alive than dead. He'll be fine to wait until we're done. We'll take Gasira eventually."

"You can guarantee me that's so?" Zezili said. "He belongs to me and he's been stolen."

Storm shook his head. "Something's not right with this. You just happen to run into a woman who says she knows who you are, and who your husband is? In a backwater in Tordin?"

"I know, but–"

"Syre!" Storm's page ran into the church, waving her arms like a woman on fire. "There's an army out there!"

Storm said, "What, pitchforks?"

"That parajista was one of Saradyn's!" the page said. "Saradyn's got an army in those woods, and they're coming this way."

29

Saradyn rode to the outskirts of the little town of Mordid at the head of a force of fifty, including six wind witches, his parajistas. He considered that entirely adequate to quash a troublesome little village and its resurrected rebel leader.

He did not count on another army already being there.

"What in the fuck is this?" Saradyn said.

The scout before him trembled. "They must have come over the border unnoticed. We're several weeks from the northern border. We couldn't possibly have—"

"How could I have no knowledge of it?"

But there was an easy answer to that, one the sputtering scout would not dare give him. The north was lawless, still. He had few sources there, and not a single town loyal to him. They still worshipped trees and giant plants up there, and had yet to come under the fist of Laine's protection. He saw Natanial picking at his teeth a few paces distant, leaning against a tree. He'd refused to ride the whole distance, but looked more refreshed than any of them. Saradyn pushed down a flare of annoyance.

"She probably has a hundred of them in the town already," the scout said, "and there are hundreds up on the hill on the other side."

"How many hundreds?" Saradyn asked.

The man's eyes were wide. "Hundreds!"

Saradyn made a note to find a scout with a better sense for counting. But even a few hundred to his fifty was far too many. He surveyed the landscape – thick woods. His men didn't know these woods any better than the Dorinahs. Saradyn motioned Tanays forward. Reinforcements wouldn't arrive for six days, at best.

"We can turn away now and come back in force," Tanays said.

"When have I ever done that?"

Tanays cleared his throat. "Lord, there is no tactical advantage here. The girl likely fled when the Dorinahs attacked. We can regroup–"

"Let's begin," Saradyn said, ignoring him. They were small enough that the initial logistics would be easy to communicate. "Wind witches – I want four of you around the village, at the compass points. I need two to stay here for the final push. Archers" – all twenty of them – "at the east and west. Bear cavalry" – all twenty-five – "I'm saving you for the end, after the witches and the archers have thinned them out. We come in with fire. I'm relying on the witches to contain it. Not an ember leaves that village, are we clear?"

He looked for Natanial. But Natanial was no longer leaning against the tree. A quick scan of the ranks told him the assassin wasn't there either. He had slipped off before he could be ordered about.

Tanays leaned over. "You'll sacrifice every person–"

"Then they shouldn't have harbored a criminal," Saradyn said sharply. "We showed them leniency the last time we were here. They may see cruelty, but I see an avoidance of foolishness. Burn it down, and every Dorinah with it."

Zezili made for the door of the cathedral. Storm sprinted past her, but it was Zezili who yelled for the scout to run back up the hill for the Sebastyn parajistas.

She broke into the town square and pivoted, trying to

figure out the plan of attack. The air thickened. She saw a shimmering wave of air out behind the cathedral.

"How many?" Storm was asking the scout. "How many?"

"I don't know. Fifty? A hundred? They're up on the opposite rise. There could be another force."

Zezili mounted her dog and rallied the women she had brought down with her. Her first instinct was to mash them all together into a defensive circle, shields and weapons facing out. The scout had seen Saradyn's men in the east, but that didn't mean there weren't more.

"West!" Zezili yelled at Storm. "Retreat west!" There was no reason to hold her position. They had come to the village for supplies, but food was worth nothing if Saradyn smashed them here between two armies. Her biggest worry was that if that was indeed Saradyn up there, he'd discovered them a full week from their destination. And if that was so, she had run out of time to figure out the Empress's intent. Saradyn would rout them before she found Anavha or destroyed the Empress's weapon.

Storm roared at the ranks, his booming voice now a useful asset instead of annoying grievance.

Zezili felt the air pressure increase. "Parajistas!" she called. "Counter!"

The village was small, but so crowded with flaming houses and terrified civilians that rallying a line to protect their retreat took longer that it should have.

Finally, the parajistas appeared behind her, two hawk-faced Sebastyns. "They're deploying—" one began.

"Counter it the fuck down then!" Zezili said. She missed Tulana, sensible Tulana who would have known precisely what to tell them. "Cover our retreat."

They fanned out behind Zezili's loose line of troops, the two lines of five, and she felt a whump of air, a blast of dirt. She hated that she couldn't see any of it.

"Shields up!" she called at the ten who'd rallied. "Shields up, lances ready. Cover and forward."

Zezili urged her dog forward as the village burned around them. If it was her on that rise and she knew she outnumbered them, she'd circle to burn them out. If she made a fast retreat, she could slip the noose.

She barreled after her forces, following the purple flag of Storm's page into the woods.

The flanking force hit her as they broke into the trees, cutting her and the ten from the main body of the retreat. The mass of them was shocking. Her people were outnumbered four to one, maybe more.

Zezili pounded through the first wave of the bear cavalry. She unseated a scrawny little man on a scraggly bear. Other men were bigger; Tordin bred its men large. They did not restrict or cull them, and it led to monstrously hairy creatures, ridiculous figures, like watching bears ride bears. But most of the fat and hair was bluster, and they died the same as any other soldier on the field.

Two bodies lay in the dirt behind her. Her shoulder was already aching. The army's blades were plain metal, like hers. Not an infused weapon in sight. A shaggy youth on a great bear barreled toward her. She deflected blows from two more already within the reach of her weapon, felling one. Then the wild youth was on top of her. She turned her dog just in time. He caught its head instead of hers.

Her animal fell under her. She rolled free, coming up, miraculously, without impaling herself on her own blade. Two more men on bears swept toward her, swinging from either side. She ducked between them. Their blades missed her and grazed one another's mounts. Their bears snarled and attacked one another, spitting great gobs of drool.

Three of Zezili's women had been knocked from their mounts and stood back to back with shields up and lances out. She limped to their little circle and made herself a part of it.

"Work toward the woods," she said, inching them forward as a group toward the trees. If they could make it deeper into the trees Saradyn's men could not come at them in groups. They could scatter and meet up with the rest of the others later.

Only one of her women remained mounted. She took point at the head of their group as five riders turned around and rallied toward them.

Zezili heard others coming down through the village, a full-on assault now, not a noose. Parajista-fueled winds blew through the tops of the trees. Zezili saw one of her Sebastyn parajistas dead, mangled on the scrubby ground. The other was nowhere to be seen.

The woods crawled with cavalry. How was she outnumbered? What was he doing taking a force this size into–

Then she saw the force making all the ruckus coming through the village – four parajistas, and two men on bears. The parajistas were making a fine show, ripping the roofs from houses, obliterating carts and kennels and grain houses. The top of the church splintered.

Five of Saradyn's cavalry ran at their position, and six more of his men came up behind them. Eleven against her four would be the end.

Zezili screamed at them, furious. Her women took up the scream all around her – fiery, shrieking warmongers all.

The cavalry crashed into their shield circle.

Bears weighed a ton, on average. Five tons of force broke their line neatly, and the six tons coming after them trampled them over.

Zezili was crushed under the weight of the two women next to her, folded behind them by the first charge. The second wave pounded right over her. Her wrist snapped. It was her left wrist. The one holding the sword. Her only good hand.

She howled.

The men dismounted and came back with swords out.

Zezili yanked a corded necklace from the woman next to her using the remaining fingers of her right hand. She pushed her sword into her right hand and used her teeth to tie the blade to her right hand, then crawled out from under the bodies of her women.

The woman on the bear had been unseated and run through with a pike. She kicked on the ground at Zezili's left, huffing blood and asking for a priestess.

Zezili distanced herself from her, edging back toward the woods while the men advanced.

Running was not much of an option, with her ragged gait. Her left hand hung uselessly beside her.

"Shit," she said aloud, because if she was going to get a last line, that sounded best.

The men swarmed her.

She pivoted and shoved the first away with her right shoulder. She thrust the blade forward, running one man through.

Someone moved behind her. She could not rally fast enough. She felt the thwack on her skull. Black spots, a burst of light. Zezili hit the ground face first.

Yelling. Not hers. She had a mouth full of loam. Her fucking wrist hurt. She spit leaves, turned just in time to see a tall, wiry man standing over her. Black hair brushing a bared collar, a beak of a nose that was still somehow attractive in the long face.

"Your name," he said.

"Fuck you."

"Anavha Hasaria," he said.

She flopped her tangled sword arm forward. He stepped on her wrist. Pain rocked up her arm.

"I've heard quite a lot about your face," he said. "I like it, but I think Anavha may find it shocking."

"Natanial!"

Another man, yelling from on top of a bear. Zezili could only see the bear's paws from this vantage.

The wiry man stood, foot still on her wrist. "Call Saradyn over," Natanial said. "We have one of the legion commanders."

30

It was Rosh, sure as he breathed. The same pinched face, the masculine confidence, the lanky frame and freckled nose. But she was without one core component, one essential element that obliterated all the rest, and gave away what she really was.

Rosh's ghosts were gone.

She was a blank canvas, a being without a past, without regret. She had left all of that on some other world. She was just a poor copy of the first.

Saradyn drew himself up and felt a smile tug at his mouth. He had feared some other madness, some new trick of Laine's come to rise with his eye, the star called Oma. But this girl was just another of the same foe he'd been fighting for six years – the darker doubles, the shadowy fey who had been encroaching into Tordin for over a decade, maybe longer. The sight Laine gave him made it easy to uncover them. It was his greatest curse, and his greatest gift.

Rosh lay in the dirt outside the ruined church, restrained by two of his men.

"I know what you are," Saradyn said.

She struggled in the dirt. "King Saradyn," she said, "I can explain everything."

"Which world sent you? Was it to destroy me?

Because I can't be destroyed."

"Please," she said. "Let me up. I'll explain."

"Saradyn!" Tanays rode over from the other side of the village. "We have one of their legion commanders."

"Who?"

Tanays looked surprised. "I don't know. Natanial recognized her."

"Stay with this one." Saradyn rode over to the edge of the village, accompanied by his page and one of the wind witches. He did not trust that the entire army had slipped his net.

He moved through a scattering of corpses, mostly civilian, but many of his and a few of the Dorinah. That bothered him. His men should have had the advantage here in their own territory, outnumbering this force. But grit went a long way on the battlefield, and the women may have had it in great numbers, being on the losing end of this one. Perhaps his men had gotten cocky. He had long ago learned not to underestimate the Dorinah. They were fueled by witchcraft.

Natanial stood over a body well away from what looked like a final holdout – four women with shields trampled into the dirt, their blood turning the soil to churning mud. A few of Saradyn's men waited around her, some mounted, some not.

He came up beside their catch. She was a filthy creature, scarred to the point of malformation. He kissed his thumb and offered it to Laine, a sign against deformity. Would that he was put down before he looked like that.

"I suggested she may be worth more to us alive," Natanial said.

"Good eye. Bring her with us."

"What of the army?" Tanays asked.

"An army without a head is no army at all. They'll go back to Dorinah, if they have any sense. But put three trackers on them. I want to know where they're headed. It's far too small for an invasion. If they're meeting a greater force, I need to know."

"You don't think she'll talk?" Tanays said.

"Look at her. You think I could do worse to her?"

"You don't recognize her, do you?" Natanial said.

"You know her?"

"That's Zezili Hasaria," Natanial said. "We have her husband back in Gasira."

"That boy becomes more and more useful by the day," Saradyn said. "Rope her up. I have two fine trophies from this venture."

Saradyn sat up with Rosh nearly a week later in a little village outside Gasira. He did not want to wait any longer for her interrogation, as the things she said about fire raining from the sky were scaring his men. Life was fearful enough now without her putting more ideas in their heads.

"How did you get here?" Saradyn asked.

She sat roped to a chair near the fire in the main room of a tavern he had generously acquired from the local innkeeper for a reasonable fee. Spring had arrived, but the nights were still cool.

She shook her head.

"I have been more than fair to you," Saradyn said, leaning forward. "Fed you, clothed you, kept my men from you. Things could have gone far differently. I could sell you off as a servant here, or a slave somewhere else. I could use you for any number of terrible purposes. But I am a civilized man. All I ask for is information. Which of the worlds sent you? Is your Empress Kirana or Sovonia?"

"Sovonia is not an Empress."

"Ah, I see," Saradyn sat back. "You are correct. She is not. She is... what, exactly? A seer, a rebel leader? You see, Empress Kirana I understand. I know her motives. She comes from a dying world. But yours is something else, isn't it? You're mere explorers. Parasites. I have even less tolerance for you."

"The transference engines—"

"What are those?"

Rosh bit her lip. He had noticed strange things about this one. She was plumper than the other Rosh, but narrower in the face, her hair longer. Small differences, but they added up. What interested him most was the similarity of names. What compelled one to name these people the same across different versions of their worlds, even when the power structures were so different? What magic was in a name?

"I have pieced together quite a lot in this little backwater," Saradyn said. "That's what one of your other little spies called it. A backwater, like a latrine, and I know there are more of you in my holds, hiding out like rats, ferrying each other information that you can use out here to get people like Zezili Hasaria onto your side. Eventually I will hunt down all of you. But I've known of your presence here since I was a child, since I could see the strangers without... strangers with differences. I saw you and pointed it out when others could not. I will always see you, you understand?"

Rosh stared hard at the floor.

Saradyn turned to Tanays. "Bring in the dogs."

Rosh raised her head. He saw the fear bloom there, like a flower.

"Something you wanted to tell me," he said, "before I leave you with the dogs?"

It was the same for all of them, from that world, this fear of dogs. He had different names for all the worlds – he had identified five of them, so far, and called them by their primary agent, numbered by the frequency with which he ran into members of their respective scouting parties – Kirana, Sovonia, Gian, Aradan, and Kalinda. It bothered him that so many primary actors were women. Why was that? Was there a message in that, something he should understand?

"We use the transference engines," she said. "They amplify the power of the stars, even if they aren't ascendant. They can call to them between worlds. That's where they go when they're not here, the stars. They don't orbit. They blink out. Between worlds."

"That's an interesting theory."

"That's science," she said.

"Science?"

"Science."

"Sounds like witchcraft."

"I have not met one sane person in this world," Rosh muttered.

"You know why you were able to come over now?" he asked.

"We can come over when our... counterpart here dies. I'm an explorer," she said. "A missionary, if you will. You don't need to treat me poorly. If you know what I am, you know that whatever the person you knew did here, I have nothing to do with it."

"And if you and your little explorers take any kind of notes at all," Saradyn said, "you'd know what I do with your kind when I find them."

She had the sense to lose a bit of color; even with her ruddy complexion, he noticed it.

"I think you should consider what you can learn from me."

"What is it you're learning from *me*?" he asked. "I know you're scuttling all around Grania, not just Tordin. Are you taking sides in this fight? Preparing for an invasion?"

"We are purely here to explore this phenomenon. You don't seem to understand how important–"

Saradyn stood. He flicked a hand at Natanial.

"That's all?" Natanial said.

"That's all."

"Seems brutish."

"So is life."

Natanial stepped forward quickly, and before Rosh could utter a single complaint, he neatly snapped her neck.

She slumped forward.

"A waste of my talent," Natanial said. "I'm an artist, not a brute."

"I'll decide what you are."

Saradyn expected a retort, but Natanial said only, "Is Zezili next?"

"No, I'm tired. As I said, it's not worth talking to her without the husband."

Natanial nodded and went to the door. Dayns and Sloe whined outside. Natanial let them in as he left.

Saradyn sat across from Rosh's body and petted the dogs. He stared at her in the flickering firelight. How did one guard against espionage from another world? It was as if some other being had shot down from the moons and started spouting off nonsense about another realm. He had trouble enough reconciling the fact that Dorinah could exist in the same world he did, let alone these aliens.

Dayns whined at him. He stroked her ears. "Hush now," he said. "Have I not kept you safe?"

Safer than he had kept any human being in his care. Rosh's limp head, the lanky hair, reminded him of the day he murdered the Thief Queen, Quilliam. She had been his ward for some years, but he failed at that, and farmed her out, and look what she had become; raised by fools and savages, running off into the woods to join with thieves and miscreants, intent on destroying all he wanted to build here. Who was she, to pass judgment on him? Just a foolish girl like this one. They blamed him for destroying her, but what choice did she leave him? What choice did any of them leave him?

Dayns whined again.

"What is it?" he said. "Come now, we are safe. We're almost home."

Sloe began to bark.

Saradyn frowned at them both and went to the door.

People were coming out of their houses, entering the damp streets; it had rained just that morning. They pointed and gasped at the sky.

Saradyn squinted at them. His vision was blurry. He called to Dayns and Sloe. They barked and ran through the line of figures, dispelling them like mist.

He huffed out a breath. Was he hallucinating an army of ghosts, now? A whole town of ghosts?

He gazed into the sky, and saw Para blazing there on the horizon. What star had those ghosts been seeing? He didn't know. He feared to guess.

He got down on his knees, and raised his hands to Laine.

Saradyn prayed for clear vision, and a gift that felt less like a curse.

31

So this was Saradyn. Not a tall man, but broad, like a tree
eclipsed by its fellows that made up for height with girth,
crowding out all those around it. Blood rushed down
Zezili's face. She told herself that head wounds were all
bluster. She wasn't vomiting or confused, not any more
than usual, but she bled all that first night, trussed up on
the other side of the fire from Saradyn, self-styled king
of Tordin, and his most intimate familiars. They were all
men, which she supposed shouldn't have surprised her,
but she had never in her life been the only woman in a
group, and it unsettled her. She was very obviously out
of place, and it wasn't just because hers were the only
bound hands.

She saw the Rosh girl occasionally the first few days,
but she noticed the girl didn't come out of the tavern
that Saradyn and his lackeys pulled her into at the end
of the week. Why hadn't they just killed her back there
on the field? Who was she to them? Zezili did not speak
Tordinian, and it put her at a distinct disadvantage. The
tall man with the big nose had known who she was,
but Saradyn hadn't seemed to until they had a rapid-
fire conversation over her body. She wasn't sure what
that meant. It crossed her mind that Big Nose may have
been the same one to take Anavha, or at least the one in

Saradyn's inner circle to recognize who Anavha was and keep him alive for ransom.

But if she, too, was their prisoner, they'd get no ransom from her. Best case, they hoped to sell her back to the Empress, then have her buy out Anavha too. As the blood caked on her face that night, she feared they would find the Empress less than receptive to that offer. A second failure meant death, and though Storm and the rest of the force still had a head start on getting where she wanted them to go, Zezili's fate was not tied to theirs any longer. She was on her own.

It was a week back to wherever it was they ended up – some no-nothing little town not much bigger than the one they'd just come from. The town stank, like they were still shitting in pots and throwing them into alleys. Plumbing seemed to be a thing of legend. The only evidence of its existence – in the past, at least – was a large, cracked fountain they passed just off the main road. It sprouted up from the center of a tiled floor of what once may have been some grand estate, but now lay in ruins, slowly devoured by the woods. The trees here were big, mostly everpines, and instead of burning out the vegetation on either side of the roads they lined them in big concrete blocks slathered in lye that ate through the concrete as surely as it did the vegetation that tried to survive there.

Everything she saw gave the impression the Tordinians were rats, maggots living on the bones of some collapsed civilization. History told her that was truth – the Empress's cousin, Penelodyn, had ruled northern Tordin for almost a hundred years, bringing civilization to great swaths of the locals. But they'd rebelled and tossed her out and this is where it left them – worshipping some mad king and shitting in buckets.

Two big male soldiers hauled her into the rickety main hold of the shitty little town. The hold was mostly wood, built on the massive stone base of some far older building.

She wasn't much up to resisting by then. She sweated and shook with fever. Her wrist hadn't been tended to, and it was bruised black and swollen. But the fever came from some other wound, something open – either the throbbing, oozing lump on her head or the blazing score on her back. She hadn't even noticed the wound in her back until hours after the end of the battle. Some ax had caught her there. It wasn't deep – her armor had resisted most of the blow – but nine days without even a wash and it was a burning brand on her shoulder now, like someone had set a hot stone on it.

They dropped her in a cell in the basement – cold, no windows – and shut the door. The darkness was total.

How long she was there, alone in the dark, she didn't know. The fever took her under. She dreamed of little black dogs with paws as big as their faces. They opened great mouths and ate their own feet. Anavha was there, writhing under her, squealing that she was hurting him, and just as she was about to reach her own release, reveling in her power, her absolute control of this beautiful body, the eye of Rhea glared down at her, filling her whole vision.

The eye filled her cell with light.

Zezili shielded her eyes. The pain left her body. She felt the blazing gaze of Rhea on her. It saw all of her worst acts – her slaughter of countless dajians, the genocide of an entire people, heaped on her willing shoulders. And the others – the dajians in her own care who she maimed and murdered; the husband she abused; the women she sent on fools' errands she knew would end in death, just to avoid the troubling politics of discharging them.

"But I did it in your name!" Zezili said. "For the will of the Empress! I am yours. I am hers. I am–"

Rhea knew what she was.

She belonged to herself. She had made her own life, forged in fire, on the bloody backs of others. No choice, though, no choice. If she was not stepping on another's back, someone else would step on hers. She had not made the world, but she had to live in it.

She had thrived only because she had given up her humanity.

The light went out.

Zezili gasped and opened her eyes. A plump man stood next to her, dressed in some white garment. He hushed her. She was tied to a table.

"What is this?" she said.

"For your own protection," he said. His head was shaved bald – his eyebrows, too.

A fire blazed in a hearth. The room was lined in clay jars, and stank of incense and cardamom and other spices she could not discern.

"Where on Rhea's tit am I?" Zezili snarled.

"Just doing a bit of cleaning up," the man said in heavily accented Dorinah. He picked up a very large saw, the length of his forearm.

Zezili's gut roiled. She looked at her left hand, her good fucking hand, the bloated, blackened flesh. "Set the bone, you fool!" she said.

"I'm sorry," he said, "it's gone to rot."

Zezili jerked in her restraints. Four big men came up from behind her. Held her down. She tried to bite them. Her fever had broken, and she was exhausted, weaker than she should be.

The Empress and her cats. Saradyn and his men with saws.

"Where is my husband!" she yelled. "Where is he? When I get out of this shit I will murder every last one of you. Every one. I'll impale you with this bloody fucking stump. I will impale the fuck out of you, cut off your fucking cocks, shove them down your cowardly throats. You'll suffocate on your own testicles, you fucking–"

Her tirade made the plump man tremble.

Then a voice from the doorway, in Tordinian, said something like an order, and again, in Dorinah,

"They'll do it."

It was the lean man who'd spoken of Anavha, the one with the beak of a nose. "They'd take your tongue, too," he said, "but Saradyn needs that, he says."

"I don't know who the fuck you are, but I'll take your fucking cock too," Zezili said. She was frothing. Spit flecked her mouth.

"You're welcome to what I have of one," he said. "My name is Natanial Thorne. I expect you'll remember it."

The saw bit into her wrist.

Zezili howled.

32

Anavha whiled away his days in the great, drafty hold playing board games and learning to play cards with the guards, both men. They thought him ridiculous, he knew, but they seemed to soften to him after a time, as if he were some child in need of tending. He learned about their families. One, a widower with six children; the other, a young man not much older than Zezili, courting a woman in a neighboring village. Anavha found himself both fascinated and horrified at their courtship practices. The young man said he'd never had sex with a woman, and intended to wait until she accepted his proposal, at the very least. Anavha admitted he had probably had sex with a dozen women before he married Zezili.

They both looked at him as if he were some horrifying insect, crawled up from gnawing on a corpse. Then the widower laughed, slapping his great knee.

"Dorinah!" he said. "What a place that must be!"

"It was not very pleasant," Anavha admitted. "It wasn't... it's not what you think."

But the younger one started joking as well. So Anavha pressed a smile onto his face – smile, smile, and pretend at joviality. He had spent much of his life smiling, but in that moment, with these two unbound, gregarious men, he found that he was very tired of smiling.

He was given new clothes, clean but plain and garish, like something a prisoner would wear, yes, but most men in Tordin seemed to wear these blandly cut trousers, tunics with square-cut collars, leather vests that fell to their knees, cinched with a belt. Drab green and brown and dark blue colors. Anavha had not seen a flash of red since they left Aaldia a month before.

In truth, he missed the Aaldians. Their broad smiles. Easy laughter. The intentness of their gazes when they spoke to you, as if what you said was the most important thing in the world. He and Natanial had spent two nights with an Aaldian friend of Natanial's, a broad-cheeked woman with an absurd yellow hat like a cone who taught him the Aaldian alphabet and numbers, all written out into practice books of expensive paper that she let him take when he left. He liked the look of the Aaldian script. It put him in mind of running rivers, and the eddies of currents. But he had lost the books during their difficult crossing of the Mundin mountains, and now he drew the symbols of the script from memory on the wall of his cell with a charred stick; the guards thought it was some kind of art.

Outside his artistic scribbling, Anavha spent a lot of time staring at the window above his bed, remembering his long days at Zezili's estate, waiting for something to happen to him. A year into their marriage, Zezili had been pregnant for a time. That had excited him terribly. The men he knew from his days in the mardanas were all fathers within a year of their marriages, raising strong, beautiful children for Dorinah. But when he met with them during the early days when Zezili was still sharing him with her sisters in the city, he had no children of his own to speak about. Their little tea house meetings – always out on the sidewalk, as unescorted men were not allowed inside – became awkward. He would listen to them talk, smiling beatifically, saying nothing, while one of Zezili's sister's dajians watched him from a nearby table to ensure he didn't get into any trouble.

As soon as Zezili's sisters bore children, he rarely saw them. Their care was relegated to house dajians. He longed to be a father, and spent endless nights after learning of her pregnancy thinking up names, and the stories he would read to her, and the trees he would help her climb, and how much she would love him, and he would love her, and they would be a family.

But that was all just dreamy nonsense. Zezili miscarried three months into her pregnancy, as she would miscarry twice more in their marriage. She was not a woman built to make life, she told him. Just take it.

That left him here, alone in Tordin with two jailers, losing time, his life, to chatter and nonsense. Nothing had changed but the scenery of the bedroom.

Two weeks into his gilded captivity, the younger guard, Mays, came to his room. Anavha glanced up from his Aaldian writing – he was writing a poem, he decided, about birds in cages. It was too early for cards.

"The King is back," Mays said, "Natanial with him. Thought you'd like to know they ran into some of your friends. Dorinahs."

Anavha had not thought Mays his friend, but it seemed a kindness, to tell him that. "Did anyone ask for me?"

"Natanial's coming up. He'll be upset you haven't gotten fat."

Much of the guards' good humor, Anavha always suspected, was because they were trying to get him to eat more than was good for him. Until now, he didn't realize it was some order from Natanial, who had pressed lard-soaked rice and pork fat at him for most of their journey in Aaldia.

"Thank you," Anavha said.

Mays hesitated, and his clear, bright face darkened for a long moment. "I'll miss you," he said.

"I'm not going anywhere," Anavha said.

"Sure, of course," Mays said.

"Can you bring me clean water? I want to wash up."

"Of course," Mays said, and shut the door.

Anavha waited for the water before he undressed. It was not Mays who brought it up, but a guard he'd never seen before. The man set the bucket down inside the door without a word. It was barely lukewarm.

Anavha sponged himself off and dressed in his cleanest clothes, the terrible Tordinian ones. Natanial hadn't even let him keep his Aaldian garments, the broad robes and heavy purple drapes and deep cowls. He admitted he missed Aaldia more than he missed Dorinah. No one treated him like a man in Aaldia. They treated him like a person.

He was reading over the poem on the wall when Natanial entered. He carried a tray of rice and buttered greens circling a gravy-soaked hunk of some kind of meat, most likely bear. Anavha hated bear.

Natanial slid the tray onto the table on the other side of the room. The table was a battered but functional piece that Anavha mostly used for the card games.

"Well," Natanial said, peering at the Aaldian script on the walls. "Are you out of paper, or run to madness already?"

"They said the historian wouldn't authorize any paper for me," Anavha said. "There's a shortage."

"We're at war with the province that makes most of it," Natanial said. He made as if to expand on that, but stopped. Motioned to the table.

"Come sit with me," Natanial said.

"I'm not hungry."

"Eat."

"I told you, I'm not hungry."

"Mays and Foryer say you haven't eaten a full meal in three days."

"I like staying slim."

"You're starving."

"Zezili likes me thin."

Natanial grimaced. "Of course she does. Starving

people are easier to confuse and control. Ask any dictator. Get up here."

Anavha reluctantly sat across from Natanial. His stomach growled, betraying him. Trying to keep his expression stoic made his whole face hurt. Natanial once listened to him cry for three hours in Aaldia, and in the end, he'd had to eat it all anyway.

"You telling me to eat is no better," Anavha said.

"Don't listen to me then. Listen to your stomach. Listen to yourself." Natanial tapped the plate.

Anavha's stomach hurt, but his stomach always hurt. Hunger was a vice. If you worked hard enough at it, you could capture and contain it. If you were strong enough, you could eliminate hunger all together.

"I don't know what that means," Anavha muttered, and pushed his plate away. He saw the blobs of glistening fat tremble on the plate. Definitely bear meat.

Natanial sat across from him. "I have good news. Saradyn agreed to leave your care and training to me, for a time."

"What does that change?"

"It means he won't turn you over to his wind witches to be beaten and tortured."

"Oh."

"Thank you would be nice."

"Thank you for–" for kidnapping me, he almost said, and bit his tongue. He told Natanial the truth of what he felt far too often. Natanial had never struck him. Maybe that made him too bold. Maybe Zezili was right, and he needed a firm hand to keep him on the path to Rhea's embrace. He certainly wasn't going to get there speaking everything that came into his head.

Natanial laughed. "You say what you want," he said. "Go on. I'm not Zezili."

"If it wasn't for you," Anavha said slowly, "I wouldn't need protection from Saradyn."

"That's true," Natanial said. "You'd be cutting yourself

open in front of a monstrous spouse who was as concerned with that as she would be with a dog that bashed its head repeatedly into its kennel. You know what she'd do with the dog, eventually? She'd have it put down."

"You don't know anything about Zezili."

Natanial narrowed his eyes. "That's being remedied," he said. He stepped away from the table. "We'll start training in the morning with a friend of mine. Get you some fresh air. If you don't eat, you'll be hungry. I'm not bringing some palanquin out here to haul you out into the woods."

"I'd rather write more poetry," Anavha said.

"Yes, well, wouldn't we all? But that's not the world we're living in. So eat up, and prepare yourself."

Anavha stared at the plate a few minutes more after Natanial left. Then he picked up the tray and dumped its contents in his refuse bucket.

For eight days, Natanial led Anavha out into the woods, a two hour walk from the main keep, to meet with his friend Coryana. Natanial seemed to have a great many women friends in many countries. Anavha would not have thought that odd except that they never seemed to visit any men, and in Tordin, the population of men and women was far more equal than in Dorinah. Anavha saw men everywhere – tall, fat, thin, short, lanky, muscular, and hairy – very hairy. But they never stayed with any of them.

When Anavha asked him about that after the first day as they walked home, Natanial shrugged. "Never thought about it," he said. "I suppose I just feel more comfortable with women, and they with me. They don't mind my... peculiarities."

"Like being an assassin?"

"Oh, that too," he said, and did not elaborate.

The third day, Anavha didn't want to get out of bed.

Natanial dragged him half the length of the hall outside his cell until he relented.

His friend Coryana was no better. However much Anavha insisted he was of no use to anyone – that someone had played a cruel joke on them and he wasn't gifted – they carried on. For hours. Their patience grated. He didn't understand it.

On the eighth day, hungry and exhausted, unable to remember the bit of poetry Coryana had been trying to get him to use to focus his thoughts, he threw himself to the warm spring ground among the wildflowers and sobbed.

"Get up, Anavha," Natanial said. "We go again."

Anavha curled up next to a stump, huffing in the smell of the fresh everpine shavings. "I can't. I can't."

"I can outlast you," Natanial said. "You get up and do as Coryana tells you. Then we get to have a rest. It's your choice. Make good choices."

Anavha keened. He could not say why his whole body rebelled, why he wanted to scream and seethe with every fiber of his body; fear and sobbing were his only tools, the only ones that didn't get him beaten. If he showed anger or violence he would be harmed. Crying was the only emotion his world ever allowed him. If he had any power, it was in his tears, and he was well versed in using them.

But Natanial remained unmoved.

Anavha lay crying until his face felt puffy and his eyes hurt. He cried until there were no more tears to squeeze out.

An hour later, Anavha was standing again, concentrating on the susurrus of Tordinian words Coryana whispered to him. Listen, repeat. Pull.

"Like breathing, a second breath," she said. "A breaking apart. A release."

Release.

Anavha saw the blood welling from the cuts in his arms, the bloody knife, the parting of the world.

Release.

He gasped.

A threading needle of power rippled beneath his skin. It felt like hot liquid seeping into his organs. He wanted to vomit it out like some vile poison.

Release.

The poetry. He repeated the poem again, sharpening his focus, and the liquid poured from his body, a bloody burst of light that tangled together like a misty ball of yarn. But instead of blowing apart the tree, or starting some fire, the misty red ball of threads dissipated in the warm air.

Anavha let out his breath.

Natanial came up beside him, arms folded, and shared a long look with Coryana.

She pressed her hand to Anavha's shoulder. "There it is. You see?"

"And you didn't even have to bleed on anything," Natanial said.

"This is enough for today," Coryana said. She was smiling for the first time, her voice full of warmth. "A controlled, first-time draw is the most difficult," she said. "The rest will come easily, in comparison."

Anavha started crying. He wasn't even sure why this time.

"Hush now," Coryana said.

"It was well done, Anavha," Natanial said. "We'll go home now, all right?"

But far from being proud, Anavha felt sick, and powerless.

Natanial hauled him back into his room – not ungently – but because Anavha refused to stand, he had to be dragged by the arm the whole way down the hall outside his cell. He was screaming the whole way, shrieking like he was dying, because it felt like dying, being pushed to do something, to be something, he did not want to be. And he was so tired.

Natanial dumped him in his room and closed the door.

Anavha lay on the floor in the dark for at least ten minutes more, sobbing until there were no tears, just huffing, choking anger.

Clouds roiled in the world beyond his little window, revealing the moons. A well-appointed prison was still a prison.

Anavha pulled off all his clothes and grabbed the empty wooden tray on the table. He smashed it against the table again and again until it splintered to pieces. He took the biggest piece and began sharpening it against the rough stone until he had a good point on it. Then he pressed it to his arm, sawing at flesh. When that didn't work, he stabbed, and the tears came again. He was completely out of control. He had no control over his life. They had taken this too, his ability to decide what he ate, and what he did to his own body.

Slivers of wood embedded themselves into his flesh. He threw the stake away. It thunked on the far wall. He sagged to his knees and bowed in front of his wall of Aaldian poetry. He pressed his hands to the words and wiped them all out, smearing his hands in char.

When it was gone, he lay still on the floor, staring at the window.

The door opened.

Natanial came in, illuminated by the bold white light of the moons. Tall and lean, his beak of a nose made bolder by the shadows, he was like some bird of prey – powerful, beautiful.

"Oh, Anavha," he said. He picked Anavha up and brought him to the bed and lay him down.

Anavha wrapped his arms around him and pressed his face to his warm chest. He was out of tears, but he trembled just the same.

"The world is mad," Anavha said.

"Yes." Natanial stroked his hair, pressed his rough hand against the nape of Anavha's neck.

Anavha pulled away, so their faces were a breath apart. What he saw in Natanial's gaze was the same unnamable thing he felt.

"Take me from here," Anavha said.

Natanial traced the line of Anavha's mouth. The desire his touch inspired coursed through Anavha's body, hot and breathtaking. For a moment he felt a terrible shame, but who was here to see them? Not Zezili. Not the priestesses. He was aware of his nakedness, and the obviousness of his desire.

"If I take you, my own captive," Natanial said softly, "a young man adrift in a strange land, then I'm no better than Zezili, am I? Power can be monstrous, can make men monstrous. I'm an artist, not a monster."

"But I..." What? Anavha thought. What did he want, really? Did he know? "I want *you*," he said, and it felt rebellious, impossible, like saying bears could dance in the clouds.

"You don't know what you want." Natanial released him. "We'll take a day or two to rest, then start again. I know this is difficult, and difficult things can be painful, but it will make you stronger, more in control of your own life, do you understand?"

Anavha did not, but he nodded.

Natanial shut the door, leaving Anavha alone in the darkness.

Anavha sat a moment more before he realized how cool the room was. He pulled on his night gown and noticed someone had put out his dinner earlier, before he returned to the room. He hadn't even noticed.

Anavha pulled up a chair. The plate was heavy with thick hunks of rye bread piled in rice and meat gravy. They left no utensils. He wasn't permitted eating sticks or the pronged implements that Tordinians used, but they usually left a spoon. Not this time. The smell of the cold food made him salivate. How long since he cared to notice hunger?

He ate with his fingers, smearing gravy on his chin,

until the food was gone.

The next morning, he dressed and washed first thing, and sat waiting for Natanial at the table. He ate his breakfast, most of it, because he really was overfull.

While he waited he murmured the words of the poetry Coryana had been intoning all week. He wrote it onto the smeared charcoal wall with his charred stick. He concentrated on calling the breath of power, until he felt it crawling under his skin, a whisper, a whiff–

The door opened, and he lost the thread of power. The mist dissipated.

He stood, smiling, but it was not Natanial. It was Mays, looking apologetic.

"You're cleaned up already?" he asked.

"Yes," Anavha said. "I'm training with Natanial today."

"Not today," Mays said, "King Saradyn wants me to bring you downstairs. He wanted to make sure you were made up and presentable."

Anavha smoothed his tunic. "I am."

"Good, all right." Nodding.

"What's wrong?"

"No one's told you, have they?"

"I've been training with Natanial."

"So he didn't say anything about it?"

"About what?"

Mays chewed his lip. "Maybe you can just–"

"What, Mays?"

"King Saradyn wants to present you to your wife," he said. "Zezili Hasaria has been our captive for weeks, and he thinks she's softened up enough to see you. They're in the dining hall. I'll–"

Anavha threw up his breakfast.

Mays rushed in. Just as he reached Anavha, Anavha bolted past him, still dry heaving. Mays slipped in the vomit, swore.

Anavha knew where the dining hall was.

33

Saradyn, the big fat man, came to her when the stump of her left hand was nearly healed. The white-frocked shitface of a "doctor" was happy to care for her wounds now that he had inflicted them. She gleefully bit off the tip of his nose during one of his checkups. He sent a younger man the next time, who wore a helmet with a face guard, as if he had come to do battle with her.

But when Saradyn finally came to see her – after how many weeks? – he brought only his dogs, two ugly runty dogs that stank terribly.

The room they put her in was something like a dining hall, a piss-poor place for an interrogation, if that's what this was.

Saradyn pulled up a chair at the table across from her. It was a vast table, and could seat over thirty people. They sat at the middle, leaving a broad length of the knotty table between them. One of the dogs came up and sniffed at her. She kicked it. It whined.

Saradyn called the dog back.

"You speak real Dorinah?" Zezili asked, "Or are you too fucking stupid for it? Everyone in this country is a fucking stupid butcher. Is that all you can do? Shit in buckets and–"

Saradyn gestured to one of his men, some little one

that Zezili hadn't seen before. He held a large book. He dipped his head at Saradyn a few times, then once at her, as if he wasn't sure how to greet her. It felt like some absurd parody. She flexed the phantom of her left hand.

"King Saradyn of Lind," the man said, in passable Dorinah, "Laine's Fist of–"

"Oh, get the fuck on with it," Zezili said.

The man said something to Saradyn in Tordinian.

Saradyn spoke, not to him, but to her. He had a deep voice and odd eyes, hazel, maybe, yellow-brown. His thick, black hair fell into his face. He paused once to push it aside and stroke at his beard, as if from long habit.

His translator said, "King Saradyn wants to know why you brought a force into Tordin, and whether or not this is the Empress's command, or yours."

"I'm a rogue," Zezili said. "Look at my face." She leaned forward, sneering at him.

The translator prattled on.

Zezili leaned back, watching Saradyn's face. Hard to believe this was the King the Empress once fucked. They said it's why he thought so highly of himself. She had come down for Penelodyn's body. He was nothing back then, just some petty lord that amused her, but he took the fucking to mean something it hadn't. A lot of people around him had, too, and this is what it made him. Some mad, petty tyrant thinking he had tamed a woman who fucked anyone she fancied because she could.

"I heard you gave up your own family after she fucked you," Zezili said. "I heard you murdered them in your bed because you heard voices, saw things, after she touched you. Women drive you mad? Is that why you had them cut my hand off? Because if that's the worst you can think of, you're a fucking fool."

Saradyn glanced at the translator, whose expression was pained. They argued for a few minutes before Saradyn appeared to peel the translation out of him. Zezili could tell it was mostly accurate because Saradyn's expression darkened. He made a retort.

"You forget that we have your husband," the translator said.

"I've heard that, but I haven't seen him. You chop something off him too? You can't break me, you old fool. I've survived worse than you."

Call and response. He said, "We'll be happy to bring him in here and cut strips off him for every further question you refuse to answer."

She grimaced, sat back. "Why should one more dead man matter to me?"

"Because you have come a good long distance to find him, have you not?"

"I don't go mad over a good fuck the way you do."

A pause. Smattering of words. Then, "Perhaps we can come to a more amicable agreement."

"We can," Zezili said, and for the first time in weeks she found the long thread of her advantage. She was not a clever person. She preferred brute force. But she had not come here to do the Empress's bidding. She had come here to thwart her. And if she was killed here in this little dining hall, then she was dead for nothing, and the Empress would get away with what she'd done to her, and the dajians, and the whole bloody country. It went on and on. Death without revenge was just death.

"If I tell you what she's here to do," Zezili said, "you release me and Anavha. You can wait until you verify the story, that's fine. But you release us."

"Of course."

His warm, bright eyes met hers as he said the equivalent in Tordinian. He even smiled, like a playful predator. A lie, she knew. She had been on the other side of the table enough times to know it was a lie. She and Anavha would both die, tortured and buried in some anonymous grave, because they were too uncivilized to burn their dead. She hoped only he would bury them together.

"She's sent us to uncover some secret of hers, some weapon she buried out here," Zezili said. "I came here because I fucking hate her. You understand what that's like, don't you? I could have said no, fucked off into my little life. But Anavha was gone, and half the dajians in the country were dead, and I knew I was going to be next, people like me. She was powerful as ever. I don't know the exact location or what it is, but it's north-east of here, hidden in some anomaly on the map. A ring of mountains? Something like that. That's where Storm, the other legion commander, is taking them."

"So there's no other army coming?"

"Not that I know about."

"And there is another legion commander. Your force still has a leader?"

"The Empress doesn't mind redundancies. She needs them, with the kind of place this is."

Saradyn watched her in silence for some time. He steepled his fingers. It took a great deal of will not to look away, but she refused to be first. Fuck him.

"You'll go back to your army," the translator said once Saradyn broke his silence. "But you'll take two of our people. We want you embedded with the army again."

Zezili thought a long moment. "What's to keep me from killing your two men?"

Saradyn laughed, and the translator interpreted his next words, "You have one useless hand. We have the other. You could bite them to death, of course. I'll be sure to tell them to cover their faces, like Saiduan children." Saradyn laughed the whole time the translator said this, as if the entire idea was the funniest thing he'd ever heard.

Heat bloomed on Zezili's face. Is that what they thought of her now? They thought her impotent. She wanted to tell them she wasn't so easily hobbled, but thought better of it. This was her only way to leave this shithole instead of being buried in it. Buried in the dirt, like refuse.

"I want to see my husband," Zezili said.

Saradyn stood, said something to the translator, and whistled at the dogs.

The translator bowed his head. "We will return with your husband, of course," he said. He left her there in the massive room with only two men at the doors on the other side of it for company.

She wanted to seethe, but she had been testing her bonds during the interview, and already worked her stump loose. It was difficult to secure someone with just one hand. She twisted her other hand free, but kept both behind her, looking for some kind of weapon.

Directly across from her was a huge hearth, big enough to stand in. Inside were two iron prongs for setting a roasting hunk of meat, and a skewer at the center fixed with curved metal tongs to hold the meat. Beside it was a metal container and what looked like a couple of fire pokers. She glanced again at the guards. Flexed her bad right hand. The remaining fingers barely curled into her fist. How to pick it up, and once she held it, keep hold of it while bashing someone in the face?

She yelled at the guards. "Hey! Hey!"

They ignored her, and it occurred to her that they wouldn't be able to speak Dorinah. She could yell at them a lot, make a fuss, but they weren't going to come over. She assessed their weapons. Swords and daggers. No ranged weapons.

Zezili rocked once in her chair. She steeled herself for a painful fall, then threw the chair over onto her right side. Pain jolted up her arm.

The guards came running. She stayed down until they were nearly on top of her, then crawled swiftly under the table, kicking the chair back at them.

She heaved herself onto the table and came right up on top of the nearest guard before his sword was out of its sheath. She headbutted him in the face so hard she saw a bank of static blur across her vision. She hooked the thumb and pointer finger of her right hand under the hilt of his sword and yanked it out the rest of the way. She braced it against her stomach, knowing her hand could not provide the needed pressure, and leaned into the chest of the second guard just as he brought up his dagger.

They both slammed into the ground. The hilt of the sword jammed badly into her ribs. She used the stump of her other hand to help get leverage on the hilt and pulled the sword out. The first guard was still hunched over, blood gushing down his face from his shattered nose. She kicked his legs out from under him.

He fell. Punched her hard. Her head whipped back. She headbutted him again.

He howled.

They flailed on the floor in a tangle of limbs and blood. She got the sword flat against his neck. She pressed a knee on either side of the sword, balancing herself on her toes, her ass on his chest, using her body weight to strangle him.

He kicked. She drooled in his bloody face.

Her right hand ached. She stared into his face, some fat bearded face, and she imagined Storm's face there, and she pressed harder, because she would have to kill Storm too, she would have to kill them all if she was going to stop whatever this all was, whatever dark thing the Empress had planned for the Dhai, for the Dorinah, for the Tai Mora, for the world.

The guard kicked one last time. He went limp, his tongue lolling from his mouth.

She continued sitting over him, panting, for a full minute. The edges of the blade had bit into the bottom of his throat, making a red line. His face was bug-eyed, the eyes reddened. He was starved of oxygen, his windpipe crushed. The other man was bleeding out from the belly wound six paces away. She didn't care to bother with him.

Zezili was trembling. She crawled to her feet, steadying herself on the table. There was no way out of here that wasn't walking out the front door, and to do that... She stared at the dead man. Both men wore helms; though they didn't cover their faces – making them terribly vulnerable to headbutting – it might get her out the door.

It so happened she knew a certain doctor who had a far better helmet for her purposes, and she knew where to find him. Without her left hand, she had no way to knot a weapon to her right. They didn't leave her with a lot of options. She glanced over at the fireplace again, and the roasting spit at its center with the iron teeth on it. What was the stump of her left arm now, but a hunk of meat?

She put her left arm on the spit and painfully twisted the tongs to tighten them, so the metal closed over the top of her arm like teeth. It was heavy, and cumbersome, but she wasn't going out into that hall without a weapon.

Zezili pulled on the padded leather armor of one of the dead men, sweating and swearing as she did it. How long did she have? Two minutes? Thirty?

She put the padded armor over her head without tightening it. All she needed was the padded bit over her chest where she could rest the blunt end of the spit. If she held her left arm low and tight next to her side, the spit turned to her chest, she could use the armor to leverage a good thrust.

Zezili strode to the doors, bleeding pain with every step. Her vision still swam. Her face ached from smashing the man's nose, and her phantom fingers hurt twice as bad, as if someone had mashed the whole hand under a boot.

As she stepped up to the door, she heard footsteps in the hall – too few for an army of guards. Maybe she still had a chance. She braced her weapon, caught the door with her working fingers, and threw it open. Lunged forward.

A young man ran headlong into her, body thumping directly into the spitted weapon. The weight of him sent her reeling back. She landed with a huff on the floor, the man on top of her. She smacked her head on the stone. Her stump thumped into his body, preventing him from sliding all the way to her shoulder, launched there with the weight of his own momentum.

The breath left her body, knocked cleanly out of her. She tried to roll clear. He moved first, pushing himself up on his hands. His dark hair hung into his face. Blood bloomed across his tunic.

Zezili thought she was dreaming. The square jaw, hollowed cheekbones, the delicate face and features – she knew him, knew him like she knew the hand she had lost.

But she could not say his name.

Anavha rolled off her, grabbing at the bloody hole in his chest.

Zezili gasped for breath and clawed toward him. She pushed her right hand under his head, pulled him close to her, and stared down at him with wonderment.

His mouth moved.

"Ah, my love," Zezili said.

More footsteps, a gaggle of men, led by Natanial Thorne.

Zezili bared her teeth. "Don't you touch him," she said. "He's mine."

Natanial punched her square in the face.

34

The stargazers were both men, slender and supple as reeds with words sweet as honey and opaque as molasses. Kirana drummed her fingers on her campaign table while they droned on about probability and the proposed speed of different types of light. Another week of war, hounding the Dorinahs to the sea, and the biting ulcer in her stomach was flaring up again, like some hungry animal. The stargazers' avoidance of her question was not helping her mood. She made camp inside some petty Dorinah lord's estate, hosting her stargazers through a rip in the fabric of the world right there in the lord's former entertaining room.

Decadent furniture carved with fanciful living shapes – wildflowers, vines, and belled faces of pitcher plants – clashed with the blood smearing the table, and her boots. She had the lord's table taken out and her campaign table put in. She did not sit at it, as the furniture in Dorinah was all too low, as if they liked to kiss the floor and the creatures on it. So she stood, impatient, while the blood of the household fueled this useless conversation.

"Six people died to get this wink open," she said. "Tell me how many worlds have entered the field of battle? It's a simple question."

"As we've tried to explain–" The elder, a bearded

fellow called Suari, made a broad, expansive gesture
with one hand, which she recognized as the prelude to
another circular lecture. He had blue tattoos winding up
his arms, twin mermen with forked tails and giant fangs.
She once asked him if they were a relation, and he had
asked if it was a serious question.

She addressed the younger instead. "Masis, tell me
what he won't."

Masis eyed Suari a long moment, stroking his scraggly
beard. Young men trying in vain to grow spotty beards
put her in mind of molting young birds playing at being
adults. He cleared his throat. "As we've discussed, there
is no way to accurately determine how many worlds
may gain access during Oma's rise," he said. "I can tell
you no world is fool enough to cross over into *ours*, at
least that we've determined. It seems quite clear our
world is one of the many that will not survive this latest
rise of Oma. But our preliminary theories suggest that
the closer a world is to the prime – the world where the
break initially occurred, making this travel possible –
the softer and more sensitive it will be to travel from
other realms, allowing the mixing and merging of people
fleeing catastrophes on other worlds."

"Plain language," Kirana said.

Masis said, "Because it's easier to get to the world
you're on, now the one where the primary break
occurred, it's statistically more likely to be the world
more people will travel to as the worlds come closer
together."

"So we could have hundreds of worlds invading this
one right now? I could have dozens of usurpers take
everything I've gained here?"

Suari turned up his nose, though she suspected it was
an unconscious gesture. She was well aware of what he
thought of her – daughter to a cobbler, murderer of half
the world. "We are stargazers, Kai, not priests."

Masis said, "There could be any number of adjacent

realities pushing into your sphere right now. It will only get worse when Oma rises. The fact that you have identified others is a bold sign, though – it means Oma's rise is very close."

"How close?" Kirana said.

"Weeks," Masis said. "Perhaps a month or two, at maximum."

"And that means travel without blood," Suari said. "So perhaps next time you could spare the six."

"It's six fewer left here to till your garden when you arrive, that's all," Kirana said. That made them both stand a little straighter. They all yearned to cross over. The toxic sky was getting worse. She had no equipment here, no safe observatory, to put them in, not until she had taken Dhai and its temples. And if she failed to close the rifts from the temples… she, too, could be overrun by some other world.

She said, "Do you have recommendations on sealing these soft areas where the other worlds are getting people through? Something we can do before we crack Dhai?"

"Only what we told you before," Suari said. "Until the machines that caused the initial break are engaged to seal it, or Oma leaves the sky – which could be twenty years or more – you will see visitations from other worlds. Perhaps twenty. Perhaps thousands."

"Why is it you never give me comforting news?"

"As I said–" Suari began.

"You're not priests." Kirana waved a hand at them. "Go, then. Get back to observing that cancer speeding across our sky. I've not given up on a solution for that."

Suari's eyes widened, but Masis just nodded. Did they think she had killed too many to go back? But killing was wearying, and she knew exactly how much more she had to do before this was all over, and Yisaoh could cross over, and they could build a real life here.

"Tell the minder to fetch Yisaoh," she said, "if she isn't engaged in something else."

The stargazers nodded and moved out of the frame. The wink looked out onto a shadowy green wall lit with smoky outlines of people. Kirana had moved her entire army closer to the equator, as the poison from the sky was worse the closer one went to the poles. The northern continent she'd murdered with plague was uninhabitable now, as were the great glass cities of the only empire that had held out against hers. They'd negotiated an uneasy peace five years before. The people of the glass cities told her their gods would save them. So when death rained from the sky, its people went out into the streets and raised their hands to it, and died there. Millions dead. Such a waste of blood.

This outpost with the green walls and shadowy memories of death belonged to a people called the Azorum who had made the most beautiful green stone temples and public buildings. They were not a warring people, and they had come out to meet her army with open palms and warm smiles and she had cast great waves of fire into their sprawling cities so powerful the blast of it seared the outlines of their terrified bodies against those same walls.

Kirana supposed they would have painted over them, in time, but they did not intend to stay in the cities of the Azorum. The band of civilizations moving to the equator where the effect of the dying satellite wasn't as toxic would wither and die soon enough.

Yisaoh moved into the frame of the wink, sitting just in front of the shadowy outline on the wall. Her hollowed face was made more cavernous as the long shadows of the evening began to creep across the room.

"The stargazers tell us we're about out of time," Kirana said.

"I remember the first time you told me that."

"It convinced your mothers," Kirana said. "They wouldn't have given permission for us to wed if I hadn't told them the world was ending."

"You have a persuasive way about you." Yisaoh smiled a mirthless smile; lips making the motions. Her eyes remained shadowed. She held her hands in her lap, tightly. She only did that when she had too much to say and a fear of saying it.

"The other worlds are here," Kirana said. It hurt to say. Her throat closed, as if she tried to swallow a stone.

"How many?"

"We don't know. We're turning away from assaulting Dorinah and going straight to Dhai, now. We don't have time to make a foothold here. If we don't begin the process of closing the seams between the worlds, we could be overrun by some other force."

"Without doing the spring planting in Dorinah, you'll be lost come summer. Many crops will already be in, but who will tend them? You said you needed Dorinah before Dhai, or we could not support ourselves there."

"I know. But I have a boon."

Yisaoh waited, brows raised.

"Nava is here. Her double. We found her in some lodging near the crossover point. That's a bit of luck, isn't it?"

"Luck?"

Kirana leaned forward. "There is luck still, Yisaoh."

Yisaoh's lower lip trembled. Kirana put her hand through the gap in the world, though there was always a fear, a danger that it would snap shut and take her limb with it. Yisaoh gripped her hand, hard. Her skin was cold to the touch, like a corpse. But the air around her was very warm.

"Luck," Kirana said.

"Luck," Yisaoh whispered.

"I will take the wall of Liona. We'll take Dhai and its temples and stop the encroachment of the others. This is our world now. We'll find your shadow. It's only a matter of time. I promised, Yisaoh."

"So many promises," Yisaoh said. She pressed Kirana's

hand to her face. Put her other hand up to the invisible wall between them, until it met resistance. Her double's existence, pushing back at her.

"And I've kept them. For you, I've kept them."

A knock at the door. A voice outside the frame of the wink. "Twenty minutes, before it closes, Consort."

Kirana squeezed Yisaoh's hand. "Soon," she said. "Will you bring the children in?"

"Yes," Yisaoh said. "They've been asking for you."

Yisaoh moved outside the reach of the wink. Kirana heard a door close. Low voices. She waited patiently.

The children came in ahead of Yisaoh – tall, leggy Moira, already twelve; curly haired Corina, ten; and little Tasia, her youngest, six.

"Can we visit now?" Tasia said.

Kirana said, "We're getting things well prepared for you. I don't want to bring you over until I have everything ready."

"Mother isn't coming," Moira said. Cool. Matter-of-fact. Kirana saw much of herself in her, though they were not her blood children. Moira and Tasia were her dead cousin's, and Corina was Yisaoh's. She and Yisaoh had raised all three since they were infants. Kirana still remembered coming home from delivering the plague-ridden goods to the docks and finding Moira toddling out to greet her. Kirana had been gone so long she had no idea she was already walking.

"I'll follow after," Yisaoh said.

"Mam," Tasia said to Kirana, "Mother says the sky isn't rotten there."

"That's right. We'll all be together soon." She thought to promise it again, but after her conversation with Yisaoh, promises tasted bad. No more promises. Action.

"Kai?" the voice of the sinajista on the other side again. "Consort, the wink's becoming unstable."

"Love to you," Kirana said. "When you arrive you'll have a big house, and rooms all to yourselves. What do you think of that?"

"It's hot here," Tasia said.

Moira folded her arms, frowned. "It better not be as hot," she said.

Kirana restrained her annoyance. Oh, to be twelve. "It's not as hot," she assured her. "The wink's going out. You take care of your mother."

"I love you, Mam!" Corina burst out, spreading her arms wide.

The wink wavered, like ripples on a pool of water.

"I love–"

The wink closed.

Kirana stared hard at the other side of the blood-smeared house, now a blank wall.

One of her sinajistas knocked, opened the door. "Kai…"

"I know," Kirana said. She hated that they knew her weakness. Did caring for Yisaoh make her stronger, or weaker, in their eyes? But they all cared for someone still on the other side. If she shared their motivation, didn't that make her more like them? Make her more trustworthy?

"We march west tomorrow," Kirana said. "Time is short."

"It's been relayed. And the force approaching from the east?"

"Not our concern. Let the Dorinahs deal with them. I want to concentrate our forces on Liona. We're taking Dhai."

"Yes, Kai."

Kirana stood over her table. The lines were blurry, the map a fuzzy nonsense thing. Teardrops on the map. She wiped her face. Foolish. Tears saved no one. A decade-long campaign was about to end. She needed to stay focused here at the very end. The end of everything, and the beginning, too. Her beginning. Their beginning. A renewal.

"Kai?"

Lohin's mewling voice. She called him in.

"I've heard we have a new destination," he said.

"Correct."

"With Nava in our custody, we could breach the walls of Dorinah in a week and–"

"How long have you known of the second force?"

"The... second force, Kai?"

"The one coming from the east? The Osadainans. A people we already thoroughly destroyed."

"I... it was purely speculative. I needed to confirm..."

"Do you think this is a joke, Lohin?"

"I... no? No, this is life or–"

"Not just your life. Or my life. But the lives of our entire people. How many times have our people fled destruction, looking for the prime world, the first world, the one with the power to stop the transitions, the apocalypse?"

"Quite some time..."

"We've tried to find this world for four thousand years," Kirana said. "Four thousand. How many Kais is that?"

"Quite a number."

"Yes. Four thousand years. And we've found it. And now you're fucking around. You're fucking this, Lohin. Fucking it terribly."

"Kai, I apologize, I was just–"

"Send Madah in here."

"Madah?"

"Do it."

He bowed once, twice, bowed as he scooted out the door, backing away from her. She waited, drumming her fingers on the map, thinking of Yisaoh's cold skin. How much longer?

Madah entered, tall and slim, young, fierce. She carried herself like someone born far better, someone of Kirana's station, but Kirana liked that just fine. Lohin squirreled in behind her, pinched little face taut, gaze downcast.

"Madah," Kirana said. "I want you to take Lohin's place. You understand?"

"Yes, Kai." Madah sketched a bow.

Lohin started. "But Kai, what do you want–"

"I want you to stay here in Dorinah and relay intelligence to me about what's happening. All right?"

"But, if hostilities are moving to Dhai–"

"You will not be needed in Dhai. We march to the wall in the morning, Madah. You are both dismissed."

Madah left.

Lohin lingered, crouching in the doorway. "Kai, please, without the army... I'm... they'll think I'm a slave. There is very little–"

"Then you must use your wits."

"Kai–"

"I have no time for baggage, Lohin. No time for bearshit, or regrets. Go."

He made a sound like a cat in distress.

They marched at dawn for Liona.

35

Ahkio kicked at the confines of his cell – and a cell was what it was, though none were supposed to exist in the temple. In his naivety he'd assumed Nasaka had cleared a storage room for Almeysia, but no, this was very clearly a cell, the like of which he'd only read about in bad Dorinah romances and references in *The Book of Oma*.

Liaro had not come down with him, but it was still his name Ahkio yelled inside the black cell. He shouted himself hoarse. It wasn't until he kicked a bucket in one corner, sending it clattering across the little eight foot by eight foot space, that the gravity of the situation came over him. He pressed himself against the floor, right up to the little sliver of air that crept in from under the door, and cried one final time, "Nasaka!"

"She won't come."

The voice was faint, and familiar.

"Who's that?"

"Don't tell me you don't know?"

He heard another sound, a faint cry that sounded like a cat, or, absurdly, an infant.

"Who is that?"

"It's Meyna, Ahkio."

The cold from the floor seeped into his bones. His cheek felt numb. But he squeezed against the seam of the door anyway, pressing his face as close as he could to try and see into the hall.

The cry came again. Then the sound of Meyna murmuring.

"Nasaka put you here?" Ahkio said. As if he needed the answer.

"She came for me after you left," she said.

"What did she want from you?"

Silence. The fussing cry. Ahkio closed his eyes. Her baby, the one she had been so close to having last summer when he exiled her, growing up in this prison in the guts of the temple while he ran around upstairs, arguing with Nasaka.

"This is a poor way to speak," she said. "I'm coming over."

"How will–"

He heard a scraping sound. Footsteps.

Meyna's eye appeared on the other side of the crack beneath the door, wide and bold. He stared at her, speechless. Heard the amusement in her voice.

"The hinges are on the inside," she said. "This isn't a proper prison. We don't have any. I busted out the hinges weeks ago from the inside, using the refuse bucket."

"How are you still here?"

"The other door is locked, the one to the hall. Hinges on the outside. I've been up and down this whole corridor. It's full of old records. No secret ways out. It would take us an age to tunnel out with our bare hands. A hundred years at least."

"How do I get out?"

"Grab your refuse bucket. I'll talk you through it."

Ahkio followed Meyna's instructions, though it was difficult in the dark. He felt his way around the hinge pins. It took two hours of sweat, a splintered bucket, and no small amount of cursing, but he managed to remove the hinges and haul the door inward.

On the other side, Meyna stood before him, thinner and filthy, her greasy hair bound back with what looked like a torn bit of her tunic. Her mouth was a puckered moue, brows drawn.

"I'm sorry you became a part of this," he said, because he could think of nothing else.

"I chose this," she said, "when I told Kirana I'd look after you. Every bid for power comes with a price, doesn't it?"

The baby wailed.

She sighed heavily.

"Do they send more than one person down to feed you?" he said. "We can overtake one together."

"It used to be Elaiko," she said. "Now it's some other one."

"Pasinu?"

Meyna shrugged. "She didn't share her name."

"If we can–"

"Ahkio, I want a bath and a steaming bowl of curried rice and yams. I want a clean swath of linen and a tunic that doesn't stink. But she sends gifted people down here. If we move on them now and fail, we'll have given our trick away, and then I'll be bound up even more securely, or killed. If they've already brought you down here, I suspect we've reached the final days."

"Final days of what?"

"You haven't figured out Nasaka's plan, have you? Ahkio, what have you been doing all these months?"

"Keeping the country together. She's betrayed us to the Tai Mora. I found out that much."

"She wanted me to bring Etena here. My mother was one of the Woodland Dhai who escorted her into exile."

"And you... didn't? You chose to stay?"

"Choice? You're so naïve, Ahkio. She'd have killed my child."

"Rhin and Hadaoh? Mey-Mey?"

"Safe," she said. "Unless you did something to them."

"We need to work together," he said.

"Then let's talk of the present. The past is rotten."

● ● ●

Ahkio stayed awake all night... all day? Time was limitless here. He had no idea how Meyna had stayed sane. She was emotionally stronger than him. It's what drew him to her from the very first.

He must have nodded off at some point, because the scraping open of the door at the end of the corridor started him awake. He crawled to his own door. He had pushed it back into place with the hinges still broken. Meyna said that when they fed her they had to open the door, which is why she had to keep replacing the hinges every night.

Ahkio tensed, listening. The clanging of a key in a lock. His door. He stood and pressed his palms lightly against the door. Waited for the click of the lock, and the give of the door–

He stepped back half a pace and put his shoulder to the door, ramming it with all his strength. The door toppled outward onto the person outside of it. The hall was too narrow, though – the top of the door stuck on the wall opposite. Ahkio rolled under it, swinging his bucket at the figure caught under the door. He smashed the bucket into the figure's face, bursting the nose, before he realized it wasn't Pasinu.

It was Nasaka.

Ahkio tackled her, pinning her to the ground. Meyna pushed her door open, wielding her own bucket. She swung. Ahkio ducked. The bucket narrowly missed his head and swung into Nasaka's face.

Blood spattered Ahkio's face. He sputtered.

"Stop! Meyna!"

She brought the bucket down twice more.

Nasaka's nose was smashed, her left cheekbone clearly crushed. Blood welled from her mouth. She spit two teeth, sputtering more blood into Ahkio's face.

"Meyna, the door!"

Meyna ran to the door to the corridor, pushed it open. "The hallway is clear!"

Ahkio yanked Nasaka up and pushed her into another of the rooms. He found the keys on the floor, smeared with blood. His hands trembled as he fumbled with the keys, finally locking her in.

"It won't hold her," Meyna said.

"I'll send someone down," Ahkio said.

"Who?" Meyna said. "You don't know how many of them are hers. She could have turned them all against you in the night. You could be walking into a trap."

"Ahkio…" Nasaka rasped.

He pressed his hands to his ears. He didn't want to hear it.

"You said Pasinu was the only other one who came down here," he said. "Lock the corridor door behind us. Even if she gets out of the cell, she won't leave the corridor."

"You'll let her die down here?"

"Grab your child," Ahkio said. "I'm closing the door."

Meyna ran back into her cell. Ahkio had expected an infant, but the bundle in her arms was a plump little nine-month-old child, sitting up in her arms, sucking on its fist. The big eyes were Meyna's, the tangle of dark hair, the broad face. It was a relief to see nothing of himself in that face; a child birthed in a prison.

Ahkio urged Meyna into the hall. "Up. We need to get to Pasinu, quickly."

Nasaka's voice, pained, slurred, "Ahkio…"

He slammed the door. Found the key, and twisted the lock. He wiped the blood from his face and forged ahead.

"You know where Pasinu is?" Meyna said. "If she's–"

"Let me think."

"You've gotten mouthy."

"You're much the same."

He glanced back. She smirked at him, and he found himself returning the smile, absurdly. He covered his mouth, but a laugh bubbled up inside him, and he could not stop it. He bent over, and laughed so hard he thought he'd retch.

"Are you all right?"

"It's just... The absurdity..."

"Hush. Voices."

He went quiet. He recognized the voices – Una and her assistant, Sabasao.

Meyna whispered, "Are we going to fight them too?"

"No," he said. He straightened and pushed forward boldly into the hall.

Una and her assistant rounded the corner, and came up short. Una's mouth hung open. "Ahkio? Kai? This is..."

"Surprising, I'm sure," he said. "You're exiled. Sabasao, you're gatekeeper of Oma's Temple."

"This is a mistake," Una said. "Ora Nasaka–"

"Is no longer with us," Ahkio said. "Get out. Meyna?"

Meyna came up behind him. The child clung to her hair.

"Oh," Una said.

"Oh?" Ahkio said. "Is that all you have to say for yourself? Go forward, Una. Sabasao, you need to choose a side right now. The one that locks up Dhai children in the temple basements, or the one that frees them. Which do you choose?"

Una started gabbling.

Sabasao was a young man, not much older than Ahkio. "It's time, then," he said. "Kai, there are so many sworn to Ora Nasaka that–"

"She's dead," Ahkio lied. "So there are fewer options."

"I need a bath," Meyna said. "Curried yams. Remember?"

"Could you give me a moment?"

"Yams."

Sabasao nodded. "Up we go, then. I can tell you who you have, but it's not many."

"Fool child," Una muttered.

Una's star was in decline, but he didn't think she was as far gone as Nasaka. If she tried something now, she had no one to blame it on but herself. If he had learned one thing in all this time trying to rule Dhai, it was that what people really wanted was to rally around a strong leader.

They pushed upstairs and into the foyer. Ahkio led Una out the front doors and yelled for a stir of militia. He found eight of them, and for one tense moment, he worried Nasaka had gotten to them first. But they were Ghrasia's still. Bold, loyal Ghrasia.

"Three of you need to escort Una out of Dhai," he said, "to Liona. The rest need to go upstairs and contain Pasinu, Nasaka's assistant."

"I'll warn you, Kai," one of the militia said. "She has Oras up there."

"So do I," Ahkio said. "Let's head up. Meyna–"

She was already forging toward the kitchens, baby hitched on her hip. "Yams and a bath, Ahkio."

He headed upstairs. The militia followed. They found Pasinu in Nasaka's study, standing on a ladder, shelving books. Ahkio yanked the ladder out from under her. She fell hard.

"Bind her and drug her," he said.

"Kai," she said. "Kai, what is–"

"You know very well," he said. "Where's Liaro?"

But she did not know. Ahkio took the stairs two at a time. He went all the way to the top, strode across the Assembly Chamber, and found Liaro passed out in the bed in the Kai's quarters. He ripped open the curtains.

Liaro raised his head, bleary-eyed.

"Get out," Ahkio said.

"Ahkio!" Liaro rubbed his eyes. "Ahkio, this is bad business."

"Meyna was in the basements. With her baby. What was Nasaka going to do with me, Liaro? What else did she have planned?"

"Where is she?"

"Dead," he lied again, and the lie was getting easier.

"She ordered all the parajistas back from Kuallina. She wants everyone back in the temples."

"She'd prefer we died at Kuallina. How many civilians dead, to ensure–"

"You don't understand. She told me–"

"What lies did she tell you, Liaro?"

"Please, I'm–"

"Hung over? Still drunk. Get out of this bed, out of this country–"

Liaro crawled out of bed. He reached for Ahkio's hands.

Ahkio pulled away. "Get out, or I'll have the militia throw you out."

Liaro dressed, tears falling freely. Ahkio didn't want to understand Liaro's betrayal. He just wanted it over. He followed Liaro out, down the stairs, cutting him off every time he tried to speak. At the big double doors, Liaro tried to plead his case one last time.

"You're the love of my life, Ahkio," Liaro said. "What I did I did to protect you. I thought it was right."

"Goodbye, Liaro." He ushered him out the door. Closed it.

Soruza crossed the foyer to him. "Ahkio, I've heard some terrible news about Ora Nasaka–"

"Recall your orders for the parajistas," he said. "Ora Nasaka wasn't working on my order. She's dead. Whatever you thought you were doing for this country, it was most likely treason. So I suggest turning things around. Recall them."

"Yes, Kai, but Ora Nasaka said–"

"I don't give a care for what she said. If it's not been clear to you until now, Nasaka is a traitor to this country. She's been aligned with the Tai Mora all this time. Every order she gave you was in service to them. Those parajistas need to be in Kuallina."

"I'm sorry, Kai. I… didn't know."

Hadn't she? Ahkio honestly had no idea. "I need

another note sent to the Temple of Para," he said. "To Caisa Arianao Raona. Tell her to meet me in Kuallina. Take the Line."

"But you just–"

"I've changed my mind. You'll find that changing one's mind in the face of new information is wise."

"Yes, Kai."

"Can I trust you to hold this temple until I return?" So far as he knew, there was no other power vying for attention in the temple. With Nasaka locked up, they had few options. It was follow him or descend into chaos. He wouldn't blame them for choosing chaos.

"I will, Kai."

He inquired in the kitchens, and was directed downstairs to the bathing chamber where Meyna was submerged, scrubbing her hair with everpine while a gaggle of novices played with her child. It was strange to watch. The novices were so unconcerned, completely ignorant of the shift in power going on above them.

Ahkio squatted next to her.

Meyna rolled her eyes up at him. "Put your things in order?"

"I'm going to Kuallina. The harbor has fallen. The Tai Mora."

"Tai Mora?"

"Have someone catch you up," he said.

"You'll do just fine," she said.

"I just said–"

"I'm going with you to Kuallina," she said. "The way by Line is hours. We'll have time to catch up."

"That sounds like a terrible idea."

"Does it?" She ducked under the water, rinsing out her cloud of dark hair. Surfaced. "If there's one person up here you can be sure isn't on Ora Nasaka's side, it's me, isn't it?"

"You hate me as much."

"Not quite as much," she said.

"The baby—"

"Every Kai led with a baby at her hip. There's a long tradition. You could, too."

"This game again?"

She laughed. It sounded genuine. She came to the edge of the pool, whispered, "Kai Ahkio, what better way to shore up your position here than with a baby of your own on your hip? You are a childless man, still. With me and your baby, you give people hope. A future. Have you considered that?"

"You're a scheming Mutao, just as Nasaka said."

"I'm right, though, aren't I?"

She was right. He chewed his lip. Liaro gone. Mohrai pregnant, but was she still alive in Kuallina?

He gazed into Meyna's dark eyes and read mirth there. She was still one of the smartest people he knew, and unlike Nasaka, he knew her motives. Her final move. If he gave it to her, she had no reason to fight him.

"Will you marry me, Ahkio?"

"You and Rhin and Hadaoh?"

She shrugged. "The more the merrier? They are in the woodland. We can address that issue when we get there."

The child shrieked with laughter. He glanced over at the grinning novices carrying it about in their arms.

"Is the child gifted?"

"It's Nasaka's grandchild," Meyna said. "I suspect it will be."

"One who can bear children, or cursed like me?"

"All signs say it will bear children," she said. Meyna had not gendered Mey-mey until she was a year and a half old, when Mey-mey started applying a gender to herself.

He held out a hand and helped her out of the bath. She was gloriously naked, but he handed her a towel quickly, to keep from thinking of it. "So you've decided to invest in me, finally," he said. "What changed your mind?"

"I was in prison for almost a year," she said. "It gave me time to think."

They married in the Sanctuary, a hasty ceremony that earned him strange looks from more than one Ora. The faces of the Oras were different – Almeysia and Una gone, Gaiso dead, Nasaka shuttered up downstairs. Only Masura was familiar, and it was she and Soruza who held the ceremony. By all laws it was an illegal pairing; Mohrai, Rhin and Hadaoh had to sign all the appropriate documents, agreeing to the match. But Ahkio wanted symbolism. He wanted continuity.

Most of all, he needed to hold up Meyna's child in the light streaming in from the dome above, colored red in the light of Oma's visage, and declare it the Li Kai, his successor.

He had three dozen witnesses to it. The child squalled at him. He held it tight, gazing into the mirror of Meyna's eyes, and mourned for Kirana, and the line of Kais that could have been.

Meyna had not expected this part. He saw it in her face.

When he returned the child to her arms, he leaned over, whispered. "I know you want to come to Kuallina. But if I die there, something needs to continue. Do you understand?"

"I'll hold the temple," she said.

He withdrew.

Friends. Enemies. It was all blurring together now.

He got onto the Line to Kuallina, into an uncertain future.

36

Ghrasia was on the wall of Liona when the Tai Mora army arrived. Scouts brought word just ahead of their arrival. She had just enough time to beg for a dozen jistas from the Temple of Para. Only five arrived ahead of the army.

News had already reached her about the fall of the harbor, and the forces headed toward Kuallina. She had sent half her army to Kuallina to shore it up, not anticipating a second Tai Mora army at her gates. Her strategy and tactics classes taught her not to fight a war on two fronts and not to divide one's forces, but with an army as massive as that of the Tai Mora, their sheer numbers defied standard rules of engagement.

When she gazed over the great wall of Liona, it did not surprise her to see her daughter Madah there at the head of the Tai Mora army, swinging a great weapon from her perch atop a low rise where she addressed the long lines of blue-clad parajistas.

She would know her anywhere – the long lean lines of her, the hatchet of a face, the heavy brow she shared with one of her fathers. When Ghrasia went home to wash and prepare her body for the funerary feast, she had looked terribly peaceful in repose, far more peaceful than she had in life.

Madah was a fighter – angry, violent. Ghrasia had kept her out of trouble by pulling a lot of political favors, and Nasaka kept that hanging over Ghrasia. Nasaka had covered up the violence, and even one accidental death. It seemed appropriate that it was she who led the army to the gates of Liona, to burn down her mother's wall with a force of parajistas so large Ghrasia had no hope of pushing them back. The parajistas on the wall with her were already sweating, holding a great wall of air around Liona, but it would not last.

Ghrasia stayed on the wall for the first onslaught from the foreign army that clogged the pass for as far as she could see, far greater than any number of refugees or legionnaires.

The wall shook so hard under the offensive that Ghrasia lost her feet.

She did not stay for the second volley.

Ghrasia strode purposefully downstairs. She felt oddly calm. The little feral girl met her as she rounded the corridor leading to her study, and sniffed at her hand as she passed, then trailed after her.

She found Arasia two doors down, yelling at a group of militia.

"Get the militia off the wall," Ghrasia said. "When the wall falls, we'll be caught in it. Regroup on the other side."

"We'll hold Liona," Arasia said.

"We won't," Ghrasia said. "But we can slow them down. Abandon the wall and regroup outside of it. They'll have to get over the rubble of the wall, and that will give us an advantage with archers and jistas."

"It won't fall," Arasia said.

The hold shook again. Ghrasia caught herself against the wall.

Arasia put out both hands. Two of the militia fell. "All right!" Arasia said. She rounded on the militia. "You heard her! Relay the order!"

Ghrasia paused at the door to her study and stared at

the big tapestry of Faith Ahya crossing over the pass into what would become Dhai. She wondered who would come out the hero of this moment.

She moved downstairs, yelling the retreat as she went, and the great fortress trembled and shivered beneath her. One hallway fell in behind her as she went, trapping those who came after. She stayed long enough to huff out a few blocks before she realized it was a lost cause, and then she was moving again, trying to drown out their cries with distance.

Heroes.

Ghrasia made it into the courtyard, falling into a mass of militia and civilian support staff streaming for the relative safety of the woods. She made her way there, calling for Arasia, rallying the confused militia.

She climbed atop a broad tree, its leaves still unfurling in the low spring season, and called at them, "The wall of Liona will fall! When it does you will hold them here. You will delay them to give Kuallina time to muster her defenses. You knew this day would come. Some must fight so others may live peacefully. You are the ones Oma chose to fight. Fight well. Die better."

She slipped down from the tree. "May I take your arm, Arasia?"

"Of course," Arasia said, and linked her thick arm with Ghrasia's slender one. She towered over Ghrasia. Ghrasia patted her shoulder.

"You have the line here," Ghrasia said.

"You–"

"I will be on the wall," Ghrasia said. "I won't let those parajistas die alone."

"Ghrasia, this is–"

"Hold here," Ghrasia said. "This Tai Mora army will crash into Kuallina from the east, and their other army from the harbor will hammer Kuallina from the north. They'll catch them in that fist and crush them hard. You understand?"

"Last stand."

"This is ours."

Arasia nodded.

Ghrasia marched back into the hold. The feral girl found her again as she crossed the courtyard, and Ghrasia yelled at her to go back.

"The people who hurt you are coming," she said. "You understand me? You may not speak, but you know what I'm saying, don't you? I will hold them. But you must go."

The feral girl sat on her haunches, head cocked.

"Understand?" Ghrasia said. "We are not all supposed to die here."

The girl gave a jerk of her head, something very like a nod, and scampered back off toward the woods.

Ghrasia let out her breath. Of all of them, that girl deserved to live.

She mounted the steps while the hold roiled around her, climbing up and up, back to the top of the wall.

The parajistas were sweating and trembling. One was already on her knees, vomiting.

Ghrasia asked permission and helped her up. Ghrasia bent, and whispered in her ear, "Hold them. I need you to hold them while we organize the militia. Give me another twenty minutes. Can you do that?"

The woman nodded. She was Ghrasia's age, maybe a little older.

Ghrasia went down the line, asking them each to hold for twenty more minutes, and in twenty minutes she went down the line again, asking for twenty more.

The two men on the end were sobbing, great heaving sobs that Ghrasia felt more than the shaking of Liona.

She went to the edge of the parapet again and gazed down at row upon row of parajistas at the front of the enemy's lines. There must have been sixty or more of them. The fact that her five had lasted nearly three hours was extraordinary.

Another woman had joined Madah on the rise. Ghrasia peered at her as she pulled the great crimson helm from her head. A confident thing to do, in the middle of a battle. It confirmed what Ghrasia already suspected – this was not a true battle, just an exercise, for these people.

The woman raised her head to the wall and stared right at Ghrasia. Though there was a great distance between them, the recognition was as stark and immediate as it had been with Madah.

It was Kirana, Ahkio's sister, former Kai of Dhai. Come to destroy Liona.

Ghrasia had felt little of anything for an hour, just exhaustion. Emotion had drained from her body like pus from a wound.

Now she was angry. Deeply, bone-chillingly angry.

She raised her voice. "Hold your barrier and prepare a second spell," she said. "Prepare a vortex. At my order, drop defenses on the wall and deploy the vortex at the center of the army. Understood?"

Weak calls of acknowledgment.

The parajista nearest her gave her a wide-eyed look.

Ghrasia pressed thumb to forehead. "An honor to stand with you," she said.

"And with you," the parajista said.

Ghrasia leaned over the edge of the wall. "Drop and deploy!" she yelled.

A rush of air filled her ears.

She saw the vortex open up at the center of the great army, just as a blast of air walloped the wall. The shockwave blew her clear across the parapet and over the other side of the wall.

Ghrasia had four seconds to experience the rush of the fall, four seconds to see the wall crumbling down after her, four seconds before her body hit the courtyard, and the wall of Liona buried what was left of her.

37

"Is he dead?" Zezili asked. "Fuck you to Rhea's eye, just tell me if he's dead!" She slumped against the wall of the closet they'd thrown her in – in the panic, no one had seemed sure what to do with her – and roared herself hoarse, but no one came for her. They'd ripped the skewer from her arm, and she felt her whole face puffing up from the surprisingly solid hit from Natanial Thorne, the man she intended to murder in his bed.

She huffed herself against the door once, twice – and much to her surprise, it burst open. She tumbled to the stones and scrambled up. She ran past startled servants and one man fondling himself in front of some old painting, looking for an exit. Her body protested mightily, but it could rest when it was dead.

Zezili broke out a side door, past a scattering of chickens, a horrified stable boy, and a young woman cutting up the body of a boar.

She made for the kennels and slammed her right shoulder into a man leading a bear across the yard. He fell. She kicked him so he stayed down and stood on his body to get the leverage she needed to mount the bear.

She slapped the bear with her good hand, keeping her seat entirely by clenching her thighs tight while gritting her teeth hard enough to make her face hurt.

There was shouting behind her. Something zipped past. Arrows, already? The bear plunged down the muddy streets. Waves of civilians scrambled out of her way.

She knew nothing of Tordin, but she knew the sky. She looked up, found the suns, and turned herself north. She rode for hours until the bear frothed at the mouth, its great forked tongue lolling.

She had not heard any signs of pursuit for miles. Zezili came upon a little farm with a dog tied up out front, and exchanged the bear for the dog. The owner appeared on the stoop just as she whistled it forward. She took off again at a lope, following a dirt track she hoped was a road.

Zezili camped that night well off the road in some abandoned barn. It worried her less than the woodland, which was treacherous, more treacherous than anywhere in Dorinah. The vegetation was dense, full of snapping, biting plant life. Her skin burned with dozens of bites.

She pushed herself into a corner of the barn, and the dog curled up next to her. She slept badly, plagued by nightmares. Anavha, beautiful Anavha, bleeding in her arms. If he was dead, what did she have left but revenge? This was the Empress's doing. She kicked awake sometime in the blackest part of the night, and sobbed. Sobbed for the loss of many things – the loss of her legion, her health, her hand, the loss of her dog Dakar, and Anavha. She had spent her life trying to convince the world she was worth something, and in the end, she had nothing.

Zezili slept in the barn for two days, nursing her aching body, living on young plant shoots and dandelions and a hare who made the mistake of coming into the barn within the length of the dog's lead.

Then she rode out – north, stealing what she needed along the way. In a little town four days out she stopped to barter for a map, but found that her reputation had preceded her.

She heard her own name whispered as she got off the dog. So she took what she wanted – with a look and sneer – and used the map and supplies to get her to the spot on the map Storm had given her. The final resting place for the Empress's weapon was nearer than ever.

A week and a half alone on the roads, talking only to her dog and frightened village people, gave her too much time to think, and to dream. But the longer she was on the road, the less she dreamed, and the less far-ranging her thoughts. Her focus was a searing brand.

Saradyn and his people were a menace, yes. But it was the Empress who had called her dajian, who had made her dance like a puppet on a string. It was the Empress who had killed Anavha. The Empress who had taken her hand.

And she would destroy everything the Empress wanted her to save. Burn it out as surely as she would a cancerous weed.

When she came within sight of the circle of mountains that marked her final destination, the fist of her drive loosened. She took her time picking out the track the army must have taken. They would have arrived here weeks before, but the trail was still fresh. New plant life curled about the edges of crushed wildflowers.

She followed the broad track around the towering deformity in the ground that marked her final destination. They were not properly mountains, but some kind of spongy matter, like a single great tree stump that ran for miles along a circular border. She followed the track around the anomaly for half a day before she found the hole.

Masses of dirt were piled up outside the hole. It looked like someone – or something – had tried to burrow under the ridge of the "mountains."

Zezili dismounted. She saw dog and bear tracks, human tracks, too, and further on from the hole, a ragged line of abandoned tents, already curled in little tufts of moss and fast-growing vines.

"Anyone here?" she yelled.

Nothing.

She tied off the dog near the hole and kicked around the abandoned camp. The supplies were all intact. She found packs of dried meat, rice, hard bread, and tubers.

Then she saw the first and only body. A crumpled, partially rotted figure, hunched against a tree. Zezili recognized the armor. It was Jasoi.

Zezili knelt in front of her to inspect the gaping wound in her side. It looked like the bite of some monstrous animal, but if that was so, why hadn't it eaten the rest of her? Wherever the others had gone, they hadn't intended to go long, and yet… She gazed over her shoulder, over at the hole. Shuddered.

She stood. "We're going to eat," she told the dog. "You remember real food?"

The dog whined.

"Me either," Zezili said. She put Jasoi's name onto her very long mental list of the dead. She had killed hundreds of people in her lifetime, but it was her foolishness, her neglect, her poor choices, that murdered most of them.

The weather was warm, but she wanted cooked rice, so she used one of the flint kits to make a fire. She yanked the vines off one of the tents and got it set up properly again. She kicked out a mean little rodent and two snakes. She stepped on the head of the biggest snake and mashed its head in. Rice and snake meat sounded delicious.

She had gotten adept at skinning and gutting animals with her three good fingers and her teeth, and she did it now, throwing together a meal for her and the dog. When they were fed, she lay there with him at the center of the abandoned camp and stared up at the moons. She sucked in a breath of warm air while the insects buzzed around her, snapping and biting, undeterred by the smoke.

It was a good final night.

She woke at dawn covered in dew and dozens of shiny green beetles. They were harmless and beautiful, like being covered in jewels.

With cool resolve, she spent nearly two hours tying a

dagger to her left arm with a long string of cord pulled from one of the tents. The stump had healed well enough that she could wrap the cord from the stump around her elbow, so that if she kept her elbow crooked, it gave her the proper leverage. She shoved the blade into the wall of the surface anomaly a few times to test it out. Then she untied the dog's lead and yelled at him to clear off.

He loped a few feet away to the edge of the camp, flicking his ears forward. At least he had a better chance at survival than Dakar.

Zezili went to the edge of the hole and peered in. She got down on her belly to try to see the other side, but all was blackness. And in that blackness she saw Anavha's pained face. The mirror exploding in the other world. The end of the fucking world.

Fuck it.

She crawled down into the blackness, pushing dirt and insects, and Rhea's eye alone knew what, past her as she went. It wasn't high enough for her to walk, so she moved along on her elbows and knees, huffing in the smell of the dirt.

The darkness stretched on. She was descending slowly. She felt the descent in the curve of the floor.

What kind of weapon was down here?

She crawled and crawled. The air still felt fresh.

A flicker of light.

She squinted and crawled toward the light. The hole was curved upward again.

Thank Rhea.

As she rose, she began to smell something bad. The unmistakable stench of rot.

Zezili huffed her way to the lip of the hole and braced herself for whatever was on the other side.

She took a deep breath and popped her head out. Then ducked back down.

Her brain frantically tried to make sense of what she'd just seen. Zezili steadied herself. She looked again.

She had come up inside the living circular barrier – the strange anomaly on the map. Great, tangled tree limbs clawed upward from the top of the barrier, obscuring the sky.

The ground was littered with bodies for as far as Zezili could see, in various states of decay. Some were merely skeletons, tangles of bone and armor. Others were bloated bags of meat and she crawled over the lip of the hole carefully, weapon at the ready. She kept low, walked over to the first body. This one was very ripe, maybe six or seven days dead. She knew the armor. The Eye of Rhea was embossed on the helm.

All around her, above the bodies, hung massive cocoons as big as cages. They dangled from the broad branches of the trees. Some of them had split open. They dripped with some kind of plant goo or mucus. The one nearest her trembled softly.

Zezili stepped back, nearly falling back into the hole.

She heard a susurrus, like a swarm of insects rubbing its wings together. A hundred paces across the broad plain of bodies, six figures moved toward her, ducking their heads, their arms moving strangely, as if double-jointed. They were golden creatures, naked, with two sets of legs and absurdly narrow waists, like wasps.

But it was their gait that gave them away, the way they moved side to side, cocking their heads at her like curious cats, green eyes blinking furiously.

They walked like the Empress. They walked like the woman who had sent for them, their… mother? Their companion? These were the Empress's weapon. Her own people.

The Empress always wore a big, beautiful belled skirt, hiding two sets of legs, padding out an impossibly small waist.

They were visitors from somewhere else, hidden in some other time for just this moment – the moment when Rhea herself was coming back into the sky, and the Empress called them home.

38

The Liona Stronghold disintegrated, like a body covered in lye.

Kirana sat at the head of her army, gaze fixed on Nava, or Isoail, whatever she called herself here. She was not as powerful as Kirana had hoped, but it was enough to turn the tide. The wall fell, a body devoid of bones, skin sloughing away. The plants that held it together sizzled. The stones flowed like water, melting. And then there was the screaming.

Kirana had heard worse screaming. A woman stood on the wall, many women, yes, but Kirana remembered one woman, standing firm on the parapet, screaming at their parajistas while Nava cut through their defenses like some horrifying specter.

All they loved, all they hoped for, all they wanted, dead in a few hours.

The steaming wreck of the wall littered the pass, a great morass of stone and blazing plant matter.

Kirana did not leap across it. She waited for her advance troops to go first, picking their way among the wreckage. Then she patted her bear over. Her weapon unfurled from her wrist. She kept it out as they crept across the stone barrier that had held back the people of Dorinah for five hundred years. Nava went first, prodded along by Kirana's loyal parajistas. Kirana kept a watch on her, looking for any sign of her turning. But what loyalty did this dajian have, to a country she had never known? None.

They trundled to the other side, passing body after body. Kirana saw mangled limbs. Grasping hands. Tattered clothing. She saw the remains of paintings and rugs and barrels and any number of things, and for a moment she lamented the waste. Surely they could have salvaged something from the destruction?

It was then that she saw the force waiting for them on the other side. At least four hundred militia and several hundred more support staff wielding sticks and stones rushed across the blasted wall to meet her.

Kirana had not expected so many to rally behind the wall, and certainly did not anticipate so many would stay once it was clear there would be no victory for them here.

It took another two hours to crush and scatter that force, which proved remarkably relentless for a bunch of pacifists.

Kirana dispatched a dozen of them herself, splattering more blood across her boots, feeding her hungry armor. When they were dispatched, Madah rode up beside her, so very young and strangely jolly.

"What do you see?" Kirana asked, because sometimes she could not trust her own sense of things.

"I see victory," Madah said, and Kirana looked at the destruction anew, now from Madah's eyes, and she saw a clear way across the rubble. They would move through the towering trees on the other side and make their passage into Dhai, then to Kuallina, and further on, to the temples, their ultimate goal, a goal her people had been struggling to reach for thousands of years, the goal that would be hers, the one all the history books would assign to her. She took a deep breath, pulling in the scent of the stone dust, the pulped plant matter. This was her achievement. This was her legacy.

They broke out across the wreck of Liona and into the clearing beyond. Kirana saw refugees running from the destruction, people caught outside the fall of the wall, or those who were camping outside it. Shrieks. Calls for mercy. Nothing she had not heard before. But as her bear trundled into the clearing, she pulled it to a halt and watched them, really watched them for the first time. She had sent many to kill these people in her stead. She had ships in their harbor, ships that had obliterated their defenses there. But here she saw them. Really saw them.

Her people.

Kirana frowned. Her weapon began to retreat into her wrist, an everpine branch that had lost its will. She curled her fingers, coaxing it back to life, and it extended. She gripped it tightly. Not her people, no. Pacifists. Cannibals. Fools. Every one of them.

"Pursue them," she barked at Madah.

"Yes, Kai."

Madah called to the squad behind her, and six dozen Tai Mora, weapons raised, galloped after the fleeing Dhai.

Kirana curled a lip in disgust. To come so far and lose her stomach now would be a tragedy. She snarled and raised her own weapon. Slapped her bear forward. She pursued Madah and her squad.

She cut down the fleeing Dhai. Great slashing hacks. A young man with a crooked nose. A grandmother carrying a small child. Three adolescents hardly old enough to fuck. She sliced them down, yanking them from the world like hunks of rice.

Kirana caught up to Madah's forces. Bodies littered the long plain from Liona to the woods. Bunches of floxflass collected around their bears' paws.

"Walking trees out there," Madah said. "Waiting for them to pass."

"How many escaped?"

"We got all we could see."

Kirana stared back at the ruin of the wall. "Hold here

in case any more escape the wreckage," she said. "I need to wait on intelligence."

"Yes, Kai," Madah said, and Kirana adored what she saw in her face – the fierceness, the absolute certainty. There was more certainty in that face than Kirana had felt in twenty years. She thought again of Yisaoh, and her heart ached. Would this all be worth it without Yisaoh?

Kirana shook the thought from her head and paced back to the bulk of her force as they streamed over the wall that had once been Liona. They were stabbing at the rubble, dispatching those who had survived the fall.

She called one of her lieutenants, and had him open a wink to Gaiso, at the outskirts of Dorinah.

"We're in Dhai," Kirana said.

"We arrived in Daorian just ahead of those fourth world travelers," Gaiso said. "The Empress is hardened against us. She has some kind of... I don't know what she has up around this wall. It's like nothing I've seen."

"Hold there. We may be able to take the temples soon."

"Timeline?"

"Uncertain. I'm getting reports that Honorin's force at the harbor is pushing the remaining resistance to Kuallina. If we can break them at Kuallina, we have them."

"Without the rice fields in Dorinah–"

"I rely on you for that."

"I can take Dorinah, but without the dajians to farm this land, we've got very little to keep us going past the fall. You know that."

"I rely on your resourcefulness."

"Kai, I–"

"There are a good number of people in Dorinah," Kirana said. "Put them to good use."

Gaiso smacked her lips. "The Dorinahs won't make good slaves."

"When the alternative is death, you'd be surprised at who chooses slavery," Kirana said. "They will submit."

Gaiso pursed her mouth. Kirana didn't like that look.

"Kai, the logistics of this—"

"When have the logistics been possible?" Kirana said. "Yet here we are. We are almost there, Gaiso. I close these gates—"

"We're still missing the instructions—"

"The temple will know me. It will speak to me. Have a heart, Gaiso."

Gaiso nodded. Curtly. Kirana flexed her left fist. They were committed. Gaiso would push to the end. They all would, the ones who had come this far. One did not destroy millions only to give up with the final twenty thousand already in the noose.

"Chin up, Gaiso. You'll get your children over. I have them on the list."

"When, Kai?"

"When we have them." She would have found and killed Gaiso's children before she found Yisaoh, she knew. But that was how it went. Gaiso's children would still be in Clan Garika, ripe for picking on the way to Kuallina.

Kirana severed the connection and galloped about the ruins with the others, running through any Dhai still living. When it was done, she called back through to Shova on the other side, and told him to try pushing through another wave of their people.

She sat on a giant boulder inside the ruin where she had a clear view of the wink while they tried to send in another wave. Eighteen more of her people were able to get through. Eighteen! How many had they eliminated in this foray, to get that eighteen?

It frustrated her that there was no clear analog between her people and the ones they killed. Sometimes the ones they killed had doubles in her world, and sometimes they did not. That meant some of her people couldn't get through, but many could. It was a stupid cosmic rule. She felt, often, as if Oma were making fun of her and her people, or perhaps making fun of the Dhai here. Who knew? But it was deplorable. Disgusting.

She made camp and settled in, but could not sleep. The killing gave her nightmares. The smell of the stone dust clogged her nostrils. When she closed her eyes, she saw Nava looking at her with accusing eyes, so black. So cold. She was tired of the cold.

She closed her eyes.

Saw Yisaoh's face.

She woke to a voice at the door to her tent. "Enter," she said, without being absolutely certain who had knocked.

A young woman stood in front of her, a hunched, awkward looking thing, with scars on her face, as if she'd been stabbed with a sharp implement. She listed to one side, as if her left leg could not properly hold her weight.

Kirana feared sounding foolish, so didn't ask her name. "What?"

"You've made a terrible mistake," the girl said.

"Is that so?"

"I will meet you in Kuallina. We must speak. This destruction has gone on long enough."

"The destruction is just starting," Kirana said. "We must burn to start over. I've told all of you this many times. Who are you?"

"You'll know," the girl said. "You'll know in Kuallina."

Kirana felt dizzy. She staggered. When she looked up, the girl was gone. She huffed out a breath. Yelled for the guards. They ran in, oblivious. She asked if anyone had been past them, and they looked at her as if she were mad.

But she knew she wasn't mad. It was the sky that was mad, and it was doing mad things to them. Everything was breaking apart – the worlds, the seams between them, the distances between people and places, even time itself, all muddled and distorted.

I'm dreaming of the Dhai, she thought, and they are dreaming of me. But those dreams will be true, soon. So very soon.

Kuallina. They would smash the Dhai at Kuallina.

39

Kuallina lay an hour distant. Lilia saw the bulk of it against the horizon from her perch on the topmost branches of an abandoned bonsa house. Tasia combed the garden below with Laralyn, looking for forgotten tubers or hidden food stores. The fires of the army still burned north of her at the harbor. The gates themselves must be on fire, not just the town, to burn like that over four days.

Lilia climbed down from the tree, breathing easy and free. Four days chewing raw mahuan had made her feel strong, weightless. For the first time in years she was nearly free of pain. Though her stomach cramped and her stool was bloody, she preferred this slow death to the faster one. She made her way carefully back down the side of the tree house, using a ladder made of trained vines. The nights were still cool, but the vines were flowering. They had passed great swaths of purple and white wildflowers on their long walk to Kuallina. Lilia insisted they stay off the road, which took longer. They had to haul Amelia out of a bladder trap. Laralyn nearly lost an eye to a lashing corpse flower. Her vision had gone misty. Tulana broke out into a rash after stumbling into some toxic flower.

Lilia had no illusions about where they were headed, or what their final fate would be. She knew in her heart – knew it and embraced it. She resolved to save nothing for the way back. There was no way back.

"So what is your grand plan?" Tulana said as Lilia kicked off the ladder.

"We need to get into Kuallina first," Lilia said. "You'll need to help with that." In truth, Lilia had no plan. But no one followed a person without a plan. She needed more than compulsion to inspire these women.

"What do you need us for?" Tulana said. "This country is lost."

Lilia glanced over at Tasia where she clawed at the remains of the garden.

"Come inside," Lilia said, and motioned Tulana into the house. The door was unlocked, like all doors in Dhai. Its inhabitants had left in advance of the army.

"I can't draw on Oma anymore," Lilia said. She made herself look at Tulana as she said it, because to do any less would show weakness, and she had never been weaker than in this moment. Saying it aloud made her mournful again. How much differently would this war have gone if she had not burned out? If Taigan was still here?

"Burned out?" Tulana said. Her lip curled. "Is that so?"

"I don't need a lecture."

"I wasn't going to lecture," Tulana said, and her tone changed. It was she who looked away. "You aren't the first arrogant little girl to destroy herself because she thought she didn't need training."

"You're still bound to me. Your ward is still good. You've seen it."

"Indeed I have," Tulana said. Her face crumpled. She wiped her face with her fists, cleared her throat. "There's a very popular story you dajians tell, about servitude. I've seen you playing at it in Dorinah, breaking your own farm implements so you don't have to work. Burning your own crops. Letting giant floxflass nests devour the puppies you're tending. It's an ugly thing, but I'm told you call it resistance, and it gives you some pleasure. It's a thing I'm coming to understand, this delight in destruction of what one has built."

"No more talking," Lilia said. "Doing."

"And how is it you intend to stop me?"

The air vibrated. For a moment, Lilia thought she could see the red mist forming around Tulana, but no. It was just the memory of it, her mind conjuring a vision to pair with the milky air.

"You really have burned yourself out, haven't you?" Tulana said. Whatever she held, she released. The air pressure normalized. It wasn't as if Tulana could move against her. The ward prevented it. But whatever she spun must have been grim. "You think your little dajian refugees love you? Just wait until they find out you're not a god, just some ugly little girl. I can tell you exactly what happens next. You get stoned to death, or thrown off the top of that hulking fortress."

"You don't know anything about Dhai."

"I know they'll eat you alive – they won't even give you the courtesy to wait until death! – if you don't figure out very quickly how to put together an army and hold a position. You've lost Taigan. I worked with Zezili Hasaria, directing legions of women and Seekers against the outer islands, and even the Saiduan. I've seen war. I know it. You'll lose."

"My intention isn't to have you fight a war on their terms," Lilia said.

Tulana crossed her arms. "What are you proposing?"

"You led the Seekers in war."

"Wait now–"

"When we get to Kuallina, I'll need you to train the Oras who will go with us. I need them trained properly, to fight as units, the way they do in Dorinah."

"You'd put me in charge of thousands of gifted?"

"There aren't that many," Lilia said. "I can get the full count, though."

"How many do you think there are?"

"There are only twenty thousand people in Dhai,"

Lilia said. "Oras? I don't know, but not more than six or eight hundred."

She saw something sorrowful pass over Tulana's face. "What is it?" Lilia asked.

"That's... we'll lose that many in the first day facing that army coming up from the coast."

"We aren't going to stay and fight," Lilia said. The plan was taking shape in her mind as she spoke.

"What will your Kai think of that?"

"It doesn't matter what he thinks," Lilia said. "They won't be following him. They will follow me."

"I have no reason to–"

Lilia thumbed at the ward.

Tulana's knees buckled. She fell. She curled into a ball on the ground. The reaction was so fast, so potent, Lilia released the ward immediately.

Tulana threw up one of her hands. The air got heavy, but nothing happened to Lilia. The ward was too powerful.

"I could kill you now," Lilia said. Her voice was steady. She placed her hands on the table. Her hands were steady.

Tulana huffed out a long breath. The expression she set on Lilia then made Lilia's stomach turn. She had never seen so much hatred in a person's face.

"Aren't you supposed to fuck each other to work out disagree-ments?"

"Will you do it, or should I kill you here?"

Tulana grimaced. "Don't expect miracles."

"That's exactly what I expect," Lilia said. "The Dhai will look for a miracle to save them. And I will give them a miracle."

Dawn.

The time of miracles.

Lilia chewed mahuan root. Tulana stood beside her, with Voralyn and Amelia just behind, and Laralyn at the back, holding Tasia's hand. They stood on a slight rise looking out at the broad camp of the Tai Mora army. The army had burned out the wooded area for half a mile in every direction and set their camp right on it. Compared to the vast army Lilia had glimpsed when she crossed to the other side, they were a small force, but by Dhai standards, the rows and rows of tents and cook fires were overwhelming, a pustulous plague of at least a thousand, including support personnel. Lilia and the Seekers had hidden from four scouting parties. The scouts were going house to house, killing everyone within and stealing whatever wasn't bolted down.

"Spectacle," Tulana said.

"People fear spectacles," Lilia said. "Spectacles can be shocking." She remembered the smoke that poured over them as they fled from the harbor. A needless spectacle.

"We have no advantage."

"They want Dhai intact," Lilia said. "The less damage, the better. They may be stealing and killing, but they aren't burning out the houses or the gardens, did you notice? Just the roads, and the harbor gate. It's why they sent smoke after us but not fire. They aren't here to pillage. They're going to make this their home."

Tulana tugged at her coat. "No one will agree to your plan. No one in their right mind would destroy their own country."

"It's just things," Lilia said. "Not people. If we destroy what they came for, we thwart them, don't we?"

"You need some adults to knock sense into you."

"Once we get to the clearing, you need to–"

"I remember," Tulana said. "We'll do it."

"There won't be much time before–"

"This isn't my first tumble, girl," Tulana said. "Trickery won't get you far."

"It only needs to get me past the army," Lilia said.

They had discussed a route around the army, endlessly, but the army was running patrols now, keeping anyone from coming into or going out of the massive protective parajista barriers that had been deployed around the hold. The refugees caught outside the walls of Kuallina but inside the parajista barrier could see eye to eye with the Tai Mora while they slept.

Lilia stepped away from them. She was wrapped in a bubble of Para's breath deployed by Amelia. She walked unchallenged to the edge of the camp, heart pounding. There was no mistaking what she was now. They would know her the moment they saw her.

And they did.

She strode out past the trees, holding a blazing willowthorn weapon aloft, infused by Voralyn while they waited on the rise overlooking the ramp.

"Disperse!" Lilia said, and she could not imagine what she looked like in that moment; some twisted, mad figure, holding a flaming brand. "Disperse or my army will rout you!"

As they had at Liona, the Seekers amplified her voice. It rolled over the camp like some thunderous god's.

Heads looked up from campfires, and peered out from tents. The army scrambled, a hive of angry bees. A horde of them attacked her outright. She held her ground. Did not budge as they swarmed her barrier.

"Get the jistas!" someone yelled.

Infused weapons uncurled from their wrists. The last time Lilia saw a weapon like that, it was hacking up her mother's body.

She strode further into the camp. The huff of air around her pushed away the crowd of soldiers before they could reach her. "Those who stand will meet the wrath of my army," Lilia yelled, and she felt profoundly foolish for a long moment. She sounded like a fool from some dramatic Dorinah opera.

Then came the illusion.

It winked into existence on the other side of Kuallina, a shimmering oval mirror half the size of the fortress, bleeding red light across the whole field. Lilia squinted into it. It was far brighter than she anticipated. The bloody light lit the whole field. It was then that they believed. It was then that they cowered.

How many other worlds were in play, now? She didn't know. They didn't either. She could be anyone, from anywhere, with as much power as she pretended.

But not for long.

"Jistas!"

A buffet of air smashed into her protective shield. She felt it vibrate. How long Laralyn held it... well, the Seekers would not sob if she died terribly in this moment.

The mirror illusion trembled. Red light burst across the field, and inside the face of the mirror was a foreign landscape – a Dorinah one, most likely, considering its maker – and a vast army decked in Dorinah armor and red plumes so realistic that Lilia feared for a long moment it was real, and that the Seekers had tricked her.

But the edges of the illusion shimmered. She knew it for what it was, so she pushed on, weapon raised, yelling at them about the mighty power of her army.

The lines nearest the mirror broke. She saw them turn. She screamed louder, flashing the sword about like it was the thing controlling the vast army about to crush them.

"Regroup!"

She heard it from the same direction as the mirror. "Regroup!"

Flags went up, great red and blue and purple standards waving left, right twice, then three times. The massive army peeled away from Lilia.

She swung her weapon again, flat out at her left side, the signal for the Seekers to advance.

Lilia did not wait to see if the Seekers broke from the trees to follow her, but strode purposefully across the scattered camp.

Every cry of "Jistas!" made her stomach knot, but she went on. They would uncover the ruse any moment. Once the jistas were assembled they would be able to see it and untangle it.

She hurried. Members of the army ran into her barrier,

and fell back, shocked. She could see their faces now, faces of every shape and hue. Tall men, broad-shouldered women, scraggly youths, even children and camp followers, their hair braided nearly as intricately as a Dorinah's. Some of the camp followers wore leather chokers, and she wondered if they were slaves, but the army was, no doubt, free. Fighting willingly because not fighting meant dying under a burning star on a doomed world.

Would Lilia have died over there, or would she have fought? In some other world she was camped here among these people, fleeing certain death.

"I would have fought!" she yelled, aloud, and realized that much of what she'd been thinking she'd been spouting out at the people rushing around her.

When she came to the other side of the camp, her throat was sore, and her feet ached. She needed a hunk of mahuan root. She dug about for one in her bag.

The barrier around her shook. She saw a man on the other side hacking at her shield with a great infused blade. Blue light sparked from the weapon. She stared at him from her side of the barrier, fascinated, like watching some deadly animal worry at a cage.

What would she do, when he burst through?

She put the mahuan root into her mouth and chewed slowly while contemplating his efforts. He did not look like the Tai Mora. He was broad and flat-featured, with sallow skin and curly black hair knotted in white ribbons. He looked very hungry. And his eyes...

Lilia stepped forward, to the edge of the barrier, and peered at him. He hacked directly at the barrier in front of her face. She did not flinch.

"Do your worst," she whispered. "I am going to outlast you."

"Jistas!"

A flurry of flags, again.

Now that she was close enough to the barrier around Kuallina, she saw curious Dhai peering at her. She shifted her attention to them.

Another soldier ran by, grabbing the one assaulting her, and they plunged back toward the illusion of the mirror.

Lilia walked right up to the edge of the barrier around Kuallina.

Tulana came up behind her, tall and regal in the morning light. "You sold that spectacularly," she said. "I think they feared you more than whatever was going to come out of that mirror."

Lilia did not say that desperation and madness were sisters, that one often led to the other. She just nodded, and called to the people on the other side of the parajista barrier.

"I am Lilia Sona!" she said, and Tulana raised her hand, palm up, and the voice carried. "I've come back from the walls of the harbor with a message for the Kai."

"I can try and force it open," Laralyn said, glancing back at the camp. The mirror image was still pouring fake soldiers onto the field, but it would not be much longer before the army realized they were merely illusions.

"Hold," Lilia said. "If we fight them, they'll see us as the enemy."

She almost laughed, and had to cover her mouth. The enemy. What did that mean, anymore?

The parajistas opened a sliver in the barrier and let them through. Someone in there must have vouched for her. Ghrasia, maybe. Lilia stumbled on the other side. Tulana caught her arm, and kept her upright as waves of refugees swarmed forward. Lilia stiffened, suddenly terrified they would tear her apart for losing them the harbor.

"Faith!" they called. "Faith! Faith!"

They raised their hands and their voices. The chant rolled out across the disheveled swarms of people camped all around the hold. As she walked forward, they did not overtake her, but moved out of her way. Children ran to the front.

Tasia came from Laralyn's side and grabbed her hand. She gazed up at her with wide, awestruck eyes. "Are you really Faith Ahya?" she said.

Lilia did not answer. She moved through the crowd until she saw a woman so familiar it brought tears to her eyes. She came up short, thinking she was imagining her.

"Emlee," Lilia said.

The old woman clucked at her and moved toward her from the crowd. She looked terribly frail, but when Lilia took her hand, Emlee's grip was firm and warm. "What have you done out here? What's happened to you?"

"I was trying to save people."

"How can a child do that, when she has not yet saved herself?" Emlee said.

"I didn't think you'd come. I thought you were dead."

"I nearly was. The rest of us followed after you, eventually. Got caught up in the madness at Liona. I'm not much of a healer without my people. And there are plenty of us here now."

"What's been happening?" Lilia asked. For the first time in many weeks, she felt like a child again. It was comforting, looking to the adults for answers.

"They say there's another army coming, from Liona. Not ours."

"How is that possible?"

"Does Gian know you're alive, or Cora?"

Lilia shook her head. "I haven't seen them. Do you know–"

"Inside," Emlee said, and her expression darkened. "Gian went inside at the head of the first wave. She said you were dead. It's been yelled all through camp for days. She has the Catori's ear, now."

Lilia frowned. "I'm sure she'll be pleased to see me."

"I'm sure," Emlee said, and she squeezed Lilia's hand when she said it, but it was not a reassuring grip. It was a knowing one. "You are very deep into this, Lilia," she continued softly. "Where is your sanisi?"

"It's all very complicated," Lilia said. "Will you come inside with me?"

"No, my work is here," Emlee said. "But when the call started I wanted to see... I wanted to make sure it was you. The true one."

Lilia made her way to the gates. The sally port was open, letting supply carts through to feed those scattered outside, but there were eight militia guarding the single entry, ensuring those outside didn't come in.

As she approached, the sea of refugees parting before her, the militia straightened. Gaped.

"Take me to Ghrasia Madah," she said. "I'm Lilia Sona. She will know who I am."

Silence. Confused looks. Finally, the nearest one said, "Ghrasia is not here. Catori Mohrai is in charge of Kuallina."

"Then take me to her. She'll know who I am, too."

"Our orders are–"

"Should I tell these people you won't admit me?" Lilia said. "Should I tell them Oma's most gifted jista is being kept at the gate?" She thought to make a threat to use Oma against them, but with Tulana and the other Seekers behind her, it felt even crueler. Empty words. Empty threats. Without access to Oma, her power rested entirely with the people behind her, and power like that, so difficult to gain, was very easy to lose.

They took her inside, and across the crowded courtyard. The Dhai from the surrounding clans had been given access to the interior of Kuallina. They wore the shorter haircuts and uniform clothing of residents. Lilia felt a needling annoyance at that. She suspected many of the Dhai from the camp had arrived here ahead of the locals, but would not have been permitted past the gates.

She told Tulana and the others to stay in the yard with Tasia, though Tasia begged to go up with her. "You can look for your parents here," Lilia said, and gave Laralyn a long look. Laralyn grimaced, but took the girl's hand

and pulled her away. If Tasia's parents survived, they would be here. Lilia was uncertain of the likelihood of that. She had no idea about losses yet.

Two militia escorted her upstairs into the heart of the hold. Kuallina was an old hold, built the same way as the temples. When Lilia put her hands to the walls she could almost feel it breathe.

She had thought Liona felt crowded, stuffed far past capacity, but that was nothing compared to Kuallina. The sheer weight of humanity around her was stifling. She was irritable, claustrophobic, but she could breathe and walk more or less straight, with just a little dragging of her bad leg, and that was something. She pulled the wad of mahuan pulp from her mouth and put it into her pocket. Her head was starting to swim.

They ushered her into a little room, more like a storage closet, and told her to wait. For the first time, Lilia felt some trepidation. Was she a criminal now? Was this prison?

She paced, walking around the room in a discreet circle, running through her argument again and again.

The door opened thirty minutes later. Mohrai pushed in, mouth firm. "What do you want?" she said. "I thought you were dead at the wall."

"I need to speak to Ghrasia," Lilia said. "If you plan to hold up here, the plan is flawed."

"Ghrasia is dead," Mohrai said. "She died at Liona."

"What?"

"Liona has fallen," Mohrai said. "We have two armies coming directly here. The one from the harbor and the one from Dorinah, the one that breached Liona."

"We can't stay here," Lilia said. "I brought Seekers with me. They are trained in war. We can use them as a diversion to plot a course to the woodland, but we must destroy everything behind us. If we burn out the stores in Kuallina and the clans, we leave them nothing to live on. If we–"

"The Kai is coming here by Line. He'll be here within the hour. He'll decide how much of your nonsense is worth listening to. I told him not to send you to the harbor. I told him I–"

"Then I will take the Dhai from the camps," Lilia said, not wanting to argue in this little room. "I will take them west, into the woodland. The army won't be able to follow us there. They can try to burn us out, but the geography–"

"We won't all become refugees like you," Mohrai said. "This is our home. You wouldn't understand that."

"It's my home too."

"Is it? Are you certain?"

Lilia firmed her jaw. "My plan would have worked," she said. "You were in charge of the harbor, and it fell. It was nothing to do with me. The Oras were untrained. The militia was not ready. And we still don't know why they attacked as soon as they did. Their emissary was still at Oma's Temple. Not even you suspected an attack without warning."

"We'll never know, will we?" Mohrai said. "Ahkio was a fool to send you to the harbor, and we were foolish to listen to you. If we–"

"Don't blame me for this," Lilia said.

Mohrai said, "Things are exceedingly grim here, and you–"

"Catori?" said someone outside the door. "The Kai is here."

"Stay here," Mohrai said, and shut the door.

Lilia leaned against the far wall and slid to the floor. Her fate was in the hands of someone else, again. She did not like these talks. Talking, talking, when what she wanted, what she needed, was to act.

It was more than an hour before someone came for her, and then she suspected they might just feed her, or kick her out. It was a young novice. Lilia recognized her – she was a companion of the Kai.

"I'm Caisa," she said. "The Kai has asked you up."

But they did not go up, they went down to a broad dining room where the Kai stood, his back to the windows – a foolish position, Lilia thought – as well as Mohrai, and half a dozen faces she did not recognize.

"What happened?" the Kai asked.

Lilia told him. Not just their original plan, and what happened at the wall, but how she had escaped, and awed the army into letting her through. What she didn't tell him was that she had burned out. If she told him that, she feared Mohrai would throttle her right on the table. When she was finished, he did not look at her, but the vast map of Dhai on the table.

Into the silence, Mohrai said, "I really think–"

"Give me a moment, Mohrai," he said.

Lilia wanted to clasp and unclasp her hands again, but stilled them. She stood as straight as she could.

"I have a plan for Kuallina," Lilia said.

He barked a laugh. "Do you?"

"I'm not a seer," Lilia said. "I'm a strategist. I didn't anticipate that they would attack us while they had an emissary at Oma's Temple. I thought we could act first. But they thought the same. It was a matter of who moved fastest. We couldn't get the sinajistas to the wall in time to build the warded spells to attach to the boats. We needed more time, and we did not have it."

"You didn't tell me about this plan," he said. "I could have... delayed the emissary."

"Do you trust every person around you?" Lilia said. She did not point fingers at those in the room, but Lilia had already met a lot of travelers, a lot of shadows. If there were none in his inner circle, she would be inordinately surprised. "If any of us sent you word, it could have been intercepted."

"Ghrasia is dead," he said. He voice broke.

"I know," Lilia said.

"And half of Asona. We've lost–"

Lilia raised her voice. "And we'll lose more if we sit here waiting for that second army," she said.

"There are injured," Mohrai said. "Sick people, elders, children. You want to take those all into the woodland, for your fool plan?"

"They'll die if you keep them here. Do you want to lose everyone here, or just a few?"

"You're a cold person," the Kai said.

"You're not cold enough," she said. "It's why we're here. What happened with the emissary? Why did they attack?"

The Kai raised a hand. "Mohrai, Caisa, the rest of you, leave us for a moment."

"Ahkio," Mohrai said.

"Just... leave us."

Lilia tried to hide her surprise. She'd expected to be thrown in the storage closet, or fed to the army.

But the room cleared out, as he asked. She stood alone with him in the broad room with its streaming light and horrifying view of the burned-out plain and the camping army.

"What are you?" he said. Cold. Keen eyes.

"I told you–"

"What. Are. You?"

"My mother hid me here," she said. "I was very young. I thought it was a dream. She opened a way between my world, the one with the burnt sky, and this one. I've lived here my whole life. They hid hundreds of omajista children here, the resistance. There's a resistance on the other side, though I haven't met many of them. Gian–" but it was the wrong Gian she wanted to tell him about, so she swallowed her words. "The woman who brought me here was one. I went to the other side to find my mother, just before we came here. They were building a great mirror there to keep the way between their world and ours open, and I destroyed it with the help of a Dorinah legionnaire. I killed my own mother there, too, when I did it. It was the only way." Her voice rose. "I killed my own mother, and I'm just like them now. I'm everything Dhai hates. I can see how you look at me, and you should. You should look at me that way. But who better to fight them than me? They took everything from me. They will take everything from you, too, if you let them."

Silence.

She swallowed hard. He turned away from her, and gazed long out the window at the army.

"I agree with you that we'll lose if we fight them," he said. "Not just this war, but the one for who we are in the future, too. If all that's left of us is the fighters, the killers, what kind of society will they build? I don't want to save the strongest, the most ruthless of us. I want to save the smartest, the most compassionate, the very best of us. Do you understand?"

She moved forward to the short end of the table, so she could hear him better. His voice was so low. "If you hold them here, they will all die," Lilia said. "The way we did at the harbor."

"Mohrai will hold the bulk of the militia here," he said, "and most of the Oras. You'll have some novices, and those Dorinahs you brought with you."

"I understand."

"You're going to need a distraction to get past that army."

"I've thought of that," she said.

"Another illusion?"

"No one falls for an illusion twice," she said. "They'll anticipate that now."

"You should go before the second army gets here."

"I can't," Lilia said. "It's better if there's a second army, because it means we'll have someone to invite to dinner."

"What?"

"You're going to invite their leader to dinner," Lilia said, "and tell her that we surrender."

40

Lilia found Gian in Mohrai's quarters, speaking in a voice so loud Lilia heard it through the door. Lilia opened the door without prelude, and stood frowning while Gian turned.

Gian's expression was difficult to read. Shock, horror? She leapt up and ran toward Lilia. Lilia did not open her arms, but endured the embrace stiffly, guardedly. Gian's hair was clean, the clothes new. Gian took her so tightly that even more of Lilia's charred clothes smeared away.

"I thought you were dead," Gian said, breathless. Lilia looked beyond her, to Mohrai.

"What were you speaking of?" A question for Mohrai, not Gian.

Mohrai stood. "Gian suggested we send her out to negotiate."

"Curious," Lilia said, tone flat. "What makes you think they would listen to you?"

"I…" Gian trailed off. Released her. "It's just that, I thought–"

"Are you theirs?"

"What? Tai Mora? No! How could you think–"

"Then why would you–"

"Emlee told me about Gian," Gian said. "Your… other Gian."

Lilia hissed out a breath. "She had no right to tell you that."

"If that Gian was part of some resistance, I could pretend–"

"You will stay out of this," Lilia said. "Emlee had no right to tell you about Gian. My Gian."

Gian's face fell. "I thought–"

"That's enough here," Lilia said. "The Kai and I have already discussed a plan. We'll do it when the rest of the parajistas arrive from the temples. He's had to call them all here. It could be a few more days."

"Lilia–" Gian's tone was wheedling. Lilia didn't like it.

"I'm having a bath and going to bed," Lilia said. "Do you have a place for me, Mohrai?"

"No," Mohrai said. "You'll have to share with Gian."

Lilia nodded curtly. "I need to have my jistas accommodated. They are prepared for war, unlike ours. I'm putting them in charge of our defenses."

"The Kai approved that as well?"

"I would not have–"

"How many is he going to marry?" Mohrai said, bitterly.

"What?"

"Is that what he offered you? Do you have some secret child, too?"

"I have no idea what you're talking about."

Mohrai waved at her. "Never mind."

"Show me where the room is, Gian," Lilia said.

Gian hung her head. Lilia felt guilty, then. Weren't they all just doing the best they could? Gian led her to a small, cramped room with two narrow beds. The slim window looked out into the central courtyard, now packed with Dhai from the surrounding clans. Lilia gazed out over them, a swarm of desperate people.

Gian closed the door. "The Kai married another woman," Gian said, "and declared a Li Kai. They're saying that's not usual."

Lilia rubbed her face. It was tingly from all the mahuan root. She was salivating again, hungry. What was a little more? "No, that's not very usual. Kais haven't had multiple spouses since…" She racked her memory for the history of it. "Since at least the first two."

Married and declared a Li Kai… he must have thought he was going to die here in Kuallina. Lilia didn't blame him.

She took a breath. "It's gone," Lilia said.

Gian stiffened. The rigidness of her body frightened Lilia.

"Oma," Lilia said. "It's… gone."

"That can't be."

Lilia started to cry. She hadn't let herself cry yet, and it all came out now, loud and ugly. "I think I burned myself out. I didn't know. I wasn't trained. That's all Taigan would say, how I wasn't trained."

Gian tangled her fingers in Lilia's hair and made soothing sounds. "It will be all right."

"Please stay with me," Lilia said.

"Of course, yes," Gian said.

"Will you hold me?"

Gian lay next to her in the bed. She pressed her body against Lilia's, spooning her from behind, but Lilia could feel the fear and anxiety in her body. It made Lilia tense too. Who was she, if not a powerful omajista? Without Oma, she was just a refugee girl with a bad leg and crumpled right hand.

She needed to show strength, or she would lose all of them – Taigan, Gian, the refugees, the Kai, the Catori, the jistas. How long could she pretend nothing was different? The only omajistas she knew were Taigan and Tulana, and Taigan was gone.

Lilia felt something lumpy under the pillow and pulled it out. It was a yellowish tuber, one her mother had warned her about. The sight of it nearly stilled her heart. "Gian! Where did you get this?" Lilia said. "You haven't eaten it. Tell me you haven't eaten it!"

Gian snatched the tuber from her. "Sorry," she said. "They grow by the river. I was just saving them. I–"

Lilia found two more of them in the bed. She took them to the window and started throwing them out.

"No!" Gian said.

"These are poisonous," Lilia said. "How did you even–" And then she stopped throwing the tubers. She held the last in her hand, and squeezed it tight. "Oh," Lilia said. "Oh, this is much better."

"Can I have it back?" Gian said.

"I'll do better," Lilia said. "I'll bring you a dozen more. But don't eat them. Not yet. Not until you understand them." Lilia kissed Gian's forehead. "I have a plan, Gian. Oh, I have such a better plan now."

"What plan?" Gian said.

"I can't tell you yet. But it's going to be beautiful."

The army came from Liona, and smashed against Kuallina's eastern defenses. Ahkio stood on the wall with Lilia and Mohrai when it happened. They were a vast force, far more terrifying than the few hundred who had come down from the harbor. This was several thousand. They bore great colored banners and wore chitinous red, green, and blue armor that made them look like a swarm of beetles. They burned much of the wood as they went, so the smoke preceded them.

"How do you know their leader is with them?" Ahkio asked Lilia.

She shrugged. "I don't. But if it were me, and I'd waited my whole life to take Dhai, and I wanted it untouched, I'd be here in person. She's with one of these armies, or someone who can speak for her is."

"I'm going down to calm the militia," Mohrai said. "I don't want panic."

"Gian," Lilia said. "Could you get me a coat?"

Ahkio eyed her sharply. The season was moving into

low spring. It was unlikely she was cold.

Gian nodded and left them.

Lilia leaned toward Ahkio. She was a head shorter than him, though it seemed like more when she hunched over as she did now, leaning on the parapet. "I can go alone, Kai. Someone needs to lead them from here."

"We should both go," he said. "Mohrai will lead them."

She put her chin in her hand. "You have another wife at the temple, they said, and a child. Maybe things being less complicated will be good."

"No," he said. "I've considered the options. If Meyna and her child are lost, there's still Mohrai and hers. If Mohrai and hers are lost, we have Meyna." He had considered every angle. In another country they may have thought multiple heirs would divide them, but all Ahkio could think of now was redundancy. What made them different than the Tai Mora? How could they use it to their advantage?

"And you—"

"If I'm lost, it doesn't matter," he said. He was surprised at the sound of the resignation in his own voice.

"Kai, I think you should return to the temples, once I go down there."

"Is this part of your grand scheme?"

"Someone needs to lead the people from the temples into the woodland. If you go at the same time I do, you can have them cleared out before her armies get there."

"I don't see—"

"More importantly… Kai, there's something you should do, have done, when you go up. You need to have them burn the fields behind them. The temples, too. Burn every orchard. Every house. Burn down everything in the temples. All of it."

"I thought you were mad before, but this—"

"They want Dhai untouched," Lilia said. "Did you consider why?"

"I know what they want in the temples."

"Then burn it down. Burn it all down."

Ahkio gripped the rail. His face was hard, knuckles clenched. "This strategy–"

"It's not nice," she said. "But when we were out there, we saw that they weren't destroying anything. They mean to live here, Kai. The only way to thwart that is to make it uninhabitable. Mohrai will lead them into the woodland here while I distract them. The Seekers will help. But while we're doing that, you need to start the burning. Only you can do that."

He pressed his fists to his face. "Oma's breath," he said.

"I've thought about it a hundred times," she said. "If we go, we have to burn it down."

He wept, then. He felt nothing when he did it, and Lilia just stood there dumbly beside him, chewing her mahuan root and gazing out at the army.

"If I hadn't broken the mirror it would be a much bigger army," she said, "one we couldn't have held even this long. One we couldn't run from."

When he did not stop crying, she seemed to soften, but that wasn't what he wanted. It wasn't what he needed. He wanted her to comfort him in some way, but she stood resolute. It was why he had given her this chance in the first place, because she was more ruthless than him. He knew it the moment he met her. He had unleashed this monster. It was the only way he could think to save them all, and what they were. She would be the monster. He would be the politician. He would not have a drop of blood on his own hands, though he would know, always know, that every life she took was his to share.

"I can do it myself," Lilia said. So certain.

"No," he said. "I should meet her."

"Why?"

"She's my sister," he said.

"Oh," she said. "I never had a sister."

A runner arrived for him, and he excused himself, grateful for an excuse to flee from her company. Farosi waited for him below with a message written on delicate green paper.

"From Yisaoh," Farosi said.

"You've seen her?"

"No," he said, "but I had the handwriting verified in Garika."

Ahkio opened the note.

If you've a desire to meet, it will be on my terms. Temple of Tira courtyard.

She wrote a date two days from the current one. There was still a clear Line path between Kuallina and the Temple of Tira. With the army blocking them in from the north, the temples of Sina and Para could be considered behind enemy lines now. Anything north of Kuallina was gone – burned and routed – the inhabitants driven south ahead of the army. Ahkio had every parajista they could muster at Kuallina now, running in shifts, backed up by sinajistas and tirajistas, directed by Lilia's omajista captain, Tulana. He had not thought they would last a day, let alone weeks, against the armies that smashed them here at Kuallina, but the Seeker ran her teams with an iron discipline, rotating them out in two-hour shifts. The constantly shifting parajistas on the wall ran like a water clock winding down.

"Can you take a response to her?" he asked Farosi.

He shook his head. "The runner who brought it said it was a one-time offer. You meet on her terms or not at all."

Ahkio let out a huff of displeasure.

Someone knocked at the door. Caisa entered. "Kai?" She had arrived with the last of the parajistas from the Temple of Para, all that were able to get onto the last Line out.

"News?" he said.

"The… Lilia would like to see you to discuss the banquet again."

"Let that lie," he said. "I need you to come with me to the Temple of Tira tomorrow."

"Why?"

"We'll discuss that on the way."

He told only Mohrai he was leaving. She was not pleased, but he pitched it as a trip to take stock of their resources at the Temple of Tira. Food was at a premium now with so much of the stores at the harbor overrun.

"No surprises," she said. "I'm sick to death of surprises."

He rode the Line south to the Temple of Tira. It took a few hours. Caisa read the whole way from *The Book of Oma*. He saw her mouthing the words and nearly started to recite along with her.

"Is there a *Book of Oma* over there?" he asked.

"No," she said. "Ours is *The Book of Dhai*. It's about our history, mostly, how we are the blessed of Oma, how Oma delivers us from evil during times of madness."

"How many times?"

"Four thousand years, two turns of Oma," she said. She leaned forward. Space in the bubbled chrysalis was tight, so her nose nearly brushed his. "Thank you for taking me back."

"You heard about Liaro. Did you know?"

"I know he loves you very much, Kai. I know… whatever happened, he thought he was doing the right thing."

"I've had enough of betrayal."

She moved back. "Kai, you know this is just starting."

"I thought it was ending."

She pointed at the sky. "Oma hasn't even risen yet. That's when things get very bad, the books all say."

He laughed out loud at that.

They arrived at the Temple of Tira under a misty rain. The Line carried them up and up through a massive tangle of trees, deep into the woodland. Perched atop a massive cliff, its great foundations spanning two huge rivers spilling over the side, was the Temple of Tira, a green-black fist of a temple with the same domed top as the Temple of Oma. Even this far into the woodland, the plants had not reclaimed the temple. It kept them away with some kind of inner defense, one the Oras had never understood. Ahkio heard it posited that the temple's living skin secreted some kind of chemical or pheromone that repelled living things, but if that were so, it would have been impossible to keep a garden within the temple grounds, and Tira's gardens were the most renowned in the country. Its walls were made of tiered gardens, spilling with red and purple and yellow blossoms.

When the bubble of the Line arrived inside the Line chamber of Tira's temple, a novice already waited for them. She threw a bucket of living matter over the chrysalis, disintegrating it all around them.

Ahkio stepped free. "I have an appointment in the courtyard," he said.

"You're expected," she said. "Please wait while I get the Elder Ora."

Masura's cousin, Aimuda – an aging man with just a thin wisp of white hair left atop his slightly conical head – stepped through the doors a few minutes later. Rumor had it a midwife had pulled him from the womb with a pair of tongs, permanently deforming his head.

"Welcome to the Temple of Tira, Kai," Aimuda said, pressing thumb to forehead. "You are expected below."

Aimuda led him down six flights of stairs, plenty of time for Ahkio to note how quiet the temple seemed. "Where is everyone?" he asked.

"Only a few of the novices and the support staff remain," Aimuda said. "The rest have been sent to Kuallina."

"I didn't realize you sent so many," he said.

"Elder Ora Soruza of Oma's Temple was very persuasive in their insistence that we send all we could spare, as the very survival of Dhai was at stake. We could spare all. We sent all."

He led Ahkio into the rear courtyard among the great tiered gardens. A labyrinth of petrified bone trees stood at the center of the courtyard. The great grinning skulls leered down at him, creatures so long extinct he had no name for them.

There, at the edge of the bone tree labyrinth, stood Yisaoh, smirking and smoking.

He expected her to look haggard, pursued, thin and wan, but she was plump as ever, cleanly dressed, her hair combed to a fine luster.

"I heard you were looking for me," Yisaoh said.

"How is it you've been here all this time?"

"I haven't," she said. "Easy answer."

"You convinced the Elder Ora to harbor you for a meeting, though?"

"It's for the good of Dhai," she said, flicking ashes. "The two of us at odds has done neither of us any good."

He stepped forward, but she retreated into the shadow of the misty bone trees, her face lost to the fog. He saw only the burning embers of her cigarette.

"I came to hear your apology," she said.

"Apology?"

"What else would you call me out here for? I want to hear you apologize, and invite me back to Dhai, so I can spit in your face and laugh. Because what country do we have to return to? A bleeding mess. Your mess."

"A mess I inherited."

"Will you apologize or not?"

"The Tai Mora are looking for you."

She inhaled a long draft. Smoke bloomed around her head like a cloud. "That is a fact I'm aware of."

"If they hate you, and they hate me, that should make us great allies."

"Enemy of my enemy, and all that?" she said. It took him a moment to understand the reference. It was a Tordinian saying.

"Something like that," he said.

She nodded, then poked the hand with the cigarette at Caisa. "You still following this madman, girl?"

"He's Kai."

"So where's my apology, Kai?" Yisaoh asked.

"I'm not here to apologize," he said. "I'm here to propose a solution to our impasse."

"This should be terribly interesting. Do continue."

"Marry me," he said.

She laughed. Laughed so hard she choked on smoke, and doubled over, waving her hand at them. "No, no, really!" she said.

"It's a very serious offer," Ahkio said. "We have a problem easily resolved. A great many women who wanted a voice as Catori."

"So your solution is to marry all of us? Oh, Ahkio, you are darling." She finished the cigarette and stomped it out under her foot.

She turned and made to enter the bone tree maze.

"I need you, Yisaoh," he said.

"Do you?"

"I need a united Dhai," he said. "Help us in Kuallina."

"Kuallina is lost."

"We know that."

"Then why ask?"

"I need you to lead the civilians out of Kuallina," he said. "You know the woodlands, and they'll follow you."

"Where are you going to be?"

"I'll go back to the Temple of Oma, and hold that position. The temples have greater defenses than the holds. But the woodlands have the best defenses, and I think you can disappear there. I think you've been planning that for some time."

"This is too bold to be your idea."

"No. There's an omajista girl, Lilia. She came up with the plan. She says we should burn everything behind us."

"She is right, you know."

"I know."

"Why not have Mohrai do it?"

"Mohrai grew up at the harbor." He thought of the lute, and her soft fingers. "She's not made for the woodlands. She doesn't know it like you do. And what Lilia has planned to delay the army while we escape... I don't think she'll survive it. Many people still trust you. A lot of those who fled to Kuallina are from Garika. They'll go with you."

"If you aren't speaking truthfully–"

"I've never lied to you, Yisaoh. You know I speak plainly."

"I'll do it on one condition," she said.

He waited. She pulled out another cigarette. He wondered how she could stand to inhale so much smoke. "You tell everyone you apologized," she said, "and never ask me to marry you again."

Ahkio broke the news of Yisaoh's arrival to Mohrai first. He found her in the great dining hall, poring over maps of the troop arrangements outside Kuallina.

"We've turned Yisaoh," he said. "She's agreed to lead the civilians if something happens to me."

Mohrai raised her head. He wasn't sure what he expected, but it wasn't for her to shake her head resignedly. " You never wanted to be Kai," Mohrai said.

"I wanted to be a teacher." Ahkio rubbed his forehead. "And you wanted to play the lute. Yet here we are, neither teaching nor singing."

He thought she might throw something at him, but she just shrugged resignedly. "What you did is done," Mohrai said. "And so are we. Let her in, and let us discuss what's next."

41

Lilia sent out word to the armies that they wanted to parley, but received no response. The parajistas pummeled their defenses relentlessly for six days.

Lilia had Tulana, Voralyn, Laralyn and Amelia running shifts, taking turns managing the jistas on the walls. Their faces were haggard after three days. On the fourth, Tulana had a screaming fit, throwing plates and cups in Lilia's vicinity and telling her this was a fool's enterprise, and they were lost, and to just let her drop the barrier. Lilia slapped her, a woman almost twenty years her senior.

But they held out.

On the sixth day, Lilia walked down to the defenses herself. She surveyed the massive ring around the refugees, and stared into the faces of their enemy. From the ground, the army was even more horrifying. The refugees had all pushed as close to the walls of Kuallina as they could. The latrine ditches were overfull. Foodstuffs were still coming in by Line, but they were heavily rationed. The people called at her as she passed, and she stopped to press her hands to people's heads and hearts and murmur courageous words.

She strode right up to the barrier with exhausted Voralyn at her side while her people looked on. She supposed she looked like a fearless woman as she did it, but in truth she felt nothing as she pressed her nose to the barrier. The misty forces that assaulted them were invisible to her. With all the parajistas from the temples funneled into Kuallina, and the Seekers keeping discipline, they could hold out for a good long time.

But Tulana was the only omajista on the wall now, with Taigan gone and Lilia burned out. Tulana was powerful, but it was the relentless volleys from the parajistas that kept them all safe.

Lilia leaned forward and gestured to Voralyn. Voralyn raised a hand. The air around her compressed a bit more. It was already a bit like soup, here at the front.

"Empress Kirana," Lilia said. "I request an audience."

Her voice thundered out across the army, and met resistance as it encountered various tangles of parajista offenses.

She repeated it twice more. Waited. The first line of infantry on the other side of the barrier raised their heads from their shields. They stood in long rows, waiting for a break in Kuallina's defenses that they could stream through, ever alert.

But no one came forward.

Lilia put her hands in the broad pockets of her tunic.

"They know they can crush us," Voralyn said. "Why should they care to parley?"

Why, indeed?

Lilia chewed her lip. She took another pinch of mahuan root. Long use killed people, she knew. Her mother warned her against it, and the Oras, all of her doctors. But it took twenty years to do it, and Lilia knew she would not make it the twenty years.

She slogged upstairs to speak with the Kai. She entered the great dining hall without announcing herself, and found him speaking in low tones with a broken-nosed woman smoking what smelled like a Tordinian cigarette.

"Their Kai isn't answering," Lilia said.

"Yisaoh has another idea," Ahkio said.

"Yisaoh?" Lilia said. She had heard of the woman, but didn't realize she was in Kuallina.

Yisaoh put out her cigarette on the table. Lilia thought it very rude. "We've held here three weeks," Yisaoh said. "It's the Feast of All Souls in just a few days. I suggest we ask for a cessation of hostilities, and a parley over a banquet."

"Isn't that what I already asked for?"

"We're going to remind her we have something she wants more than Kuallina," Ahkio said.

"What's that?" Lilia asked.

Yisaoh said, "Me."

When Lilia went out onto the plain this time, Voralyn at her side to give her words strength, she said, "Empress Kirana. I am the daughter of Nava Sona, speaking for Kai Ahkio Javia Garika. We propose a parley on the Feast of All Souls. We have news of Yisaoh Alais Garika."

Three hours later, Kirana sent a messenger to parley.

42

Zezili crawled into a nearby cocoon, sliding in its mucus. She grabbed a moldering body and yanked it up against the opening to the cocoon, shielding her from the view of the approaching monsters. She could just peer over the back of the stinking corpse and see the alien women hissing past her, close enough that she could throw a rock and hit one.

They sniffed the air as they approached. Zezili froze. They swung their heads about. Zezili stopped breathing.

They exchanged rapid-fire clicks and guttural sounds – some kind of language.

Then the gaggle of figures moved on, and Zezili let out her breath.

She needed to find out where Storm had gone when he breached this barrier. Waking up these things was supposed to require some kind of ritual. It was why they brought the jistas. So where had he performed it?

Zezili crawled out of the cocoon and loped across the field, keeping low. She paused often to flatten herself against the ground whenever she heard or saw one of the strange women. She made for what looked like a ziggurat at the center of the anomaly. At first she'd thought it was some plant-plagued hill, but now that she was closer, it was clear it was a building that had been reclaimed by the woods.

The bodies made a neat trail to the structure, and they got fresher. She recognized three women from those she'd brought with her, and one of the Sebastyn jistas. They had lost at least one jista back in that stupid town, Mordid. That left three to do whatever needed doing to wake up these things. How many would it take to put them back to bed?

Zezili found the doors of the temple – was it a temple? A fortress? – open. They were massive slabs of stone. She wasn't sure how Storm had gotten them open. The jistas, maybe? She stepped inside and pushed the arm with the dagger ahead of her. Inside, great bronze mirrors reflected the light from the entrance, spilling back and back, further than Zezili could see. What she could make out was a broad foyer with a massive ceiling painted in strange geometric figures. The room had six broad exits – not counting the one she walked in from. She saw that the mirrors directed the light to just one of the entrances, at her left.

Inside were more bodies, all less than a week old. The odor was so strong that Zezili's eyes watered. She picked her way across the bodies and made for the archway. As she rounded the corner, she saw another body ahead of her jerking erratically on the floor. A breath of horror escaped her. Then a bloodied face rose from the flopping body – it was some serpentine creature with great black fangs and eyes the color of silver. It had four front limbs. She saw the lash of a black tail. She had never seen anything like it.

Zezili put the wall at her back. The creature rose up. It was at least twice as tall as her. It moved so fast she had no time to retreat. In a breath it was on her. It clamped on her thigh. She stabbed it in the eye. It howled, and released her. She stabbed the other eye. The tail lashed, and caught her across the face. She fell and stabbed it in the torso. It was thrashing now. It was the thrashing that would kill her, that fucking tail–

Zezili stabbed it in the throat. The face came at her again. She batted it away with her left arm and stabbed with her right. The blood was black, and made her skin itch. She hissed. The tail smashed her face. She stabbed at the eyes over and over, splattering black, irritating blood until it stopped moving.

Zezili took great gasping breaths. She drooled into its mashed face, and spit black ichor. She got up, and stumbled past the body. The tail thumped. She hollered at it, kicked it, but it was just reflexive nerves. It flopped on the floor.

She pushed on, deeper into the ziggurat. She was definitely headed below ground now, following the slightly sloping floor. The creature's blood burned her skin. She wondered how poisonous it was, and if she'd be dead before she got to the end of this fucking maze. She spat. The blood made her mouth tingle.

Down and down she went, passing great open doors inscribed with strange writing. They reminded her of the stories she'd heard of Tordinian tombs. The open doors led to rooms the size and shape of her wardrobe at home, and the walls were covered in mucus. She saw great plant-like protrusions covering the interior of each. Like the cocoons outside, the tombs glowed with a faint green bioluminescence. She tried to imagine spending… what? Two thousand, a thousand years cradled in one of those things? This must be where the Empress had buried her kin.

The corridor opened up. Zezili walked into a broad, spherical room. The room was lined in the same sticky tentacles as the tombs she'd passed, and the floor was green. It roiled like something alive, and lights rippled across its surface. She saw what remained of her three Sebastyn jistas on the edge of the pool, their skin charred. At the center of the pool was a great dais, and on top of the dais was what looked like a silver throne made of skulls, all coated in silver. She did not recognize the skulls of the creatures that made up the throne. They looked vaguely human, but distorted. Some had three eyes, or four eyes, and massive bulbous foreheads, and jutting mouths. A few even looked like they had horns. They were some parody of humanity, some dark vision. On top of the throne was Storm, slumped forward with chin on chest. Zezili could not see him well, but suspected he was as dead as the jistas.

"What the fuck?" she muttered aloud, because none of it made any sense. She was not gifted, and suspected there must be some kind of barrier or switch or something she couldn't see.

Zezili looked around for something to throw into the pool, and settled for yanking a satchel off one of the jistas and tossing it in. The pool was not a pool – the bag sat on it like it was a solid surface, disturbing only the light. But it didn't hiss or eat it or burst into flame.

Zezili squared her shoulders and tested one foot on the green surface. She'd come all this way, why stop now? The light flickered, but it was solid. She crept across the surface to the throne and peered up at Storm's body.

She raised her foot to mount the silver steps–

And Storm's head jerked up. He gabbled at her, jerking about like a puppet on a string. Zezili jumped back, shoving her daggered hand ahead of her.

Storm swung his head toward her, and the gabbling became something she could understand. "Do not defy her!"

"What happened?"

"Do not defy her!"

Green bile dribbled from Storm's mouth. His eyes were unfocused. His flesh looked moldered, to her. It had taken on a greenish tint.

"Storm?"

"Do… not… defy…"

His chin slumped back to his chest. The body relaxed,

as if the puppet master released the strings.

Zezili stepped gingerly around the back of the throne. The top of the throne was attached to the back wall by a giant, pulsing thread of green tentacles, all fused with the silvery throne. She thought of the Empress's silver throne back in Daorian. Fashioned after this one?

That's when she heard the whispering.

Zezili crept behind the throne and hid under the massive pulsing tentacle. She peered around the other side, back the way she had come.

It wasn't whispering. It was hissing.

The Empress's people were clicking and muttering and sliding down the hall toward her. The shushing sound grew louder and louder.

Zezili thought she might lose her shit then, just dribble out there behind the throne. Her gut churned so bad she wanted to vomit.

But this was what she wanted, wasn't it? Some glorious end, fighting impossible odds?

Zezili pushed her daggered hand forward, and stepped out from behind the throne.

43

Maralah had not confined many people to prison. Prison was where a coward put you when they didn't know what to do with you. If she were in Morsaar's place, she'd have had herself killed immediately, the way she'd killed Alaar's heirs and wives and the heirs and wives of the Patron before him. The few she kept alive had to swear fealty to the new Patron within days of the ascension.

But no one asked her to pay fealty. No one came to her.

They locked Maralah in the south tower, with a narrow slit of a window that showed her the sky, three feet higher than she could jump. She spent most of her time sitting at the opposite wall, staring out that window, watching Para move across the sky. It was not a proper gaol – that would have been the lightless passages below. Nor was it some lushly appointed place one would put the loved one of a rival, waiting on a ransom. It appeared to have been a storage room of some sort, hurriedly emptied to accommodate her. She saw scuff marks on the floor, tattered onion skins, and shriveled hasaen tuber stalks scattered across the floor. Someone brought a heavy bear skin up for her the first night. Water and food came up once a day. She expected it would be another sanisi who would look after her, but they simply sent up a slave, a new one each day. They cut a hole in the bottom of the door so they could push it through. The entire affair felt odd, ill-prepared. She had not taken Morsaar for a usurper.

The season dragged on. When she realized they weren't going to kill her immediately, she planned for a long wait. It was entirely possible, if they kept her alive a few weeks, that they'd keep her alive a few months. And that gave Taigan time to answer the fiery ward she'd used to recall him some time ago.

Maralah measured time by the chill in the air, and the extended amount of daylight in the sky. Low spring came and went, became high spring. She listened to the ice melt, the water drain from the roof. She watched Para circumnavigate the sky each day. She started up a routine. Food came in the early morning. After eating, she went through her defense forms, and then basic sword craft. She napped through the afternoon, then played strategy games with onion skins and shreds of bear fur until dark.

Prison left time for contemplation, which was the worst part of it. If she was not careful, her mind could wander to her fate, or Rajavaa's, or the country's. It would lead her to wonder what would happen if they just left her here, abandoned in a cell, while they retreated south to Anjoliaa after all. As the snow melted, she began to wonder if Morsaar meant to stay here and fight, if this was the last stand. But she didn't think a man who couldn't even muster up the courage to kill her had the determination to stand fast in front of the greatest and grimmest army the world had ever known. She spent too much time, perhaps, going over her mistakes. When all one had was time, it was inevitable. If she had come up the stairs just a little sooner, before Kadaan killed Alaar, things would be different. If she had sent out Taigan to find omajistas sooner, perhaps... or moved this legion here and that one there during the first assault... or if she had known the tears in the sky for what they were, maybe, she could have prepared better... but those thoughts did not change her situation. They did not free her from the present. They trapped her in the past.

She was not easily lost to ennui, even now. If she was lucky, they would take her out of here eventually instead of forgetting about her and letting her starve to death. Getting taken out and killed seemed like the best possible result. It also meant that the moment she was out, the moment something changed, she would need to move, and quickly, if she wanted a chance at something other than death. She could rely on no one but herself now, and perhaps the possibility of Taigan, unless he was dead already.

So instead of preparing for her eventual starvation, she prepared for the day the door opened. It was the same way she fought the war with the Tai Mora. You fought for the day it was over, but you got there by fighting one battle at a time. In this little cell, the battle she fought each day was against herself, and her own despair.

It was why she was ready the day the cell door finally opened.

"Hands out," the sanisi said. He was young, not far past twenty. A sanisi did not complete their training until at least twenty-two, but he looked far younger. It wouldn't surprise her if they were pushing them through training faster, here at the end. Two other sanisi stood behind him. Parajistas, all, if she had a guess. Morsaar wouldn't risk moving her with anything less, would he?

"Where are we going?" Maralah asked.

"Hands out," he repeated. The air grew heavy.

She complied. He bound her hands in copper-threaded rope; expensive stuff. Also more difficult to burn through even for a sensitive sinajista, let alone one like her who was in far decline.

The sanisi led her into the hall. She recognized Kovaas and a short, long-faced ataisa named Arakam who had come in with Rajavaa's force.

That left her Kovaas. "I'm fine with dying, Kovaas," she said. "But at least have the courage to tell me so."

He did not look at her.

"Beheading, then?" she said.

He lowered his chin.

She continued marching forward. Beheading wasn't so bad. There were worse ways to die. It surprised her that Morsaar wanted this to be so public. If she were in charge, she'd have killed someone like her with a squeeze of parajista-controlled air and burned whatever was left. A public killing meant he wanted to make a show of his strength. It was fitting, that after all this she'd be killed by her own army. She'd outlived most sanisi. Many died in battle, or during some power shift like this one. Living to forty-three, outlasting her brother, her child, every relative she'd ever known – that was something. Clutching a win from the jaws of disaster. She smiled grimly.

The younger sanisi led, and Kovaas took up the rear. They descended the long spiral of stairs to the massive courtyard below. It was as they entered the yard, the younger sanisi over the threshold, leaving Maralah and Kovaas, briefly, inside, that Kovaas leaned over and said, "Rajavaa is still alive."

Maralah stumbled into the light. The days were brilliant now, still cold, but much longer. The double suns were high in the sky, piercing white. Para rode the western sky, a flaming blue brand. The slap of fresh air filled her lungs. She stared out at a great cutting stone in the yard, and a basket of fresh, bloody heads. A cart of bodies. She did not recognize the man at the stone. From the look of his clothes, he was an infantryman, probably one of Morsaar's.

There were eight more sanisi in the courtyard, two at each door. Maralah thought it a poor use of sanisi, with a Tai Mora army marching for Harajan. At least twenty more regular soldiers lined the parapet overlooking the courtyard. It made her wonder just how many people – how many powerful people – Morsaar planned to kill today, or had already killed. But all she had was Kovaas's whisper about her brother being alive. It was precious little to go on to understand what was happening, or whether or not Kovaas would back her if she bolted.

Maralah considered herself a fair tactician. Her odds, even with Kovaas, a parajista, were poor. Not unless he'd manufactured some grand escape for her, and she could see no reason for that. She glanced back at him. He avoided her look.

"You going to give me a reason?" she said. "Why now?"

"The Tai Mora are outside," Kovaas said. "They asked for blood."

Maralah's skin prickled. "You all know they're liars," she said. "They'll have us kill ourselves, and then come in to finish the rest. You know these Tai Mora. You know what they are."

The young sanisi jerked at her bonds. Maralah headbutted him. He reeled back.

The air thickened.

She called for Sina, Lord of the Underworld. Sina's breath came immediately, too easily for a descendent star, then disappeared. She held it under her skin and set her bonds aflame. She twisted at the copper wire while the rope blazed.

Arrows buzzed past her. She ducked and ran back toward the tower. Tripped. Kovaas threw himself in front of her. Took two arrows to the chest. Then a third.

Maralah hunkered behind his body. Shouted, "You know me! You know what they are! They will turn on you."

The words felt foolish, even to her desperate ears. More arrows thudded into Kovaas. She needed to move to cover. The air around her grew thick. She flattened herself against the ground, her only defense against a parajista attack.

As sanisi at the doors opposite advanced, she realized what a stupid way this was to die. Beheading was neat and elegant. Dignified. Now she was just a bear cub flushed into a kill hole. Maralah grabbed Kovaas by the back of his trousers and heaved him with her to the door back to her cell. A tangle of air ripped the coat from his body.

She lost her breath. Heaved again. She tumbled back into the tower with Kovaas, and kicked the door shut.

He was still breathing. Blood smeared his mouth. His eyes were wild. A whump of air thundered at the door.

"Poor thing to die for," she said. "They'll kill me either way."

He gaped something at her. Pointed at the ceiling.

She glanced up, saw nothing. "What's really happening, Kovaas?"

He gulped air, wheezed, "Stargazers. Sina."

Outside the door, someone cried out.

The air became thick as soup. She gasped and grabbed at Kovaas's infused blade. She crawled to the door, like swimming.

Outside, the sky was violet-crimson, as if the sea was on fire. Para still hung in the sky, but it had been joined by a second body, eclipsing it – the mangled, irregularly shaped violet body of Sina. Everyone in the courtyard gaped at it; a miraculous happening, even by the standards of their irregular sky. As Maralah watched, Para flickered in the sky, flashed like a coin, and then simply... disappeared, as if blinking out of existence. In its place, Sina blazed a powerful, eerie purple.

Maralah raised her infused blade to the sky and opened herself to Sina. Blue fire crawled around the Para-infused blade. It spat and hissed at her as she forced Sina's power to subsume that of Para. The blue flames surged, and were overcome with violet mist. Purple heat emanated from the blade.

Maralah laughed, and sang the Song of Unmaking out loud.

44

Roh smelled sulfur. The scent was so odd, so unexpected on the rolling white tundra, that he reined in his dog and stopped. He and Luna had gone north for three days before turning south, trying to shake their pursuers. For a week they had moved across a featureless tundra, eating mostly rice. Roh tried to gag down the fish Luna caught, but his stomach rebelled, and he vomited it all up. They had been plodding so long on this featureless land that he knew his brain was bound to start making things up. Roh thought he might be going mad when he smelled the sulfur.

"Behind us," Luna said, pointing.

Roh saw a cluster of dark figures coming around a low snow drift. They had not lost their pursuers after all.

"Why do they care about us?" Roh said. "It makes no sense to follow us."

"The Tai Mora are thorough," Luna said.

Roh turned his dog forward.

"We should be careful," Luna said. "That smell–"

Roh's animal trundled up to what looked like a cliff. Roh halted him, and gazed out over a massive crater so large he could not see its end. In the crater below, roiling pools of bubbling gray water steamed in the frigid air. Tangles of frozen steam glittered on the sides of the crater. Ice coated the branches of scraggly trees like spun sugar.

"Any other way across?" Roh asked, stupidly, because he could see there was not. It stretched on and on, this misty, bubbling crater, like a massive giant had taken a huge bite of the world and left spittle and bile behind.

"I've never been out here." Luna looked over his shoulder again. "They'll follow."

Roh slapped his dog. It grumbled at him, annoyed, and waggled its head, but obeyed, shuffling over the lip of the tundra and onto the pockmarked crater full of pools.

"Are these boiling?" Roh asked.

"Why don't you test it out?" Luna said.

Roh frowned at him, but it was a fair response. Roh knew he was just making noise. The sound of his own voice was comforting.

Moss and spindly grass grew between the pools, leading Roh to believe the ground, at least, wasn't as hot as the water.

Roh had never seen water boiling on its own before. "Will it kill us?" he asked

"Not before the Tai Mora," Luna said.

Roh called Para and came up with nothing. It was like sucking at an empty spoon, expecting warm broth and getting a mouthful of air. He pulled again, mouthing the litany instead of just repeating it silently, and Para bled into him slowly, reluctantly. He held the breath beneath his skin and waited. He glanced behind them again, and counted the figures. Five. How many were parajistas? Surely not all of them. Why send powerful people after two... his mind wrestled with what he was, what Luna was, but he had to look at himself the way they would. He and Luna were just slaves, not sanisi, or diplomats, or anything else useful. He had taken on Ora Almeysia, a powerful tirajista, a woman with a star in decline, and since then he had fought the Tai Mora twice – at the banquet hall in Kuonrada and in Shoratau, and he was still alive. He could get them through this.

"I'd say we should hide," Luna said, "but there isn't anywhere to go."

Roh stared across the bubbling pools. The Tai Mora were gaining, and they would not stop until they caught them. He looked at Luna. Luna knew how to survive here, and he'd been carrying Roh all week. What had Roh done for Luna?

The air pressure increased. Roh pulled on Para again. It came sluggishly. He pulled until he seethed with power, then murmured a litany to place a protective wall around the two of them. He saw a blue ball of brilliant light speed toward them from the Tai Mora. It burst against his defenses.

The dogs barked and circled. Roh struggled to keep control of his while maintaining the barricade.

The Tai Mora yelled, and their dogs came after them at a sprint.

Roh made his decision, though fear boiled in his gut. "Go, Luna."

"There's nowhere to go."

"Ride! You have the book. Go."

Luna twisted back and forth between the Tai Mora and Roh.

"If you don't go I'll kill you myself. It's better than what the Tai Mora will do."

Luna hollered at his dog to run. He slapped its heavy flank and they were off across the boiling crater, the animal loping through the spaces between the massive pools.

Roh turned on the Tai Mora and let loose a tangle of Para's breath, a dangerous skein of needled air. It moved so fast it would skewer them alive in half a breath.

Something flashed in the sky at his left. He focused on binding his next attack. His first offense crashed into the Tai Mora defenses. They still barreled toward him, weapons snarling from their wrists. He could see their faces now – grim, determined.

He called Para. Nothing.

Roh concentrated harder. He opened himself to the star, and was rewarded with a thin trickle of breath.

The sky flashed again.

A thunderous boom rocked the air, so hard his dog bolted. Roh fell hard on the ground, and lost his breath.

He gazed into the brilliant lavender-blue sky, blinking rapidly. Was he seeing double? There were two stars in the sky, brilliant blue Para and another – a star not due for a year or more, one he had never seen before, but he knew it just the same.

Purple Sina blazed down at him like a bruise.

And Para winked out.

It happened so quickly Roh thought he dreamed it. But with Para's absence in the sky, he also lost his grasp on Para. All he had of Para now was what he held beneath his skin. He held Para's final breath tightly beneath his skin. He felt it burning him up from the inside. Sina stared balefully down at him, unblinking. One final litany. One left, and then... then he was theirs.

The Tai Mora reined in their dogs. He saw their leering faces, and the slobbering dogs. Roh launched himself up onto one shoulder, rolled over, and reached out to Luna's fleeing form. He whispered the Litany of Protection, and released it just as a searing fire blazed across his skin. He screamed.

When Roh came back to his senses, he saw a woman stood over him waving her hand. The air tensed, though he saw no blue mist. She called a star he could not see.

She called Sina, the ascendant star.

"Wait!" Roh said. "Wait! I have–" What? What did he have to offer them, but his own death? Dance, he thought, dance the way you always do. "I can prove very useful," he said. "I was a slave under the Saiduan. Anything is better than being under them. Anything."

A lie – Kadaan had always been kind – but the idea of slavery, of having his hair cut, his clothing chosen for him, his body pushed and pulled at the will of another, was repulsive enough to add weight to his words. His Saiduan was accented. They must be able to hear it in his voice. But if the Saiduan took him a few years before, he would still have it. It fit his role. He pulled off his hood, showed them his shaved head, and then he pressed his forehead to the warm dirt at their feet, the way Dasai had pressed his head to the floor in front of the Patron.

The woman muttered in that not-Dhai language. Roh lifted his head and watched them talk. The taller woman was on his side. He could see it in her face. But the smallest was leery, and the man wanted him murdered. All it took to know was a look. They weren't stoic Saiduan. They didn't fear showing their true faces.

"I'm no threat," Roh said. He didn't dare try to draw on Para now. Its absence still hurt. He was trembling, feverish, though from fear or the shock of losing Para, he didn't know. No one had told him what happened when one's star descended so suddenly. He should have had months of warning from the stargazers. He felt naked, completely vulnerable, in a way he had not felt since he was a child. Two years of Para's ascendance was a lifetime for him, the difference between ages thirteen and fifteen. At twelve he had gone from a gangly, spit-upon nobody to a boy with a chance at becoming something more, something extraordinary. Without Para, what was he?

They talked on. He pushed them. "I have information about the Dhai," he said. The admission came upon him suddenly, like a sickness. "I can help you defeat the Dhai. I know the Kai's cipher." He almost did vomit, then, but what was he without what he owned? He was dead. Dead right here, obliterated in this roiling, nightmarish land.

No more voices. He watched their faces. They knew what the cipher was, then.

"I know it," he said, bumbling on, trying to buy time – for Luna, he told himself, but really, it was for him, he knew it in his heart. "I can help the Tai Mora, your Kai. I have... all sorts of information about the Dhai." He was sweating, and it had little to do with the warm air.

They conversed amongst themselves. The man turned away. The tall woman pushed toward him. She leaned over him, and he cowered, yes, he cowered in front of her, because even if he could fight, fighting was nothing when the person you faced stood under an ascendant star.

"Get up," she said.

He scrambled to his feet. She towered over him by a head. "I'll do anything you say," Roh babbled. "I'm not dangerous."

The other woman said something. Roh thought it sounded very like something in Dhai about being "pretty." They both laughed.

Heat moved up his face.

The tall woman grabbed his chin. Held it firmly. He didn't resist. She tried to meet his look, but he stared at the ground. Luna would tell him to be meek, to stand down. He would not have tried it with Kadaan, but with the Tai Mora, the people who had murdered every Saiduan from the north sea to Anjoliaa...

She licked his face.

Roh stiffened. He willed himself not to tremble.

"Fine, then," the shorter woman said. "But if you run, you understand? If you run, I will cut you open myself, and fuck your corpse."

Roh worked some spit into his mouth. "I understand."

"Go get the other one," the man said.

When the two women left in pursuit of Luna, Roh sank to the ground. The man stood over him, staring. "If you're lying about the cipher, or your temperament, they will do worse than fuck your corpse."

"I know," Roh said. And he did. Oma knew, he did.

45

A prickling skein of power slid across Luna's skin. Luna fell forward, and nearly lost hir grip on the dog. Something felt strange, as if ze were covered in spider's webbing. Ze looked back and saw Roh collapsed in the mud, the Tai Mora hunched over him. One of them looked up at Luna, and gestured at hir.

A whump of air struck Luna. Ze toppled. Hit the ground hard. Lost hir breath. Ze rolled right into a boiling, murky pool.

Heat suffused Luna's body, but ze did not feel wet. Hir face was dry. Ze sputtered to the surface, splashing. Water rolled off hir body in little droplets. Ze had some kind of protective coating over hir. Luna saw the Tai Mora advancing, and gazed across the broad pool. Luna kicked below the surface and swam hard for the other side of the pool, a good forty paces distant. The coating of air around hir made hir buoyant – staying under the surface was a struggle. Ze paddled hard for the other side, all the while looking for a root or spur of rock to hold onto, to keep hir under and away from their roving eye. Roh must have wrapped Luna in some parajista spell.

Luna came to the other side, exhausted, and glanced back, keeping only hir eyes above the water. The steam and roiling bubbles of gas obscured hir view, but that was good. It would make it harder for them to see hir, too.

Hir two pursuers – the others must have stayed with Roh – spoke in loud voices on the other side of the water. Hir bear had stopped at the next pool, and watched the Tai Mora with sticky yellow eyes.

The tallest one, broad in the shoulders, gestured across the pool toward Luna. Luna submerged again, treading hard to stay below the surface. Ze was sweating terribly in the heat; it soaked hir clothes, dripped down hir face. How long would this spell last? Ze was going to drown in hir own sweat before long. Luna had a sudden urge to urinate. But dying at the hands of the Tai Mora looked a fair bit worse than drowning in urine, right now.

The water was stifling. It was like being stuck inside a cave roiling with steam. Hir head crested the top of the water, and fresh air flowed around hir skin. Ze tried to breathe, and sucked in foul-smelling air. The skin was breathable.

Ze peeked hir head up. The Tai Mora were advancing, each taking a side of the pool.

Luna ducked again.

The press of the water made it difficult to breathe, even knowing Luna could. Ze pushed a single finger to the surface, let it skim the top to refresh hir air. Luna took shallow breaths. Waited. Ze expected hands on hir arms, or a great gout of air, yanking hir from the water. But Para was descendent now, and they would not use air, but fire. They'd burn hir up and leave hir a charred husk on the plain.

Seconds ticked by. The air ze managed to suck in was warm, but felt stale. Ze started to hyperventilate. Calm would not come. Luna was drowning, like ze had when ze fell off the boat in the Haraeo sea as a child – falling, falling into a blackness alive with vast sea creatures larger than any building. Luna thrashed.

But to surface… to surface was death, or worse.

Darkness licked at hir; warm and inviting. Hir body, starved for oxygen, rebelled. Ze surfaced.

The protective barrier around hir burst.

Hot water soaked Luna's clothes, and dragged hir under. Ze felt no bottom. Luna kicked and clawed for the edge of the pool. Ze found purchase and hauled hirself out. Luna lay on the bank, gasping. Ze looked for the Tai Mora, but saw no one over the misty swath of the pools. This soaked, ze couldn't leave the protective warmth of the hot springs, not until ze dried out.

Luna scrambled forward in search of hir dog; the animal would be carrying some dry clothes, a blanket, hir fire-starting kit. Ze circled the pool once, and saw no Tai Mora, no dog. Luna walked on, fearful to whistle or clap hir hands in search of the dog in case the Tai Mora were still close.

No dog.

But ze did see the Tai Mora. They were tall figures moving through the mist. Ze pressed hirself to the ground. The air wasn't blistering cold, but it had begun to cool hir watery clothes. Luna was already shivering.

The Tai Mora had five dogs now. They pulled Luna's and Roh's behind them. Ze looked for Roh among them, but did not see him before the whole party was swallowed up by the mist.

Luna rolled over and started yanking off hir clothes.

Ze was alone somewhere on the Saiduan tundra, without food, dry clothes, fire, or mount.

As ze stripped, ze remembered the boat, and the bloated arms of hir dead parents.

Ze had been in worse places than this, and survived them.

Luna wrung out hir clothes, shivering in the cool air. Ze found one of the spindly pines nearby, and hung them out to dry. Ze unwrapped the book, ensuring it had not gotten wet, then slipped into the warmth of the hot springs. It would take hours for hir clothes to dry. It would be night by then.

Ze closed hir eyes. Luna had been in worse places.

If Luna repeated it often enough, ze might soon believe it.

46

Lilia's first plan had been to serve the Tai Mora their own dead and set the whole table on fire as a massive distraction, believing that was appropriate, but Ahkio's face at her suggestion put that idea to rest. When she found the forsia tubers among Gian's hoarded food, she had a far better idea. Most of the refugees were eating plain rice now and little else, but Lilia proposed they spread out a proper banquet with fresh food shipped in via the Line from the Temple of Tira. If they pretended they were well stocked and eating well, it told the Tai Mora they were comfortable with a long siege. And the tubers would be just one dish among many.

The Line had become a front of sorts for the battle of Kuallina – the Tai Mora had already severed the lines going to Asona Harbor, Liona, the Temple of Sina, and the Temple of Para, leaving only the routes to the Temple of Oma and Temple of Tira intact. Lilia had Laralyn protecting the remaining two lines. Those who took the second shift were weaker, less experienced. It was only a matter of time before the Tai Mora hit them when the second shift protected them, and then they would be completely cut off.

The banquet they planned was one Lilia would have eaten at the temple during the high spring festival season

– honeyed fiddleheads, curried yams, caramelized onions and salted weed plantains, marigold blossoms in buttery cilantro rice, soft braided bread braised in garlic, and fried edamame.

For the final dish, she walked with little Tasia along the creek bed running behind Kuallina. The creek was now festering with the piss and shit of the great army, which used it as a latrine. Kuallina itself had a well, so it didn't threaten their own water, but the waste had polluted the stream, killing various types of fishes, toads and other, more delicate creatures, and that made Lilia angry. She had worked personally to oversee the digging of the latrines for the refugees outside the wall. Shitting in a creek was wasteful, irresponsible, filthy.

Her anger made it easier for her to put up with the stink and mess of it on her shoes as she waded in and pulled out the great knobs of the dormant forsia lilies growing on the little islands at the center of the stream. Tasia carried them in a big sack that eventually dragged across the ground. Lilia needed one for every guest, and a half dozen more for practice.

"Never eat these," Lilia told Tasia as she put them in the sack, just as her mother had said to her when she was small.

"But you're going to eat them," Tasia said.

"They are poisonous," Lilia said. "They have to be prepared the right way, and divided up and eaten correctly. Until you learn how, they will kill you. Understand?"

Lilia hauled the forsia tubers back into the kitchens of Kuallina, and stood at the sink with her sleeves rolled up and scrubbed them herself. They had a spiny outer skin and soft, sweet-nutty interior. Lilia liked the idea of serving the Kai and her people some weed that grew in their own shit. Liked it very much.

She cooked one of the forsia tubers in the oven, then called down Gian and the Kai to teach them how to eat the tubers without killing themselves. Yisaoh and Mohrai came down with the Kai, watching him and each other like predatory birds. War had a way of bringing people together.

"This needs to be done correctly," Lilia said, "or it will kill you." She said it in the same tone she'd used with Tasia.

Lilia carefully removed the skin of the root and put it aside. "Don't eat this part," she said. "This next is most important, though." She took the knife and gently tucked it into the center of the tuber, and pulled the knife all the way around its stiff core. She pulled apart the two halves, revealing a sticky black center from which radiated three dark tendrils.

"This whole black center must be removed," Lilia said. "These tendrils, too. You must not eat this part. Not even a taste. It will kill you." She began to de-vein the tuber.

Mohrai examined the skin of the tuber. "We should at least have Ahkio's already cleaned."

"It will give us away," Lilia said.

"What will happen if he dies at that table?" Mohrai said. "It took a year to unite the clans. Succession now, especially after that... performance in the temple, will be contested. This is much riskier than I thought."

Yisaoh shrugged. "Let him do it."

"You would say that," Mohrai said.

"How serious is this poison?" Ahkio said.

Lilia neatly pulled the first black thread away, and set it aside. "An hour, maybe two. They can burst if you don't handle them carefully."

"Can we wash them?" Ahkio said.

Lilia sighed and set down the knife. She wiped her hands on her apron and then rubbed her aching head.

"If we think they will fall without a head," Mohrai said, "their... leader is certainly thinking the same thing. If this doesn't kill Ahkio, sending him down there surely will. I'm having second thoughts about this. It sounds bold here inside, but out there—"

"Kai?" Lilia said. "You thought this a fine idea when I proposed it."

Mostly fine, anyway.

Ahkio folded his arms, tucking his hands under his armpits. It was an annoying, defensive gesture. He looked at the table as he did it, weighing and considering.

Lilia smacked her hand on the table. "Now is not a time to talk," she said. "Now is a time for action."

"I hate to say it," Yisaoh said. "But Mohrai is right. Do you really think you can sit at that table and kill your own sister, Ahkio? We know she's down there. I don't think you can."

Ahkio raised his head. Lilia saw his answer. He was not a ruthless man, not a killer. It infuriated her more than she thought it would. She had given him a way out before, but he insisted on being part of this, and now, when the time came, he became a coward. He would not follow through.

She stared hard at the knife on the table. "I have given a lot of things to fighting these people," she said. "You—"

"Revenge," Ahkio said.

"It's not revenge," Lilia snapped. Reflexive. Of course it was about revenge.

"I'm sorry about what they did to your mother," Ahkio said. "I'm sorry about your world, your village, your leg. But destroying them fixes none of that."

"This is not about revenge, it's—"

"We'll have a banquet," Ahkio said, "without the poison. We'll meet them like civilized people, and accept what happens. The more I've considered this duplicity, the more I dislike it."

"It's the only way," Lilia said.

"Is it?" he said. He seemed disappointed in her. They all did. She was disappointed in herself, too – for failing at the harbor, for burning out, for not telling them. "Ghrasia wouldn't have agreed to this," he said. "It was compassion that had her open those gates for you. The same compassion that would stay her hand now."

"You can't speak for the dead," Lilia said.

Yisaoh interrupted. "We'll do as the Kai says." She pulled a cigarette from a leather case in her tunic pocket. Lilia wondered if she would run out soon, and whether or not she would be so mellow, then.

Lilia picked up the knife and jabbed it into the table. "Fine, then. But I won't be part of it. This was my idea, and this was the only way it was going to work."

"The way it worked at the wall?" Mohrai said.

"It would have–" Lilia stepped away from the table. "Do what you like. This isn't my battle anyway."

She stormed out of the room. Gian ran after her, grabbing at her hand.

"I'm sorry, Li," Gian said.

Lilia pushed away her hand.

Lilia went to her room and curled up on her bed. No one but Gian and Tulana knew she could no longer call on Oma, but even with no power, with nothing but bluster, she was willing to do this – to sit with the leader of the Tai Mora and feed her poison and risk the consequences. Because this was their only option. The illusion that shielded the retreating civilians was already going to be difficult to sell after the bold one she had used to cross the great army. She knew her plans sounded extreme, desperate, and they were. But doing nothing was worse.

Gian came in to sit with her, but Lilia yelled at her to get out. She was increasingly agitated now, anxious. She chewed more mahuan root and lay alone in the dark room. Hunger gnawed at her belly, but she did not get up.

Taigan was right. She should have gone to Saiduan. The Saiduan, at least, would do what needed to be done. The Dhai were cowards, just like she had been. They lived fearfully, like she had. But cowards never changed anything. Cowards didn't win.

She didn't remember sleeping, but she must have dozed. She woke to the smell of Tordinian tobacco.

Her door opened, slowly. In the pale light of the moons, she could just make out Yisaoh's long face, the crooked nose.

"I've drugged the Kai," she said. "You and Mohrai are going out tomorrow, with Gian and Mohrai's cousin, Alhina. I'll lead the civilians out while you distract them. Ahkio will go back to the temple, when he's awake."

"What happens when he finds out?"

Yisaoh shrugged. "I'm telling him you drugged him. If you succeed, he'll have to forgive you. If you fail, we'll say you went rogue and manufactured this yourself. Fair enough?"

"But–"

"I know what it is to be driven by revenge," Yisaoh said. "You're the only one of us foolish enough to do this."

The active assault of Kuallina's defenses ceased the day the Empress accepted their parley, but as Lilia stepped through their own still-active parajista shield, her heart hammered so loudly she thought Mohrai, walking beside her, might tell her to turn back for being cowardly after all.

They made an odd party – Lilia and Gian, Mohrai and Alhina. Gian held tightly to Lilia's hand. It sweated terribly in hers, but Lilia dared not let go, not now.

Behind them came the staff who had prepared the banquet. They carried dish after steaming dish.

Two great tables had been moved from Kuallina, and set in a narrow space between the two barriers that protected each of the forces. Behind Lila's side were the refugees, so close she could reach them in just fifty steps. And behind Kirana was her camped army, tent after tent aligned in neat rows, as if a siege were the most normal thing in the world.

Lilia and her companions came up beside their chairs on the dais. The cooking staff spread out the food.

Lilia waited. Gian nervously tugged at her hand. Mohrai coughed a few times, and whispered something to Alhina.

"Will they come?" Alhina asked Lilia.

"She'll come," Lilia said.

They had attracted crowds from both armies. The army on the other side of the table, the Tai Mora, all sat outside their tents, watching. Some stood, sipping tea from metal cups. It seemed to Lilia like an extravagant use of metal.

There was a ripple among the army further back; Lilia followed it with her gaze.

The crowd parted, and two women and two men strode forward. The woman at the front wore chitinous red armor, but no helm. Beside her was a woman wearing a Dorinah-cut dress. The men behind both wore armor as well. The armor was the blue she associated with parajistas. Lilia had wanted to bring parajistas too, but knew that if things went very badly at this table, no number of parajistas would save her.

The two women at the front she knew. The woman in the armor was the Kai, the one who had attacked her mother with a willowthorn sword while Lilia stood on the other side of the rent between the worlds, screaming. The other was Isoail, the woman who wore Lilia's mother's face here, the one who had happily sent Lilia off to the slave camps before realizing she was more useful than she first realized.

Lilia's stomach knotted. She had to let go of Gian's hand, then, because she was going to grip it hard enough to hurt her.

As the Kai approached, Lilia reached for some sense of calm, the same calm she had when others were grievously injured and she had to concentrate wholly on their problem. She felt her fear bleed away. Her hands ceased to tremble.

The Kai was just a woman. Women died.

And Isoail… she should not have been surprised that Isoail had switched sides.

Kirana reached her seat. Placed her hands casually on the back of it. "I was promised your Kai, ugly bird," she said to Lilia.

"I am the Catori of Dhai," Mohrai said. "I speak for the Kai. You must excuse his absence. He was called away on other matters."

"He lost his nerve, you mean," Kirana said. She sat in her seat, and waved at the rest of them. "Sit, sit. Let's get this over with."

Isoail sat beside Kirana, but the men did not sit.

Lilia sat opposite Isoail. Mohrai sat opposite the Kai, with Alhina to her right. Gian sat at Lilia's left.

The serving staff removed the covers on the food. The smell of it made Lilia's stomach growl. She had not eaten properly in days. She could not keep herself from looking at the piles of the forsia tubers, their honey-smelling steam dominating the other scents.

"You know I won't eat anything," Kirana said. "I'm not so great a fool as that."

"Eat what you like," Lilia said. "But it's polite here, to parley over a table, especially during this festival season."

"A festive season." Kirana laughed.

"You and I know one another," Lilia said. She asked Mohrai to pass her one of the forsia tubers. Mohrai raised her brows as if to ask "So soon?" but she passed it nonetheless.

Gian took one as well, though her fingers trembled as she did. Mohrai and Alhina did the same before adding other dishes to their plates – the fiddleheads and rice, the honeyed onions and oily kale.

Kirana touched nothing. Lilia started to panic. If she would not eat, it meant they needed to drag this distraction on a very long time, long enough for the civilians pouring out the back entrance of the temple to make it a good way to the woodlands. Hours, maybe. She could not imagine sitting with this woman for hours.

Kirana tapped her glass. One of the men came from behind and filled it with something from a flask at his hip. "Do I know you?" she said. "I know many people."

"You killed my mother," Lilia said. "So I destroyed your mirror."

Kirana smiled broadly. It was Isoail who looked like she wanted to bolt. "You did?" she said. She drank the amber liquor in her glass. Smacked her lips. "You killed your own mother in the process. How did that feel?"

"I could tell you, if I felt anything anymore," Lilia said, "but I've given that up for embroidery."

Kirana laughed. It sounded like a genuine laugh, deep and long. For a terrible moment, Lilia imagined a world where they could have been friends, or lovers. Different worlds. Different choices.

"Isn't it right that we get along?" Lilia said. "We both love this world."

Kirana smiled. "Let me take a stab. Poisonous, is it?" she said. She pushed at her plate again.

Mohrai and Alhina were already eating, but neither had dared touch the tuber.

"There's nothing wrong with any of it," Lilia said. "You insult me." She began to carefully cut up the tuber. Gian watched her plate, too intently. Lilia should have left her in Kuallina. Taigan had a less easily read expression, but Taigan had abandoned her, and Gian had only run from her. Lilia tried not to smile too broadly as she ate the first bite of the rich, spongy interior of the tuber. It tasted nutty-sweet. Like revenge.

Kirana peered at Lilia's plate. Lilia's stomach squeezed. It was very possible they had the same kind of plant over there. If it was recognized, they'd take Lilia's head now. She may as well take it off herself.

Instead, it was Isoail who took one of the tubers from

the plate. She set one on Kirana's as well, and served her rice and fiddleheads too.

Isoail did not exchange a single look with Lilia. She began to cut up the tuber. She removed the skin, as Lilia had. But as Lilia watched her cut it up she noted Isoail missed the translucent, veiny spine of it. The part filled with the poison. Isoail took a careful bite. Rolled it around on her tongue. Her eyes lit up. Surprise. Joy.

"That's very fine," Isoail said. "Just as I always read."

"Yes," Lilia said, though what Isoail was tasting was something Lilia never had. Her mother said forsia was the most delicious delicacy in the world. The most sublime. Unforgettable. The inner, edible tuber was nothing compared to the ecstasy of the poison. And Isoail knew what it was. She ate it gladly. Isoail was not a traitor. She was another captive, with no way out.

Isoail continued eating while Kirana talked. Lilia tensed with each bite Isoail took. Lilia ate her own, de-veined tuber slowly. Each bite tasted like stones now.

"Let's get to the point of this meeting," Kirana said. "I believe we're to have an exchange. What is your proposition?"

"We ask for immediate cessation of hostilities," Mohrai said. "In exchange we are willing to turn over a woman of some interest to you. Yisaoh Alais Garika."

Kirana took a long, slow drink. "Why should I cease this assault for just one woman?"

"If she is of no interest to you, then we are at an impasse," Mohrai said. "We will send her home."

"She is in Kuallina?" Kirana said. Too quickly.

Lilia knew, then. Yisaoh was someone to her. The double of someone close to her.

I know your weakness, Lilia wanted to squeal, but Isoail was washing down the poisoned tuber with more water. Refilling the glass. Extreme thirst was the first sign of poisoning. Lilia could do nothing. Could not speak. Could not yell. This was Isoail's choice. The woman with her mother's face.

"Water?" Gian asked. She was filling their glasses. Lilia nodded absently.

"She has asked for harbor in Kuallina," Mohrai said, "but if we cannot work something out, I suspect she will return to the woodland."

"You'll just turn her over to me, like that?"

"We understand our position," Mohrai said.

"It seems like a very easy choice," Lilia said, "but you can think on it here as you eat. We'll have drinks, after, and decide then."

"I have no interest in dragging this out," Kirana said.

Lilia stopped eating her tuber and picked at her rice. As she scooped a bit of it to her mouth, she saw a black thread in it, right before eating. Her stomach heaved. It was a bit of the poisoned vein of the tuber. She set it back on her plate.

"We are in no hurry," Mohrai said.

Kirana leaned forward. "Is that right? Well, I am. If this is a serious offer, let's say this – you bring me Yisaoh, alive or otherwise, it makes no difference to me, and we withdraw for one hour. We let your civilians leave the fortress. But your jistas and your militia stay. Their lives are forfeit."

"Unacceptable," Mohrai said.

But Lilia wondered, for a long moment, if they should take it. They were here risking their own lives to save those civilians, to give them a few precious hours to escape. Could they not turn over Yisaoh? Yet the Kai would never permit it. Mohrai would know that too.

"That is my offer," Kirana said. "Convenient as it is for you to deliver Yisaoh to me, even if she runs, I will find her eventually. I find all those who oppose me, and I give them a fitting end."

Her gaze swept the table. She made some imperceptible nod and served herself up some kale and weed plantains. Lilia tried not to stare as she poked at the tuber on her plate.

Lilia concentrated very hard on her own food, making a moat around the tainted rice.

Alhina spoke, suddenly, words spilling loudly, "You will love the forsia tuber," she said. "It is such a delicacy."

Lilia stiffened. Fool.

Mohrai said, "I will consider the offer. We will, of course, have to speak to the Kai."

"I doubt that," Kirana said. "You forget we share faces as well as temperaments. My brother was always a coward. I suspect this Ahkio is no different."

"In that, you are wrong," Mohrai said. "He is one of the most compassionate, honest and trustworthy human beings I have ever had the pleasure of knowing."

Kirana raised her brows. "There are some differences, then," she said, and laughed a little as she began to skin the tuber.

Lilia tried to measure how much time had passed since they had left the hold. Nearly two hours? The Kai would be awake now, and angry, but Yisaoh would have already begun the retreat into the woodlands.

"Did you recover many omajistas?" Lilia asked Kirana. "The ones the rebellion sent to other worlds?"

Kirana paused in her peeling. "We recovered a great many," she said. "They were on the wrong side of this conflict, and all of them knew it. It's too bad you yourself burned out."

Mohrai and Alhina turned to stare at Lilia.

Heat moved up Lilia's face. "Why do you think that?" she asked.

"Because Isoail here has had you in a palisade spell this whole time, and you have yet to attempt to counter it," she said.

Lilia met Isoail's look across the table.

Isoail's gaze was warm and very frank. She did not look away as she pulled the black mushy center of the tuber from its heart and pushed it into her mouth.

Of course Isoail knew what forsia was.

Isoail gagged almost immediately. She vomited on the table, so violently it splattered Mohrai and Alhina, who shouted and pushed away.

Lilia pressed her hands to her mouth, but did not move.

Beside her, Gian gagged. She knocked over Lilia's wine glass. Fell to the floor. Began to convulse.

Lilia stared at her, not comprehending. She grabbed Gian's plate and saw the broken tendrils of the of the forsia plant mixing with bits of her rice and fiddleheads. Gian had accidentally eaten it, just as Lilia had almost ingested it herself.

"Gian!" she scrambled after her, and held her in her arms. Gian vomited black bile. It splattered across Gian and Lilia both.

"Parajistas!" Kirana's voice.

The voice that called for the destruction of Lilia's village, for the enslavement of her mother. The voice that would bring the whole world to its knees.

Now that voice would smite her, once and for all.

Something flashed in the sky overhead.

Lilia held Gian's convulsing body close. Black bile oozed from her mouth and nose now, and her eyes were glazing over, so very dark, just like the other Gian... the other Gian... so many Gians, all dead. So many worlds, all dead.

Flickering in the sky. A wash of violent light.

Lilia looked skyward. Two stars blazed in the sky where there had only been Para a moment before. As she watched, Para blinked out, leaving the great purple mass of Sina blaring balefully upon them. A great, thunderous rumble shook the clear sky.

"Gods," Lilia said.

The parajista walls. The barricades around Kuallina. Their entire defense relied on Para's breath.

Kirana started shouting again, a different order. She had left the platform. Mohrai and Alhina, too, had fled, running back toward Kuallina through the broken barricades.

"Sinajistas! Raise the flags! Raise the flags! Burn that fucking hold down while it's vulnerable!"

Lilia held Gian a breath longer. She ran her fingers through Gian's long, silky hair. On the other side of the table, she saw Isoail's prone form covered in black bile. They were the only three still on the dais.

Lilia – ungifted, forgettable once again. Her greatest gift was appearing too ordinary and powerless to bother killing when there was a whole defenseless stronghold at one's mercy, and she had already murdered all of her greatest allies.

47

Heat and darkness. Roh saw the world in bands of color – blue-lavender sky, the white slash of the tundra, a yellow wrap against a woman's brown skin. Voices in Dhai, and then not-Dhai. It was a language so close he felt he must know it. Maybe he didn't understand it because he was stuck in some kind of dream. Some nightmare.

He thought ascending to Sina would be faster and less confusing. But the journey continued while he shook and sweated and screamed at bulky violet apparitions bleeding great gouts of orange light from their mouths.

When his fever broke, he was unsure of the season. He wasn't even certain where he was, until he heard one of his captors say, "Caisau." They were so far north that seasons felt meaningless. All he knew was that most of the snow was gone. It persisted only in rotten patches in the shade of stunted undergrowth. He saw no trees this far north, but the implacable tundra was gone, too, replaced by jagged pillars of stone that snarled up from the rocky ground like the teeth of some band of snarling animals. He knew they were in Caisau because it was the only word that his captors spoke that he understood.

Roh spent a long time trying to work out their language every night, peering at their mouths and gestures. It was close enough to Dhai that he should have taken to it easily, but some terrible thing in him had shifted, and now the world looked very dark, and every task seemed difficult. Even though the days were absurdly long, he found it hard to wake up in the morning before he was kicked. He wanted to sleep forever.

The first time they tried to humiliate him, throwing stones at him until he took off his clothes and ran from them as they wanted; too weak to go far and easy to capture again, he cried when they caught him and beat him. It should have been easy to fight them, if he had a full stomach and Para at his call – but Para was lost to him, and he was so weak and exhausted he could barely lift his head most days. Whatever sickness had burned through him, it took much of his strength with it, and the pace they kept did not let him recover properly.

Caisau rose up from the snarled pillars of the rocky landscape, a massive living hold so breathtaking that even Roh – in his depressed, exhausted state – felt a surge of awe. Caisau, once called Roasandara, the seat of the Dhai two thousand years before. It was like stepping into some history book. They broke through the forest of pillars and onto a wide bowl of stone like a shallow crater. Caisau was made of dozens of linked domes and spiraling towers that encircled a central dome so great it seemed to touch the sky. The skin above the great red sandstone walls was blue-green, and shimmered like the skin of the Dhai temples. Far past the vastness of Caisau, he saw the sea, still bobbing with great icebergs, and a harbor filled with bone boats that looked like crooked finger bones.

Around the walls of the hold were artisans' houses, merchants' stalls, and homes made from the same brown stone as the jutting pillars. For a city the size of Caisau, it did not seem very busy. As they moved through the great main streets, tiled in red stone, he saw why – there were no Saiduan here. They were all Tai Mora. A few looked up as their party passed, but most ignored them, faces open and boisterous. Roh had only seen the worst of their soldiers, but these were clearly civilians, or at least soldiers out of armor, and the way they laughed and carried on business brought tears to his eyes because it was like walking through some other world where the Dhai had never lost Caisau.

The Tai Mora had come home.

His captors brought him through the great shuttered eyes of the round gates. He kept thinking he would see signs of Dhai culture here, some art style or architecture that he recognized, but the fortress was completely foreign to him except for the living skin of it. Massive creatures carved from red stone and smoothed nearly featureless by wind and time leered at him from the walls. Some of the frescos had clearly been defaced and redone. They carried stories of Saiduan battles, not Dhai ones.

They passed into a foyer so high it made Roh dizzy to gaze up at it. The ceiling was patterned in green and blue geometric shapes, faced with mirrors that spilled light from its windows all across the floor.

His captors conferred with a tall, regal woman in a bulky fur-lined coat stitched in silver. She sat behind a bronze podium speaking to two pages. They argued for some time. The woman peered around them at Roh.

The woman was Tai Mora, but the pages or servants or assistants or whatever they were didn't look like Tai Mora. They were finer featured, paler, with brown hair and yellow eyes.

"We'll wait here a few minutes," one of his captors, the broad, pock-faced woman they called Kosoli, said.

"Longer than that," the man, Borasau, said.

The group of them sat against the far wall on a ring of benches. The little brown-haired assistants brought them tea and sweet cakes. Roh was starving, and they let him eat. He hated that he was so grateful for it.

An hour passed, maybe two, before one of the servants came back and called them further up into the hold.

They climbed through broad, open halls filled with

light. How the hold could be so filled with light and still so warm, Roh was uncertain. Servants and official-looking people moved past them. He passed great libraries, most of them empty. The empty libraries were the only sign that there had been any sort of violence or upset here at all. The Tai Mora had held Caisau for nearly two years now, and must have cleaned up much of it after the invasion.

The assistant came to a great glass door. The light was so bright that Roh squinted. This time of year, it would hardly get dark at all this far north. They entered a warm, humid atrium so vast it felt like walking into the open air.

Roh stared upward. They were under the massive dome at the center of the hold. All around them were huge, broad-leafed trees and twisted vines with leaves larger than Roh's head, full of tangling gardens of flowers and fleshy succulents that Roh had no name for. He sweated in his coat, and peeled it off. The others did the same.

The servant led them through the meandering gardens. Roh heard the sound of running water. They passed a massive waterfall poking up from a clotted nest of vegetation. It sprayed a cool mist. Little birds flitted about the flowers. Yellow and orange birds, birds with stalks for eyes, birds with great long threaded tongues that they used to sip at the flowers. Birds with claws at the ends of their wings. Birds... so many birds...

They rounded the waterfall and came to the center of the atrium and a little park. Silver benches lined the walkway. A blue patterned walk made a large circular path at the center. In the center grew an enormous petrified bone tree so tall it blotted out much of the light. Roh gaped at the massive skulls. They had come from creatures with heads as big as he was. Bones twice as tall as him made up the trunk. The tree was as big around as six people standing side by side. He saw shapes moving up and down its length – tree gliders hopping quickly from bone to bone, branch to branch. That's how he knew it was petrified, not alive. It would have eaten them all, and him too, if it still breathed.

Sitting across from the tree was a wizened old man. The servant came to him, bowing so low Roh thought her head might touch the ground.

Roh's captors met him and they too bowed. As Roh reluctantly got to his knees to do the same, he met the man's look, and froze halfway into his bow. He coughed or cried, he wasn't sure which.

The man peered at him with black eyes in a heavily wrinkled face, a face with just one expression, an expression Roh knew well.

It was Dasai, his dead mentor.

Roh huffed out a breath and struggled to his knees, because saying Dasai's name aloud won him nothing. He pressed his head to the floor so the man could not see the tears streaming down his face. The stone floor was very cool. He pressed his palms there too, and did not raise his head even as the man spoke to their captors, talking in Dasai's voice – his Dasai – but in the language of the enemy, the people with their faces.

"Look up at me, boy," Dasai said in Dhai now, and Roh rubbed his face and did what he was told. He looked at the man whose head he had watched hacked from his body.

"You know the Kai cipher?"

"Yes," Roh said.

"We have books here in the Kai cipher," Dasai said. "I expect you can get to work translating those for us."

Roh wondered how they knew the books were in the Kai cipher, and how those books had gotten to Saiduan, but decided fewer questions were better. He would translate them from the cipher into Dhai, and presumably someone else would translate them from Dhai into Tai Mora. That was a tremendous amount of work for a few old books. The Tai Mora had one advantage above all else, and that was that there were more of them and those they had subjugated than any other nation Roh knew. Why had he ever thought they had a chance against these people?

"Can you do that?" Dasai said, more forcefully this time.

Roh had been staring right through him. "Yes," Roh said. "I can do that."

"Good. You'll be bathed and given suitable clothes." He said something else to his captors in their dialect, and Borasau nodded and said something in the affirmative.

Roh needed to learn their language, but it was like picking flies out of honey. His mind didn't want to tangle with them.

His captors stood, so he scrambled up as well. Once they left the atrium, they chattered among themselves, seemingly in good spirits.

Borasau pushed Roh away from the group as they rounded a turn, and told him to sit on a bench. "Someone will come for you," he said. He took a chain affixed to the wall. It was attached to a collar.

Roh jerked away from him when he saw it, but Borasau caught him. He clipped the collar around Roh's neck, patted his shoulder, and left him.

Roh shoved his hands under his thighs and waited. He needed to urinate, badly, and there was nowhere to go. Twenty very long minutes later, a tall woman wearing a long skirt and fur-lined leather tunic arrived. She had a high forehead, a twist of dark hair, and kept licking her lips.

"Dhai?" she said.

He nodded. "I'm told I should—"

"I know what you're here for," she said. "I'm to get you cleaned up. My name is Vestaria. We can do this kindly, or madly. Which way is up to you. I'm going to take off this collar and replace it with a warded one. The ward won't permit you to leave the hold. You understand?"

He nodded. He knew what wards did.

"Lovely," she said. "If you struggle, if–"

"I have to urinate," he said, too quickly. "Please. I'll do whatever you ask. Just let me piss in some place properly."

His captors thought it funny when he pissed himself.

Her face softened. Pity. He saw it in her face and guilt roiled over him, guilt that he had come so far, and done so much, but was happy to do whatever some foreign force wanted of him, some evil people killing his, if only they would let him piss in a pot instead of on himself.

She clipped on the new collar, a leather one that chafed. It was too tight. Swallowing was uncomfortable. She led him to a latrine and he urinated sitting on it like a real human being, and even though she was right outside the door he let himself cry, just once, because he feared he wouldn't get another chance.

Then she led him to a bathing room and scrubbed him clean like a child and helped him dress in new clothes.

"You are no doubt exhausted," she said, "but I'm afraid you must come to the libraries now. It's time to earn your breakfast."

Roh expected her to take him to the libraries they had passed before, but she took him deeper into the hold instead. Deeper and deeper until they arrived at a set of double doors, already peeled open to reveal a vast room.

He stepped inside and gaped, for all around him, as far as he could see, were shelves and shelves of books. And, at the center of the room, milling about the shelves, were hundreds of collared slaves like him, not just Dhai but other people, too, from Dorinah and Tordin and Aaldia, and maybe other places he hadn't heard of. Roh turned to Vestaria, trying to form a question.

"The ciphered books are here," she said, leading him to a table already occupied by three other slaves, all Dhai. "These have worked on them for some time, but they were not as close to the Kai. I do hope you're telling the truth, boy, because there is much work to do."

The table was stacked with at least a hundred and fifty tomes, great things bound in green and black leather, each as thick as his palm was wide.

"All of these...?" Roh said.

She patted the top of the nearest stack. "Two thousand years of Kais kept records here," she said. "Let's hope for your sake that the Kai cipher hasn't changed much. Get to work."

She walked off.

Roh felt he should introduce himself to the others at the table, but they did not dare look at him.

Roh's hand trembled as he picked up the book nearest him. He opened it. And there were the familiar Dhai characters. He traced his fingers down the first column. They were nonsense words as written. He grabbed at one of the blank books at the center of the table, and picked up a squib of a pen. Counted out the letters as he would for the cipher, and wrote the first sentences in clear Dhai:

We lost sixteen ships today, and whatever it is that's falling from the sky is getting closer. The creature of Caisau tells me we are too late.

He laughed softly.

All that time they worked in Kuonrada, and the Saiduan had lost much of what they needed during the taking of the first city, the first incursion. They would never have been able to unravel all this, though, if Roh had not come here, if Roh had not tried to make his own fate.

Too late, Roh thought. They were all too late. He stared out at the massive library swarming with scholars, and thought how foolish the efforts that he and Dasai and Kihin, Aramey and Chali, had made looked by comparison. They had always been a hundred steps behind the Tai Mora.

He pulled the book into his lap.

The creature of Caisau.

48

Maralah yanked the souls from every living thing in the courtyard. The shrieking filled her ears. Purple blasts of Sina's breath enveloped the unprepared sanisi and infantrymen. There was no time for them to run. Morsaar had sent only parajistas for this task, and that left her the most powerful person on the field. She spared just one, a skinny tirajista who she wrapped in a field of violet flame.

She pointed at Kovaas. "Let's bring him back."

The tirajista shook his head. Maralah urged the purple flames closer. Burned at his heels. "You'll spend the rest of the war encased in this weapon otherwise. You understand?"

He spat at her. "I am a sanisi," he said.

"So you are." She yanked his soul from his body. The wispy lavender essence of him came free, and the flesh that remained crumpled. Her weapon consumed the soul's energy.

With enough souls at her command, she didn't need any allies. The last known sinajista who could manipulate souls the way she could died a decade before. So long as Sina rode the sky, she was the most powerful person in Saiduan.

Maralah clung tightly to her weapon. It was not

a willowthorn branch, so it would not respond to her touch. It did not slide around her wrist, nor would it hold Sina's power indefinitely. These souls would bleed out in days if she didn't use them.

Good thing she didn't expect to hold onto them that long.

Maralah called Sina and held a wave of power beneath her skin as she marched across the courtyard. She burned the infantry in the hall, then the three sanisi who charged at her. The shock on their faces warmed her stomach. She was a filthy, stinking wreck, her hair a matted tangle. As they burned around her she found her face had taken on a grinning rictus. The small muscles of her face hurt.

She made her way to the Patron's wing, burning as she went. It was two floors before she met resistance. Two sinajistas put up a wall of purple flame that singed her clothes. She flashed up her sword in a broad arc, sending a wave of fire out in turn. Their sinajista-spun defenses tangled in the narrow corridor, sparking and hissing.

Maralah cut her way forward, calling wave after wave of Sina's breath and twisting it to her will. The door to the Patron's quarters was locked and warded. It was an old sinajista ward she had put on herself for Alaar. She untangled it now with a deft tug of six long threads. The door was locked. She blasted it open with a burst of purple flame. Eight sanisi stood ready, flanked by twenty members of the Patron's broodguard. Four of the sanisi were wrapped in purple mist, sinajistas ready to unleash a final defense.

She pushed forward a wave of purple fire and held it just inches from their faces, because she saw something there that gave her pause. Three of the sanisi were hers, or had been, months ago.

"Is Driaa behind you?" Maralah said. "I have something special for hir."

The sanisi and broodguard stood with weapons raised.

"Is Rajavaa alive?" she asked.

Sovaan, a tall man at the far end – one of hers – said, "Maralah, it is Patron Rajavaa who said we must keep you from this room."

Maralah admitted she'd had months to consider that possibility. Morsaar was not a usurper. He didn't have the gall. He had done all of this at Rajavaa's order, which is why she'd been left alive this long instead of killed immediately.

So typical. So Saiduan. So be it.

"And who is your Patron, Sovaan, when Rajavaa is dead in a month?"

This was the moment. The moment she had avoided all her life. Or perhaps the moment she had been building up to all these years. She was too old for this, and she knew it. She should have moved twenty years before, instead of holding Alaar's hand.

"I'm going to burn this place down around me," Maralah said. "If you're too young to have seen me do it before, you'll see it now."

Three submitted, and bowed their heads. The rest she killed. While they smoked she said, "I need a sinajista and a tirajista to raise a man from the dead in the yard," she said. "Kovaas, you know him?"

Two sanisi pulled away at the end and trotted down the stairs.

"Hold this position," Maralah said to the last. He bowed.

She pushed open the door to Rajavaa's room.

Rajavaa lay halfway off the bed, weapon clutched in his swollen hand.

Morsaar swung from her right, leaping out from behind the door. Maralah skewered him through the gut. She kicked him off her weapon, and strode to Rajavaa's side.

Rajavaa should not have been alive. She'd half

suspected Kovaas was luring her into some bigger plot.
But no.

"Rajavaa, you fool," she said.

"Morsaar!" he gasped.

"You could have asked me to leave," she said. "It
would have suited me better than prison."

"You'd… never leave… never. Let them come… for
me. You killed him. You…"

"We're not all going to die here, Rajavaa."

"Morsaar," he said. He clawed at the sheets and began
to weep. The weeping became coughing. Blood spattered
his beard.

"You're not getting out of this so easily," she said. She
yanked the bedding up and bound him in it. He was so
weak he hardly struggled. She knotted him up at the
chest and the feet.

The door opened. She tangled a breath of Sina into
a protective wall, but it was only the returning sinajista
and tirajista, dragging Kovaas with them. But he was still
very dead. They dropped him on the floor.

"What is this?" Maralah asked.

The sinajista bowed. "I don't have the skill. I've
never… seen Sina rise."

Maralah waved them both over. She knelt next to
Kovaas's body. "You've done a resurrection?" she asked
the tirajista.

Another shake of the head. Of course not. They were
both barely into their twenties.

"I can get his blood flowing again. I'll pull his soul
back into his body." She tapped her weapon. "It's stored
here. When I do that, he'll just die again unless you heal
up the worst of the wounds."

"Tira is descendent. I'm not sensitive."

"Then you'll work harder," Maralah said. "You don't
have to heal everything. Just the killing blow. You
understand? Start now."

The tirajista's hands moved over the body.

Maralah placed her blade on Kovaas's chest and knelt before him, calling on Sina deeply, until purple mist suffused her whole body. She expelled the breath, and sang the Song of theDead, the Song of Unmaking, the Song of Souls, lacing each spell together with deft, delicate accuracy. She had feared that to lose Sina for so many years meant losing her knowledge and skill with it, but some things were learned by the body and the mind, and what the mind forgot, the body remembered.

She pulled the strength of the souls from the blade and into the meshed spell of resurrection she had created, then let go of it.

Kovaas's eyes opened. He gasped. Arched his back. Screamed.

The tirajista jerked away from him.

"Mend the wound!" Maralah said.

The tirajista concentrated hard, muttering several songs Maralah knew now by heart, after years on the battlefield bringing back the dead.

Finally, the tirajista sat back, spent. "That's all I can do," he said.

Kovaas lay panting on the floor. Maralah took her blade from his chest and peered at him. Sometimes the dead came back bad. Sometimes it was too late.

"You know who you are?" she asked.

"Maralah," he said, breathless. He gazed at her as a man would gaze at his ascendant star.

"You," she repeated. "Tell me your name."

"Kovaas," he said. "I... you've brought me back."

"Come up now," she said. "I need you to help me." She glanced at the other two sanisi. "What of the Tai Mora army?"

"We can see them from the walls," the sinajista said. "A few hours at best. Coming from the northeast."

"No flanking force to hem us in?"

"Runners say no. Just one force."

"Take six slaves. Twelve sanisi. Twenty infantry. Rally

those and go out to meet the Tai Mora."

"We've got those invaders a few hours from the gates. They'll see this as running."

"It's preserving the line."

"The Patron wanted to die here."

"Now he doesn't. Do you?"

The sinajista glanced over at the rolled-up form of Rajavaa, wriggling and grunting on the cold floor. "I'll rally them."

"You too," Maralah told the tirajista. "We'll be here."

She waited until they'd gone, then told Kovaas they were retreating.

"Help me take the Patron," she said.

"The others?"

"Just us," she said.

He was still too weak to help her with Rajavaa, so Maralah hoisted her brother over her shoulder. He was much lighter now, but she was not in the best shape after months in prison. She kicked open the latch that opened up the panel near the mantel. A wedge opened up, just big enough for her to huff Rajavaa into it and squeeze after him. She closed the secret door behind her and took Rajavaa by the ankles. She dragged him down the long, dark hall. She had been this way only once before, with Alaar, during an attempted coup. It was a long way to freedom from here.

Maralah dragged him for a good hour, down stair after stair, until he stopped struggling and she was dripping with sweat. Kovaas was finally able to help her toward the end, and it made the going easier. She had no supplies and only the glimmering of a plan. Getting the others to rally a small group, thinking she was waiting on them, bought her time. By the time they realized she had gone off on her own, the Tai Mora would be at the gates, and they would have bigger problems than her.

She collapsed at the entrance to the long tunnel at the bottom of the hold. Kovaas went to scout ahead to ensure the tunnel was clear. She had another mile to drag him. Her whole body shook, and she was breathing hard. She leaned against the wall. Listened to Rajavaa mumble. She pulled back the sheet from his face.

"Thirsty," he said.

"Not taking liquor with us."

"Let me die."

"Not a chance. I can resurrect you now, you know."

"And I'll die again. I'm not... your monster."

"That's precisely what you are," she said.

"Usurper."

"That's the best you have? All these months you imprisoned me, and that's all you came up with?"

He spat at her. Misty flecks that merely wet his own face. Fresh air moved over them, coiling down through the passage.

"Cheer up, brother," she said. "We're going to Anjoliaa. Taigan will meet us there. Just as I promised."

"Too late."

She showed her teeth, gritting them so hard her face hurt. "Feel free to die as much as you like on the way there. Over and over and over again. I'll bring you back, Rajavaa. And then Taigan will heal you."

"I want to die... with Morsaar."

Maralah covered his face back up. He mumbled at her. She stood. "I wanted to stay out of prison," she said. "We don't all get what we want."

She took him by the heels again, and dragged him into the dark, damp corridor after Kovaas.

49

"Wrong," Korloria said, and slapped Roh's hands with a switch. He sat with the other hundred captive translators in a huge dining hall while Korloria and three other attendants walked their lines, ensuring everyone's hands were in their laps, attention fixed forward. When the four attendants were pleased with the captives' behavior, they went to the high table and hit a gong, signaling that it was time to eat. The translators attacked their food as if it were their last meal, and sometimes it was. By the time Roh ate that first meal, he had not eaten in nearly a day. He wolfed it down so fast it nearly came back up again.

Hierarchies thrived on ordered systems. Roh had learned that in his classes on governance. The system that controlled Roh and his fellow captive translators was a perfectly structured one, even though it must have been less than two years old. A gong woke them before dawn. He learned that he could not talk to anyone without punishment, so he learned the routine by watching them. The few voices he did hear were after dark, hours after bed check, when some of the more rebellious dared to exchange whispers.

He made his bed and washed his face and put on his clothes the same way everyone else did. They wore the same drab gray robes, like temple drudges. The gong signaled every new task – get to breakfast, tea and hard bread. Get to the library for six hours of research work. Break for more tea and hard bread and half a citrus fruit of some kind. Six more hours sitting in hard chairs with dusty books. Gong for dinner, meat and vegetables, which Roh didn't eat for the first week, until hunger overcame him and he choked down the dead animal flesh with the same abhorrence he would have had for eating his own vomit. Gong for bed. The monotony made him want to crawl out of his skin.

His escape from the drudgery lay in the texts themselves, the records of some Kai two thousand years dead who talked to him of a Caisau that was much warmer than this one, almost tropical. She talked of great frilled fishes in the sea. Massive land animals that moved across the tundra in the thousands, so large that just one of them fed the people of Caisau for a week. And cities… she spoke of cities spiraling out across what was then a semi-tropical plain. What he knew of geography and weather confounded her accounts, because it seemed impossible that a continent this far north could ever be warm, but what did he know of the world before it broke?

He brought his translations to Korloria at the end of each day, and she took them without comment. One day two of the translators got into a fight in the archive room. Roh raised his head, so shocked that anything different was happening that he didn't react for a full minute.

Then he leapt up and ran to the tussle. Two middle-aged women wrestled on the floor; the larger, dark-haired one had the smaller one in a chokehold, legs locked around her torso. She yelled obscenities. Roh recognized the language as Saiduan, or some dialect of it. He made out something about cheating, or falsifying records, and then Korloria moved through the masses, and everyone ran away, back to their desks. They were faster than Roh. He didn't take the hint.

Korloria swiped her fingers at the two on the floor

and they screamed, broke away, and writhed on the floor as if being flayed. Roh bolted back to his desk then, and sat hard in front of his books while they screamed and screamed.

At day's end, when Korloria took his translated pages, she smiled at him and said, "Your keepers said you were a fighter. What do you think of how we manage fighters?"

"It's efficient," Roh said. He did not meet her gaze when he said it.

That night, at dinner, Korloria clapped her hands before the start of dinner and announced they would have a bit of fun.

"Since you all enjoy fighting so much," she said, in Saiduan, "let's have real stakes. That's what you all wanted, isn't it? Some excitement."

She called the two women from the day's fight over, and brought them up in front of the high table.

"End your disagreement here," she said. "I can throw you both in confinement for three weeks, or one of you can kill the other here, now, and have an end of it."

The women shifted their feet. Exchanged looks.

Korloria threw a cup of tea at them. Roh flinched. What was she getting at? What was the point?

"Or I can kill you both here," Korloria said. "Fight! Go on!" She flicked her fingers, and both women bowed over in pain.

Roh turned away and stared at his plate. This is not my fight, he thought, over and over again, while the women keened. He heard one throw up her dinner.

Quiet, Dasai had told him. Be quiet, Roh. Bow. Subservience. He had never been so good at being quiet.

Roh leapt up from the table. "Enough!" he said. He strode toward the high table, already tense, anticipating Korloria's counterattack. "You want someone to fight? Why don't you fight me?"

Korloria squeezed her fist. The women crumpled like rag dolls, dead on the floor.

Roh stopped halfway to the table. All eyes were on him.

"On your knees," Korloria said.

She came down from the high table. "Kneel," she said. "Know your place."

"Fuck you," he said. Saiduan had the vocabulary for it. Dhai didn't.

She squeezed her fist.

His knees popped. He heard it before he felt it. He was on the floor before the pain registered, before he understood what had happened, before a sledgehammer of fiery needles shot through his knees. He squealed, a horrible sound like some dying animal. He couldn't believe it came from his own throat.

Korloria stood over him, expression bemused. "This is what happens to those who fight."

"Confinement" was a concrete box in the ground in some forgotten courtyard. They threw him down there for six days. He knew because he could see the suns rise and fall. Night was only four hours now. The searing pain in his knees was so bad, so deep, he could not sleep. On the sixth day they hauled him out and brought him to a doctor who chewed her lips and clucked her tongue and spun some tirajista trick that she said would heal him faster, but then they put him back in the box, and he was there another two weeks lying in his own shit and piss. They hauled him out once a week, hosed him down, and tossed him in again.

It was during his confinement that he began to hear the voices. Whispers, first. Then laughter. Sometimes he gripped the bars of the top of his cage and tried to break them. He spent a long time just screaming. He screamed that he was mad, hurt, thirsty. He screamed that he knew things, and that he was important. He screamed because he needed to convince them that his life meant something.

He couldn't walk without help when they pulled him out. The doctor proffered a crutch. When he came back to the library, no one looked at him.

Korloria was there, though, smiling. She brought him a stack of books. "It's a shame," she said, "a boy so pretty, so fragile. It's lucky you have such a talent with these, or we'd have had no further use for you."

He just stared at the stack of books. He had missed the books. He had missed going somewhere else. Anywhere else. Roh opened them and began to translate again, though it was slow going. He was not well. He had a low fever, and the pain in his knees was constant, even when he wasn't trying to walk; a cold nerve pain. He lived in dread of the idea of walking, fearing with every step that bubbling pain would get worse. And it did, sometimes.

The creature of Caisau says the invading armies will not cease until we shut the way between the worlds, but these transference engines she references aren't on any map. I think she's as mad as we are.

Roh woke that night to the sound of squealing laughter. He lay awake in the dormitory, fists clenched in his sheets. The squealing continued, but it wasn't coming from inside the dormitory. It came from behind him. Behind the walls.

Roh pressed his hand to the wall. The warm skin of the hold seemed to sigh at his touch. He felt the tremulous vibration of the laughter. He pushed himself closer to the wall, and pressed his ear against it.

The laughter became a voice, young and high, like a precocious child.

"Where are you, Patron? Why have you not asked after me? Do you not love me? I love you."

Roh shivered and moved away from the wall.

A few days later he turned over his pages to Korloria and she said, "Stay here, you. You'll come with me. Keeper Dasai wishes to see you."

He limped after Korloria down the long hall, expecting

she would take him back to the great atrium. Instead, they stayed there in the library until all the other translators had gone. She told him to sit at his desk. He did.

Dasai entered from the front door, walking confidently toward their table. Two tall, robed women accompanied him.

"You have translated a good many books, boy," Dasai said, and sat easily beside him at the table. "The work you've done has pleased us."

Roh tensed, uncertain what new horror they were cooking up. When he had first arrived, all he wanted was a shift in the monotony. Now he knew that any change in routine led to something terrible.

Roh just nodded, knowing the likelihood that he'd say something stupid that would ultimately lead to more pain.

"So after all this translation, what is your opinion of this Kai, this woman who wrote all these diaries?" Dasai asked. "Trustworthy accounts, do you think?"

Roh wet his mouth. He looked at Korloria, trying to find some guidance, but she just smiled.

Roh said, "I'm just trying to do as you tell me."

"And now I'm telling you to *think*," Dasai said. His eyes were black, the gaze piercing. It was so like the look Roh's Dasai gave when he was scolding him that Roh had to stare at the floor. "Was she a mad woman?"

"The temples in Dhai are living things," Roh said. "Maybe these holds are too. Maybe they used to talk to her. Maybe she wasn't so mad."

Dasai leaned forward. "And why is it they won't talk to *us*, boy?"

The words bubbled up, "Because you're not Dhai."

Dasai smiled as if he found the idea amusing. "That's quite likely," he said. "Tell me, how is it you're so good at translating these books. Not every Dhai knows the Kai cipher."

"I knew the Kai," Roh said, and came up with the rest of his lies on the spot. "I spied on him, his papers, and I learned it. It was on a dare." Lies came easily when you spent most of your time with nothing to do but come up with stories and translate those of others.

Dasai glanced at one of the robed women beside him, a tall woman with large hands and a lopsided face. Roh couldn't tell if she had been born with her face that unbalanced or if it was the result of an injury.

They spoke briefly in the Tai Mora dialect. Roh had gotten better at understanding it; many of the other translators spoke it.

"I told you it would be easier to tap into the heart of Caisau with a Dhai," Dasai said.

"There is no discernible difference between us and them," the woman said. "It should make no difference to who can hear the heart and who can't. This boy must be a relative of the Kai. It's all that makes sense."

"I've heard it said the King of Tordin can pick out those from neighboring worlds. Clearly some can see a difference between us."

"I've heard there are bears who can fly," the woman said.

Dasai laughed, a boisterous bark of a laugh so happily unguarded that Roh marveled at it. His Dasai had never laughed like that.

Dasai turned back to Roh, and said in Dhai, "If you were a relation to the Kai, it would make you very valuable to us. There's no danger in admitting the truth."

"I'm not," Roh said. "I wish I could say I was, but I'm not."

Dasai slapped his knee and stood. "Ah, well," then, in the Tai Mora dialect, to Korloria, "You keep at the work you're doing. The Empress has Dhai in her fist, now. What we can't uncover here, she may be able to uncover there. The boy here will prove useful."

"I can awaken the heart of this hold without the boy,"

Korloria said. "It's already murmuring. You've heard it."

"I have," Dasai said, "but my mother has murmured nonsense for years about pirate treasures and secret inheritances, and yet here I am, still a magistrate."

"There's no use getting access to the engines in those temples if we don't know how to use them," Korloria said. "The heart of Caisau knows how to use them."

"I agree," Dasai said. Roh noticed for the first time that Dasai carried no cane, and did not wince when he bent his legs. "Let's hope this little menagerie isn't for nothing."

Dasai and the tall woman bent together to talk in yet another language, one Roh didn't follow at all. Dasai nodded, and they walked back out of the library, leaving Roh alone with Korloria.

Roh started to get up.

"Stay seated," Korloria said.

He froze.

Korloria caressed his cheek. "You are a pretty boy, has anyone told you that?"

Roh stared at her midsection, fixated on the eye of the silver belt that held her outer robe closed.

She leaned over him, pressed her cheek to his, and whispered, "It pleases me when you please them."

Korloria stepped away. "Come now, it's time for dinner, scraps. That's a fine name, isn't it? Scraps. What's left of the Dhai. Go on."

Roh didn't have to be asked twice.

After dinner he lay awake with his ear pressed to the warm wall of the hold, listening for the voice. Instead, he heard voices inside the dormitory. Two giggling translators. It was rare enough to hear his companions speak, let alone laugh. He sat up. Slim windows lined the top of the southern face of the room, and nighttime now was just a blush, a dusky haze while the suns rode the edge of the horizon, so he could see two figures tumbling together in the sheets of one of the beds.

Roh lay back, trying to ignore the twinge in his knees, and thought of Korloria's breath in his ear. He had learned something of hierarchy now, and power. There were many kinds of power.

The next day, when Roh gave Korloria his pages, he made sure to brush her fingers with his. When she came to him that morning with more books, she leaned over him, and he pressed his knee against her thigh. She made no mention of it, but she lingered there, far longer than she had in the days before.

Roh felt nothing at all when he was near her – at best, he felt disgust and fear. But when he quailed at what he knew he needed to do, he thought of Dasai's story about the slave who bowed, and pressed his head to the floor and waited for his moment, and gained his freedom.

The sky moved, and the days passed. Korloria held him after the others went, finally, and they did not wait for anyone else to enter. She pulled him into the stacks, and pushed him against the wall, and kissed him, pinning him there. Roh thought of Kadaan, his finger wet with wine, wiping the rouge from his lip, and he let Korloria do whatever she wanted, though his knees ached, and he threw up in the hall afterward.

Press your forehead to the floor.

A few days later, Korloria swept into the dormitory with the three other archive administrators and called up two young men. Roh recognized them as the ones who'd been tangling in the sheets after dark.

She whipped them both, and while the whole dormitory watched, one of the other administrators castrated them with an infused blade that cauterized the wounds. Roh smelled burnt flesh.

"Let this be a lesson," Korloria said, and her gaze swept right over Roh, "there will be no fornication here. None. You are here for one purpose."

One purpose.

Korloria brought Roh up to her rooms the day he

heard Caisau call his name.

Roh ran his hands along the hall as he followed her up, stomach knotted with dread. He heard the burbling laughter again, and glanced at Korloria's back to see if she had heard it too, but she didn't react.

"Rohinmey," the voice whispered. "You are running out of time."

Roh offered Korloria aatai from her great liquor cupboard, and she drank until she was pleasantly tipsy, but not drunk. He could not overpower her, not as he was, with two bad knees, badly malnourished. Her behavior around him was so practiced that it gave the impression that she took advantage of the young translators often.

The liquor was enough to make her sleep, and when she was snoring, Roh slipped out of bed and went into the room adjacent. He found her papers at her desk, all written in what he assumed was their Dhai dialect. It was impenetrable.

He rifled through the desk drawers, and finally found one that was locked. He worked at the lock with what he took to be a stylized letter opener on the desk until it opened. There he found what he was looking for – a map of Caisau.

And he didn't need to understand the language to read the map.

Roh tucked the map into his belt. The lock on the drawer was broken. She'd notice it. She'd know it was him. When she woke up, she'd use the ward to murder him, if he was lucky.

Roh took the letter opener from the desk and went back to the bedroom. He stood over Korloria. Raised the weapon.

She opened her eyes. Grabbed his arm.

Roh climbed on top of her, though his knees sent sharp needles of pain up his thighs.

"You think I'm stupid?" she snarled. She pushed him off. He fell hard on the floor.

The collar around his throat burned. A shock of pain lit down his spine. He bent back, screaming. Another jolt, like someone had yanked his spine from his body and now dangled it above him, and set it on fire.

Korloria knelt next to him. She took a fistful of his long hair, twisting his head back. "Don't think–"

He brought up the letter opener in his other hand and stabbed her through the heart.

Korloria let out a huff of breath. She released him. Clutched at her chest, slumped against the bed.

Roh lay on the floor, shaking, while the memory of the pain throbbed through him, wave upon wave. When it subsided, he crawled across the floor to the bed and used it for leverage to pull himself up.

Korloria was slumped to one side. Her eyes were open, one hand still hanging onto the weapon in her chest.

Roh stumbled to her wardrobe and pulled it open. He found one of her robes, a head wrap, a silver belt. He dressed carefully, arranging the yellow wrap on his head the same way the other Tai Mora women in the hold had. If they didn't ask him to speak, he could pass.

She had no proper weapon in her room, so he yanked the letter opener from her chest, cleaned it off, and hid it in his sleeve.

He kept the map close at hand, but knew vaguely where he was going – down.

Roh grabbed his crutch and limped into the hallway, closing Korloria's door firmly behind him. The first two people he passed were servants, and both looked back at him. He had kept his eyes lowered. He had learned deference. But a Tai Mora wouldn't. A Tai Mora would walk through the hall like she owned it.

Roh came to the big main stairwell, the same one he had last come up without assistance before Korloria destroyed his knees. The stairs looked like an incredible obstacle, an impossible cliff face.

He remembered Lilia in Oma's Temple, navigating

the scullery stair every day without a complaint, and he firmed his resolve. He grabbed the rail tightly, and started down.

Within the hour, he was lost in some storage room, hungry and increasingly terrified about what would happen when they found Korloria's body and him gone from the dormitory. He pressed his hand to the wall of the hold.

"A little help?" he said.

Nothing.

Maybe he really had imagined the voice. He was mad, then. He'd made it all up. Roh opened door after door, looking for another stairwell. He followed the map to a dead end – a dark corridor with just one flame fly lantern, and only two of the flies still alive.

Roh wondered what would happen if he just died down here. It was better than whatever was up there.

He twisted back around to go back the way he'd come. But the entrance was gone. A blank wall stared at him. Roh turned around again. Where there had once been a dead end, he now saw a gaping hole in the skin of the hold.

Roh staggered forward. He ran his hand along the wall for balance. A stone ramp spiraled down and down, as far as the flickering light of the flame fly light reached. Roh took the lantern from its holder in the wall and brought it with him.

As he stepped over the threshold, the wall sealed behind him.

He was alone in the darkness, with no way back.

Roh limped down and down, because the only way out was forward.

50

The hissing, chittering monstrosities poured into the room like golden insects, grinning and ducking their heads from left to right, as if trying to draw Zezili's fire. Not that Zezili had much of anything to fire. She backed up into the green pool, weapon out. It was going to be like dying at the claws of the cats, only she wasn't getting up this time.

It'd been a good run.

Zezili slashed at the first one who reached her, drawing blood. Another creature came from her left and bit her hard on the shoulder. Bit her! Zezili stabbed it in the face. They swarmed her then, hands and feet and faces pushing her to the ground. One bit her thigh. She kicked. Slashed.

Somewhere at the rear of the mob, one of them screeched. Then she heard curses. Human ones. Had some of her force survived?

The swarm turned away from her and attacked the group behind them. Zezili crawled back around the throne, dragging her leg, and peered out at the melee. She recognized the armor of Saradyn's men. He had come after her, then, and she hadn't even noticed. She had grown too soft out here in the woods, too wrapped up in her own woes. Saradyn's men hacked at the creatures, and she wasn't sure which she wanted to prevail. If she got lucky they might just kill each other and end all of her problems, but that was too easy. Rhea had never once blessed her with providence.

Saradyn himself pushed free of the mob, lunging with sword and shield. He moved fast for a big man. Three of his men fell, and five of the women. One of the creatures scuttled off, injured and keening. Only Saradyn remained, backing up toward Zezili, feinting at the last creature. Blood streamed down his arm. Zezili half thought she might cut the rest of his arm off herself, but what was that going to accomplish, now?

The creature had him pinned. It used one set of legs to grip his sword, and took him by the neck with its hands.

Saradyn gasped.

An arrow zipped into the room, followed by two more. They thunked neatly into the creature's back. It released Saradyn and turned just in time to get an arrow through the eye.

Natanial, the beak-nosed man, strode into the room, carrying a short bow and two more arrows in his drawing hand. He said something in Tordinian, and gestured at Storm's body in the throne.

"They woke something up," Zezili said, pressing the stump of her arm to her bleeding leg.

Natanial raised the bow, strung an arrow, and peered around Saradyn to get a good look at her.

Saradyn sneered at her, and said something that probably wasn't complimentary.

"They're like the Empress," Zezili said. "But you knew that, I guess, if you fucked her. They'll eat us up, starting with Tordin. I came here to stop it."

"Tordin is mine," Saradyn said.

"So you can speak a civilized language after all," Zezili said.

"They murdered the whole force we brought through the hole," Natanial said. "If our interests are aligned—"

"Go eat your cock," Zezili said.

"Pleasurably," Natanial said. "After I'm out of this festering pit."

"Your sinajistas outside?" Zezili asked.

"Fire witches," Saradyn said.

"Bang stones. Make fire. Yeah, yeah, fucking *witches*," Zezili said. It was like talking to some superstitious dajian.

Natanial lowered his bow. "How are you still alive?"

"Been asking myself that," Zezili said.

"You're blessed of some god," Natanial said. "Just not mine." Natanial frowned at the two of them, clearly disappointed in his odds. Zezili horked out a laugh that loosened something in her chest. She spat phlegm.

"Fight out," Saradyn said.

Natanial shrugged, said something to him in Tordinian. Saradyn laughed.

"What?" Zezili said.

"He says we cut whatever's keeping your friend here upright and run back across those killing fields," Natanial said. "But that's about as tactical as Saradyn ever gets."

Zezili glanced up at the big silver throne. "You think he powers them, maybe?"

"They need all these bodies for something," Natanial said. "I expect they were hungry after they came out of there."

Zezili crawled to her feet. "Good enough plan as any," she said. She smirked. "Well, Saradyn. *You*'ve got the biggest sword."

He frowned, muttering something under his breath as he approached the throne. He barked something at Natanial. Natanial pointed at Zezili, made a retort.

Saradyn held out his sword to Natanial.

Natanial took the blade and got behind the throne. Zezili and Saradyn took a few steps back, inching toward the door. Zezili kept Saradyn in the corner of her eye, concerned he'd pull a knife. He never took his eyes off her.

Natanial brought up the blade.

Zezili cringed.

The blade came down on the tangled root mass behind the throne. It thunked solidly into it, as if the pod were a tree trunk. A wound opened up in it, bleeding sticky green sap.

Natanial cut again.

Storm bolted up in the throne again. He screamed.

Saradyn pulled his dagger out and held it in front of him like a talisman. He kissed his other hand and made some kind of warding gesture.

Storm leaned forward in the throne, both hands gripping the armrests, gibbering green blood. Natanial hacked again.

"She sees you," Storm says. "She sees you. She is here."

Natanial's blade sliced through the final thread of the giant root.

Storm's body went limp again. He tumbled off the throne, landing in a pathetic heap at its base.

Zezili exchanged a look with Saradyn. "Time to run?" she said.

"Run," he said.

The three of them ran hard up through the tunnel. Zezili favored her injured leg. Natanial could have outrun them both, Zezili knew, but he stayed behind her, guarding the rear. As they broke into the clearing, Zezili noticed something in the light had changed. She gazed up into the sky where Para should be, but Para's light wasn't blue. It was violet, and its heavenly body was the wrong shape.

"The fuck–" she muttered, but Natanial came from behind her, urging her forward, and suddenly what had happened in the sky wasn't so interesting anymore.

Saradyn made for the great hole Zezili had come in. Halfway there, Natanial yelled at him, "They've got a swarm there!"

Zezili swung behind a big tree. Saradyn slowed. Sure enough, there was a group of at least forty of the gold-skinned women between them and the hole. They were arranged in a loose circle, clicking in that strange language of theirs.

Saradyn swore. Zezili searched the scattered ground around them, trying to think of some other way out of this fucking kill pit. She saw the great cocoons hanging from the branches, oozing their slimy sap. She followed the pods – low, higher, highest – and found a neat chain of them that ran up the side of the mountainous anomaly that encircled them.

"The pods," Zezili said. "Climb those up and over?"

Natanial stared at her hands – the three fingers and the dagger. "Can you?"

She brandished the daggered stump. "Makes for great climbing, I'm sure."

"Follow me," Natanial said.

Zezili was happy to let him draw the first of them off.

Natanial stayed in cover for half the length of the run across the center of the clearing before he broke into plain sight.

Zezili staggered to keep up with him, but she was flagging. Saradyn slipped ahead of her.

She heard the hiss of the women the moment they saw them, and it spurred her to run faster.

Natanial caught the end of the swinging cocoon and climbed up it like some kind of arboreal creature.

Zezili jabbed her dagger into the cocoon and clawed for purchase with the three fingers of her other hand. Pain jolted up her arm. She almost vomited. But the women were barreling after them now, advancing fast across the clearing, pushing bodies out of their way, and that fate would be worse than the pain.

Saradyn's big ass was just ahead of Zezili. She hooked her fingers into his belt. He kicked at her.

"Stop!" she yelled. "You kick again I shove my dagger

up your ass, you hear me?"

Saradyn must have understood, because he didn't kick at her again. With Saradyn climbing and her hooked onto his belt, she could push herself up with her legs while he pulled.

Saradyn got to the top of the first cocoon. She pushed herself up next to him. They stood side by side, watching Natanial clawing for a root on the side of the mountainous barrier. They were just twenty feet from the top.

"Swing the cocoon!" Natanial yelled.

"Want to dance, then?" Zezili said, and cackled. She rocked her body weight forward. Saradyn did the same, swinging the cocoon until Saradyn could grip the other one. Zezili leapt after him. They swung again, to the next, and by then Natanial was scrambling up the side of the mountain.

Zezili went to make the jump after him, and slipped. She yelled. Saradyn swore. She still had hold of his belt. Her legs swung out over the side of the cocoon. The horde of women had arrived below. Four of them tried to leap onto the first cocoon, but they were too heavy. It broke, and they toppled. Zezili swung herself from Saradyn's belt out toward the edge of the mountain, aiming for the root Natanial had used.

She took a breath and released Saradyn's belt, flailing with the daggered stump and her fingers, praying one found purchase.

The dagger thumped into the mountain, scraping down the side of it as she fell. She caught the end of the root with her three fingers. She swung her legs forward, clamping hard onto the rest of the root with her legs. She stopped falling.

Zezili panted and sweated. She yanked her dagger out of the mountain and plunged it up again, relying almost entirely on her legs to push her up the top of the mountain.

Saradyn was yelling at her, but she didn't pay any attention to him. Her legs were shaking. The women milled below her, hungry.

Zezili pushed with her legs, up and up the length of the root until she saw a whole, lean hand thrust in her face. She looked up.

Natanial held out his hand. She shook her head. What was she going to grip it with?

He got down on his knees and took her by the front of her shirt and lifted her the last foot up to the top of the mountain.

Zezili lay there, panting and hugging the loose dirt.

Saradyn climbed up next to her, his face poking up. He spat something at her. She made a face.

"I'm going to prepare the witches," Natanial said, and slid down the other side of the mountain. It was so steep he mostly tumbled down it, reducing the speed of his fall by grabbing onto shrubs and roots on the way down.

Zezili stared Saradyn in the eye as he grabbed at the top of the mountain. She saw him grip a loose clod of dirt. He loosed his other hand, relying on the clod to hold him. It didn't.

Saradyn slipped. He yelled.

Zezili edged up to the side of the mountain and stared down at him. He still had hold of the root with one hand. He dangled out over the horde of women.

"I'd offer a hand," Zezili said. She held up her stump. "But it doesn't look like I've got one to spare."

Saradyn sputtered at her. He kicked at the side of the mountain. She figured he'd get a foothold.

He didn't.

The root tore.

Saradyn's face crumpled into that of a fearful child – horrified, angry to learn that the monsters his parents always told him weren't real were, in fact, waiting for him, and had always waited for him.

Zezili's mouth hung open.

Saradyn lost his grip, and fell into the hungry arms of the women below.

Zezili crawled across the broken ground, listening to Saradyn's cries, until she could get to her feet. Then she slid down the other side after Natanial, mind still reeling from Saradyn's demise.

Natanial was standing among a group of six men and four women in purple robes – the sinajistas, Zezili supposed. They argued.

"What's wrong?" Zezili asked. She didn't get too close. Being set on fire sounded like a bad way to go.

"They need line of sight in order to kill the women," Natanial said. He pointed at the glowing violet body in the heavens. "Even with a flash ascendance, they always need line of sight."

She looked up the way she'd come down – it was too steep to climb. The only way back was through the hole. "They afraid of getting dirty?"

Natanial said, "If they go in, they know they aren't coming out." He peered behind her. "Where's Saradyn?"

"Needed to take a piss," Zezili said. "I'll go."

"Where? To piss?"

"No, into the hole. A delayed burst. Not sure what they'd call it." She made a circular motion with her arms, trundling them around each other like she was wrapping yarn. Her body was still shaking, the muscle memory of the climb. "You twist the fire spell around a living thing, then send it into the enemy. It's set with a delay. Gives you time to get inside before it's triggered. Pretty popular tactic of mine." Of Tulana's, really.

"When have you ever done something like that?"

Zezili showed her teeth. "Did it to dajians all the time," she said. She remembered the runner she had sent up to scout the top of that living mound, happily sending him to his death. And more. She'd sent so many more.

"Burned like fucking torches," Zezili said, "but they took out a lot of the enemy, too."

"I'm missing something."

"Not at all," she said. "I'll do it."

"Where *is* Saradyn?"

"That's what I said. I'll do it."

She was caught, every which way she looked. Standing here with fifty of his men, this predatory assassin, a gaggle of sinajistas, and Saradyn dead, well – there was no way out of it. She had come here to thwart the Empress's plans. She had come here to die.

Natanial's look was piercing. "Saradyn," he said.

"Didn't make it," Zezili said.

"Tell me why I shouldn't kill you here."

"Because you can kill me in there."

Natanial barked orders to the sinajistas. They obeyed. Zezili felt the air around her condense. She took a long breath, like breathing soup. Her skin tingled.

"How long do you need?" Natanial said.

"As long as it takes to get through the hole and into the center of them," Zezili said. "When all that food's gone in there, I figure they're going to start coming out."

Natanial said something to the sinajistas.

Zezili waited until the sinajistas gave her the nod, then walked back to the hole. They all followed her – Natanial, the sinajistas, the fifty men of Saradyn's still on this side. She felt like some kind of blood sacrifice to a vengeful god, and she supposed she was. She always wondered what it felt like, knowing you were going to die.

She came to the mouth of the hole, and stared down.

"Changed your mind?" Natanial said.

"So you can gut me?" she said. "No."

"They do far worse to king killers."

"That man was no king," Zezili said. "Just one more foolish bag of meat who thought he was fucking special."

"Like you?"

"I don't think it," Zezili said. "I know it."

She started down into the hole. The journey felt shorter this time, maybe because she knew what to expect. She raised her head and peered out over the clearing. The women were on the other side.

Zezili ran toward them, waving her arms. She wasn't quite sure how long the sinajistas had given her before she burst apart. Maybe she wouldn't die at all. Maybe Natanial had just said it so he could watch her get eaten up.

The women heard her. They raised their heads.

Zezili stopped, out of breath.

Finally.

What were people supposed to think about, before they died? She didn't know. She thought about how tired she was, and how much she stank. She missed her fucking hand. Her leg was still bleeding. She leaned over to catch her breath while the swarm of the Empress's people advanced on her position, like something from a Dorinah opera.

She straightened as they came at her.

"Zezili?" Natanial stood in the mouth of the pit. What a fool. He'd burn up if he didn't run.

The first line of creatures hissed at her, so close she felt the heat of them.

Natanial cupped his hands to his mouth. "Anavha's alive," he said, and dropped back into the hole.

Zezili snarled. "Son of a–"

She burst into flame.

51

Taigan sailed into Anjoliaa at the stern of a broad Aaldian ship. She held onto the rigging and leaned out over the sea, inhaling the musky reek of the harbor. After the mess in Dhai, Anjoliaa appeared, on first blush, untouched. But as the ship neared the port, Taigan caught her first whiff of fear. The docks were crowded – not just dock workers and fishmongers and slaves, but citizens of every class, in every state of distress. Men with tattered vestments and calloused hands. Women with muddied robes and frayed hair. Ataisa in their long trousers and tunics coming apart at the knees and elbows. Children who should have been veiled, running about with little more than scarves on their heads. All shared the same hungry faces, and wide, panicked eyes. Taigan supposed that was a good sign, that they still had the energy for panic, but as she peered deeper into the crowds she saw the listless ones packing the dark corners, their eyes glazed over and all hope gone.

They sat with hands outstretched, babies in their arms so dehydrated and malnourished they'd ceased to cry. What remained of her people had come to Anjoliaa to die, pressed against the sea by the Tai Mora. She imagined that when the end came, the sea would turn red with their blood.

Taigan watched the faces of the Aaldian crew. Most Aaldians were dark people, gray or green eyed, with hemp-stained hair coiled into elaborate dreadlocks, and broad, flat faces. She knew them to be a fractious but largely peaceful people, yet as the clawing hands of the desperate Saiduan came for the side of the ship, the captain did not hesitate, but leapt across the deck and gave orders for her crew to beat them back with the mallets at their hips.

Taigan slung her pack over her shoulder and hopped from the stern to the pier. She landed hard. The crowd around her scattered. Hungry children covered their eyes. She still looked the part of the sanisi, even after all this time in exile.

One of the men on the pier offered to sell his youngest child to the Aaldians in payment for passage. Taigan glanced back once, just in time to see the look of disgust on the captain's face.

"We're not slavers or cannibals," the Aaldian said. "We deal cleanly or not at all."

Of course, if he'd offered her a corpse or a pint of blood, she would have considered it a fair trade. Morals were funny things. Moving among so many different people, over so many different times, Taigan could take none of them seriously.

She enjoyed a clear walk up the pier for a few paces until the crowd got used to her, then she had to resort to shoving them out of the way. Hunger and desperation always overcame fear, in the end.

Taigan made her way away from the pier, and the crowd thinned out. She suspected many Saiduan had already fled to neighboring islands, or gone east to the far continents, or south to Hrollief. Every people had its breaking point, and she suspected that the flight of the Patron from Harajan to Anjoliaa had been a clear sign that the time for stubborn national pride was over.

She made her way to a tea house. The insistence on

paying customers meant it was less packed than the
streets, but the atmosphere was no less fearful. Groups
of men and ataisa spoke together in low tones. It was not
until she was halfway across the room that she noted she
had come in the wrong entrance – the women's entrance
had been on her right. Of course, she didn't expect any
of them to try pulling off her trousers to combat her
claim, at this point. She was whatever she said she was.
She expected a good number of the men and ataisa were
women dressing the part in an effort to avoid too many
questions. She tapped at the front counter until the
proprietor came up from the back.

"I'm Taigan," she said.

The proprietor was a plump, heavily bearded man. He
looked her up and down once, but didn't challenge her.
"Of course. This way, please."

He led her up a twisted set of steps, a long hall, and
then up another narrow flight. He knocked.

"Taigan, Your Eminence," the man said.

The door opened.

Maralah stood in the narrow frame. She was much
thinner. Taigan saw it most in her face, as the rest of her
was heavily swathed in several layers of dark robes. She
wore blue and violet, not sanisi black. Taigan saw the
glowing hilt of her violet weapon sticking up from a slit
in the back of her clothing, and her boots were the same.
Her hair was newly braided, glossy, as if she'd just had
it done.

Taigan stepped toward her, thinking to say something
witty about how hard it must be to find a good Anjoliaan
hairdresser with the city in disarray.

Maralah put a knife through her gut.

Taigan huffed out a breath. The tea shop proprietor
squeaked and ran back down the stairs.

Taigan leaned against the wall, clutching her bleeding
stomach. "Was that necess–"

Maralah took Taigan by the collar and hauled her

into the room. Taigan instinctively called on Oma and pulled a skein of breath beneath her skin. But even as she prepared a defense, the ward on her back burned, and her hold on Oma vanished. She snarled.

Maralah flung her against the wall. Taigan crumpled, curling in on herself. Maralah stabbed her in the face, through her right cheek. Stabbed her chest. Taigan flung out her arms. Maralah cut her open like a stuck pig. Taigan screamed.

Maralah cut open Taigan's stomach and yanked out her intestines. Even as she did, the wound she'd inflicted in Taigan's face began to hiss and bubble and heal. Maralah sweated and seethed. She hacked and pulled. She cut out Taigan's liver and flung it across the room. She drove her knife into the lying, duplicitous woman's heart, yes, woman, she could see the breasts now that the clothes were ripped and torn and bloodied. Taigan the abomination. Taigan the impossible. Taigan who could not die.

Taigan's intestines began to coil back into her body. Maralah pulled her infused weapon from her back. She cut off Taigan's left leg, then the right. Cut off both arms. Sliced her head in two. She called on Sina and burned the mangled, shredded body to a charred ruin.

She dropped her weapon, then, and sagged to the floor, breathing heavily. She leaned against the large trunk at the end of the bed and watched the seething, blackened ruin pull its fleshy pieces back together. Hunks of charred meat drew together to form the torso. The liver remained on the other side of the room, but the rest of the pieces fused back together and began to reknit themselves, like something from a nightmare. She watched the husk become a human-shaped glob again. The whole meaty mess trembled, then spasmed. Gasped. The spine arched back. Screaming. Screaming. Screaming. Unending.

The char flaked away from the skin, revealing a fresh new layer of a deep russet brown. The body regenerated in a matter of minutes, and came back smooth and hairless as a newborn babe.

The screaming stopped. Taigan stared at the ceiling, huffing deep breaths, and flexing her hands.

Maralah tugged at the ward she'd imbedded in Taigan so long ago, and felt it respond. The ward was intact, then, bound to the flesh firmly. How lucky for them both. Her body felt heavy. She held her weapon loosely, legs splayed, just staring at Taigan, wondering at all the choices that had brought her here.

"Rajavaa is dead," Maralah said.

He had been dead for two days, but this was the first time she had said it aloud. He sat in the bathroom at the end of the hall, the body preserved in salt. She'd thought to preserve him for Taigan, thought if she could resurrect him twice a day she could save the higher functions of his brain. But by the twentieth time she resurrected Rajavaa on this long trip to Anjoliaa, she had brought back only a gibbering shell, a non-person, a sack of meat. Even if Taigan had come a week sooner, she'd only have preserved the body – a breathing vegetable.

"Everyone dies," Taigan said, and laughed. She laughed and laughed until it came out a hacking cough. She turned onto her side and hacked up gobs of blood onto the floor.

"You failed me," Maralah said.

Taigan spit bloody bile. "I've failed a lot of people."

"You were not allowed to fail *me*."

"*Allowed*?" Taigan said. "What a vain, power-mad woman you are, to believe your desires shape the world."

"Desire is the only thing that shapes the world."

"The gods shape the world. Not you. Not me. Only the gods." Taigan pointed to the sky. "Only the heavens."

"We are the instruments of the gods."

"You believe that?"

"Yes."

"More fool you."

She lifted her weapon. "I will cut you up again."

"You were not the first," Taigan said. She sat up and winced, as if her new skin were still tender. She rested against the wall, breathing heavily. "I expect you won't be the last."

"How old are you, Taigan? How many Patrons have you watched die and ascend? How many empires?"

"What is age, really? Time." Taigan's gaze rolled up to the ceiling. "In my village, when I was very young, we still knew of Oma. Oma was not a myth. Oma was the dark god. The vengeful god. Oma was the god who cursed me."

"How long, Taigan?"

"Hundreds of years, likely," she said. "Give or take."

Maralah stared at her, this hairless freak, this monstrous omajista who had shown up at the Patron's court twenty years before with stories of Oma's rising. Alaar's predecessor had thought her mad. Alaar had not.

"Why did you betray Alaar?"

"Alaar, huh," Taigan snorted. "A weak Patron for a time that needed a strong one. He was not right for what was coming. You know that now, but you didn't then. I did."

"You would have killed him."

"Of course. Just as you did."

"I didn't."

"You allowed him to die. It's the same thing."

They sat for several breaths in silence. Taigan said, "What next?"

Maralah had spent the last month asking herself that very question. She had gone over possibilities again and again, coming up with terrible answers, each more empty than the last.

"There is no hope in Saiduan," she said. "What

remained of the army, and the last of the sanisi, were killed in Harajan."

"You took no force with you?"

"I was betrayed."

"Ah."

She grimaced at the way Taigan said it, like it was an inevitability. "Some say what remains of the more powerful families are making bids for Patron. But most are simply fleeing now, like gnats."

"I expected you to fight in Anjoliaa."

She laughed bitterly. "With what? These filthy refugees, throwing roof tiles? There is no army. What little order they have here is orchestrated by the city guard, and they're beyond corrupt. More and more flee each day. Soon the city will run itself, right into the sea."

"If you have no use for me," Taigan said, "release me."

"After all this? No."

"There is hope, still."

"Not here."

"In Dhai."

"With the maggots? I thought you hated them. And where is your little worldbreaker, eh? All the omajistas you promised me."

Taigan shrugged. "You summoned me before I was done."

"You left them in Dhai."

"The Tai Mora offered them a peaceful resolution, before they burned the harbor. How many peaceful offers did they make us?"

"Do they feel that bad about killing themselves?"

"I think they wanted Dhai untouched, in a way they did not with Saiduan. They came here to destroy, but they are going to Dhai to occupy it. The final battle will not be fought in Saiduan. It will be fought in Dhai."

"You want me to release you so you can go back to Dhai? You'll run off to some fishing village, like a coward." Like her. Staying in Anjoliaa meant death, being run through against the sea. She knew it. Taigan knew it. But calling Taigan a coward was easier than calling herself one.

Taigan shrugged. "Do what you will. When you are dead, the ward is released. If you want to die here, that suits me very well, too. I have a lot of patience."

"Why did you fail me?"

"The task you gave me was to find a worldbreaker so we could close the way between the worlds. But we had yet to understand how to do that. I think the Dhai know. We need both to succeed."

"Give up everything and throw our lot in with the Dhai? Is that what you're saying?"

"You do what you like. I ask only that you release me."

"No."

"Very well."

They sat in silence for some time more. Maralah was aware of the murmuring noise from the street, and the steady drip, drip of a leaky pipe somewhere in the guts of the building below her.

She got to her feet. Sheathed her blade. "Get yourself a room." She tossed Taigan a couple of coins. "And new clothes."

Taigan stood, naked, and went to the door. "For the love of the empire, Taigan, put on something." She grabbed one of Rajavaa's robes and threw it to her.

Taigan dutifully pulled it on, staring at Maralah the whole time. She opened the door. Left her in silence.

Maralah wasn't sure how she'd expected to feel, on seeing Taigan, on punishing her for her transgressions. She had won something, surely, by getting her unkillable healer back, but she had no worldbreakers, no Patron, and no army. Just she and Taigan, and Kovaas downstairs, drinking his sorrow from a deep cup. They had all looked to her, and she had failed them again and again. The Tai Mora no doubt knew what she was only now beginning to realize – the Tai Mora had won. Saiduan was dust, like the Dhai before them, and the Talamynii before them, and on and on, back and back for how long, how many cycles?

All she had to choose now was how she wanted to end it.

A knock at the door. The blackest part of the night, when Maralah slept the least. She reached for the long dagger at her bedside.

"Announce yourself."

"Kovaas."

She had no light, but he had brought a lantern with him. She held tightly to her dagger, because the light was blinding, and she thought perhaps he'd come to end it. She saw he had a steaming bowl of something in one hand.

"You'll sleep better if you eat," he said.

"Are you a nursemaid now?"

"It would make for a pleasing change of profession. What are you?"

"Not a war minister, that's certain." She took the bowl. It was warm, which was nice, because the chill had seeped into her bones. It was curried rice and fish heads. It smelled divine. "Where did you get this?"

"I have my ways."

"You cooked it yourself?"

"Killing is not all I'm good at."

She broke apart the flatbread tucked into the edge of the bowl and ate with her hands. Her stomach murmured.

"Rumor says the Tai Mora are four, five days out," he said.

"The city's been quieter."

"A few have joined with the local guard, put up defenses. But I suspect those won't last. There's a very vocal group that wants to surrender."

"They've seen what the Tai Mora do to towns that surrender." Well, perhaps they hadn't. But *she* had. It was no different than what they did to cities that fought. Perhaps the fighters died more quickly.

"And what will you do?" he asked.

"Don't know," she said. "You?"

"You should lead them," he said. "It would be a fine change of profession."

She wiped the bowl clean and stood. She poured water from a pitcher into the basin on her night stand and washed her fingers, considering. "They won't follow a woman."

"You're not a woman. You're the Minister of War."

"I've been around and around this dozens of times."

"Sometimes our stories erase women who lead," he said. "It doesn't mean it never happened, only that we refuse to remember. There are folk stories of–"

"There are folk stories about men who turn into bees," she said. "There are stories of time-traveling dogs and shepherds with wings. They won't follow a woman." She sat back down next to him.

"I did," he said. In the dim light, broad shadows played across his heavily bearded face. The beard made his expression hard to read. Big, bright eyes, broad, generous face. A face she had brought back from death – for loyalty, if nothing else.

"You followed Rajavaa," she said. "Not me."

"I followed *you*. Not Alaar, not Rajavaa, not Morsaar. *You*, Maralah."

She pressed her hand to his cheek. He leaned into her touch. "I'm tired of fighting," she said.

"Then let's not fight," he said.

She pressed her lips to his, and he responded in kind. Not urgent or demanding, but gentle. The kindness of the kiss was so unexpected that it lit her up like a torch. When was the last time she had been touched with kindness? They made love in the cool evening like much younger people. She had been past the age at which she concerned herself with pregnancy for some time, but had not been able to take advantage of it. The freedom it gave her was nothing short of miraculous. Kovaas drank her like a thirsty man, as if she was the last woman in the world, and perhaps, tonight, that was what they were – the last two sanisi in Anjoliaa, drunk on the inevitability of death. But not yet, not yet…

After, he lay sprawled beside her, breathing low and soft, and she traced the broad scars on his back and wished they had met under some better circumstance. But Maralah the Minister of War would not have taken another sanisi to bed. The politics of that were too great. She would have relied on celibacy or hungry young men from the villages. Never equals. Never potential rivals. She had not lived this long by acting like a foolish girl. Yet here she was.

She thought of Rajavaa's body in the tub. And Taigan in the room below. She wondered if Taigan had heard them. Taigan, more broken than any of them.

Kovaas rolled over. Caught her hand in his, drew it to his breast. "Will we part tomorrow, then?"

"Or tonight, under cover of dark?"

"They will follow you, Maralah."

"And you?"

"You know my answer."

"Even if I am a woman without title who leads no army and holds no power? You find that interesting?"

"You will always have power. Over an empire, a village, an army, or perhaps just over a man."

"Sentimental," she said, but she wrapped him in her arms, and rested her face on his broad chest, and, for the first time in weeks, considered a future that did not end in death.

52

Ahkio was on the wall, cursing what felt like a terrible hangover, when Sina entered the sky. The double satellites hung there for one blazing, fearful moment, then Para winked out. The parajistas on the wall wailed. It was like a knife cut cleanly through the line of them. Tulana was screaming at one of her Seekers, a sinajista. The smoky walls that barred the view of their retreat dissipated, revealing the empty field below where the refugees had been.

"Oma's breath," Ahkio said, and ran down the line to see how far Yisaoh and their retreating forces had gotten. He could not see them from here, but their tracks would be easy to follow.

He had not called any sinajistas from the temple. They were completely defenseless.

Ahkio yelled at the parajistas. "Off the wall! Retreat!"

Tulana barreled toward him. "We hold this wall!"

"With what? We have one sinajista and three hundred militia. That's the last of us."

"Then we die here," Tulana said.

"I said–"

She grabbed him by the collar, shook him. "I don't answer to you. I answer to that little cripple, and I tell you now, I would rather be dead than a slave." She released him, and yelled at her people.

"Voralyn! Fire wall!"

Ahkio bolted down into the hold, and found the leader of the militia, Farosi, coming up the steps. "Is it true?" Farosi said.

"Para's down. We need to retreat."

But Farosi climbed up past him. Ahkio went after him. They stood on the wall together, staring out over the low fire wall that now ringed Kuallina, held there by Tulana's single sinajista.

Farosi placed his hands on the wall, and nodded grimly. "All right," he said.

"We need to retreat," Ahkio said. "They'll bust through that ring in–"

"We'll stay here," Farosi said. "We need to cover you. Get to the Line room, quickly."

"Farosi, you'll die here–"

"Of course," Farosi said. "That was the plan all along, was it not, Kai? We distract so the others may flee. It just so happens we distract a few moments less than we hoped. Come along."

"I can't–"

Farosi called two parajistas over. They were trembling badly, already exhausted and now shaken. "Take the Kai back to Oma's Temple," he said. "There's room in the Line for three."

They did not have to be asked twice.

"Can I take your hand?" Ahkio asked.

Farosi nodded. They clasped wrists.

"I need you to burn it behind you," Ahkio said. "Send a small force south to follow. Burn everything. Every village. Every field. Every orchard."

"I have fifty on the ground. I'll move them as soon as you're out."

Ahkio nodded. The parajistas came behind Ahkio and hurried him over to the Line room. "Caisa!" Ahkio said. "I can't leave without Caisa!"

But everything was happening very quickly. The

tirajista in the Line room poured the chrysalis components into the divot in the floor, and it bubbled up around them, and off they went, Ahkio and two powerless parajistas, swinging back over the trees, speeding away from Kuallina. "Get Caisa out!" he yelled, but the others were already turning back into the hold to fight.

Ahkio pressed his face to the northward side of the chrysalis, watching as the army came alive outside Kuallina. A wave of fire burst up from the foreign army, a plume twice the height of the wall. It engulfed the fortress. As the wave passed, the Tai Mora army swarmed, like a thousand insects devouring some corpse. For a moment he wondered if Lilia and Mohrai had survived it. He knew Yisaoh would, fool woman. Yisaoh would survive anything.

The Line passed above the trees, higher and higher, giving him a clear view of the army's assault on the gates of Kuallina while Sina's baleful purple glow illuminated the field. It was the same journey he had taken the year before, tucked inside the Line with Nasaka, after she had told him his sister lay dying. Now it was not his sister who lay dying. The whole country was burning as he watched on.

"Maybe… the temples…" one of the parajistas said. She met Ahkio's look and stopped speaking. She was young, not much older than him. "Perhaps we can… the temple of Sina, at least…"

"We're retreating," Ahkio said. "Dhai is lost."

She began to cry.

Ahkio could not bring himself to comfort her. He saw Sina's light reflected in her eyes, and he gazed toward Oma's Temple with a heavy sense of dread.

Sina had risen.

Nasaka was a sinajista. One of the most powerful. She would not be happy, and she would have burned her way out of those cells the moment her star entered the sky.

Whatever waited for him at Oma's Temple would not be much better than Kuallina.

•••

Four hours later, Ahkio and the parajistas arrived in the Line room at the Temple of Oma. Ahkio saw no flames above the temple, no burning plateau, nothing to give him any idea of what was happening inside.

There was no one to meet them, so they had to wait for the chrysalis to dissolve on its own, which was maddening. The three of them shouted for another hour before the chrysalis began to lose its integrity. They peeled it away with their fingers, and Ahkio bolted out the door.

"Come with me," he told the younger parajista, Mihina. And to the elder, Sulana, he said, "Round up the sinajistas. They need to know we're retreating and burning the temple behind us."

"The temple?" Sulana said. "Kai–"

"You want to leave it to the Tai Mora?" he said.

She shook her head.

"Then go," he said.

He and Mihina went down the scullery stair. He burst onto the sixth floor where the novices should have been training, but the rooms were oddly empty. Ahkio kept descending, checking halls as he went. His sense of unease intensified.

Ahkio plunged down the steps, finally coming out in the foyer. It was packed, clogged with novices and Oras. Some were crying.

He called at the first he saw, a boy with a pocked complexion. "Where's Meyna?" he asked. "Meyna and the Li Kai?"

The boy burst into tears. "Kai! Kai!" he cried, and the cry went up, and the room seethed like a living thing.

"Where are they?" he yelled.

"She's in the Sanctuary!" someone said, and Ahkio pushed his way through them, jostling the crowd rudely. The doors to the Sanctuary were open. He barreled inside.

There was Nasaka at the center of the room, holding a bowl full of blood.

"Nasaka!" he said.

She looked up. So did the woman who knelt in front of her. Ahkio came up short.

He knew the woman at Nasaka's feet, though he had not seen her since he was a child.

"Etena?" he said.

His aunt rose, a narrow slip of a woman with his mother's broad forehead and pert nose, pulling at the cloak around her shoulders. "Ahkio?" She glanced at Nasaka. "You said he was dead."

"Where is Meyna?" Ahkio said.

Nasaka dumped the blood over Etena's head. Etena gaped, sputtering.

Ahkio ran to the platform, wondering whose blood that was. His child's? Meyna's? "It won't work!" he said. "You think you'll just make a new Kai, you think—"

A blast of heat took Ahkio off his feet. He slammed against the far wall. The crowd screamed around him, and parted like a sea for Nasaka. Ahkio was suddenly sick, and vomited all over the floor. Fire. Why was it always fire?

Nasaka strode past the crowd, pulling her willowthorn sword from the sheath at her side.

"Stop! Nasaka!" Etena came down the steps, one hand held high. How had Nasaka found her after all this time? Even with Meyna's direction, it should have been impossible. Etena had stayed hidden because she didn't want the seat any more than he had.

Ahkio coughed. His eyebrows were singed. He scrambled to his feet and tried to keep his head about him. The memories were pouring back – his mother, the fire, Kirana's arms pulling him to safety in the Dorinah camp…Nasaka's expression now was fearful, not angry. But fear was worse.

Etena caught up to Nasaka and grabbed at her tunic.

Nasaka turned stiffly and ran her through, then set her on fire.

Etena burst into flame, like some horrible specter come to life.

Ahkio screamed, screamed like he had the day in the camps, and for the first time he questioned who had really started the fire that killed his mother. Was it really the Dorinah legionnaires? Or someone with a far more intimate knowledge of what fire could do? Oma's breath, he thought, she made me a puppet from the day I was born.

He ran into the foyer. People screamed and scattered. He slid around the banister and went up the scullery stair, taking the steps two at a time. He had no idea where to go – just away, away, as far and as fast as he could.

He smelled smoke. He was sick again on the stairs.

Ahkio pushed into a door on the fourth floor, hoping he shut it fast enough that Nasaka didn't know what floor he came out on. He looked for a place to hide, and then wondered at the absurdity of that. Hide from her until when? Until some other sinajista dared to face her? Until the Tai Mora came?

He ran down the hall. These were the rooms for the novices and they stretched out across this whole floor of the temple. In a fit of inspiration, Ahkio ducked through the door to the latrine and pressed himself against the wall just inside. There was a bank of four stone seats under which flowed a steady stream of water.

Ahkio ran to the latrine and looked down. He could probably fit. He'd lost weight like everyone else, but even so navigating those dark, filthy tunnels all the way down to the sewer dregs would be dangerous. He turned around and yanked the door open to run again – just as Nasaka strode down the hall. He slammed the door.

Too late. Too late by far.

Ahkio backed up against the wall. He was out of ideas. He heard Nasaka's footsteps outside.

She opened the door, and came in sword first.

"Why not wait for the Tai Mora to kill me for you?" he asked.

She pointed her sword at him. Her expression – he

thought she would look mad, but no, it was the same expression she always wore – grim certainty. Absolute faith.

"Etena," he said. "Why call Etena from the woodlands?"

Nasaka shook her head. "You aren't real," she said.

"What?"

Nasaka swung at him.

Ahkio ducked. He tried to get around her, but she was well trained, and he was unarmed. The sword caught him in the side, and ripped open a great gash.

He stumbled and grabbed at his side.

She raised her weapon.

Ahkio punched his head into her stomach, ramming her against the wall. She swung again. Caught his arm.

Ahkio hit the floor. Blood gushed from his right arm. Soaked his sleeve.

"Nasaka, please, this is… a mistake…"

"They killed you," she said. "My real son. You're some imposter. Liaro said you were different after you came back from the basements. I can see that now."

"I'm not, Nasaka. I never was. Please." He grabbed her wrist with his left hand, trying to take some control over her weapon. His wounds burned, but fear and adrenaline burned brighter.

She kicked him in the gut and swung.

He rolled away, but not fast enough. The weapon bit into his leg and cut deep. She swung again. He screamed and yanked himself forward. She took off his left leg at the thigh.

Ahkio shrieked. Blood gushed, so much blood he swooned and crumpled on the floor. His vision swam, and ran to black at the edges.

Nasaka appeared above him, holding his leg. She threw it down the latrine.

"Nasaka…" he said. "Mother, please–"

The last thing he saw was the blazing purple light of her weapon swinging for his head.

53

Taigan sat on the roof of the boarding house, staring out at the spinning spire of Sina in the dawn sky. The sky turned a blushing lavender as the double suns broke across the horizon. Unlike Para, Sina rose before the suns, and set just after them. It amused her to read the tomes of astronomers desperate to understand why the divine satellites did not adhere to a strict, regular path the way the heavenly bodies did. They were not fixed things, the astronomers said, but visitors from someplace else, the divine realm, thrust through the seams between things at uneven intervals. The powers they brought with them were equally unpredictable.

She smoked a Tordinian cigarette, a rare luxury now, and wondered how the battle went in Dhai, or if she had already missed it. It had been weeks since she was pulled back here to Anjoliaa, weeks waiting for the Tai Mora army. She thought she could see the first sign of them now, in the very far distance. The smoke of cooking fires. Far more interesting, however, were the tears in the sky. Along the western horizon she saw broad ripples. As she watched, one tore open to reveal a bloody amber sky on the other side. She called Oma, and the breath that flowed beneath her skin came more easily and with more intensity than it ever had. Stargazers could predict little. She tracked Oma's rise by how easy it came to her. Not long, now.

The window behind her opened. Maralah said, "We're leaving."

Taigan crawled back into the window, and dropped to the floor. Maralah and Kovaas were there, both looking very clean and overdressed.

"Twenty minutes," Kovaas said, and gave Maralah a little bow. He picked up a pack and left them.

Taigan put out the cigarette on the window frame and preserved the butt of it in her coat pocket. The weather had warmed considerably, but even this far south, there was still a chill in the air at sunrise and sunset.

"What is my task?" Taigan asked.

"You're to stay in this room until tomorrow morning."

Taigan raised her brows. They'd begun to grow back, darker and thicker this time. They nearly met over her eyes now. "And then?"

"And then you'll know what to do."

"You could have told me that before I put out my cigarette." More long distance messages, then, playing runner to whatever strange scheme she was up to now. Did she plan a final stand? Taigan hoped so. She had listened to her and Kovaas fucking the last few weeks, and knew something about her had changed. She no longer looked like a walking corpse, a dead person with no family, no hope. Taigan wondered what it felt like.

"Those are vile things," Maralah said.

"It's not as if it will kill me."

"No," Maralah said. She turned on her heel. "Until tomorrow morning."

"Are you leaving me money to eat, at least?"

"The proprietor has been paid in advance for your meals and your room. But only until morning." She hesitated at the door. Glanced back at her, mouth partly open, as if she wanted to give one last order, one final piercing comment. But she did not. She stepped through the door and left Taigan alone.

Taigan went back onto the roof. She spent her day watching the sky, and the approach of the Tai Mora army. They were another day, perhaps two, out, but the city was broiling. Some were shoring up their houses, but many more had left. Only the very stupid or the very desperate stayed – the elderly, the infirm, the stubborn. Watching a city preparing for an army was like watching them prepare for a natural disaster, an imminent storm far too big for them to understand.

She spent the evening in the main tea house playing a game of screes with a very old man whose beard was stark white. She had played screes with Lilia a few times, but it was the first she had seen it in Saiduan. She supposed Anjoliaa, being a port city, was most likely to have picked up the game. The pieces were arranged on a square, checkered board. Twelve white pieces in the middle, twenty-four black pieces arranged around the edges. It was easy to see the lesson in it – the white pieces had to win by outmaneuvering a much larger force that surrounded them on all sides, as if in an ambush. Taigan had had enough of being ambushed, so she played the black pieces, and the old man played the white. She admitted to herself early on that she was not good at the game as the white pieces began to trump hers, one after another. The game was not one of attrition, which she thought was interesting. Instead, the goal for white was to move the tall white Leader piece to one of the corner squares on the board without being overtaken by a black piece. Taigan's goal was simply to eliminate the Leader piece by boxing it in on all sides with her superior number of black pieces.

Taigan lost the first game, and the second. As dusk fell and the proprietor came around with some watery soup and weak tea, they began a third game. They were the last two people in the tea house. The old man was another boarder.

As Taigan sipped her tea and surveyed the board she understood why this was Lilia's favorite game. It was not about superior numbers, but isolating one piece. If you isolated just one piece, even if it meant sacrificing all of your own pieces, you would win the game. It was all about the Leader piece.

Taigan nearly dropped her cup. The game. Lilia's game.

The realization came over her so suddenly that it made her a little giddy. Without her power, Lilia was just a strategist. A smart strategist would play the game that would best topple the board. She could play white – outnumbered, but sacrificing all to save the Leader piece. That was a good strategy for the Saiduan, it was the game Maralah had tried to play, but it wasn't very Dhai. If Lilia was playing to win, she would play to put herself next to Kirana. She would box her in. She would play to capture the Leader piece, and watch the rest fall.

That was the moment Taigan felt the ward that had bound her for over a decade break.

She let out a huff of air. Spilled her tea. The old man started. The wound on her back went ice cold, then – nothing. She felt no pull, no push, no heavy gauze around her thinking or her gift and the use of it. It was as if she were lighter. Freer.

Taigan set down her tea. Placed both hands on the table.

"You will lose the third," the old man said. His Leader piece was just two places from the corner square.

Either Maralah was dead, or she had released Taigan voluntarily. Taigan bet on dead, knowing what waited for them outside the gates. But she was not going to waste her newfound freedom finding out.

She stood. "I concede," she said.

The old man grunted. "Poor loser."

"I don't believe in losing," Taigan said, and went upstairs to find her weapon.

Maralah gazed out over Anjoliaa from the height of the eastern foothills. Dusk cloaked the valley. Sina was still ascendant, bathing the world in a purple glow as the moons began to rise and dominate the sky. The great satellite was larger than the largest moon, but only just, and it glowed with its own intensity, not the reflection of some other star. She held its power easily beneath her skin, with hardly a thought; the concentration required now that her star was ascendant, with her at the full capacity of her power, was negligible. From this distance she could also see the Tai Mora army on the other side of the city.

She meant to hold Taigan until morning, giving her a good head start in avoiding her, should she be eager for revenge. In her position, Maralah would have sought vengeance immediately. But as she gazed at the Tai Mora army, her resolve, for the first time in her life, faltered. It was the army they both fought. The army that had come to destroy them.

Maralah had fought it with everything she had, sacrificing everyone she cared for, even Rajavaa, to its bloody extinction. Now she stood on a hilltop with just thirty families, Kovaas beside her, leading them to some rotten, remote fishing village where she thought they could weather out the rest of the war. She wondered if the Tai Mora would hunt them down and kill them, the way her people had with the Dhai, or forget about them. Once the Tai Mora crossed over, what use was there in murdering her people? None. None at all. But she had some experience with armies used to killing. When the killing ended, one needed to have plenty of other work to keep them occupied, or they'd turn on the civilians. She had seen it a hundred times. She knew what she would do.

Maralah glanced back at the families on the ridge. They sat in the broad clearing, resting for a few minutes before the next push. They were quiet as ghosts. She and

Kovaas had spent the last week putting together this sorry little band of refugees and encouraging them to flee the city. She and Kovaas had found other sanisi in the city, and given them the location of their final destination – a remote fishing village far to the northeast, one of the early settlements routed by the Tai Mora. Why would the Tai Mora return to a place they had already burned out?

It was a place Maralah knew well, the city her daughter was born in, so many years ago, when she still thought about the future, perhaps too much. She could have ended the pregnancy, but Alaar was... himself on learning of it, and simply assigned her to a remote part of the Empire for a year, at her request. Some days she wondered why she bothered.

Maralah had not raised her, just left her with some fisher family. She had become a skull dancer in a local city temple to Oma, and died soon after it was overrun by Tai Mora. Maralah had not seen her since she was six months old. She did not miss her, not in the visceral way women often said they missed their children, but some days she missed the idea of her.

She wondered if that's all regret was, missing the idea of a thing.

"Maralah?" Kovaas took her hand.

She did not pull away.

54

Anjoliaa burned black as pitch, as if the Lord of Unmaking had rained fire from the sky.

Luna smelled it long before ze saw it, but the revelation was still shocking. When ze crested the northern hills, following the broad muddy track of the road past a massive, clawed tree, the smoke seemed to rise up forever.

Shoratau to Anjoliaa had taken hir five weeks. If high summer had come later, ze would have frozen out there. Shoratau to Harajan nearly ended hir. At one point ze hadn't eaten for nine days. But the Tai Mora had cut a broad swath of destruction from Harajan to Anjoliaa, and ze was able to pick through what they left behind. Though the armies were hungry, Luna had the advantage of knowing where many people hid their foodstuffs. Homes burned, but the simple root cellars surrounding the remains generally stayed hidden under melting snow and mud. Hir feet were bruised, and ze knew ze'd lost at least a couple of toes. Ze hoped it wasn't more.

From this distance Luna saw the tangled ruin of the city stretching on and on, all the way to the harbor. Two tall ships lay smoking there, and ze could see three more sturdy ships in the distance, whether Tai Mora ships or foreign ones assessing the damage, ze was uncertain.

Anjoliaa was supposed to be the last intact harbor in the south, Luna's only way off the continent for hundreds of miles. Back in Harajan ze thought ze'd beat the army there by at least a week. But hunger and illness had gotten the best of hir, and that left hir standing here in the muddy tracks of an army that had burned the city below and was now nowhere in sight. Ze saw no camp outside the city, and no movement inside it.

Luna stopped at the edge of the road. Ze carried a stout walking stick to help steady hir. The frostbitten foot no longer hurt, but made it difficult to walk. The road ze had followed since passing by Kuonrada – also burned out and empty now – went another forty paces ahead, then met a massive sea of muddy tracks at least half a mile wide. The muddy churn flowed from the top of the rise all the way into the city, as if some massive beast or force had plummeted from the sky and onto the hill, then run screaming into the city.

A warm wind buffeted hir, pushing up from the sea. Ze picked hir way forward. Ze had come too far to stop.

As ze descended toward the city, ze saw a party of three figures coming from a copse of trees about three quarters of a mile distant. Ze paused to assess them. They looked tall and tattered from here. They didn't have mounts. Refugees. Ze shifted hir route so ze angled further away from them, heading toward another part of the city. When they shifted their course, too, ze walked a little faster.

They began to run.

Fear knotted hir belly. Ze had no cover out here, and only the stick to ward them off. Luna glanced behind hir at the broad, scaly tree ze had passed.

Luna scrabbled across the muddy ground, making for the tree. Hir pursuers gained. Ze hurried faster.

They neared. Luna heard the slap of mud. Hir breath sounded loud, so loud. Ze could not feel hir feet. They felt like two wooden blocks at the ends of hir legs, propelling hir forward. If Luna fell ze would break.

Ze slipped once and found hir balance. Fingers tangled into hir coat. Ze slid out of it. The cool air struck hir. Ze stumbled. Clawed for the tree.

There were no branches within hir reach. So ze launched hirself at the trunk of the tree and jumped, stretching hir arms and fingers like a bird about to take flight.

Hir hands found the branch. Ze crawled up. Hir first pursuer grabbed Luna's shoe. Ze kicked out of it and climbed higher. Luna was smaller, lighter. Ze climbed. Higher and higher, until the slippery yellow branches bent dangerously under hir weight.

Below hir, hir pursuer had slowed. The two men on the ground yelled encouragement.

The branch beneath the man bent. He reached for Luna's bare foot. "Maggot!" the man said.

Luna kicked the hand away. Crushed his fingers.

The man lost his balance.

The branch snapped. He pinwheeled his arms and fell.

He fell with a bloody thump to the ground below. His companions went to him, calling, "Rasaa, Rasaa!"

His leg was bent unnaturally beneath him. Luna saw the broken white bone poking up through his knee.

The two men gazed up at Luna. One yelled, "We're coming back and burning you out, maggot!"

One of the men went off, back toward the burning city. That worried Luna more than anything, because it meant there were more than three men. They most likely meant to sell hir, after they did whatever it was with hir that amused them. Now that one of them was injured, they would be angrier, and Luna knew all about what angry people did to those they had power over.

Luna listened to the man wailing below. He wailed for a long time. The sun moved across the sky, low. The days lasted much longer now; if ze was further north, it wouldn't truly get dark, just fade to dusk for a few hours each day. Winter in Saiduan. Ze wondered if ze would ever see one again.

Hir thoughts drifted. Roh yelling, face perfect and beautiful, even pinched in hunger, hair greasy after weeks without washing. Brave, confident, yes, but confidence that made him so very stupid. He had never been owned. He didn't know what he was giving up. Pressing the book into Luna's hands. Wide eyes, and fear, yes, but the confidence was still there, the belief that death was for other people, not for him.

Luna's heart hurt.

The tree shook.

Luna jerked hir head up, realizing with a surge of icy fear that ze had started to nod off. Hir arms and shoulders hurt; hir legs ached. The two men were still there. The uninjured one had settled against the trunk. He no longer looked up at Luna, but out toward the city where his friend had gone.

Luna huffed out a little breath. Ze gazed down the length of the trunk, and found a clear path through the bare branches to the man's head, thirty feet below. Luna took one stiff arm away from the tree trunk and grabbed the utility knife at hir belt. Hesitated. If ze waited until dark, the man might bed down under the tree, giving hir a greater chance of stabbing him somewhere vital instead of just angering him. But his friend might return by then.

Ze pulled the knife. Got a line of sight on the man's head. Ze began to uncurl from the tree, shifting as quietly as ze could.

Falling was going to hurt.

Luna dropped the knife.

In the next breath, ze released hirself from the tree trunk and fell after it.

Ze banged into branch after branch, slipped and slid, hanging just long enough at each level to break hir fall. The man below shouted.

Luna landed on him. Luna grabbed the man around the neck with both arms and squeezed. Ze put hir legs around the man's torso. Hung tight.

The man roared. Blood gushed from a wound on his head. The knife had grazed his skull. Luna saw the knife in the grass and squeezed harder. The man was bigger, stronger, but like Luna, he was hungrier and leaner than he should be, tired, and Luna had the advantage of surprise.

Ze held on. Whenever the man breathed out, Luna gripped tighter. The man clawed at Luna's arms. Smacked hir into the tree. Luna leaned forward, over the man's shoulder, so he couldn't hit Luna's head against the tree.

The man stumbled. Fell to his knees.

Squeeze. Hold on.

Do you want to be someone's flesh again, bound to another?

Squeeze.

The man's fingers found the knife.

Luna felt hot, sharp pain in hir left shoulder. Ze turned his face away, to the right.

Squeeze.

Luna saw a vein on his shorn head throbbing, throbbing. Heard the wheezing. Pulled tighter.

The man collapsed.

Still, Luna hung on.

Ze held the man tight while he twitched, held him close until the fight left his body, the muscles relaxed, until the man became meat.

Luna released him. Hir arms were stiff. Ze rolled off the body. Grabbed and sheathed the knife. Ze crawled a good distance from the body and caught hir breath. The injured man lay another few paces away. He had shouted himself hoarse, and now lay silent. If he dared move, the ruined leg beneath him would shift.

Leave him or kill him?

Luna pulled the coat from the body and replaced hir

own with it, though it was much too big. Ze used the man's belt to knot it securely around hir. Took the man's pack. Found some food, fire-making tools, more than ze had owned in weeks.

As ze threw the pack over hir shoulder, ze heard a muffled thumping behind hir, and turned just in time to see the dark form of a bear rider cresting up over the rise.

Luna ran the other direction, away from Anjoliaa and up the coast. Ze might lose him in the trees there, ze might–

Luna tripped. Fell headfirst on the muddy ground. Mud filled hir nose and mouth.

The rider caught hir by the collar of the massive coat and pulled hir up.

Luna yanked out the knife, and waved it at him.

"Luna?"

The rider was tall and lean, hair butchered to shoulder length, knotted against his scalp in braids. He wore a long black tunic and leather trousers under a dog hair coat. Luna hardly recognized him, even swinging from his grip.

"...Kadaan?" Luna whispered.

"Where is Roh?"

Kadaan lowered Luna to the ground. Luna panicked. Would he leave Luna here, if Roh wasn't with hir?

"The Tai Mora have him," Luna said. "He told me to bring the book to Dhai."

"The book? You lost Roh, but not the book?"

Luna started to pull off the too-big coat.

"Don't," Kadaan said. He glanced back at the dead and injured men near the tree. "Their friend is just behind me, with three more. Pushed into a tavern saying he had a Dhai up a tree, maybe a Tai Mora. They will eat you if you stay."

"How did–"

"Come with me."

Luna bent at the knee, and made an awkward attempt

at the two-fingered salute of subservience.

Kadaan caught hir up again, and pulled hir up on the bear behind him. "No time for that," he said.

Kadaan circled the bear around the other side of the tree and took off toward the coast. They rode all the way to the beach, where the sea had carved out great caves. Luna saw people down on the beach. When the walkers caught sight of them, they scurried back into the caves.

"Who are they?" Luna asked.

"Refugees from the city. A few were able to flee ahead of the army."

"Were you here?"

"No, I was staying in the city. What is left of it."

"How did you know–"

"I put out word I was looking for two Dhai traveling from the north. One of my runners said a man burst into a tavern saying he had a Tai Mora up a tree. I believed that highly unlikely."

"Are there no Tai Mora in the city? Where did they go?"

"They used gates," Kadaan said.

"This far south?"

"Oma is rising. I suspect they can do what they want, now. Who knows where the army is, now?"

"Why did you wait, Kadaan?"

He did not answer.

"There's no use going into the city," Kadaan said. "I heard Aaldian and Tordinian ships have come by this beach the last two nights."

"Payment?"

"Expensive, but not set. They'll take whatever we have of value."

"We don't have anything of value."

"I'll speak to them."

Luna slept and ate, curled in a tiny uninhabited cave, more like a divot in the stone, one of the few that offered a buffer from the wind that wasn't occupied. Kadaan woke hir at midnight, which rolled in with the tide.

He led Luna down to the waiting rowboat. Luna trembled, listening to the men haggle with the shivering families on the beach. Jewelry and coins traded hands, and when there were not jewelry or coins, Luna saw parents sobbing over their young children, then turning around, shaking their heads. No, they would rather stay here than give over their children as slaves. Luna's heart raced.

The big man beckoned Kadaan over. Luna hung back, watching the Aaldian man speaking. He gestured at Kadaan, then back at Luna. Luna stared at Kadaan and wondered what terrible bargain Kadaan would make, now, to ensure the book went to Dhai. When Kadaan glanced back at Luna, Luna lost hir nerve, and turned away. Ze ran across the rocky beach.

"Luna!"

The rowboat, the mix of Saiduan accents, the sound of Aaldian, the smell of the sea.

Kadaan caught hir. Grabbed hir around the waist. "Luna! Where–"

"I won't go! You won't sell me!"

"Luna, stop. No one's selling anything. You want to get to Dhai? Luna!"

"You're a liar!"

Kadaan pinned hir against the ground. The stone bit into Luna's shoulders. Hir heart pounded. Hir whole body shook. The smell of the sea, the sound of Saiduan…

"Enough." Kadaan held hir arms. "They'll take my weapon, Luna. My infused weapon, in exchange for your passage. Do you understand? You are free. Free to go to Dhai. Deliver the stupid book. Understand?"

Luna stopped struggling. "I'm not a fool. Just tell me."

"I've told you. You want freedom? This is freedom. You'll be alone, you understand? You get on that boat, and you're alone. The blade is only good for one passage, though it's worth an estate. They have us at their mercy."

Kadaan's grip eased. Luna sat up.

"You hear me, Luna?"

"Yes."

"The harbor in Dhai is closed. The Tai Mora have invaded. But this ship is going to Dorinah. From there you'll need to get to Dhai."

"I can't go to Dorinah. The Dhai are slaves there, too."

"The only other option is Aaldia, then. They're traveling from Dorinah to Aaldia."

"Then I go there. I can find a way to Dhai from there."

"You won't know the language. You'll have no money–"

"I'll find a way."

"You'll be alone, Luna."

Luna met his look. "I have always been alone, Kadaan. Don't you know that?"

Kadaan stood. Held out his hand. "Let me put a ward on you, at least."

"What kind? I can't be bound–"

"Not that kind. A ward of protection. It will help protect you against the gifted arts. All right?"

"For Roh?"

Kadaan waved a hand at hir. "Does it matter?"

"That's why you're not going, isn't it? You waited here for Roh."

"If I find Roh and I tell him I abandoned you here, what would he think of me?"

"Set the ward," Luna said. Hir heart clenched. Luna could not imagine anyone ever loving hir so much as to travel over a thousand miles to find hir.

A few words, a wave of Kadaan's hands, and the ward was set. Luna's skin prickled. Then Kadaan led hir back to the Aaldian rowboat.

Luna watched Kadaan unsheathe his glowing blue weapon and hand it over to the second man in the boat, this one stouter than the first. The man murmured something over it, and nodded. The other beckoned to Luna.

Luna climbed into the rowboat with four other refugees, the only ones able to pay the price.

Kadaan stood on a rocky spur a few paces away and watched as they pushed off. The moons were out. The night was bright. So Luna knew Kadaan watched all the way across the water, until the rowboat met the side of the great Aaldian ship. Luna climbed up after the others. When ze got to the top of the deck and gazed back, Kadaan was gone.

55

Anavha recovered from his injury in Coryana's house outside Gasira. He bled badly, but she said there was very little true damage. Her worst fear was infection. She packed his wound with honey and lemon juice and some other terrible things just to be certain.

Natanial had picked him up after punching Zezili senseless, and said he was taking Anavha to the infirmary, but he didn't. He rolled Anavha into the back of a bear-pulled cart and paid a boy to take him to Coryana's.

"Be quiet and wait for me." The last thing Natanial said to him.

Days dragged into weeks, and summer brought with it heat and muggy days. News came from the north that Saradyn's army had suffered a terrible loss. The rumors caused unrest in the town, and Coryana made it clear through her gestures and the limited number of words they both knew in one another's languages that she didn't want him to go far. He worked with her in the garden, and practiced his concentration exercises in the afternoon. In the evening, he wrote poetry, and though Coryana understood none of it, she nodded as he spoke, and smiled like one of Zezili's sisters humoring him.

The day Tanays, Saradyn's second-in-command, declared himself king of the region, Anavha sat out on the stoop with Coryana drinking sugar water and watching red birds flit through the forest canopy. He could stay here and wait for Natanial forever, or for Zezili, or for Tanays to find him, or Saradyn – if he still lived. His whole life had been here, sitting on this porch, waiting for someone to tell him what to do.

That night, he said goodbye to Coryana and thanked her for her kindness, and she nodded and smiled like she knew what he was saying and tucked him into bed like a child.

Anavha waited until she had put out the lights and the moons had risen. Then he rose from his bed, packed the few clothes and books and papers he had traded for, and walked into the middle of the garden, barefoot. He carried his shoes in one hand. He wanted to feel the dirt under his toes one last time.

Then he opened a door.

Tordinian poetry, not beautiful, but what it unlocked in his mind was lovely – a path to another place, another life. He peered at the sky on the other side, fearing he may have wound the snarls of Oma's light into the wrong configuration. But no, that was his sky. His moons.

And there was a little rocky path leading down to a tiled city lit with a thousand lights, all twinkling like the stars come to the ground.

He stepped through the door. The air warmed. It was hot, almost sticky out here. The drone of the insects was loud. He glanced once behind him, at Coryana's house, and saw someone on the porch.

It was Natanial.

Natanial did not move from the porch, though. Just watched him.

Anavha raised his hand. Greeting or goodbye? Both. All of it.

Natanial raised his in turn.

Anavha remembered their last day together, before Natanial went after Saradyn and the army.

"What am I supposed to be out here?" Anavha had asked. "What am I without her?"

"Power is a funny thing," Natanial said. "You get to decide what to do with it."

"The way Zezili did?"

"She made her choice. Now you get to make yours."

"I'm not... I don't... that's not who I am."

"Then don't make Zezili's choices."

Anavha released his hold on Oma, and the door between Tordin and Aaldia closed, and his past with it.

56

The sea of women descended on Saradyn like a snarling plague of field rats. He fell hard onto their bodies, buoyed by their strong arms, which reached out to rip him limb from limb – or so he believed – until he found himself carried aloft while they hissed and clicked around him. When he struggled, one of them bit his arm. Another twisted his leg. He felt the bone snap. Saradyn screamed, overcome with visions of being roasted and eaten alive by these creatures from some other world.

They carried him across the corpse-ridden field, then down and down, through the long, twisting corridors of the ziggurat.

When he saw them rip the gibbering body of the Dorinah legionnaire from the floor, Saradyn started screaming again, because he knew what they meant to do with him.

The great twisted root that connected the throne to the wall had repaired itself. It pulsed now with an eerie green light that glimmered from the pool at his feet as well as the walls. The light shimmered across the throne, and made the women's snarling faces all the more horrifying.

The women heaved him onto the great throne. It exerted a powerful force, pulling him into its grasp as they pushed him into it. His fingers gripped the arms of the throne of their own volition. He sat straight and tall, still screaming. A jolt of pain ran through him, and then there was darkness. Silence.

And from the dark and the silence, a pinprick of light. A voice.

"Saradyn, it has been too long."

He knew the voice. Knew it as he knew his own. If he still had a body he could feel, he would tremble and curse and beg her to let him be. But he was nothing, now, just a wisp of consciousness propelled by some dark force.

Saradyn gazed upon the Empress of Dorinah, her face peering into his awareness as if she peered into a mirror. Behind her was a stone wall capped by a shimmering red carpet of something organic, some living thing that was creeping toward her, slowly but relentlessly.

"I knew you could not resist my legionnaires," she said. "I knew you could not resist following. You were always so curious. I'd hoped Storm and Zezili would lead my people, but Storm was not strong enough to reign here alone. You, though? Yes, you will do."

He tried to speak, but he had no body. Yet he screamed at her, still, screamed as he had the day she cast him out of her bed and he went home to conquer his nation and prove his worth. *I WON'T.*

She smiled. "Oh, you will."

Saradyn surfaced from his fugue among the crowd of women. Were they women, even, or did he call them that only because they horrified him? He heard a great roaring above them, and high-pitched screaming from outside.

"They are burning them," the Empress said, "all they can find. But you are safe here, with those who remain. The temple protects you. Have no fear. There are more of my people here, still slumbering. We will wake them together."

Saradyn tried to claw his way off the throne. In control of his voice again, he said, "I serve no one!"

A prickling pain rode along his spine. Words bloomed in his mind, *"YOU SERVE ME."*

"No!"

He found his fist in his mouth, but had no memory of putting it there. He began to gnaw at his knuckles. He tasted his own blood. The Empress's voice crowded out his thoughts.

"Did you think you were hunting me? No, Saradyn. You are the only one who can put the people of Tordin to work for my women. You are the only one who can unite them to my purpose. And you *will serve me."*

Saradyn toppled off the throne. He let out a tangled sob, but it was still muffled by his fist in his mouth. He lay on his side in the center of the green pool as the women stood around him in a silent circle. Saradyn wept as the Empress of Dorinah compelled him to gnaw off his own arm.

57

The Aaldian ship was a living thing, like a Saiduan fortress. Luna had thought that was impossible. No Saiduan or Dhai knew how to ensoul a hold anymore, but when ze tried to ask the crew about it, they turned up their hands at hir and smiled bright white smiles. Only the man on the beach spoke Saiduan. Luna pressed hir ear to the hull at night, shoved into the packed hold of the ship with the other refugees, and listened to it breathing. The surface of the ship was spongy and slightly sticky, like undercooked bread.

Aaldians were strange people. Luna knew little about them. They left their country only to trade. They sent no travelers but those in the ships, and none of them ever stayed behind when they docked. Where they had come from, no one seemed to know. Perhaps they had always been in Aaldia, hiding from the Dhai and Dorinah and Saiduan.

They were lean, dark people with twisted hair the color of burnt wheat that they wore in tight locks, intricately woven into knotted crowns. Their sex, let alone their gender, was often difficult to tell, and Luna gave up on it. With no common language, Luna had no way to ask them what was polite or proper. Those on the ship seemed very young, for sailors. Ze did not see a single person older than thirty.

The storm came upon them suddenly, driving great curtains of rain from the northwest. Luna stood on deck when it came, heaving the contents of hir breakfast as ze had done for the last six days. The wind knocked hir back from the rail, and nearly took hir from hir feet. One of the Aaldian crew called out from the main top, and the rest of the crew took to the rigging to bring down the sails.

Luna slid below deck just as the deluge opened from the heavens. Ze clattered down the steps with a wave of water, instantly soaked. Ze ran to the long storage hold ze shared with the other refugees and pulled on hir coat. Ze huddled next to a barrel of salted fish, pressed hard against the spongy hull. Ze was still nauseous, and the rolling of the boat didn't help. Another of the refugees, a little girl called Sola, vomited her meager breakfast. Luna gagged at the smell.

Luna heard a great cracking overhead. A thump. The whole ship shuddered.

Water poured into the hold.

Luna made for the stairs. Ze got to the top just ahead of those behind hir, just as a great wave smashed into the side of the ship, sweeping hir overboard, heaving the ship over with hir.

Water embraced hir.

Come all this way, this far…

Luna gasped for air. Swallowed water. Gagged. Darkness.

Clawed for the surface.

Hir hands broke into the air.

Luna's head came up. Ze gasped. Got a mouth full of water. The waves pummeled hir. Ze splashed in the roaring sea, adrift. Saw wreckage. Paddled for a bobbing bucket. Grabbed it. The wind roared. Rain fell, nearly horizontal, like a shroud.

Ze needed a miracle, Luna knew. But Luna only had hirself.

Luna heard someone calling. Looked for the voice, nothing, but there... ze saw a shoreline. A coast. That's what it was, wasn't it? That long black bar gave the suggestion of land, a black sand beach. Ze held onto the bucket and kicked – it was futile, though. Luna was carried by the waves, buffeted, a buoy on the open water.

The book was a heavy burden. Ze shrugged out of hir coat. Ze could lose the coat, not the book. Not after all this. Not when ze was so close.

The sea fought hir.

Ze fought back.

Hours passed, though it felt like days. It had to be hours because ze saw the gray light of dawn, the burning brand of Sina piercing through the heavy cloud cover. Fog had descended sometime during the night. Luna couldn't see much past hir outstretched arm. Just hir and the bucket, floating in a borderless sea.

Ze was a ghost, unbound, and Sina would not take hir.

Five years old, six years old, when the Saiduan took hir, but ze remembered so little of it, and so little before that. Hir first memory, this flat sea, blazing hot, the water so blue, and the horizon stretching out so far it looked like a painting. One mother dead, the other gasping like a fish, so thirsty, squeezing the last bit of dewy moisture she had wiped from the inside of the boat into Luna's thirsty mouth.

Luna was too young to ask why she bothered, why she persisted, in the face of certain death for all of them. Hope. Hir mother had hope. Hope drove the world, and despair destroyed it.

Luna jerked awake, splashing.

Ze had nodded off, slipped from the bucket. Ze kicked and pawed after it in the heavy surf.

Hir legs hit something soft. Found purchase.

Luna stood on the sandy bottom. Ze clawed forward. The fog thinned, and ze saw the black sand beach of northern Grania stretching before hir. Ze slogged up onto the beach, pummeled by the surf. Luna collapsed a little ways up the beach, and crawled a few more feet forward, just out of the reach of the encroaching tide. If the tide was coming in, it meant ze would have to move at least a mile and a half more to escape the rising water, but hir exhaustion was so deep ze could not move.

Luna put hir face into the crook of hir arm and made a terrible sobbing sound. Ze shed no tears, just made the noise, shuddering there in the sand until the feeling passed and ze could begin moving up the beach.

Ze crawled and crawled as the fog cleared and the high tide line drew nearer. When ze finally collapsed, Luna had forgotten that there was anything in the world but this – struggling across the black sand to the tide line, hands scratched by black sand.

When ze woke, massive black gulls circled the sky, screaming.

"What's this?" Voices, speaking Dhai.

"Another body from a wreck. Storm must have taken several ships."

"Dhai ships? There are no Dhai in the water now. Ours?"

Luna felt someone kick hir. Ze rolled over. Two Dhai faces peered down at hir. One short and fat; the other smaller, leaner, with a meaner face.

"Ours?" the smaller one said.

The fat one crinkled up her face. "Those are Saiduan clothes." She switched languages, something that sounded very like Dhai, but wasn't. Then waited expectantly.

"Is this Dhai?" Luna said, in Dhai.

The fat one sighed. "Dhai." She pulled at a weapon on her hip.

"Wait, wait!" Luna said. Ze pushed hirself up.

"You have news for me, Dhai?" the fat one said.

"Saiduan. I have news of Saiduan."

The leaner woman laughed. "You hear that, Gaiso, she has news of Saiduan."

"I have all the news I need," the fat one, Gaiso, said. "I organized the final purge of Anjoliaa myself."

"Where am I?" Luna asked.

"Where do you think you are?" Gaiso said. "You've got yourself washed up on Dorinah, the first commonwealth of Tai Mora reborn."

Above them, something red and malevolent seethed in the sky.

58

Nasaka did not believe in losing. She never had. It was why, when Kai Javia's second child died just days after birth, Nasaka made the decision to give up her own child to Javia and her Catori – Nasaka's brother Rishin. Javia's elder daughter Kirana, a favorite for the seat, was in poor health. Kirana had been sickly from the moment she was born, and they needed another child to ensure the line of the Kai remained unbroken, at least in the eyes of the people. Tir and his family in Garika were already making noise about Javia being unfit to rule. But Javia was, Nasaka thought, more malleable than Etena. Etena knew too much about the coming invasion. So even if it caused some strife, Nasaka convinced Javia to have Etena exiled.

So many people. So many pieces. And for what? To preserve the peace of Dhai. To ensure the existence of a country built on principles the rest of the world thought were unreasonable. But if you were committed to an ideal, you gave everything for it, and Nasaka had, time and again. She preserved Dhai at all costs, even when it meant turning her back on the very ideals she supported. Someone needed to make the hard choices. Someone needed to do the killing, the manipulating, the threatening, to save the others from those things.

She was obligated to wear that mantle, and she wore it proudly, if heavily, every day of her life.

She wore it now, as she looked across the advancing Tai Mora armies stretching across the plateau. She had manufactured this. She was part of this. But it was because of her that any would survive. If Ahkio had gotten his way... Ahkio...

She pressed her fists to her eyes. Etena dead, Ahkio cut to pieces and dumped down the latrine, Mohrai overwhelmed in Kuallina; that left just one final player for the seat of the Kai that she had to eliminate before the new Kirana called her debt repaid, and allowed Nasaka and the few she had chosen to live in the new Dhai she had planned.

Nasaka cleared her eyes and took a long breath. She already had several people out looking for Meyna. How had she escaped the temple when Nasaka burned her way up from the basements, Nasaka was uncertain, but she would be dealt with.

A creaking sound came from behind her. Odd, as Pasinu would have announced herself. She turned–

And a knife plunged into her left breast.

Nasaka gasped, so shocked at the surge of pain she reeled backwards.

"My child," Meyna said.

Nasaka's lips moved in a litany. Meyna stabbed her again.

Nasaka fell hard. She saw her own blood flowing across the floor, fast as that from a gutted pig. She had seen one once, in the woodland, when they fed the blood of a boar to the thorn fence. The blood was thick and black.

"You nearly killed me, my child, you horror!"

Blood flecked Nasaka's lips. She gurgled and grinned, and her chest heaved. Trying to call Sina, but the pain came again and again, breaking her concentration, the knife stabbing and stabbing, throwing bloody flecks across Meyna's face.

Meyna had not run. She had hidden here, in Nasaka's study, for just this moment. Nasaka admired it. It was something she would have done.

"Formidable woman," Nasaka said. "Should have been Kai."

Meyna's hand came down fiercely, *thwack, thwack, thwack*.

Nasaka tasted copper. Meyna was sobbing and yelling. Nasaka could not make sense of the words she spoke; gibberish, rants, anger... The world began to bleed to black.

Nasaka lay on her side as Meyna withdrew. She heard noise in the hall. Shouting as the army arrived, and Nasaka's supporters uncovered and eradicated the small groups of resisters. Meyna breathed heavily. Tears and sweat soaked her face and her tunic. She wiped her bloody, drool-smeared chin with her trembling hand.

Meyna hissed at her. Hers was the last face Nasaka saw, and the last words she ever heard.

"Curse you," Meyna said, "and everything you built."

59

Rohinmey.

He had not heard his full name aloud in a very long time. Since arriving in Caisau not one person had used any version of his name. They called him boy, or scraps, or nothing at all.

Roh descended into inky blackness until he lost all sense of time. His knees ached. He paused to rest often. Finally, he came to the end of the long descent, and paused before a great door inscribed with a symbol – six circles traversed by a triangle. He raised his lantern, and saw writing in living green text circling the doorway. It glowed eerily.

He looked for a knob or a latch, but saw nothing. Roh came up to the door and pressed his hand to it. It opened easily, as if made of nothing but air. The great portal yawned open. He smelled honeysuckle and lavender. A brilliant blue light suffused the room. He shielded his eyes.

"Welcome, Patron."

Roh walked into the room, trying to make out shapes in the blue light, but saw nothing.

"I'm not the Patron," Roh said. "I'm Rohinmey Tadisa Garika." It felt good to say it aloud. He had a name. A purpose. "You're the creature of Caisau," he said.

"I've been called many things." Tinkling laughter. He kept trying to see something in the blue light, but it was like looking into a star.

"If I am a creature, you are a Patron," the voice said.

Roh remembered the slaughter in the tower room in Kuonrada. He remembered picking up the blazing weapon from the floor, hurling it at the Patron, and pinning him to the wall. "By law, you're Patron," Kadaan had said. And no one was to know. But Caisau knew.

"Who says I am?" Roh asked.

"I am the keeper of Caisau," it said.

"The creature."

"That sounds so dangerous," it said. "You must give me a name."

"You don't have one? Then you're a creature."

"Is that how it works? Those without names are creatures? Well, I cannot argue. It's how you have traversed through me, all this time, a nameless piece of meat. What do I know of your culture? Perhaps this is all normal. All things pass on, in time."

"You've been talking to me," Roh said.

"You've been talking to *me*," it said. "They have poked and prodded, but there are rules, are there not? I have been bound by many rules. I was bound to the Kai before the Saiduan, but when the Saiduan came they bound me to the Patron, but soon they, too, forgot about me. What am I? No one cares to know until the end of all things."

"The Kai spoke to you when this was still Roasandara," Roh said. "Why couldn't she turn things back? Why couldn't she stop it? I read her journals."

"The world broke before she could get to the transference engines."

"What are those? Is that how we keep people from other worlds from coming here? Can we stop it? The Tai Mora think you can stop it."

"Not from here."

"From where, then?"

"At the center of the world there are five temples..."
A blazing map appeared in the air above Roh. He hopped
back, banging his knee. Pain shot up his leg.

The map painted itself in the air in green and gray,
like a parajista-trained illusion. Roh had been learning
to build those, before he left the temple. He saw a
strange continent. The top half looked like Saiduan,
but the bottom was something else. It wasn't until the
map unfurled, pressed itself into his vision, that he
recognized Mount Ahya, the spur of the plateau where
Oma's Temple rested, and the mountain borders of Dhai.
But in this map, Dhai was not part of the island called
Grania at the tip of the Saiduan continent. It was *part of
the continent.*

"There are four temples in Dhai," Roh said. "Not five."

"That is unfortunate," the creature said. The map
winked out.

Roh started. "What, is that all? That's all you have to
say? It's unfortunate?"

"The world broke," it said. "I cannot see all futures."

"How do we work the transference engines?"

"You will need a guide," the creature said, and its
voice sounded close now, right in his ear. He flinched.

A warm breath of air moved over him, sending a shiver
through his body. "You are that guide now, Patron."

"I don't understand."

"The creature on the plateau will know you," it said.
"Step into her circle, and the map will unfold. You carry
the map now. You are the guide."

"I can't get back to Dhai," Roh said.

"That is unfortunate."

The blue glow around him stuttered, like a disturbed
lantern of flame flies.

"Please," Roh said, "say something I can understand."

"Five parajistas, five omajistas, five tirajistas, five
sinajistas – one of each to power the great hearts of the

creatures there at the center of the world. Then you need a guide, a key, and a worldbreaker."

"And I'm the guide? Who are the others?"

"That is for the other creatures to decide," it said. "I have done my part."

The light went out.

Roh stood in the darkness, cold and alone. He raised the lantern and saw that inside, the room was just cold stone, unadorned.

"Wait!" Roh said. "How do I get to Dhai?"

The voice, tickling his ear, thrumming through the walls. "Most people walk."

Then silence.

Roh yelled, "All this way I've come, for riddles! All this way, and we're going to die, and you don't care. You didn't care when we died the first time. So what use are you! What use are any of you?"

He hit the skin of the hold with his crutch. The crutch sank through it, like butter.

Roh gasped, yanked it back.

He pressed his hand to the wall. The skin of it became pliable in his hands.

"Where in my hold do you wish to go, Patron?" the creature whispered. Tickling breath.

"The dormitory," he said.

"Then step through."

Roh had taken many things on faith. This was one more.

He stepped through the skin of the hold – and into the far end of his dormitory, coming through the wall as if the spaces between things were nothing. Roh hurried to the privy and took off his stolen clothes. It was nearly daylight already and someone might have seen him. He pulled off all the Tai Mora clothes and stuffed them down the latrines. Washed his face.

He limped back to his bed, knowing there were eyes on him, so many eyes. Roh slipped into bed, pulled the sheet over his head, and lay very, very still.

The creature's laughter still moved through the walls.

"Can you take me to Dhai?" Roh whispered.

"Only through the seams between things here," it said, "and any other living engine you may encounter. Alas, the rest is up to you."

He lay awake still when the morning gong sounded. He raised himself from bed, dressed and smoothed his bed flat and washed his face again. He went through it all like some kind of dream.

They came for him three hours later, when he sat at his desk working on another series of translations. He had barely gotten through a page.

"Come with us." It was one of the other translation administrators.

Roh rose slowly. "I need to see Dasai," he said.

"I'll decide who you need to see."

"It's very important."

"I'm sure."

As they led him out, every pair of eyes in the room looked up at his passing. Roh wanted to raise his voice and tell them to fight, wanted to tell them the Tai Mora were finished, that their time was running out, that if they all fought together, they could overwhelm them. But that would ruin everything he planned, and cause a disturbance that would ruin him as surely as it would ruin them.

"Tell Dasai I remember the story about the dancing," Roh said. "You tell him that."

A fake. A shot in the dark. That's all he had now, though – darkness.

They put him in a holding room.

He knew the punishment for fornication.

He had yet to see the punishment for murder.

The administrator came back some time later. Roh raised his head, hopeful. The man punched Roh in the face.

Roh fell over. He hit the floor hard. The man kicked him four more times, and put a heavy foot into Roh's face. Roh's teeth loosened. He spit blood.

The administrator leered over him. "That was for Korloria," He said. "The rest can wait."

Two guards hauled him out of the cell. He was too weak to walk. They dragged him down a series of steps. He spit again. Two of his teeth rattled onto the steps. He probed the gap left behind – the canine and incisor on his left side.

Pretty, they all said. He looked forward to the day he was no longer pretty.

He tried not to think what they would do with him. He stared at the walls of the hold as he passed, and he thought he heard twinkling laughter. But all the creature had given him was the ability to move through the hold. He could not walk to Dhai. He could barely get up and down stairs.

A hot, muggy blast of air hit his face. He gazed into the great atrium, bathed in yellow light. He saw the winking face of Sina there on the eastern horizon, and pulled his gaze away, already dazzled. Summer had peaked some time before; he had hardly noted its passing inside the walls, but with the nearing of autumn he could see now that the way the sun moved in the sky was changing. The days were already growing shorter again.

Dasai lay at the end of a meandering path of red stones, lounging on a hammock. He raised his head as Roh approached, and folded his book onto his chest. The woman with the lopsided face sat on a living bench opposite him, legs crossed, tracing something on a printed paper.

The guards dropped Roh in front of Dasai. Roh stumbled, trying to keep his feet as needles of pain shot through his legs.

"Dancing?" Dasai said.

"Your story," Roh said.

"Do tell me."

Roh shook his head. "I needed to see you."

"The man you knew is not me," Dasai said.

"I know," Roh said.

Dasai sat up. "It's true I knew a boy like you," Dasai said. "He is dead, alas, or I'd have killed you when I first set eyes on you, because he was a far fiercer boy. He would not have ended his days here."

"I really am related to the Kai," Roh lied. "You were right. I know how to work the transference engines, but you have to take me to Dhai."

Dasai sighed. "And why would I do that?"

Roh got down to his knees, painfully. He pressed his head to the floor. The pain was so bad he thought he might pass out. He hissed out the words – "Because the creature of Caisau wills it. You read the journals. You know it was once tropical here. The land stretched from here to Hrollief without a sea between it. Grania was not an island, it was the heart of the continent. What did that? Oma. The rise of Oma. The breaking of the world. It's coming for us too. You want to stop it. So do I."

Roh raised his head.

But Dasai was not looking at him. He was looking up at the great height of the atrium, mouth agape. The woman beside him turned her head away, and suddenly the room was bathed in a bloody red light.

Roh raised his head and stared up at the heavens. A baleful red eye stared down at him, like the eye of a god, a great gory world-breaking god.

Roh heard the creature laugh.

60

Lilia left Gian's side and ran from the rush of the army after Sina's rise. She fell into a massive tent. It collapsed on her. She wrapped herself in it, willing herself still and silent so she could prepare for what she had to do next.

Heat scorched the air outside. Sweat slathered her body. But she waited. Quiet.

Boots. Blasts of hot air. Yelling armies. She waited for silence outside, counting the beats of her heart. When the waiting got to be too much, she palmed a piece of mahuan root and let her mind wander.

Finally, the din wore down.

She crawled from the stifling tent and peeked out. The plain was churned with mud. A small child watched her from a tent opposite – too-big eyes in a starved face. Lilia pressed her finger to her lips.

When she staggered up and took in the measure of the camp, it was mostly empty. The big banquet table was a mess, scorched in places. Gian's body still lay there, smoldering. Her hair, her beautiful hair, had been burned away, the scalp charred. Lilia felt nothing at all, as if her heart had been burned away with Gian's hair.

Lilia walked across the devastated camp. It still smoked in places. Her people had gotten off a few good gouts of flame before being overrun. She glanced back at Kuallina only once. She did not linger to watch it burn. The massive Tai Mora army had already exploded through the gates, and now they were merely cleaning up. Smoke rose from the keep.

She felt a hot, needling pain in her side, and scratched at it. It took her a moment to realize what it was. She tugged at the wards she had on the Seekers and found – nothing. The Seekers had already perished. She was alone.

Lilia stumbled across the camp and made for the trees. There was more burning to come, and she was its catalyst.

On the other side of the camp, Tasia waited for her in the creek bed, still and silent as a cat. There was a dirty, snuffling figure beside her. Lilia recoiled.

"Where did you find that?" Lilia asked.

It was the feral girl who had followed Ghrasia around Liona, now curled up in a ball next to Tasia.

"She saved me," Tasia said. "I got lost trying to find you like you asked me to, but she led me here. She found the bear. I couldn't hold it myself. I was afraid."

Lilia frowned. The feral girl raised her head, cocked it in Lilia's direction. "You're a filthy thing," Lilia said.

The feral girl muttered something, though not in any language Lilia recognized. How had this girl escaped Liona?

"Did you tell anyone when you left?" Lilia asked.

Tasia shook her head. "Good girl," Lilia said, and she took her hand and together they mounted the bear and rode west through the trees, to the woodland, to catch the last of the Dhai before Kirana's great army turned south for the Temple of Oma. Lilia thought they could outrun the feral girl, but she took to her feet and ran after them, faster than any blind creature should have been able to.

Lilia looked back at her once, and resigned herself to the girl's company.

•••

It took two days for Lilia to catch up to the fleeing refugees, in part because she had to stop often to hide from Tai Mora scouts. A cry went up when the refugees saw her, as if she were a hero coming home. She rode to the head of the column, expecting to find Mohrai there, but when she asked, everyone directed her to Yisaoh.

Confused in the rush of bodies, she waited until the group camped before going off to find her. Tasia ran to keep up with her, the feral girl trailing behind. Lilia had been trying to figure out a name for the feral girl, but came up with nothing.

She found Yisaoh standing over a map drawn in the dirt. Mohrai's cousin, Alhina, and the parajista from the wall of the harbor, Hasina, stood with her.

"I thought you were dead," Hasina said.

"Exaggerations," Lilia said. "Where is Mohrai?"

"Bad pregnancy," Yisaoh said. "Barely made it back to the hold after that fiasco." She took a long drag on her cigarette. "So you lived after all."

"Will Mohrai be all right?"

Yisaoh shrugged. "Most likely. She needed some time to sit. Got some blood. Hopefully nothing."

"That doesn't sound like nothing."

"Are you a doctor?"

"I am, actually."

Yisaoh narrowed her eyes. "You're a lot of things."

"Where is the Kai, then?"

Yisaoh shook her head. "We have reports that there are groups ahead of us, fleeing the clans and temples, doing the same as we are. I put out runners so we can meet up with them. He may be with them."

"We shouldn't meet."

"Shouldn't we?"

"As one force, we're easy to kill," Lilia said. "If we stay split up, it makes us difficult to track down."

"Fair," Yisaoh said, and then Lilia liked her, because she knew she was not a fool. Lilia had suspected there was some sense to Yisaoh, when she drugged the Kai and sent Lilia down to the table.

"The map?" Lilia said.

"Options," Yisaoh said.

Lilia looked at the map. She pointed to the finger of the peninsula, the place where her village had been. "I know this place. It once supported a village of five hundred. It will be suitable for us."

"Have to go further south, around Mount Ahya," Hasina said. "I know this topography. If we go north, it looks shorter, but the terrain is rugged. We have too many young and infirm with us."

"South, then," Lilia said. "It will take us past Oma's Temple, though. We may pick up some other refugees."

"If this place only holds five hundred, we can't take any more," Yisaoh said.

"No, but we can start creating networks," Lilia said. "We can be disparate, but we'll need ways to speak to each other. If we can't speak, we can't organize."

"Organize," Alhina said, "for what?"

Lilia cocked her head at her. "To take back Dhai, of course."

None of them said anything.

Yisaoh just stared at her, smoking. The silence stretched.

"Well?" Lilia said. "Anything else? Let's go, then."

Lilia bent and wiped away the map with her hands. She took Tasia's hand and led her back to the bear.

That night, she slept better than she had in a year, though the feral girl whined and farted in her sleep rather terribly.

Lilia stood among the last of the low summer poppies, breathing in the heady scent of them. Above her, the first of the adenoak leaves were just beginning to change. From here she could see the Temple of Oma, and the great Tai Mora army marching across the plateau to take up residence there. They had already begun setting up tents. Her group had indeed had to come south, around Mount Ahya. The journey had taken much longer than it should have – over three weeks through angry, spitting woodlands with the sick and young and injured in tow. Their route, despite their caution, took them perilously close to the temple, which they had learned by now was already fallen. She assumed the Kai and his second Catori and child were dead. Still, after weeks of exhausted trekking in the woodland, Lilia wanted to see it one last time. The army she saw now was the great Dhai army in the valley, the one she remembered hearing about as a child. This was the Dhai she had expected from the very start, and her worlds had collided.

Emlee came up beside her. "The others are asking for you," she said. "You know those Tai Mora will send scouts up here, once they are secure in the temple. We must be swift."

Lilia placed her hand on Emlee's arm, and wished, for a breath, that it was Kalinda Lasa there, Kalinda who told her what to do, where to go, or Gian, who believed in her, who had secrets Lilia would never unravel.

"We'll come back," Lilia said.

"You are the only one of them who says that. No one says that now. You sound a fool."

"Not a fool," Lilia said. "I have faith."

"A fool," Emlee said, patting her arm absently. "Come along, now. Your people are waiting for you."

Lilia turned her back on the temple and the great Dhai army, and plunged deeper into the woodland, just as the sky above her exploded.

EPILOGUE

Oma's Temple, seat for five hundred years of the descendants of former slaves Faith Ahya and Hahko, was an enormous green claw soaring toward the blushing sky. Its reflective glass dome caught Sina's light, turning the plateau and all who walked upon it a fiery lavender.

Kirana Javia, descendant of conquerors and flesh dealers, entered Oma's Temple through the front gates, bathed in Sina's light. The doors opened for her and her retinue without force or violence. This was the one plan she had needed to go off without incident, and it pleased her to find it working perfectly. It had taken her army most of the summer season to clean up Kuallina and clear out the villages between there and Oma's Temple. Many orchards and fields were burned by the Dhai in their retreat, and cleaning up the fields and planting a late autumn harvest had been one of her army's higher priorities. Now, on the cusp of autumn, she had arrived. Kirana slipped off her bear in the front gardens and passed the reins to kennel keepers who were clearly not her people, but cowering, wide-eyed Dhai. Until she could replace them, they would need some cowed Dhai to remain in service.

She expected to see Nasaka at the bottom of the grand tongue of the steps, eagerly awaiting her, but instead she found a mincing little boy called Pasinu. He said he was Nasaka's assistant, and apologized for Nasaka's absence. Kirana suggested they go up and find her, as Kirana was in a jolly mood, and she wanted to meet Nasaka here in her own world, finally, in the flesh, and conclude their decade-long deal for the handover of the Dhai temples.

Pasinu led her upstairs, where she saw the first of the bodies – all children and young people – their limp forms stacked neatly outside classrooms like corded wood. They had died without much fuss, which Kirana counted a blessing. She had ensured Nasaka had enough help to wipe the place clean well ahead of her arrival. She marveled at how well the taking of the temples had gone – clearing out all the full Oras, tying them up at Kuallina for weeks, giving them just enough time to feel they may triumph before she crushed them, had made the temples easy to infiltrate and control with a minimal amount of damage. Remarkable, that after all this time some grand scheme of hers had finally paid off. Walking through this temple after a decade of war and strategy and planning, after so much had been lost, after so many failures, was deeply satisfying.

She pushed open the door to Nasaka's study. Nasaka's body lay prone on the floor in front of her desk, riddled with at least two dozen stab wounds. Blood smeared the floor, the desk. Bloody footprints came all the way from the desk to the door. She even saw blood on the bookcases. It was the most brutal death she'd seen in the whole temple.

"I see she finally ate what she sowed," Kirana said.

Behind her, Pasinu gasped. "Who–"

"Settling grudges during coups is a popular pastime," Kirana said. "I suspect whoever assaulted her escaped cleanly."

"Perhaps it was a novice–"

"No," Kirana said. "This was very personal." She stepped away, and shut the door behind her. It made things easier, though. "As her assistant, I expect you to give me a full briefing," Kirana said.

"Of course."

"We have great plans for this little temple, and its sisters," Kirana said.

It took a day to clean up the temple in a way that Kirana deemed presentable. She went through room after room, reassigning quarters to jistas, her squad commanders, the stargazers, logistics, supply heads, and various support staff. She walked into the great Assembly Chamber at the top of the temple and admired the sky writ large in the atrium.

As they prepared to open a gate to admit her family, she tarried in the Kai quarters, sighing over all the things that needed to be replaced. She pulled open the curtains and stared out over the vast woodlands. Reports told her that many had retreated there. She already had squads in pursuit. She still needed Yisaoh.

Yisaoh. She turned away from the window. Something flashed in the sky, and she went back, squinted. Sina blazed merrily in the sky, but something was folding in on itself just to the east of it, pushing into the sky like a fist through wet tissue paper.

The sky flashed red, and the blazing eye of a star she had seen only in books appeared in the sky.

Kirana ran from the window, yelling for her omajistas.

"Up here!" she called. "Open the wink here! Call my children in! Let them see this!"

The two omajistas came up the stairs, huffing.

"Can you feel it?" Kirana asked.

Oma, finally risen after all this time. It was glorious.

"Heaven above, yes," the woman, Mysa, said. A smile split her haggard face. "You want a wink, Empress?" She held out her hands, and parted the seams between the world as if carving through a brick of warm lard, with not a drop of blood in sight.

Kirana clapped her hands like a child. She caught herself, but only just. She laughed so hard she put her hands over her mouth to stop herself. The omajistas, too, were merry, perhaps too merry, but after all the horror of the last decade, it was welcome.

She saw Yisaoh on the other side, sitting up from her work.

"Oma!" Kirana said. "Yisaoh! Send the children! Oma is risen!"

Yisaoh rushed outside Kirana's frame of vision.

Kirana called to the other omajista. "Go downstairs and open up a wink on the plateau. Start bringing them through, anyone you can. All of them. What we can't support here, we'll send to Dorinah."

Gaiso would have Dorinah in hand soon enough. They already controlled half of that country.

Yisaoh returned with the girls. The two youngest clung to her, but the eldest, Moira, came boldly forward.

Kirana strode through the wink, popping out onto the other side, and embraced her family. Yisaoh held her tightly. The children grabbed fists of her clothes.

"We took the temple," Kirana said. "It was almost easy. You wouldn't think that took a decade of planning."

Yisaoh met her look. Kirana knew the question. She shook her head. "Soon," she said.

"Take them," Yisaoh said. "It's time."

"I'll come back for you."

"I know."

"Travel is easier now. With Oma risen, we are the most fearsome force–"

"We have been very fearsome," Yisaoh agreed, but Kirana heard the implied question: *if we are so fearsome, why can we not kill one woman?*

Kirana kissed her and stepped back through the wink, holding out her arms.

"Moira, Tasia, Corina, come through."

"Go on," Yisaoh said.

The children gazed back at Yisaoh once, twice, until she pushed them through, herding them like wayward cats.

Kirana opened her arms to welcome her children home.

It was not until Moira and Corina were safe in her arms, weeping and trembling, that she realized Tasia was not with them. Kirana looked to the wink and saw Tasia still stuck on the other side, her face pressed against the wink, fingers splayed on the invisible barrier between them. Yisaoh held Tasia's shoulders, her face stricken.

This was not the vision of the future that Kirana had promised herself.

Kirana stood in a new, vibrant world with two of her children, while one child and her wife remained on a toxic wreck of a world she had killed millions to free them from. For the first time since the beginning of the Great War, the Empress of Dhai, Divine Kai of the Tai Mora, wept – and the baleful eye of Oma bathed her in bloody light.

After all this time, the war Kirana had waged for the survival of her people was not over.

The war for this world had just begun.

GLOSSARY

Aaldia – Country on the southwestern shore of Grania, led by a conclave of three queens and two kings, each representing one of the five former independent states of the region.

Aaldians – The people of Aaldia, a country on the southwestern shore of Grania, known for their passion for mathematics.

Aatai – Saiduan liquor.

Abas Morasorn – A Saiduan dancer at Kuonrada.

Adenoak – A type of yellowish hardwood tree commonly grown in Dhai.

Ahkio Javia Garika – Son of Javia Mia Sorai and Rishin Garin Badu. Li Kai. Brother to Kirana Javia Garika.

Ahmur – The largest of Raisa's three moons.

Aimuda Mosifa Taosina – Elder Ora of the Temple of Tira. Masura's cousin.

Alaar Masoth Taar – The Patron of Saiduan; eighth in the country's current line of rulers. A tirajista.

Alais Sohra Garika – Birth mother to Yisaoh Alais Garika. Married Garika clan master, Tir, and Moarsa, and Gaila.

Alasu Carahin Sorila – A Kuallina militia member found dead in Clan Sorila.

Albaaric – A city in Saiduan on the coast. Home city of Maralah Daonia.

Alhina Sabita Sorai – Mohrai's cousin.

Almeysia Maisia Sorila – An Ora and the Mistress of Novices at the Temple of Oma. A very sensitive tirajista who can call upon her powers even when Tira is in decline.

Aloerian – A city in Dorinah near a dajian camp.

Alorjan – An island nation currently claimed by both Saiduan and Dorinah forces. Both nations removed their forces to deal with Tai Mora matters.

Amelia Novao – A Dorinah Seeker. Recruited and bound by Lilia to help her get the dajian refugees across the Dhai border.

Anavha Hasaria – Zezili Hasaria's husband. Son of Gilyna Lasinya. The Empress awarded Anavha to Zezili as a token for her service.

Anjoliaa – A port city in southern Saiduan.

Aradan Foswen – A leader in an alternate version of Raisa.

Arakam Solaan, Ren – An ataisa sanisi.

Aramey Dahina Dasina – A Dhai scholar. Married to Lanilu Asaila Sorila.

Arasia Marita Sorila – Temporary keeper of Liona Stronghold.

Arisaa Saara – One of Alaar Masoth Taar's wives. Known as his most formidable wife, Arisaa is the mother of Alaar's most beloved sons and provides him with valued advice.

Ashaar Toaan – A Saiduan scholar.

Asona Harbor – Harbor on the Hareo Sea, in Clan Sorai. This defensive structure was built by Faith Ahya and Hahko in anticipation of raids from Saiduan and Dorinah.

Azorum – A dead people conquered by the Tai Mora on their world.

Bael Asaraan – Record keeper for the archives at Kuonrada. Native of Caisau.

Battle at Roasandara – A battle between the Saiduan and the ancient Dhai at the city of Roasandara, taught to every member of the Saiduan military.

Bendi – A strategy game played in Dhai.

Bleeding pen – A pen made from the stamens of claw-lilies.

Blinding tree – A tree that emits a deadly acid that numbs flesh and can eat through skin, bone and armor.

Bone Festival – One of the winter festivals held in Saiduan.

Bone tree – A tree with yellowish bark and spiny branches, made of bone. It catches small animals in its branches, and secretes a poisonous sap that kills its prey.

Bonsa – Large, yellow-barked trees trained to become living establishments in Dhai. Saplings are also used to create weapons infused with the breath of Para.

Book of Dhai – A written set of religious practices, codes and laws followed by the Tai Mora. The book states that when Oma rises, one world will die and another will be transformed. In the book, omajistas are referred to as the hand of Oma, and will decide the fate of the worlds.

Book of Laine – The holy book of Tordin.

Book of Oma – A written set of religious practices, codes and laws followed in Dhai.

Book of Rhea – A written set of religious practices, codes and laws followed in Dorinah.

Borasau – A Tai Mora, one of Roh's captors.

Broodguard – The Patron of Saiduan's personal guards.

The Cage – A mountain range in Dorinah, near Lake Morta.

Caisa Arianao Raona – Novice at the Temple of Oma now working as Ahkio's assistant. Parajista.

Caisau – A city in Saiduan just south of Isjahilde. Caisau's hold is a living building, but has been repaired so many times over the years that it is a patchwork of organic and inorganic material. Two thousand years ago, Caisau was the seat of the Dhai empire.

Caratyd – A city in Tordin.

Casa Maigan – An old acquaintance of Dasai's who has talamynii blood and can read old talamynii. Was part of Alaar Masoth Taar's harem in Isjahilde. Casa was left behind by the prior Patron, and inherited by Alaar.

Casanlyn Aurnaisa – Empress of Dorinah. Long ago, her people crossed over from another world, but many were left behind. She seeks to bring the rest over now, with the help of the Tai Mora. Other titles – Eye of Rhea, Rhea's Regent, Lord of the Seven Isles.

Castaolain – A city in Dorinah.

Catori – Spouse of the Kai. The current Catori is Mohrai Hona Sorai.

Chali Finahin Badu – Brother of Roh; they share two mothers and three fathers but are not related by blood.

Cholina – A city in Dorinah, located northeast of Daorian.

Clan Adama – Named for one of Hahko and Faith Ahya's children, Clan Adama's primary exports come from its orchards, generally in the form of olives, apples, cherries, and apricots. Also known for its rice production.

Clan Alia – Primary exports of Clan Alia include textiles. Also known for its rice production.

Clan Badu – Clan bordering Clans Garika and Sorila, in Dhai. Politically close to Clan Garika.

Clan Daora – Clan Daora, like Clan Badu, has a skill with forged pieces, including tools and weaponry, though it is much more well known for its craftsmanship and attention to detail. Their jewelry pieces are highly sought after in Saiduan and Aaldia.

Clan Garika – Known as the most powerful single clan in Dhai, Clan Garika is the birthplace of three Kais and four Catoris. Often at the center of challenging the power and autonomy of the Kais, the clan is also an economic center and trading hub for the whole country. Goods coming up from the harbor in Sorai are generally brought to Garika for distribution and sale across the clan. Much of the population makes a living as merchants, traders, and in other skilled professions such as plumbers, hedge doctors, and clan law specialists.

Clan Mutao – Smallest and least economically powerful of the Dhai clans, Clan Mutao provides some exports in mushrooms, coal, and copper, but mostly ends up working in reserves overseen by neighboring Clan Nako. Their status as a dwindling clan requiring subsistence from others to survive has led to a petition in recent years to combine clans Nako and Mutao.

Clan Nako – Neighboring Clan Mutao, Clan Nako holds much of the country's wealth in copper and other metals. The sale of these materials is regulated by the clan, which manipulates supply and demand as necessary to ensure the best exported price. Such market manipulation for goods meant for sale within the country is not permitted, but exports are exempt.

Clan Osono – Central clan in Dhai. Chief commodity is sheep.

Clan Raona – Originally comprised of two different clans – Riana and Orsaila – Clan Roana is just a century old, and was created in an effort to tamp down the fierce feuding between the Riana and Orsaila clans, which resulted in nearly a dozen deaths, the most unnatural deaths outside of war time that the country had ever experienced. Clan Roana is loosely aligned with clans Saobina and Taosina. Primary exports include rice and wine. Raona also raises most of the sparrows used as messengers in the Dhai temples.

Clan Saiz – Dhai clan. Chief commodity is timber and artisanal goods.

Clan Saobina – Clan Saobina exports timber and plantstuffs – including herbal aids and medications – which it grows and mixes in its own fields and workshops. The clan borders the woodlands, and so its members tend to be called on to consult on poisonous or dangerous plant outbreaks between the clans.

Clan Sorai – Named after the powerful son of the third Kai, Clan Sorai is often allied with clans Adama and Saobina in political affairs. They are also the clan responsible for the safety and security of Asona harbor, the country's single largest trading link to the outside world. The clan is generally allied closely with the Kai, and has a notorious rivalry with Clan Garika. The clan's leader is Hona Fasa Sorai.

Clan Sorila – Clan nearest the Temple of Oma, in Dhai. Primary export is timber.

Clan Taosina – Named for Faith Ahya's second daughter, clan Taosina – like clans Saobina and Sorila – borders the woodlands. Pottery and complex, plant-derived technologies such as bioluminescent floor or ceiling lighting solutions, self-cleaning fungus floors and the like are generally created and installed by Taosina crafters.

Concordyns – A province in Tordin.

Cora – A dajian who lives with Emlee.

Corina Yisaoh (Tai Mora) – Yisaoh's daughter, being raised by the Tai Mora versions of Kirana and Yisaoh.

Coryana Puyak – A friend of Natanial's who trains gifted on how to draw on the satellites' powers.

Dajian – In Dorinah, enslaved Dhai people are called dajians. Often they are branded with the mark of the family that owns them.

Dakar – Zezili Hasaria's dog mount.

Daolyn – Owned by Zezili Hasaria, housekeeper and dajian.

Daorian – The fortress seat of the Empress of Dorinah. A city of the same name rose up around the fortress on the ruins of the former Saiduan city of Diamia.

Dasai Elasora Daora (Dhai) – An elder Ora, over a century old. One of Ahkio Javia Garika's teachers. In Dasai's youth, he was a slave to the Patron of Saiduan at that time.

Dasai Elasora (Tai Mora) – Tai Mora magistrate in charge at Caisau.

Dayns – A runt dog belonging to Saradyn.

Dhai – Small country located on the northwest corner

of the island of Grania, an island at the far tip of the Saiduan continent. Also the name of the people inhabiting this country. Modern Dhai was established five hundred years ago by former slaves fleeing their masters in the neighboring country of Dorinah. It's said the satellite called Sina was especially powerful during that time, allowing Dhai sinajistas, who outnumbered sinajistas among the Dorinah, to escape their servitude.

Dhai has been led by a series of leaders given the title Kai. The title is hereditary and passes through the mother's lineage to the child with the greatest ability to call on the power of the satellites.

Dhorin – A unit of currency used in Dorinah.

Dorinah – A matriarchal country on the northeast shore of Grania, ruled by a long line of Empresses. The country is roughly eighteen hundred years old, and relies on the enslaved labor of Dhai people – known locally as dajians – to sustain its infrastructure and economy. The flag depicts the Eye of Rhea on a purple background.

Driaa Saarik, Shao – An atasia sanisi. Sent to Alorjan to shore up the island for Saiduan's retreat. Recommended by Maralah to meet with the Dhai party sent to Saiduan. Born in Tordin.

Dryan – A city in Dorinah.

Elaiko Sirana Nako – An Ora at the Temple of Oma and assistant to Nasaka Lokana Saiz.

Emlee – Gifted healer and midwife in a dajian camp, now liberated.

Empresses of Dorinah – The line of Empresses in Dorinah

began eighteen hundred years ago, when a violet-eyed foreign sorceress expelled Saiduan from the fortress of Daorian.

Enforcers – Members of the Dorinah military who capture wandering men or dajians and return them to where they belong.

Esao Josa – Granddaughter of Nirata Josa. Esao is killed when a gate summoned by her grandmother closes on her.

Etena Mia Soria – Ahkio Javia Garika's aunt, Etena was driven mad by her own power and supplanted as Kai by her sister, Javia Mia Sorai. Exiled from Dhai.

Everpine – The scent of this tree dissuades bugs and most sentient plants. Travelers through the woodland apply the scent to sleeping rolls and other supplies they want to remain undisturbed.

Faith Ahya – Faith Ahya is regarded as the mother of the newest incarnation of the Dhai nation, founded five hundred years before when she led an uprising of Dhai slaves in Dorinah. With her lover Hahko, she established the Dhai nation in one of the most contaminated areas on the planet, one few other nations would touch. For five hundred years, the descendants of her eldest and most gifted children have ruled Dhai as the Kai, or "First Dhai."

In the dajian version of the legend, Faith Ahya was betrayed by her lover Hahko, killed, and hung from the ramparts of Daorian. She then ascended to the peak of Mount Ahya and was engulfed by the light of Sina. It is said she will return to the world when she is needed.

In a story in *Fifteenth Century Dhai Romances*, Faith

Ahya was a slave from Aaldia. She carried the child of an enslaved Dhai, and was a pitiful and self-serving character.

Faith's Rally – A Dhai song about Faith Ahya establishing the first clan.

Faralis Mosa Daora – A member of the Liona militia.

Farosi Sana Nako – A militia man, leader of a group of Oras and militia sent out to search Dhai for assassins. His group located and killed five of the assassins. Head of the militia at the Temple of Oma.

Faythe – A story from *Fifteenth Century Dhai Romances*, in which Faith Ahya was a slave from Aaldia. She carried the child of an enslaved Dhai, and was a pitiful figure.

Faytin Villiam – A Tordinian historian who recorded events during the time of the Thief Queen.

Fellwort – A plant trap that consists of a pit filled with poisonous green bile.

Festival of Para's Ascendance – A festival held on the day when parajistas are at the height of their power.

Fifteenth Century Dhai Romances – A book of Dhai history written by Dorinahians. Includes the story "Faythe."

Finahin Humey Garika – One of Roh's mothers.

Flame flies – Flies that create light, used in lanterns.

Floxflass – A yellow, thorned plant that moves to constrict prey in its tendrils.

Forsia tubers – A tuber that is poisonous if not deveined. Root of forsia lillies.

Foryer Galind – One of Anavha's guards in Tordin.

Fouria Orana Saiz – A Kuallina militia member found dead at the bottom of a well in Clan Sorila.

Fox-snaps – Plant defenses used outside Woodland Dhai homes to protect them from dangerous wild plants.

Gaila Karinsa Pana – Near-mother to Yisaoh Alais Garika. Married to Alais, Tir and Moarsa.

Gaiso Lonai Garika (Dhai) – Elder Ora of the Temple of Oma in Dhai. She was responsible for the overall functioning of the temple and care of the people therein. Cousin to Tir Salarihi Garika. Replaced by Ora Soruza Morak Sorai.

Gaiso Lonai (Tai Mora) – Tai Mora parajista company general. One of Kirana's four line commanders.

Gasira – A city in Tordin; the seat of Saradyn's power.

Ghakar Korsaa – Dance teacher at Kuonrada.

Ghrasia Madah Taosina – Ghrasia's mother was originally of Clan Mutao, but relocated to Taosina and named Ghrasia for that clan. Ghrasia went on to become a hero – the Dhai general who defeated the Dorinahs during the Pass War. She is currently the head of the military forces stationed at Kuallina Stronghold and Liona Stronghold. An old friend and lover of Ahkio's mother, Ghrasia is allied with him.

Gian Mursia – Former dajian servant in Daorian with

latent skill in calling on the satellites.

Gian Mursia Badu (Tai Mora) – A tirajista Tai Mora raised on Raisa prime in Clan Badu, and directed to accompany Lilia Sona by Kalinda Lasa.

Gonsa trees – Great trees which are hollowed out by tirajistas for use as homes in Dhai.

Gorosa Malia Osono – Head of the hold at Kuallina.

Grania – The island continent that is home to the countries of Dhai, Dorinah, Aaldia, and Tordin, located at the far tip of the Saiduan continent.

Guise of the Heart – A Dorinah romantic political thriller set in Daorian a century ago.

Hadaoh Alais Garika – Husband to Meyna Salisia Mutao and brother to Rhin Gaila Garika, Lohin Alais Garika and Yisaoh Alais Garika.

Hague Gasan – Steward at the Gasiran hold.

Hahko – Hahko was a former slave in Dorinah, and aided his lover Faith Ahya in leading the uprising of the Dhai slaves from the scullery of Daorian. The two became the first rulers of the independent Dhai state, the first in over years, after the defeat of the Dhai by the Saiduan roughly the same time ago. Like many slaves in Dorinah before and since, Hahko had only one given name.

Halimey Farai Sorila – A young parajista who works with Ghrasia to look for Tai Mora assassins living in Dhai. A member of the Liona militia.

Haloria Tarisa – Syre Storm's second-in-command.

Harajan – A city in Saiduan, south of Kuonrada. Contains an old hold built by the Talamynii that borders an underground sea.

Harina Fiaza Taosina – Newly appointed Ora. Sinajista.

Hirosa Mosana Badu – Clan leader of Clan Badu.

Hofsha Sorek – One of the Tai Mora with the ability to open gates between worlds.

Hona Fasa Sorai – Leader of Clan Sorai.

Honorin Sholash – A Tai Mora military leader.

Hrollief – Southern continent on the western half of Raisa.

Huraasa Firaas, Ren – Sanisi in charge of shoring up the Saiduan retreat to Anjoliaa.

Isaila Larano Raona – Tir Salarihi Garika's apprentice clan leader at Clan Garika. Her mother was clan leader before Tir. Isaila was given the clan leader seat after Ahkio exiled Tir and his family.

Isjahilde – A city in northern Saiduan, Isjahilde has been the country's political center for thousands of years.

Isoail Rosalina – A powerful parajista living near Lake Morta in Dorinah. One of the Empress of Dorinah's Seekers.

Jakobi Torisa Garika – Ahkio's third cousin. Chosen to accompany Ahkio to Clan Osono to meet with the clan leaders.

Janifa – A city on the coast in Dorinah.

Jasoi (Januvar) of Lind – Native to Tordin, Jasoi's title among the Dorinah is Syre. She is Zezili Hasaria's second-in-command.

Javia Mia Sorai – Former Kai of the Dhai. Ahkio and Kirana's mother. Javia became Kai after exiling her sister Etena, who was so gifted that she went mad.

Joria – An outer island to the north of Dorinah.

Jovonyn – A coastal city in Dorinah.

Kadaan Soagan, Ren – A sanisi, and one of Maralah Daonia's first students. Left hand of the Patron of Saiduan. Called the Shadow of Caisau. A parajista.

Kai – Honorific used for the leader of the Dhai people. The title of "Kai" means "First," and was used in reference to the eldest daughter of former slaves Hahko and Faith Ahya, who are credited with founding the country. The line follows the most gifted in a family, no matter their sex or gender. Though the Kai is the leader of the Dhai, they do not have absolute rule in the country; they are held accountable to clan leaders, their Ora advisors, and the people themselves. The Kai's duties are as a religious and political figure, negotiator of contracts with other countries, and arbitrator of disputes between the clans.

Kai Saohinla Savasi – Kai sometime before Kirana. Visited the heart of Oma's Temple after the battle of Roasandara.

Kakolyn Kotaria – A legion commander in Dorinah whose estate was sold off to pay her debts. Her title in the Dorinah military is "Syre." Kakolyn was ordered by the Empress to purge Seekers from Dorinah.

Kalinda Lasa – A parajista Tai Mora who has traveled to many worlds. She was the keeper of a way house in Dhai on the road to Garika, and was killed by Tai Mora. Kalinda grew up with Nava Sona, and aided Lilia when she was separated from her mother.

Karoi – One of four kinds of nocturnal scavengers in the Dhai woodlands. The karoi is a vicious black raptor.

Karosia Soafin – Local priest and tirajista in the region of Zezili Hasaria's estate in Dorinah.

Keeper Takanaa – Keeper of the Patron of Saiduan's house.

Kidolynai – A city in Dorinah.

Kihin Moarsa Garika – A novice at the Temple of Oma. Tir Salarihi Garika's youngest son. He was killed in Saiduan.

Kimey Falmey Nako – Defensive forms teacher in Clan Osono.

Kindar – A cooperative game of strategy played in Dhai. Pieces are wooden figures that represent family members.

Kirana Javia Garika (Dhai) – Former Kai of the Dhai. Sister to Akhio Javia Garika. Daughter of Javia Mia Sorai.

Kirana Javia (Tai Mora) – Kai of the Tai Mora. Said to be the savior of the Tai Mora, this version of Kirana seeks to save her people from the destruction of their world. A tirajista with some sensitivity to Oma.

Korloria Fanis – Tai Mora attendant to the slaves translating texts in Caisau.

Kosoli Mashida – One of Roh's captors.

Kovaas Sorataan, Ren – A sanisi in Maralah's trusted circle.

Kuallina Stronghold – Hold where Dhai militia are stationed, captained by Ghrasia Madah Taosina.

Kuonrada – A mountain city in Saiduan, built for cold weather and strong defense.

Ladiosyn – A city in Dorinah.

Laine – The god that many pray to in Tordin, and the preferred religious figure of King Saradyn of Lind. The satellites are known as Laine's Sons. Oma is called Laine's Eye.

Lake Morta – Lake in a remote part of Dorinah. The lake is the subject of many Dorinah stories, and is considered to be a holy place blessed by Rhea. It is a spot where it requires less energy to travel between worlds. As a result, people from other worlds often appear here.

Lake Orastina – A lake north of Lake Morta in Dorinah.

The Lament of Hahko – A very old Dhai ballad.

Laralyn Maislyn – A Seeker who ends up in the same dajian camp Lilia is in. Recruited and bound by Lilia to help her get the dajian refugees across the Dhai border.

Larn – A dajian who lives with Emlee.

Lasli Laodysin – See Syre Storm.

Li Kai – Successor to the Kai.

Liaro Tarisa Badu – Ahkio Javia Garika's cousin.

Lilia Sona – Scullery maid (drudge) at the Temple of Oma, originally from mirror Raisa. Daughter of Nava Sona. An omajista.

Line – A sort of living transportation system in which people travel in chrysalises.

Liona Stronghold – Hold that occupies the pass next to the valley that cuts through the mountain range separating Dhai and Dorinah. The building itself is a construct of parajista-shaped stone and tirajista-trained trees and vines. The forces stationed here are captained by Ghrasia Madah Taosina.

Litany of Breath – A litany that helps focus the user to draw on the power of the satellites.

Litany of Sounding – Defensive litany used by parajistas.

Litany of the Chrysalis – A litany that condenses the air around a parajista into a solid bubble.

Litany of the Palisade – A litany recited by parajistas to construct shields made of air.

Litany of Unbinding – A litany to break a binding trap set by another jista.

Livia Hasaria – Zezili Hasaria's mother. A tirajista who

specializes in the creation of mirrors infused with the power of Tira. Resides in the city of Saolina.

Lohin Alais Garika (Dhai) – Husband to Kirana Javia Garika. Brother to Yisaoh, Rhin and Hadaoh. Former Catori of the Kai. Killed in an attempted coup.

Lohin Alais (Tai Mora) – A Tai Mora infantry commander's squire and intelligence officer.

Lord's Book of Unmaking – A book with appendices that include love poetry written to Oma by a sixth century Saiduan scholar.

Luna – A Dhai bound to Saiduan and a scholar of Dhai matters. Once a Woodland Dhai, Luna was caught by a Dorinah raiding party and sold to the Saiduan.

Madah Ghrasia Mutao – Ghrasia's daughter.

Madah Ghrasia (Tai Mora) – One of Kirana's four line commanders in the Tai Mora army.

Mahinla Torsa Sorila – A dying woman from Raona.

Mahuan powder – An herbal treatment for asthma, mixed with water and then ingested.

Maralah Daonia, Shao – Sanisi, one of the Patron of Saiduan's generals. Sinajista. Sister of Rajavaa Daonia. Also known as the Sword of Albaaric.

Mardanas – Brothels in the religious quarter of Dorinah cities where male prostitutes serve Rhea by pleasuring women. Also called "cat-houses."

Marhin Rasanu Badu – A Kuallina militia member,

lover of Ahkio, found dead in Clan Sorila.

Marister Fen – A Tai Mora infantry member, originally from a country called Osadaina there.

Masis Avura – A Tai Mora stargazer.

Masoth Chaigaan Taar, Shas – A sanisi and Alaar Masoth Taar's eldest son.

Masura Gailia Saobina – Elder Ora of the Temple of Tira, Masura oversees everyday management of that temple. Was once a lover of Javia Mia Sorai.

Matias Hinsa Raona – Ora and doctor at the Temple of Oma. Now deceased.

Mays Krynn – A guard at the Gasiran hold in Tordin.

Meyna Salisia Mutao – Ahkio Javia Garika's housemate and lover. Wife to Hadaoh Alais Garika and Rhin Gaila Garika. Meyna and her family were exiled from Dhai by Ahkio, for their kinship to Tir Salarihi Garika.

Mihina Lorina Nako – Parajista.

Moarsa Fahinama Badu – Near-mother to Yisaoh Alais Garika. Wife to Tir, Moarsa and Alais.

Mohrai Hona Sorai – Catori of Dhai, married to Ahkio. Daughter of the leader of Clan Sorai, Hona Fasa Sorai.

Moira (Tai Mora) – Kirana and Yisaoh's child. Adopted from Kirana's cousin.

Mora – The small red sun in the sky over Raisa.

Mordid – Village in Tordin with about three hundred residents.

Morsaar Koryn – Rajavaa Daonia's best friend, lover, and second in command of what remains of the Saiduan army. Started his military career as an assistant cook for the army when he was young.

Morvern's drake – Broad-leafed plant which grows in boggy areas whose roots are crushed and used as a sudsing agent for scouring and cleaning.

Mount Ahya – A mountain in Dhai, located to the east of the Temple of Oma.

Mundin Mountains – Mountains at the northern border of Tordin.

Mur – One of the three moons of Raisa, Mur is irregularly shaped.

Mysa Joasta – Tai Mora omajista.

Naldri Fabita Badu – Elder Ora of the Temple of Para.

Naori Gasila Alia – A powerful parajista. Ahkio's third cousin once removed.

Nasaka Lokana Saiz – An Ora at the Temple of Oma. Ahkio Javia Garika's aunt. Religious and political advisor to the Kai. Sinajista.

Natanial Thorne of Yemsire – A Tordinian man who kidnaps Anavha Hasaria.

Nava Sona – Lilia's mother, from the world of the Tai Mora. Led a rebellion that took two hundred omajista children and hid them across many worlds.

Nirata Josa – An omajista. Kin to Gian Mursia Badu.

Ohanni Rorhina Osono – A parajista and dance teacher at the Temple of Oma.

Old Galind – A city in Tordin.

Oma – The dark star, a heavenly body which appears in the above Raisa every two thousand years (or so). The light it shines is red.

Omajista – Sorcerers with the ability to channel Oma. Those with this power can open gateways between worlds and across distances, raise the dead, enhance the powers of others, call fire, and perform many other feats as yet unknown.

On Violence – A political philosophy book by Empress Penelodyn, former ruler of Tordin. Saradyn had it translated and carries it with him.

Ora – Title/honorific for a Dhai magician-priest, who is able to channel the power of Oma, Sina, Tira, or Para. Oras often act as teachers in the temples of Dhai.

Osadaina – A country on Empress Kirana of the Tai Mora's Raisa that has no equivalent on prime Raisa.

Pana Woodlands – A woodland area in Dhai near the Temple of Oma.

Para – Para, Lord of the Air, one of the satellites that appears sporadically above Raisa. Para's light is blue.

Parajista – The common name for sorcerers who

can channel Para when it is ascendant. They can manipulate the air, levitate, affect weather, or form shields, barriers, or vortices. In Tordin they are often called wind witches.

Pasinu Hasva Sorai – Nasaka's new apprentice. Near-cousin to Mohrai, on her third mother's side.

Pass War – A war in which the Dhai, led by Ghrasia Madah Taosina, defeated Dorinah. The war started when eight hundred dajians escaped Dorinah and came to Liona Stronghold, begging for mercy and entrance to Dhai. Ghrasia would not let them in, and they were slaughtered by the pursuing Dorinah.

Patron of Saiduan – Leader of the Saiduan. Powerful Saiduan families have traditionally gone to war for the Patron seat. Since it was established, eighteen different families have ruled Saiduan. When a new family rises to power, the prior family's adults are killed and the children raised as slaves.

Patron Osoraan Mhoharan – Patron of Saiduan before Alaar Masoth Taar.

Penelodyn – Sister to the Empress of Dorinah. Ruled Tordin before being unseated by the Thief Queen.

Pherl – A dajian man with a flesh-eating disease who is cared for by Emlee and Lilia.

Pol – A boy in Old Galind who gives away the rebels to Saradyn.

Rainaa – A slave of the Patron of Saiduan.

Rajavaa Daonia – Maralah Daonia's brother, and

captain-general in charge of a Saiduan military regiment. Rajavaa becomes Patron after Alaar Masoth Taar is killed.

Ranana Talisina Saiz – The defense forms teacher at the Temple of Oma.

Rasaa Goara – Saiduan man who pursues Luna.

Rasandan Parada – A dancer at Kuonrada.

Rasina Tatalia – Tai Mora infantry commander. Lohin's mother through marriage.

Ren – A title among the Saiduan sanisi indicative of relative talent. Most powerful are Shao, then Ren, Tal and Shas.

Rhea – The goddess of Dorinah religion. Para, Sina and Tira are said to be her daughters. The Empress of Dorinah is also known as Rhea's divine. In Dorinah scripture, Rhea's Eye is a name for Oma.

Rhin Gaila Garika – Husband to Meyna Salisia Mutao and brother to Hadaoh Alais Garika, Lohin Alais Garika and Yisaoh Alais Garika.

Rimey Lorina Riona – A former student of Ahkio's from Clan Osono. Relocated to the Temple of Oma to serve as Ahkio's assistant.

Rishin Garin Badu – Javia's Catori and Nasaka's brother.

Rohandaar – A dead city from Tordin's history.

Rohinmey Tadisa Garika – Novice parajista at the Temple of Oma, with the ability to see through wards. Son of

Finahin Humey Garika, Tadisa Sinhasa Garika, and Madinoh Ladisi Badu. Brother of Chali Finahin Badu.

Romey Sahina Osono – A former student of Ahkio Javia Garika's, whose body was found in a sheep field in Clan Osono. Presumed to have been killed by Tai Mora agents.

Rosh Mev – A young woman who started a rebellion in Old Galind.

Ryn – A city in Dorinah.

Ryyi – A leader among the Seekers.

Sabasao Orsana Adama – Assistant to Ora Una.

Sagasarian Sea – A sea to the north of Dorinah.

Sai Monshara – One of the top generals of the Tai Mora, Monshara is tasked to work with Zezili Hasaria to eradicate the dajians in Dorinah. Monshara is the daughter of the former Empress of Dorinah on the Tai Mora version of Raisa. One of Kirana's four line commanders.

Saiduan – Large empire which rules the northwestern continent on Raisa. The continent itself is also called Saiduan. The empire is led by the Patron, the eighth in the country's latest family line of rulers. Powerful Saiduan families have traditionally gone to war for this seat. Since it was established, eighteen different families have ruled Saiduan.

Sanctuary – A room at the heart of the Temple of Oma where the Dhai clan elders traditionally meet to discuss issues of government.

Sanisi – The conjurer-assassins of Saiduan. Sanisi carry weapons infused with the power of the satellites.

Saofi – The Empress of Dorinah's dajian secretary.

Saolina – A small town in Dorinah where Zezili Hasaria's mother lives.

Saolyndara – A dajian camp in Dorinah.

Saradyn of Lind – King of Tordin, he is struggling to unite the constantly warring factions in the country. Can see "ghosts," which he believes to be a cursed power bestowed on him by one of the satellites.

Saurika Halania Osono – Clan leader of Clan Osono.

Sazhina – A dajian. Pherl's sister.

Screes – A strategy game played in Dhai.

Sea of Haraeo – The sea that separates Dhai and Saiduan.

Seara – A winter month in the Dorinah calendar.

Sebastyn – An outer island to the north of Dorinah.

Seeker Sanctuary – The training location for Dorinah's gifted. Seekers in Dorinah have their licenses to practice magic renewed here.

Seekers – The Empress of Dorinah's assassins. The Seekers have the ability to channel the satellites, a rare talent in Dorinah.

Sel oil – A flammable oil.

Shanigan Saromei Dasina – A senior Ora and mathematics teacher at the Temple of Oma.

Shao – A title among the Saiduan sanisi indicative of relative talent. Most powerful are Shao, then Ren, Tal and Shas.

Shas – A title among the Saiduan sanisi indicative of relative talent. Most powerful are Shao, then Ren, Tal and Shas.

Sindaa Mokaa, Shao – Commander of the sanisi at Harajan.

Shar – The large double helix "sun" in the sky over Raisa, actually twin stars which exchange mass as they rotate one another. Also called "the sisters."

Shodav – A dancer and old friend of Dasai and Luna. A former slave.

Shoratau – A prison in Saiduan, located northeast of Kuonrada. Shoratau houses prisoners who were thought to possibly be useful later.

Shova Hom – A Tai Mora omajista.

Siira – The Dhai name of a winter month of the year.

Silafa Emiri Pana – A young, newly appointed Ora, part of Ahkio's most trusted circle.

Sina – A satellite that appears over Raisa, also called the Lord of Unmaking. Sina's light is violet.

Sinajista – Sorcerers who can channel the power of Sina when it is ascendant. Their abilities may include calling fire, raising the dead, transmuting or transforming substances, removing wards, and prophecy.

Sloe – A runt dog belonging to Saradyn.

Sokai Vasiya – A Seeker who ends up in the same dajian camp Lilia is in. Recruited and bound by Lilia to help her get the dajian refugees across the Dhai border.

Sola – A young girl refugee on boat escaping Saiduan with Luna.

Song of Davaar – A song used to focus power to create an intricate net.

Song of One Breath – A song used to control the power of Oma, taught to Lilia by Taigan.

Song of Sorrow – An omajista litany.

Song of the Cactus – An attack litany.

Song of the Mountain – An offensive litany.

Song of the Pearled Wall – Defensive litany.

Song of the Proud Wall – A defensive litany.

Song of the Water Spider – An offensive litany.

Song of Unmaking – Litany that cuts a person off from their ability to draw on a satellite. Temporary, and easy to counter once one has become skilled.

Sorana Hasaria – Zezili's youngest sister.

Sorat – Emlee's nephew.

Soruza Morak Sorai – Replacement for Gaiso in overseeing Oma's Temple. A jista from the Temple of Tira.

Sorvaraa – Saiduan city south of Harajan.

Soul stealer – Saiduan term for a sinajista at the height of their power. Some sinajistas can capture and harness the soul or life essence of those they slay in their infused blades.

Sovaan Ortaa, Ren – A sanisi.

Sovonia – A seer and rebel leader on another version of Raisa.

Storm, Syre – The Empress of Dorinah's only male legion commander. Not permitted to fight, but commands others. Given name – Lasli Laodysin.

Suari Febek – A Tai Mora stargazer.

Sulana Ofasa Daora – Parajista and Ora.

Tadisa Sinhasa Garika – One of Roh's mothers. Also mother of Chali Tadisa Badu.

Taigan Masaao, Shao – An outcast sanisi aligned with Maralah, bound to her with a ward, after she was able to spare Taigan's life when Taigan betrayed the Patron. Taigan has since been tasked with finding additional omajistas to help the Saiduan fight the Tai Mora.

Tai Mora – The invaders. The Tai Mora seek to escape through a permanent gate from mirror Raisa before their world is destroyed by the ascendance of Oma.

Tal (person) – A dajian. Pherl's sister.

Tal (title) – A title among the Saiduan sanisi indicative of relative talent. Most powerful are Shao, then Ren, Tal and Shas.

Talamynii – Former allies of the Dhai, when the Dhai were a powerful nation. The Talamynii tamed wolves and used them as mounts. More fearsome than the Dhai, they were wiped out by the Saiduan. The few who remained intermarried with Saiduan people and their culture was subsumed by the broader one.

Talisa Gaiko Raona – Leader of Clan Raona.

Tanasai Laosina – Near-cousin to Zezili Hasaria. Tanasai was raised as part of Zezili's family after the death of her mother, but was seen as a burden by Zezili's mother.

Tanays Heydan – Saradyn's second-in-command.

Taodalain Hasaria – Zezili Hasaria's sister. Daughter to Livia Hasaria.

Tasia Gohina Garika (Dhai) – A young girl separated from her family.

Tasia Gohina (Tai Mora) – Kirana and Yisaoh's child. Adopted from Kirana's cousin.

Temple of Oma – A temple dedicated to Oma. Located in Dhai at the tip of the Fire Gate peninsula. The building itself is a living thing, made of some unknown combination of organic matter.

Temple of Tira – A Dhai temple located deep within the woodland. Somehow repels nearby dangerous plants. Its grounds contain the most renowned gardens in Dhai.

Thief Queen – Unseated Penelodyn and attempted to take power in Tordin. Was killed by Saradyn of Lind. Also known as Quilliam of the Mountain Fortress, Quill of Galind, Quill the Thief Queen. Was once Saradyn's ward.

Tir Salarihi Garika – Clan leader of Clan Garika. Father to Yisaoh Alais Garika, Hadaoh Alais Garika, Rhin Gaila Garika, Lohin Alais Garika and Kihin Moarsa Garika. Exiled.

Tira – Name of the satellite also referred to as Lord of the Living. Tira's light is green.

Tirajista – Sorcerers who can channel the power of Tira when it is ascendant, which gives them the power to heal flesh and grow/train plants and other organics. Tirajistas are also skilled in the creation of wards.

Tolda – A dajian.

Tongue Mountains – Mountains in Tordin.

Tordin – Country on the southeastern shore of Grania, led currently by a king named Saradyn of Lind. Constantly in a state of civil war. Was led by the Empress of Dorinah's sister, Penelodyn, before she was unseated by the Thief Queen. The country is difficult to unite because of its geography—cities are far apart, and the terrain is hilly. Dangerous plants spring up again quickly after being cut.

Tulana Nikoel, Ryii – Leader of the Seekers hiding in the dajian camp where Lilia is held. An omajista.

Una Morinis Raona – Gatekeeper of the Temple of Oma.

Vestaria Mauvia – A Tai Mora at Caisau.

Voralyn Jovyn – A Dorinah Seeker recruited and bound by Lilia to help her get the dajian refugees across the Dhai border.

Water lily spiders – Semi-sentient plants that filter water when they breathe.

Willowthorn – Thorny weeping tree with small leaves which grows up to 175 feet tall. Saplings are infused with the power of Sina to create infused weapons.

Wind witches – Name for parajistas in Tordin.

Woodland Dhai – Those who have been exiled from – or who chose to exile themselves from – the Dhai settlements in the valley. The Woodland Dhai have a different dialect than those in the valley.

Wraisau Kilia, Ren – A sanisi.

Yisaoh Alais Garika (Dhai) – Yisaoh once contested Javia Mia Sorai for the title of Kai. Daughter of Tir Salarihi Garika. Sister of Rhin Gaila Garika, Hadaoh Alais Garika, Lohin Alais Garika and Kihin Moarsa Garika.

Yisaoh Alais Garika (Tai Mora) – Married to the Tai Mora leader, Kirana Javia.

Yivsa Afinisla – One of Kirana's four line commanders.

Zezili Hasaria (Raisa Prime) – Captain general of Dorinah's eastern force. Zezili's mother, Livia Hasaria, is a titled Dorinahian and her father a dajian, making her half Dhai. Her title is Syre.

Zezili Hasaria (Mirror) – Incited a revolt against the

Tai Mora and killed Kirana Javia's Tai Mora father. Worked on the massive mirror the Tai Mora created to facilitate entry to prime Raisa, but was eventually killed for refusing to cooperate.

Zini – The smallest of Raisa's three moons.

ACKNOWLEDGMENTS

This was an extraordinarily difficult book to write on an extraordinarily difficult deadline. Many thanks to Marc Gascoigne at Angry Robot for fully supporting the book and my endless tinkering with it right up until page proofs. I keep thinking writing novels will get easier, as this is the fifth book I've published and the fourteenth I've written, but I tend to set extreme challenges for myself with every new work, and this one – with its multiple worlds and multiple versions of dead and living characters – was the most challenging yet. Whether this book and the series as a whole succeeds or not is now up to readers. Thank you for taking a chance on it.

I set myself a high bar, and I had a lot of people supporting me in my attempt to reach it. Many thanks to my agent, Hannah Bowman, for going over this grueling book time and time again, and for buying me scotch. Thanks to my editor, Amanda Rutter – I know this series is a pain in the ass. Special thanks to Mike Underwood for his continued support of the books on the Angry Robot sales and marketing side, and for being a great person all around. Thanks to Caroline Lambe and Penny Reeve for publicity wrangling, Phil Jourdan for keeping it moving editorially, and Paul Simpson for swift copyediting work.

There was a lot of behind-the-scenes work here again from my assistant, Danielle Horn Beale, and I want to thank her for helping me hit these seemingly impossible deadlines. I would have lost my mind several times already this year without her to help me muddle through. Many thanks also to Jayson Utz for long talks about plot and supportive sanity checks, as well as his continued support and patience for my two-career life. I couldn't ask for a better partner.

Finally, thanks to all of *you*. Thank you for reading my work, for telling your friends, for debating my stories endlessly on social media and in online forums and in book clubs and libraries and everywhere else. Thank you to everyone who has hand sold my work in a bookstore or at a convention table, or passed on a copy to a friend, or requested a copy from the library. Thank you for the fan letters, and the love.

It's a tough time to be an author (it always has been), but your enthusiasm and support ensures I can keep telling weird and wonderful stories for you.

Can't stop the signal.

The Big Red House
Ohio
Summer, 2015

Previously in the Worldbreaker Saga

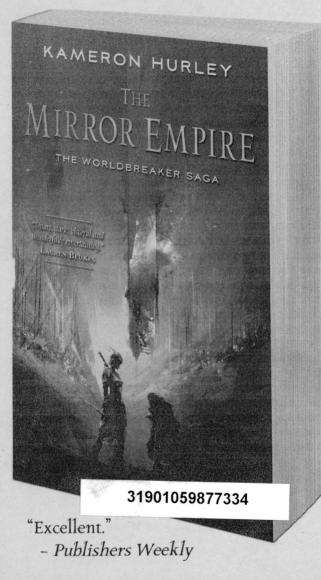